THE
BUCHAREST DOSSIER

THE
BUCHAREST DOSSIER

WILLIAM MAZ

OCEANVIEW PUBLISHING
SARASOTA, FLORIDA

ISBN 978-1-60809-544-5

Published in the United States of America by Oceanview Publishing

Sarasota, Florida

www.oceanviewpub.com

10 9 8 7 6 5 4 3 2

PRINTED IN THE UNITED STATES OF AMERICA

To Chrissy

ACKNOWLEDGMENTS

I would like to first thank Stacey Donovan, my wonderful editor, whose critical eye, advice, and magnanimous efforts to help me publish this novel made it all possible. I would no less thank my good friend Warren Grodin, for his many years of reading my writing, editing, encouragement, and camaraderie. My thanks also go out to the wonderful people at Jericho Writers in Oxford, England, for their editorial advice. I am grateful to Meryl Moss, Maria Konstas, and the rest of the team at Meryl Moss Media, for their enthusiasm and great efforts to market the book properly. I extend my appreciation and thanks to Bob and Pat Gussin, the owners of Oceanview Publishing, as well as to Lee Randall, Lisa Daily, Kat Daue, and the rest of the great Oceanview team who brought the book to life. And last, but not least, I want to thank my wife, Chrissy, for her belief in my work during these many years.

CHAPTER ONE

Harvard University, Cambridge, Massachusetts
December 1989

PROFESSOR ANDREI PINCUS left through the rear door of the Harvard Faculty Club wearing another man's coat. He had chosen it at random, as he had been trained, eyes closed, taking the first coat his hands grabbed. It was not luck that caused him to choose a man's coat. He knew that very few female professors used the Faculty Club, a fact that he regularly bemoaned. The coat was a short parka lined with fur—normally, he wouldn't be caught dead in it. He preferred the old European-style black cashmere topcoat that reached down below his arthritic knees.

Still, he had to admit that this American style was more practical. The fur made it warmer than his own, and the hood, which he had pulled over his head before leaving the club, provided protection from the bitter wind. The East Coast had been suffering under an arctic blast for days, the biting cold driving his colleagues to scurry from one building to another, finally settling into the plush red leather chairs of the Faculty Club with a glass of hot cider and a pipe to finish off the day. But the hood had the added virtue of obscuring his face from prying eyes, which had become of vital concern to him lately. He would return the coat in the morning with apologies.

It was silly of him, really, and he hoped that no one, especially the Agency, would ever hear of his behavior. And yet, lately he had felt the need to fall back on his old spycraft. He was convinced he was being followed, even though he hadn't actually seen any signs of it. In the old days his instincts had been legendary, and he had learned to trust them. Still, that had been decades ago. For the past twenty years all he had ever been asked to do was recruit an occasional Harvard man or woman for the second-oldest profession. For that he was grateful, for he knew his aging heart could no longer take the rigorous exploits of his younger days.

He plodded down the snow-covered pathway through Harvard Yard and onto the side streets of Cambridge until he reached an old Colonial house, the faculty housing that he had called home for the past thirty-four years. He could have afforded something larger, but what was the point? The house was full of memories of his beloved wife, and leaving it would mean abandoning her. If anything, the house now felt too large and empty. And with his recent premonitions of something dire about to take place, the house felt almost daunting. Still, he decided that if he had to die, he would die here, in this familiar space, where he and his dear wife of fifty-two years had been so happy.

He'd never thought that he would be so lucky, that America would welcome a Jew from Romania with such open arms. And with a full professorship at Harvard, no less. Yes, he taught one of those obscure Eastern European languages that no one heard of and, yes, it paid less than he would make in one of those international corporations that did business in Romania. But there was only one Harvard in the world, and he was part of it.

He climbed the wooden steps to his house and unlocked the door. For a moment he thought he was greeted by a waft of warm air redolent with the smell of cooking, his wife's stuffed cabbage or famous schnitzel. He heard the television, which he left perpetually on, whether or not he was at home. It gave him a sense of being part of the world, among friends he wished he could have but knew he never would. When he turned on the light, he thought he saw his wife sitting on the couch watching reruns of *Perry Mason* and trying to figure out the identity of the murderer. He blinked a few times, causing his wife to metamorphose into a man dressed in a black overcoat and wearing gloves. He was smoking a cigarette and dropping its ashes into a glass of water.

"Come inside, Professor, and get warm. The night is too cold even for a dog." The man spoke Romanian like a native.

Pincus stood frozen, shocked and yet not surprised. His instincts had warned him, and now here it was. The arm of the Securitate, his nightmare, had reached all the way to America.

The man dropped the cigarette butt into the glass and stood. He was thin and tall, in his fifties or so, with graying hair. His face was all bone and angles, his skin tight, yet marked with shallow crevices. An aged, experienced collector of souls.

"What is that silly coat you're wearing? You look ridiculous in it."

"Why have you come for me?" Pincus asked in Romanian, then slid onto the couch, his knees hurting as he bent them.

"The chickens have come home to roost, Professor," the man said, now towering over him. "For years you've been agitating with false propaganda against your country, writing articles, giving speeches. Now you are even on a White House committee, spreading your filthy lies to those in the highest levels of the American government."

"I am simply stating the facts," Pincus said, though he knew the man had no interest in facts.

"You have been convicted *in absentia* of treason," the man continued, "and we all know what the sentence is."

The man held up a bottle of *tsuika*, Romanian plum brandy, which Pincus kept in his cabinet, and poured a glass for Pincus. He then picked up his own half-drunk glass and raised it. "*Noroc!* Have your last glass of *tsuika* with me to remind you of the country you have betrayed."

"You are the betrayers, you and the other criminals who have run our once-beautiful land into the ground." Pincus swallowed the *tsuika* then banged the glass on the table. "Thousands killed and starved, and for what? You will go down in the dustbin of history as an abomination."

The man laughed. "You are a gifted orator. I don't understand why we haven't taken care of you earlier."

"Why now, then?" Pincus asked. "It makes no difference if I live or die. You're finished either way."

"Just tying up loose ends, Professor."

"You want information, is that it? Tell me what you want."

"I'm not interested in any information, Professor. I'm just here to carry out justice. I can't count on God to do it."

"There is money," Pincus said, his voice betraying a faint hope. "America is swimming in it. I can get you however much you want: a million, two million? You don't have to do anything but walk away and report that you accomplished your mission. I'll just disappear. You'll never see my face again."

"What will I do with all those dollars?" The man laughed. "If I try to spend it in the West, they'll find out and hunt me down." The man shook his head.

"Do what you want with me, then," Pincus said. "But your soul will boil in hell, if God is at all just."

"Damn God and damn my soul." The tall man spat, placed the glass on the table, then removed something from his jacket pocket. It took a moment for Pincus to realize that it was a syringe with a long needle. *Good. Death will come quickly.* In a moment he would be with his dear wife, which he now realized was where he had been craving to be ever since her death.

In one swift motion the man grabbed Pincus's white hair, pulled back his head, and plunged the long needle into one of his nostrils. He felt a sharp pain, then a fire exploded somewhere deep inside his head. Within seconds the muscles throughout his body began to contract, each muscle fiber seeming to twitch and slither independently, like worms. Then it all stopped. His arms and legs relaxed, followed by his chest muscles, and finally his diaphragm. He slumped into the soft cushions, still awake and aware, yet unable to take a breath. He saw the man standing over him, smiling, waiting. He tried to calm his mind, to prevent the panic. A flash of memory of his childhood nightmares, waking up partially paralyzed, but this was worse, much worse. His mind was now screaming for air but his body didn't respond. A voice in his head started laughing. *I will be caught dead in this silly coat, after all.* A wave of panic now overtook him, his mind frenzied, crying out. *Is this it? The end? Please, God, let it be quick.*

And then, as if his prayers were answered, it all grew quiet. As he felt himself drift off, he saw his wife, young again, the way she had been when they met, smiling and beckoning him with open arms.

CHAPTER TWO

New York City
December 1989

To SAY THAT it was a normal day in December was not to do it justice. Yes, there was the usual patina of snow covering the grass in Central Park. And the slippery ice patches on the pavement caused Bill Hefflin to slip and almost fall. And, yes, he was taking his usual morning walk down the usual path near the Metropolitan Museum, past a row of green-painted benches with brass plates honoring wealthy donors. And, yes, the usual tinge of nostalgia accompanied this morning's walk. Central Park reminded him of a similar park in Bucharest, Romania, called Cismigiu Park. There, twenty years ago, as an eight-year-old, he had accompanied Pusha, his first and truest love, down similar paths.

The park lacked one essential element, though: the peculiar aroma of a certain plant or tree that he hadn't been able to find in any other park but Cismigiu Park. Nevertheless, Central Park came close enough for him to choose an apartment only a block away, so that he could pretend, at least for a few minutes each morning, that he was back in the city of his birth, the place where he had been happiest.

Though he had been following this morning routine for years, certain signs, missives from the gods, now foretold a day of realignment, maybe even of destiny.

First, a black cat sitting by the side of the path decided to cross in front of him just as he was approaching. What was a cat doing outside in twenty-degree weather? And what were the odds it would be totally black? The instructors at the Farm had taught him that, in his line of business, there were no coincidences. Tanti Bobo, an old gypsy, had instilled in him the same lesson at the age of six. The black cat had been waiting specifically for him, that was clear.

Second, a rumble of thunder rolled out just as he was coming up to a specific tree, a bass clarion call to ensure that he didn't miss the white chalk mark on its rumpled bark, a mark that hadn't been there the previous morning. The moment he saw it he felt a tightening of his chest, a mixture of excitement and dread. These runes appeared only three or four times a year, and never accompanied by such dire warnings. The chalk mark was diagonal, from top left to bottom right, which meant the package was to be found under the ninth tree counting from the second bench on the right.

He erased the chalk mark with a handful of snow, then casually walked on, counting the benches and then the trees, then recounting them twice more. When he was certain he had arrived at the appropriate tree, he paused to make sure that no one but he and the black cat were crazy enough to be walking in the park in such cold weather. He spotted a couple walking down the path, hand in hand, and felt a twitch in his heart. That couple could have been he and Pusha. He brushed away the thought as he spotted another figure a hundred feet away, a bearded man dressed in a ragged wool hat, old coat, and tattered boots pushing a cart laden with bundles, all his worldly possessions. A homeless person.

He waited for the couple to pass then decided to ignore the homeless man. He kneeled on the left side of the tree, brushed away the powder of snow from the ground, and began digging with the key to his apartment. The ground was frozen, and the digging hurt his hand. Why couldn't the dead drop be indoors? A library, perhaps, or a café. Even a subway station would be warmer than Central Park in December.

He soon found it, however, the spike, just where it was supposed to be. He quickly dug it out, replaced the dirt, brushed some of the adjacent snow over it, and left.

On the path heading toward Fifth Avenue, he took the spike out of his pocket and examined it. It was the same as the previous ones: a four-inch pointed hollow tube made of dark metal, with a company logo stamped on it—Gunne Metal Co.—and a model number. Langley had tried to track it down once, spending months following false leads, only to find there was no Gunne Metal Company anywhere in the world that produced hollow spikes. The logo and serial number were meant to send the Langley propeller-heads on a wild goose chase.

Boris had a sense of humor.

Hefflin unscrewed the top of the spike and emptied the contents into his hand. He was surprised to find not the usual roll of microfilm but a single piece of paper. On it a message, written in longhand: "Vasili, you must come to Bucharest to create history. Time is critical." Below that line were instructions. "Stay at the Athénée Palace where you will receive my call. I will say, 'Let's get together for a vodka.' You will respond with 'Usual place?' If I answer yes, it means in an hour at The Red Barrel Bar. If I say no, it means the coffee shop at the Gara de Nord train station."

Hefflin stopped in the middle of the path and reread the message. A fury of conflicting emotions swirled through his mind. Bucharest to him meant his childhood, his paradise lost, at least as he imagined it, intermingled with the pain of lost love and lost innocence, of subsequent torment, and the beginning of a difficult new life. What the hell was a Russian agent like Boris doing in Bucharest? And why would he ask him to go there? No matter. There was no way he was going back to Bucharest to dig up his past, despite what Boris wanted.

As he arrived at his office at the CIA's Clandestine Center, located on the fourteenth floor of a nondescript high-rise on Third Avenue, a message was waiting for him on his computer. As he sat down at his desk, he felt the same tightening of his chest that he had felt earlier that morning. He sensed that the day was not yet ready to return to normalcy, that the black cat was now insisting on further fulfilling its prophesy. He cursed the superstitious nature he had absorbed during his childhood from that gypsy woman in Bucharest.

The message was from Dan Gorski, his supervisor: "Professor Andrei Pincus was found dead this morning in his home at Harvard. He's been dead a couple of days, it seems. Autopsy pending, but it looks like natural causes. Wasn't he your original recruiter? Condolences if he was."

CHAPTER THREE

Harvard University, Cambridge, Massachusetts
January 1980

THE FIRST TIME Hefflin ever spoke to Professor Pincus at length was during office hours at the end of the first semester of his freshman year. The middle-aged expat was a thin man with a full head of silver hair and the lined face of someone who had worked outdoors all his life. But as Hefflin entered the office and saw the layers of blue smoke floating in the room, he realized the fine wrinkles were the result of lifelong heavy smoking. Pincus lit up an unfiltered Camel and offered him a chair.

"It always gives me great pleasure to speak my own tongue with a native," Pincus said in Romanian. "I recognized it was your first language the moment you spoke it in class. But your name threw me off. Hefflin is not a Romanian name."

"I'm Greek," Hefflin answered in Romanian. "Both my parents emigrated from Greece to Romania as teenagers."

"Hefflin is not a Greek name either," Pincus said.

Hefflin squirmed in his seat, disliking this interrogation. "I changed it before applying to college. I prefer not to be pegged as an immigrant."

"Ah, I see. And what do your parents think of this?"

"They're fine with it." He shrugged.

The truth was that he had dreaded telling his parents. But to his surprise, his father had a very different reaction than what he had expected.

"What's in a name?" his father said when he told him. "You're still my son. Our family name was made up anyway. The way the story goes, my great-grandfather traveled from Crete to Epirus as a young man. He was an orphan, and relatively illiterate. I don't know if he didn't know his last name or if he never had one. Anyway, he was in his twenties but already had silver hair. So they named him Argyris, Greek for 'silver-haired.'" He laughed. "If it will help you get ahead in America, then I'm all for naming yourself Rockefeller or Carnegie or Smith. America is the land of the self-made man." He sighed with satisfaction. "From an illiterate orphan to a Harvard man—all in four generations. Not too bad."

His father's upbringing in the class system of old Europe, where advancement was slow and generational, strengthened Hefflin's resolve to shed his immigrant roots and become fully immersed in the American dream of the self-made man. His mother was less sanguine. "I know what your father said, but I think deep down you hurt him. Not because of the name. He is afraid you are turning your back on your roots, on the people who love you."

Perhaps he was, but he couldn't tell his mother that the community of immigrants was a swamp that sucked him down and suffocated him with a kind of spiritual fatigue. These bands of rootless people were fearful, isolated, out of touch with the society in which they now lived, suspicious of new things, and slow to adopt new ways. They had gone through cultural shock so many times that they'd eventually given up and settled into their own subculture of displaced persons. In an attempt to hold on to their identity, they ossified old traditions to preserve them, even as those same traditions continued to evolve in their homeland. They insisted on their children marrying members of their own culture, even if the children had to go back to the original country to find a mate.

This was the stifling society of Worcester, Massachusetts, in which he had grown up. Why wouldn't everyone want to escape that quagmire? But objectivity was not at play here. The community saw his leaving as a rejection of their heritage. To them his desire to become a real American was an act of treason.

So it was with this new identity as William Hefflin, which he had created from scratch, that he began his Harvard career. How had he picked that name? From a magazine.

He discovered the name "Hefflin" came from a long line of deposed royalty, whose seeds had been spread far and wide throughout Central Europe. Of course, if anyone really wanted to find his true identity, it wouldn't be difficult. This legend was not meant to hide his past, merely to obscure it with layers of coats that he could put on or take off as he pleased.

What he found in his first weeks at Harvard was that no one asked him about his background, a unique and liberating experience for him. Throughout his childhood in America, he'd had to constantly explain where he came from, what languages he spoke, and how to pronounce his Greek family name. For the first time in his life, he was now accepted as an American.

"Understandable, in a way," Pincus now said. "You want to blend in, especially since your English has no accent. You must have come here at a young age."

"We left Romania when I was eight," he said. "We lived in a refugee camp in Greece for a year, where I had to learn a new language, new norms, and form new friendships. We then immigrated to America where the process started all over again. At this point, I don't know if I'm Romanian or Greek or American. Anyway, we spoke Romanian in the house, but my vocabulary needs improving. That's one reason I took your course."

"How much of Romania do you remember?" Pincus asked.

"I prefer not to look back," Hefflin said as he squirmed in his chair. "Life moves forward, and so do I."

Pincus let out a deep sigh, tinged with exhaled smoke. "That's the American view . . . no sense of history, no learning from old experiences. But you took my class for a better reason than just to improve your vocabulary. You must still be interested in the language and culture of your birth. Language is more than just words used to transmit information. It forms the way you view the world, the way you think, even."

Hefflin shrugged. "I thought that knowing a second language well, even the Romanian language, would help me in my career, whatever that turns out to be."

"Very well, if that's what you tell yourself. Your Romanian is practically that of a native, apart from a few idioms that come from the streets, as it were." Pincus chuckled. "For example, one day in class you used the slang *gagica* to refer to a girlfriend."

"Should I have used *amanta*?"

"*Iubita* would have been better. It's less formal than *amanta* and not as base as *gagica*. The word *gagica* comes from the gypsy *gadje* meaning a non-Gypsy, similar to *goy* in Hebrew. The word eventually morphed in Romanian to mean 'chick' or the British 'bird.' It's not exactly derogatory to women, but not a term of respect either."

"You should have corrected me." He shifted in his seat, embarrassed, yet feeling a growing respect for the professor.

"I enjoyed listening to your childhood expressions," Pincus said, "almost like observing a time-traveler from the past. It gives one a perspective on history. For example, you used the word *jidan* to refer to a Jew."

"That's the word I know from my childhood."

"I'm not surprised. Romanians have always been anti-Semitic. The equivalent English word for *jidan* is kike. The word you want to use is *evreu*."

"Sorry. I didn't know." He realized that the professor himself was Jewish. He wanted to slink out of the office now, deeply embarrassed and unsure of how much more criticism he could take.

"Of course you didn't know." Pincus waved his hand. "No offense taken. So, tell me, how did you like my course? You certainly aced it."

"I loved it," he said. "I discovered Romanian writers: Eminescu, Caragiale, Sadoveanu, Blaga. But—"

"But?"

He didn't know how much to tell this professor, whom he hardly knew. "The language brings back memories of a time when I was happy," he said. "Nostalgia is a killer. It makes one weak."

Pincus sighed again. "Hence your reluctance to look back at your own history. Yes, that's the immigrant's drama. Once we leave our country—no matter how miserable it was—some of us pine for it, want to return to it, while others feel forever unanchored, no longer a Romanian and yet not fully an American either."

"One leg here, one there. Permanent impermanence," Hefflin said. "Does everyone feel that way?"

"Those who are self-aware," Pincus said. "Most are just concerned with making a living. Angst is a luxury they can't afford."

"A blessing, in a way."

Pincus moved behind his desk, opened a drawer, and took out a bottle.

"It's past five o'clock: happy hour." The professor beamed. "And now that the drinking age in the state has been lowered to eighteen, I can legally share this with you. Not that it would have been an obstacle otherwise." He let out a chuckle, then removed two shot glasses from a drawer and poured. "I think you'll recognize it."

Hefflin immediately smelled the familiar aroma of plum brandy. "*Tsuika.* I haven't had any since I left. The immigrants in Worcester have forgotten how to make it."

"European friends bring me a bottle now and then." Pincus handed him the glass and raised his in a toast. "*Noroc!* To a free and prosperous Romania."

The moment the liquid hit his tongue, a wave of memories washed over Hefflin—his father drinking *tsuika* with his uncle and letting him taste it from his glass; his mother boiling a cup to get rid of the alcohol, then serving it to him as he lay in bed with a cold.

"I can see you appreciate it," Pincus said. "It's homemade, a high quality."

Pincus settled in a chair across from him and placed the bottle on the coffee table between them. "Have you been back at all?"

He nodded upward, along with a "tsk" sound of his tongue—the Romanian gesture for "no." The *tsuika* was bringing back bodily expressions that accompanied the language.

"Why not?" Pincus asked. "You spent the first eight years of your life there, the most formative years. Your way of thinking, of looking at the world, was formed by the language and culture around you."

What could he say? That the thought of Romania always brought on a sickening feeling of loss, that the memories of Pusha, his first love, had to be kept pure, insulated from the miserable realities that he knew he'd find if he ever went back?

"What would I gain by going back?" he asked. "Indulging in nostalgia for a lost childhood?"

"You might cure yourself of that nostalgia, for one." Pincus eyed him closely, as if trying to look around the corners of his mind.

"Maybe I don't want to cure myself," Hefflin said, then regretted it.

"You prefer to suffer?" Pincus downed his *tsuika* and poured himself another. "Maybe you're afraid of what you'd find. You still have relatives there?"

"A cousin, Irina, a well-known stage actress in Bucharest, but I haven't written or spoken to her since we left." He chose not to mention Pusha.

"Don't you think that's strange?"

"Making contact with her isn't like writing to a friend in California, simply a matter of distance," Hefflin said. "It's also a trip back in time."

"Well put. But in your mind, she has become frozen in time. The truth is she has moved on, as you have. Your cousin is now an adult suffering under Ceausescu's brutal regime."

The same applied to Pusha. But he couldn't bring himself to think of her as anything other than a young girl with golden hair who had befriended and then enchanted him.

He shrugged. "What can I do about it?"

"The struggle against communism takes many forms," Pincus said. "I have no doubt the West will win in the end, but that may take a long time if matters are simply left to themselves."

Pincus shifted in his seat, appearing to be thinking, trying to decide on a course of action. He abruptly turned the conversation to Hefflin's knowledge of world affairs. What did he think of the Vietnam War, Soviet hegemony, Nixon's China opening? Was democracy a viable system, or did he think communism would sweep the world?

Hefflin considered himself relatively well versed on most issues, having judiciously read the *New York Times*, and having had daily arguments at the kitchen table with his parents and other immigrants. He responded with what he thought were thoughtful, reasonable opinions. The Vietnam War was a catastrophe, Soviet hegemony was on the rise, Nixon's China opening was an inspired move by a well-known anti-communist, democracy was the only system that would survive in the long term since it tried to meet people's need for personal freedom and accomplishment. Communism, though based on altruistic ideals, had been so corrupted by totalitarian regimes that it would eventually collapse from within.

Pincus nodded, letting out a few satisfied grunts, and went on. Did Hefflin have relatives still living in Romania other than his cousin Irina—no; friends his father might still have living there—none; and was Hefflin affiliated with any political parties in America—none.

In a momentary lapse in the conversation, Hefflin tried to turn the focus on Pincus.

"When did you leave Romania, Professor?"

Pincus's face darkened. "In '38, before the War, when Romania still had the remnants of a constitutional monarchy. I had seen the writing on the wall for years—the German Brownshirts, the Romanian Iron Guard. I knew the Nazis would sweep over Europe sooner or later. My wife and I decided to go while the going was good. First to Paris, then to America. It broke my heart to leave my parents behind, but they refused to come with us. Even though they were Jews, they considered Romania to be their country. I heard they were rounded up at some point and brought to a concentration camp. I don't know what eventually happened to them, but I can guess." Pincus's gaze drifted into the distance.

"I'm sorry," Hefflin said.

"When America finally joined the war, I enlisted in the Air Force," Pincus continued. "I flew a dozen or so missions over Ploesti, bombing the oil fields that, at the time, were supplying the German tanks. Romania was on the side of Germany until 1944, as you know. Then they had a change of government and joined the Allies. But the Russians never forgot what the Romanians did to them at Stalingrad and raped Romania of its natural resources when they invaded at the end of the war."

"My father was drafted into the Romanian army as a doctor," Hefflin said. "I don't think he saw any fighting, though. He doesn't talk about it."

Pincus's eyes grew misty. "No, I suppose he wouldn't. In those days we tried not to bring the horrors of war back home with us. It's different now. The American public saw the Vietnam War in their living rooms every night like a macabre soap opera. No wonder they revolted."

As the conversation came to an end and Hefflin rose to go, he said, "I prefer to keep my history private, if that's all right."

"Your secret is safe with me," Pincus said. "But when you get an invitation from the Fly Club, consider joining it."

As he walked back to Lowell House, Hefflin realized that Pincus had never asked him his real name. He had the feeling that Pincus knew more about him than he had let on, and that

Hefflin had been seduced with the old language and *tsuika* while being interviewed for a job, though Pincus had never alluded to one. It was only as the puzzle pieces started to fit together that Hefflin realized he was being groomed for another life.

It began with the Fly Club.

CHAPTER FOUR

Cambridge Cemetery, Cambridge, Massachusetts
December 1989

HEFFLIN STARED AT the mahogany casket, suspended on straps over the gaping gullet of the grave, and thrust back the rising rage.

It was bad enough that they had murdered an old man, but Pincus wasn't even a field agent. The rules of the game had been breached. Spies rarely killed other spies, and certainly not recruiters or intellectuals. It was part of an unwritten, but honored, protocol.

Then he remembered Pincus's lecture on Stalin murdering all the intellectuals, followed by a joke: Why do Soviet spies always travel in threes? One to read, one to write, and the third to keep an eye on those two intellectuals.

He perused the crowd—over two hundred, he estimated—made up mostly of Harvard faculty and students, huddled together, their coat collars up against the biting wind. A beloved professor, a mentor, deserved such a showing. He knew his own *bon voyage* would be a much smaller affair, but he didn't care. Dust to dust.

It had been years since he had gone back to Harvard to see his old professor. The last time, in fact, had been for his wife's funeral two years earlier. The couple had been married fifty-two years.

Hefflin couldn't imagine two people being together for that long. But Pincus had been part of the Old World, with its old rules and mores, like his own father.

The rabbi, an old man with a long beard, recited in Hebrew the traditional prayer, *Tzidduk Hadin*, as several men lowered the casket into the ground. Some people recited the Mourner's Kaddish, the few who knew it.

Hefflin felt the bile of guilt and self-recrimination rise up into his throat. He should have gone back to see old Pincus on a regular basis, to provide some company at least, perhaps share a glass of *tsuika,* to remind the professor of the mother country. At least Pincus had lived long enough to see the dominoes fall among the old communist states, to witness the beginning of the end of the Evil Empire. The entire Soviet Union was now teetering. Those events surely deserved some *mititei* sausages to go along with the *tsuika.* With his wife gone, the old man had likely no longer been feasting on the traditional Romanian dishes, but had probably relegated himself to eating institutional food in the Faculty Club.

Hefflin knew this to be one of his own failings, an aversion to looking back on his life. He abandoned friends, lovers, apartments, cities, and memories before they could abandon him. The feeling of being temporary never left him. He had never even put up any paintings on the walls of his apartment. Paintings meant stability, permanence, sensations he hadn't experienced since his childhood. Nostalgia was his longtime nemesis, and he was determined to avoid it.

He eased out of the crowd and made his way toward his car, the communal display of grief making him uncomfortable. His would be a private mourning, perhaps attended only by his lawyer and accountant. As he approached the street, he saw the stretch limo idling at the curb. A man wearing a black coat and sunglasses was standing next to it.

Ah, hell, now what?

The man opened the back door, and Hefflin leaned to look inside. Three men in suits. He knew them all.

"Come in out of the cold, Bill," Dan Avery said. As the director of operations, he had the entire back seat to himself.

"Thanks for attending the funeral," Hefflin said, not bothering to hide the sarcasm. He sat next to Avery and the door closed. The limo began to move.

"Sorry to bother you on this solemn day," Avery said. "I know how close you and Pincus were. You have our condolences."

Hefflin nodded, a half-hearted acceptance of a half-hearted apology.

Avery put away his reading glasses. A file was spread out on the seat next to him. "I know you understand that it would not have been wise to have the director of operations of the CIA photographed attending the funeral of a Harvard professor."

Hefflin acknowledged this with another nod. "Do we know the cause of death?"

"We've narrowed it down to a paralytic agent, succinylcholine, most likely. It is metabolized quickly and doesn't leave a trace, as you know. They tried to hide the needle mark by injecting it into his nostril, but it caused some bleeding."

Pincus had been conscious up to the last moment, struggling to breathe. The thought made him shudder.

"We have pictures from surveillance cameras outside the house." Avery handed him two photographs. The first showed a man wearing a dark overcoat and short-brimmed fedora entering the Pincus home. The time stamped on it read 7:12 p.m. The second showed a man in a parka, the hood covering his face from the camera, entering the house. That was stamped 8:05 p.m.

"The first man is the assassin. We believe the second man is Pincus," Avery said.

"But that's not his overcoat. He had a long black coat that he loved," Hefflin said.

"Apparently, he took someone else's coat when he left the Faculty Club," Avery said. "Either he was confused or—"

"Pincus was not confused," Hefflin snapped. "He must have suspected someone was following him."

Avery returned to the pictures without comment. "The assassin was there for almost an hour waiting for Pincus. The pictures are grainy, taken at night with only the light from the front porch. Makes no difference, though, since the assassin's face is turned away from the camera."

"So, do we have an idea who he is?"

"We know he's a Securitate agent brought in for the job," Avery said.

"The Romanian secret service, at Harvard?"

"We have a recording from inside the house," Avery said. "Don't look so shocked, Bill. We often leave a bug in the homes of our operatives for situations such as these."

And to make sure they don't flip. But Pincus wasn't an operative, just a recruiter.

Avery clicked on a machine next to him. Hefflin could hear the distinct voice of a man speaking Romanian.

"The chickens have come home to roost, Professor. For years you've been agitating with false propaganda against your country, writing articles, giving speeches. Now you are even on a White House committee spreading your filthy lies to the highest levels of the American government."

"I am simply stating the facts."

"You have been convicted *in absentia* of treason," the voice continued, "and we all know what the sentence is."

Avery clicked off the machine. "You don't want to hear the rest of it."

Hefflin could barely hold his emotions together. He felt his eyes watering, his throat tightening. *Fucking Ceausescu.*

"It's an audacious act, even for scum like Ceausescu, to kill a member of a select White House committee. And it will not stand!" Avery's face was beet red, his heavily lidded eyes now wide with fury. He gathered the photos and replaced them in his file, then inserted the file into his attaché case. He glanced up at Hefflin. "Now, let's get to a more urgent matter. Boris. Do you have any idea why he wants you in Bucharest?"

"I only know what you know," Hefflin said. "I have no contact with Boris other than the intel he delivers, all of which you have."

Avery lifted a decanter from the bar, poured two glasses, and handed him one, ignoring the other two men. "We've always suspected Boris must have a cutout. I don't see him traveling to New York every time he wants to deliver your package. He's got someone else bringing it in and planting the spikes. We've even named him: Hermes, the messenger of the gods. Which brings us back to Pincus."

Hefflin looked at Avery, then at the other two agents. "What? You think Pincus was the cutout?" He let out a forced laugh. "Pincus was just a recruiter. I don't think he had left the country in decades. Probably didn't even have a valid passport."

Avery shifted in his seat. "No, it expired years ago. Hermes has to be someone else. Still, two days after Pincus is killed, you get a message to come to Bucharest. A coincidence? I stopped believing in them years ago."

Hefflin wondered the same thing himself but couldn't imagine any connection between Pincus's assassination and Boris.

"That's another reason why this setup with Boris stinks to high heaven. Boris only deals with you." Avery smirked. "He has made you into a star at the Agency, practically untouchable, the only analyst with his own personal asset, the best Kremlin mole the CIA has. God is a fucking prankster."

Hefflin knew it had been a thorn in Avery's side for years. That no one knew Boris's identity, or why Boris had chosen him as the sole recipient of his intel, had been a dilemma for the CIA from the beginning, prompting several operations intended to discover Boris's identity. None had been successful. Boris was only an operational name Hefflin had given him. It did not refer to Boris and Natasha, the old cartoon characters from *Rocky and Bullwinkle* that lampooned Cold War spies, as his superiors had assumed with some amusement, but to *Boris Godunov*, the opera Hefflin had been attending when Boris first made contact. As the intermission lights went up at the Met and the swarms of people rushed by him toward the bar, he felt something stick to the back of his neck. It was a piece of tape with a black dot on it. It turned out to be a microdot with a list of KGB agents deployed in Washington DC. It also included the proviso that Boris would deal only with him.

"I don't know who Boris is or his motivations," Hefflin now said. "I'll go through the lie detectors again, more interrogations, whatever will satisfy you."

"No need for that, Bill." Avery's face lit up with his spook's smile. "We've already put you through the ringers, and we're satisfied. But you're wrong about one thing. You're not just an analyst. You're our top analyst on Eastern Europe. That, in itself, may have been the reason for Boris choosing you. Boris didn't want his intel to fall on deaf ears." Avery waved his hand. "All that is water under the bridge. The intel he has given us has been top notch. He has become our highest quality asset in Eastern Europe. And these are critical times, I don't have to remind you. The Soviet Empire is crumbling; all of Eastern Europe is changing before our very eyes. Romania is the only one left standing."

"I'm not a field agent. What good would I be in Bucharest?" Hefflin protested. "How do we even know that this isn't a trap, that Boris hasn't been blown?"

Avery pointed to the glass, which Hefflin hadn't even touched. "Drink that down, Bill, and think about this logically."

Hefflin sipped his drink then, recognizing Johnny Walker Black, gulped it all down.

"Good. Now, first of all, Boris used the name Vasili, the Russian translation of William," Avery said. "If he were under duress, he would have used Bill, as he arranged a while back. Second, you're right, you *are* just an analyst. Which means you're not that important, in the whole scheme of things. They wouldn't go to the trouble of setting you up. Hell, they probably don't even know you exist." Avery swallowed the rest of his drink, then twisted his face as the scotch burned its way down. "The issue is that we've never had an asset whose identity we don't know. That's a problem on many levels. We can't monitor him, provide aide if he puts up a flag, or influence him if he starts to waiver. He's totally in charge. He gives us what he wants when he wants. We don't even have a way of contacting him. It's totally a one-way street."

The perfect setup. Impregnable.

"So, Bill, one reason to go to Bucharest is to establish his identity once and for all," Avery said. "Besides, if he wants you there, he might want you to see firsthand what's really happening with Ceausescu."

"You have Stanton and his team for that," Hefflin said.

"Yes, Stanton is a good man, but he's not a native," Avery said. "He barely speaks the language. We need to have a clear view of Ceausescu's situation, of what the Russians are planning. This is a chance to find Boris's identity and milk him for all he's got." Avery took out his handkerchief and wiped his glasses. "As far as being a field agent, you received the same advanced training. On your insistence, I might add."

"That was years ago, and only as an intellectual exercise, to know what they go through to get the intel," he said.

"We'd love to give you a refresher course, Bill." Avery smirked. "But Boris makes it clear that time is critical. Besides, you aced your field training, if I remember. We even tried to convince you to be a field operative, but you refused. You'd be perfect for the job. You're tall, dark, and handsome, as the saying goes. Political correctness aside, we know that personal attractiveness makes it easier to get people to trust you. Beyond that, you're athletic, and you've continued your training in the martial arts to this day, I believe."

Everything Avery pointed out was true. But Hefflin knew he couldn't take being posted all over the world, learning yet more languages, feeling even more alien. He needed a home base.

"Anyway, field abilities come back quickly, we've found," Avery added. "Like riding a bicycle."

Hefflin looked at the three men, their blank faces, unrelenting. *Romania? In the middle of winter?*

"You'll have carte blanche while you're there," Avery added. "You can travel as you please, speak to anyone you please. The rules of engagement won't apply to you. And you might even get a chance to avenge Pincus's murder."

Fucking Avery. He knows how to add that extra zing. But Avery was right. Hefflin already felt the poison of revenge surging in him. And then there was Pusha, his first and purest love. Over the years she had evolved into a mythological figure, a goddess who demanded fidelity and worship even more than love.

Pincus, Boris, Pusha, his fractured childhood, all suddenly converged on Bucharest. Only Catherine remained outside of it. His heart twisted in agony. He had to trace this down until the open, festering wounds could heal. This could be a chance to finally purge himself of his demons. And it would give him a chance to see his cousin Irina again, maybe even Tanti Bobo, the old gypsy, if she were still alive.

"All right, Bucharest it is," he said. "Make it happen before I change my mind."

"Phillips here has all the documents you'll need." Avery smiled triumphantly. "You're booked on tonight's TAROM flight, non-stop JFK to Otopeni. I'll even fly you to New York in the company jet."

CHAPTER FIVE

TAROM flight—New York to Bucharest
December 1989

IT STARTED WITH the Romanian language—different from the corrupted argot that the immigrants in Worcester whispered among themselves. The moment Hefflin stepped onto the plane and heard the flight attendant utter the words, *"Buna seara,"* he immediately felt drawn back into the old world, the world of his childhood and his dreams. The language rattled off by these flight attendants was pure, authentic, and it tugged at his heart, threatening to let loose an avalanche of repressed memories. Then there were the attendants themselves—tall, broad-shouldered men of military age who used their hands as they spoke, less expressively than Italians, more subtly, an Eastern European style. Finally, it was the all too familiar state of their uniforms that warmed his heart: white shirts yellowed at the neck, jackets dangling loose threads, frayed cuffs, imitation leather shoes polished but misshapen and repeatedly resoled. Unable to afford new clothes or even uniforms, most Romanians repaired their clothing over decades, trying in vain to retain some self-respect, some pride.

"Coat, please?" The flight attendant beside him switched to English. He was young and tall, with a broad smile. "I hang up so no wrinkles. Okay?"

Hefflin let the man take his coat, knowing full well they'd go through the pockets. They would find a Three Musketeers bar in the right one and an unopened pack of Kent cigarettes in the left, both of which would disappear by the time they landed.

He placed his carry-on in the upper compartment and settled into his seat next to the window. Avery had not even allowed him to go home and pack, no doubt fearing that he would change his mind.

"Buy a carry-on at the airport and fill it with essentials," Avery had told him. "We have clothing and suits of all sizes at the embassy in Bucharest."

He was traveling economy class knowing it would make no difference—the plane was only going to be a quarter full, at most. Not many people traveled to Romania, certainly not as tourists, and certainly not in December. He unfolded the *New York Times* he'd brought with him and settled back, a patient resigned to an operation he knows will leave him permanently altered.

Though he had traveled a few times to Europe for his job, this was the first time he was going back to his homeland, and it left him unhinged, much as he felt when he had left Romania. The memory came back now, accompanied by a hint of nausea: the massive Gara de Nord in Bucharest, the black locomotives hissing their steam like giant dragons, the pungent smell of tar, the frenzied rushing of people, the fear that the train would leave without them. And then the rhythmic ticking of the train as it gained speed, the growing feeling that it may be true, that they were actually leaving.

"Passports. Passports," a morose soldier demanded, standing at the door of their train compartment. He was wearing a ragged green uniform, a leather belt across his chest, and a gun in a worn leather holster.

"Passport, please."

Hefflin awoke from his reverie, his chest still tight as the image of the Romanian soldier faded through the palimpsest of memories. Another flight attendant was now looking down at him—graying hair, a formal bearing, different from the rest.

"Passport, please," the attendant repeated.

"My passport?" Hefflin asked, confused.

"Yes, sir. It will be returned to you before landing."

The man's English was impeccable. A different caliber from the rest of the attendants. He saw the stack of passports collected from the other passengers, so he reached inside his jacket pocket and handed him his.

"A diplomatic passport." The attendant looked at him with interest.

"I'm State Department attaché to the American Embassy in Bucharest," he said. "On official business."

The attendant turned a few pages. "You have not been in Romania recently."

"My first visit." His first lie.

The man smiled. "Well, then, let me be the first to welcome you to our country. Though I would have chosen a more propitious time."

Was the man referring to the winter weather or the historic convulsions occurring throughout Eastern Europe? Still, Hefflin was impressed by the use of the word *propitious*. This was no ordinary flight attendant, though he knew none of them were. They were all Securitate, Ceausescu's dreaded security agency.

"Duty calls." Hefflin shrugged.

The man smiled again. "We are all slaves to duty."

After collecting the remaining passports, the attendant retired to the rear of the plane, no doubt to run the names on those passports against some list of their own. They wouldn't find William Hefflin, at least not on the first round. If they dug deeply enough, they might discover his name on a list of minor State Department functionaries, his official cover, though he doubted their sources were that good. Still, they weren't stupid. Any embassy attaché anywhere in the world was presumed to be a spy unless proven otherwise.

The door closed and the pilot's voice welcomed the passengers in Romanian, followed by English, to their nonstop flight from New York JFK to Bucharest Otopeni Airport.

Hefflin looked around the cabin and counted thirty-two people. There was no one in the business class compartment. Outside, light snow was falling. December had been one of the coldest on record, both in New York and Bucharest. The plane was de-iced, then it began taxiing toward the runway. The captain announced they were tenth in line, so Hefflin began reading the *Times* in earnest. An article mentioned Secretary of State James Baker's sense of urgency regarding the unification of Germany after Chancellor Helmut Kohl proposed his own vision to the West German parliament without first clearing it with Washington. A second article mentioned that Alberto Tomba, two-time Olympic gold medalist in skiing, would be sidelined for at least a month due to a fall that resulted in a broken collarbone. Another article reported that the Soviet Union had changed its confrontational policy in the Middle East and would now cooperate with the United States in constructive diplomacy.

Gorbachev. A forward-looking leader, a prophet, or a fool? Hefflin, and more importantly, the Agency, hadn't yet figured him out. Under his rule, the Soviet Empire was crumbling. Ever since he'd relaxed his grip by introducing *glasnost* and *perestroika*, the wave of political reform had begun sweeping across Eastern

Europe. Last year Janos Kadar had been replaced as General Secretary of the Hungarian Communist Party. In Poland, the anti-communist Solidarity Party had captured ninety-nine percent of the parliamentary seats and Tadeusz Mazoweski became the first non-communist prime minister in the Eastern Bloc. Hungary, East Germany, Czechoslovakia, and Bulgaria quickly followed with their own quiet revolutions. Only Romania remained frozen in the past.

As soon as the plane was in the air, the No Smoking sign was turned off and the passengers immediately lit up. He lit one of his own, a Kent, four packs of which he had stuffed inside his jacket pockets. For some reason Kents were the American cigarettes most familiar to the Romanians. He knew American cigarettes were almost impossible to find in Romania, being sold only in official Tourist Shops for foreign currency, which Romanians were forbidden to own. The black market smuggled some in, though most of the Kents seen among locals were garnered from foreigners who used them as an alternate form of currency. A pack of Kents could buy dinner at a local restaurant; two packs would get a car and driver for a day; five was more than enough for a woman for the night. He had bought three cartons at the airport and stuffed them in his carry-on, leaving little room for much else. He knew the embassy in Bucharest would provide all he needed.

He caught the attention of a flight attendant and asked for a drink, "Scotch, Johnnie Walker Black, neat, if you have it."

"I am sorry, Mr. Hefflin, but we only serve alcoholic beverages in business class."

He knew that was a lie. More important, however, was that the flight attendant already knew his name. His official rank had already gained him a privileged status. He removed an unopened pack of Kents from his pocket and placed it on the seat next to him.

"Your business class is empty." He pointed with his chin.

"It is a shame not to use it," the attendant said with a blank face.

"Perhaps you can share this pack with your colleagues."

"I am sure they will be very grateful, sir." The attendant slipped the pack into his pocket and extended his arm as an invitation.

The seats were standard business class. A glass appeared by his side, a scotch on the rocks. Though he'd asked for it neat, he accepted it anyway, not wanting to make a fuss. Once the precious bottle had been opened, the attendants and, no doubt, the pilot and copilot would share much of it. *That American sure had a thirst. I've never seen anyone put it away that fast.*

So now they all had cigarettes and drinks, the beginnings of a party, brought about by a $1.25 pack of Kents and a $2.00 glass of whiskey. A small price, by Western measures, but luxury items for the Romanians. But there was no room for camaraderie here. They were enemies, after all. These small bribes were only the mechanics of social intercourse, Romanian style.

He settled back and let the scotch linger in his mouth. It wasn't Black Label, but some cheap brand he didn't recognize. That was why they'd added the ice, he realized, in the hope of masking the brand. Maybe they just didn't have Black Label. But a moment later he saw it listed on the menu stuffed in the seatback in front of him.

He lingered with the drink, reluctant to ask for a second, but soon there was only ice in his glass and he pressed the button for service. After a few minutes, the same attendant appeared, and he ordered a second scotch.

"Make it Johnnie Walker Black this time, no ice." He smiled.

"Of course, sir." Did the attendant's lips twist up into a subtle smirk? Was the bitter aroma of whiskey exuding from the man's breath or his own? A moment later his drink arrived with no ice. But then he noticed there were two, one in each hand, held not by the same attendant but by the older one who had taken his passport.

"I believe there was a mistake in your first drink, Mr. Hefflin," the man said. "My apologies. May I sit and share one with you?"

A flight attendant allowed to drink while on duty? Or was this an admission that the man wasn't what he pretended?

"Be my guest," Hefflin said as he collected his drink.

"*Noroc*," the man toasted—"Good luck" in Romanian—and clinked his glass.

Hefflin feigned ignorance and responded in English, "Cheers." He immediately recognized the taste of Black Label.

The attendant took out a pack of Romanian Carpati cigarettes. Hefflin offered him a Kent from his open pack.

"No, thank you, they are too mild for me," the attendant said. "I prefer the Carpati."

Was this true or an intentional slight to put him in his place? *Not everyone can be bought by your miserable cigarettes.*

"So tell me, Mr. Hefflin, what are your duties as an attaché?"

"Etiquette," Hefflin said with a straight face.

"Etiquette?" A histrionic raising of the eyebrows. "Oh, we certainly need more of that in Romania. You will be a busy man if you try to teach etiquette to our people."

"Diplomatic etiquette," Hefflin said, though he liked the way this Securitate agent was toying with him. Was he going to have to play the straight man?

"That is certainly a useful profession," the attendant said. "And you come just at the right time, in the middle of winter, and when the whole of Eastern Europe is in such turmoil."

"Winter, summer, etiquette is always needed to . . . avoid misunderstanding."

"Of course, by all means, we must avoid misunderstanding." The man chuckled. "So, is that what you do in America, also?"

"Etiquette is needed everywhere. It oils the wheels, like a pack of Kents." He took out an unopened pack and placed it on the little table in front of him.

A new skin fold appeared on the man's left cheek. "I see you are already familiar with our corrupt ways. It is a remnant from the Turks, God curse them. The *baksheesh* has never left the Romanian psyche."

"I don't judge," Hefflin said. "In the Congo it may be a sack of flour, in Brazil a few *reals*, in America a lot more."

"In America they don't waste time with small bribes, hey?" The attendant let out another chuckle.

"All that matters is that you know the system. In a way, that is also part of etiquette."

The man burst into laughter. "So, all this time I thought we were corrupt but, really, we have just been engaging in etiquette." He slapped his thigh. "I like you, Mr. Hefflin. You have a European sense of humor. I wish there were more Americans like you." The man finished his drink and stood. "Keep the Kents. You will need them in Romania."

Hefflin watched the attendant approach one of his comrades and whisper to him loudly enough for Hefflin to hear. *"Ce dobitoc!"*

Hefflin made sure his face didn't lose its smile. The man had just called him a quadruped, an idiot. He was convinced the old spy had done so to see if he understood Romanian—not the diplomatic language he may know as an official, but the street argot. He raised his glass in a salute, a caricature of the stupid American, his smile opening up as between new friends. The man nodded back with his own golden smile.

Had he pulled it off, or had the trained Securitate agent noticed small, unconscious changes in his expression? Had the remark about his European sense of humor been meant to convey that the agent knew he was not a native American? He was sure a dossier on him was already being created.

No matter. He was only traveling as an observer, he reminded himself. Even as he thought this, he was bothered by the word Boris had used: "Vasili, you must come to Bucharest to *create* history." He was convinced Boris had not chosen the word by mistake. Avery must have also noticed it. What was Boris thinking? Were these revolutionary words?

He decided to put away his speculations and focus on what was more important in his life. He had not allowed himself to properly grieve for his old professor. He typically compartmentalized his life, and had thus saved his mourning for the long flight. But he could not think of Pincus without Catherine. The two were intricately entwined.

Against his better instincts, he closed his eyes and began to retrace his history with Pincus and Catherine, the shapers of his destiny. Together they had made him into the man he now was.

CHAPTER SIX

Harvard University, Cambridge, Massachusetts
January 1980

IT WAS A few days after his meeting with Professor Pincus that he found an envelope waiting for him on his dorm room desk. It had to have been hand-delivered, for it bore no postage markings or stamps. Inside was an embossed invitation from the Fly Club.

He knew very little about the Harvard gentlemen's clubs. They'd always had a mystique about them, which they perpetuated through the sworn secrecy of their members. He had occasionally seen men in suits and ties accompanied by women in flowing gowns entering the Fly Club manor, which was adjacent to Lowell House, his on-campus residence. The female guests later alluded to grand parties catered by some of the best restaurants in Boston and live bands providing music until the early hours of the morning. Each of the clubs had their distinct pedigree and notable past members.

He had always distrusted groups, any groups, especially those composed solely of men. His image of college clubs was that of fraternities he'd heard about at other colleges, with beer-guzzling, loud-mouthed guys talking trash about women they'd dated, and living from one debauched weekend to another.

"Punched by the Fly Club?" His roommate, Cliff, stood wide-eyed. "How the hell did you manage that?"

"Punched?"

"That's what they call being wooed, or at least teased, with membership. It's quite exclusive."

Cliff rummaged through his desk and found a notepad filled with his own handwriting from which he began reading. "The Fly Club, established in 1836. It has a slew of notable members in its pedigree: James Bryant Conant, Abbott Lowell, Charles Eliot, Franklin Roosevelt, John and James Rockefeller—"

"Stop. That's ridiculous. I don't fit among those guys."

"That's just for bragging rights. Most members are just the sons of the wealthy or politically connected."

"I'm neither of those. Why would I get punched?"

"One of the upper classmen must have submitted your name." Cliff described the process: you get invited to lunches, dinners, parties, during which they decide whether they like you enough to invite you again. About two hundred or so students were punched every year. After each event, the members vote and the numbers are cut in half. Only about twenty or so make the final cut. "But this is really weird," Cliff said. "First of all, punching season is in the fall, not in January. Secondly, you're a freshman. Most students are punched in their second or third year. And thirdly, this is your first invitation, when the parties are supposed to be off-premises, at some restaurant. You've been invited directly to the manor."

Cliff stared at him wide-eyed, a look of awe spreading over his face.

Hefflin felt like he was suffocating, out of his depth. "So what do they actually do in the club? Is it just a fraternity?"

"Definitely not a fraternity and you should never use that word," Cliff said. "No one lives in the club manor. It's for socializing only, with guys you might find interesting, and for making contacts. A lot of these guys will be important men in the future."

Making lifelong friendships with future leaders of industry sounded appealing, and intimidating. His self-image was that of a loner, a man who didn't belong.

"They must want you for some special reason," Cliff said. "Just go, and find out what it's about. No one turns down an invitation to a men's club and certainly not the Fly Club. Besides, if you do get in, maybe you can put my name up for next year's punch season."

*   *   *

The Fly Club building was a two-story brick structure with white Greek columns flanking the entrance. As he approached, he felt his palms sweating. His starched shirt collar chafed. With each step he took toward the front door, his instinct to flee grew stronger.

A middle-aged man wearing a butler's uniform appeared at the door. Hefflin hesitated for a moment, still toying with the idea of turning around and fleeing, then drew a deep, steadying breath and handed the man his invitation.

"The gentlemen are waiting for you in the dining room, sir," the butler said, then asked him to follow.

The dining room was larger than Hefflin had expected, with brown wooden beams crisscrossing the ceiling. A moose head stared down at him from one wall; framed paintings of notable past members hung on the others. Three young men were sitting at a round table holding cognac snifters. They were all wearing jackets and ties. He had put on a suit and tie, not knowing what to expect.

They stood to greet him.

"Mr. Hefflin, a pleasure," one of them said, extending his hand. "I'm Tyler, Reginald Tyler. These men are Tom Drier and Allen Gainsworth the Third, or is it the Fourth? I can never keep it straight. We all address each other by our last names, here—why I don't know—tradition, I guess, but there you have it."

They shook hands, then settled around the table. Tyler was a tall, skinny fellow, with brown hair and dark eyes behind horned-rimmed glasses. The other two were stockier, muscled, probably on the rowing team.

A snifter of cognac appeared by his side, and the other three all raised theirs.

"To our new club candidate," Tyler said. His companions echoed with, "Hear, hear!" then swirled the cognac in their snifters and sipped.

"Thank you for inviting me, it's an honor," Hefflin said, trying to hide his insecurity.

"Normally punch season is a long, drawn-out affair," Tyler said, "but this isn't a normal punch. You don't have to prove to us your brilliant wit or the quality of your tennis game or the royalty in your pedigree."

"I never intended to try," Hefflin said. "But why do I get special treatment?"

Tyler shifted in his seat. The other two looked down at their drinks.

"Every so often we get a request, shall we call it, from an alumnus," Tyler began. "You see, all the men's clubs, which includes the Fly Club, are funded by alumni. Oh, we have minimal monthly dues—forty dollars, I believe—for our present members, but that doesn't begin to cover the cost of maintaining this venerable institution. The costs are born by well-heeled alumni—and they're pretty much all well-heeled. It's not purely altruism on their part, I might add. These social clubs help form relationships among men who will be tomorrow's leaders. It's in the interest of the alumni to continue to expand their network, which may personally benefit them in the future."

"An alumnus asked you to invite me?" Hefflin felt like a little kid on his first day at school. He tried to hide it by sipping his cognac.

"It was more of a demand, actually," Tyler said.

Hefflin was stunned, unable to imagine what previous Fly Club member would even know he existed.

"Who is this alumnus?"

"Well, that's the thing; he prefers to remain anonymous. In fact, even we don't know his identity."

"Then how were you made aware of this request?"

"Our money managers in New York informed us. The alumni donations we receive every year are considerable, in the hundreds of thousands. We have a Wall Street firm that collects this money, invests it, and pays our expenses. Our celebrated parties alone cost over one hundred thousand dollars a year. Most donors don't want their names to be made public—only to members and then only on their terms. Apparently, this donor is one of our most generous supporters and one of our most discreet. You seem to have a secret admirer, Hefflin." Tyler raised his glass. "To great expectations."

It was at the first party that he met her.

The Fly Club was ablaze. A four-piece jazz band was playing in the grand ballroom. Couples were swaying on the dance floor. He had brought Emily, a Radcliff classmate, a "Cliffy," as his date. As soon as they stepped inside, they parted company, she going off on a safari to hunt down the most eligible bachelor—one of tomorrow's leaders hoping to spread his seed on crisp Fly Club sheets as he plotted how to earn his first million. The Porcellian Club, the most select of the men's clubs, even promised to donate the first million to any of its members who hadn't earned one on his own by his thirtieth birthday. To anyone's knowledge, that had never been necessary.

He spotted her standing by the pool table holding a cue stick. She had the look of a French flapper—tall, thin body; short, dark hairdo that came to a point by her left cheek; heavy Cleopatra eyeliner that extended well beyond her eyelids; and thin lips painted a bright red that matched her nails. She wore a black, knee-length dress with spaghetti straps and black stilettos. Her long fingers held the cue stick like a pro. He could see she was carrying her partner, Joe McGillam, a novice who couldn't keep his eyes off her.

She played well enough to win the game without giving away her ability. He could see by the way she acted with McGillam that she wasn't interested in him, treating him more like a waiter whom she constantly sent to fetch her a drink.

Hefflin lifted a martini from the silver tray of the liveried waiter, a prerequisite to compensate for his timid nature, and waited for it to take effect. During one of McGillam's errands, he approached her.

"Where did you learn to play?" he asked.

She turned to him with a blank stare, as if offended that he'd approached her without being properly introduced.

"Don't worry, I won't tell," he said. "You fooled the rest well enough."

"Mais pas toi?"

"Non, pas moi. It's the way you hold the stick." He returned to English. "Like—"

"A phallus?" She did, indeed, have a faint French accent.

"A gun."

"Same thing. I also shoot."

"You still didn't answer my question."

She said she'd learned to play in her father's library in Paris, if he must know. His face must have shown surprise for she added, "I grew up in Paris. Your accent is pretty good for someone who has never lived there."

He apologized for his five years of high school French.

"No, the accent is very good. You must have an ear for languages." One raised eyebrow. "How many others do you know?"

He told her French was his fourth, and weakest, if she must know.

That seemed to impress her, for she took him by the arm and pulled him toward the rear exit. "I frantically need a cigarette, and they have this silly club rule."

They found their coats and stepped outside. The evening was clear, and a cold breeze was wafting snow up from the ground. He offered her one of his filtered Dunhills, which he had bought for the occasion, but she pulled out a pack of unfiltered Gitanes from her black opera purse. He lit hers with a silver lighter that he carried to impress, then lit his own. They stood under the stars like two spies sharing secrets.

"My name is Bill," he said.

"Catherine," she said, without extending a hand. "But your name is Vasili, in the original Greek. It means 'king,' I believe. You are Greek, are you not?" She smiled. "I had a Greek boyfriend once, for an entire summer. Your faint accent reminded me of his."

He felt slighted. He didn't think he still had an accent.

"Oh, don't worry, it's barely noticeable. Only people like me can hear it." She winked.

"People like you?"

"Gypsies, who have roamed the world. I learned some wonderful swear words from my Greek lover. My favorite is *malaka*. He told me it means 'chronic masturbator.' Is that true?"

"Yes. Is it a turn-on?"

"Of course. I imagine this gorgeous boy never feeling satiated, stopping in the men's room between classes, on a train, in a plane, living in a constant state of orgasm."

"Men have limitations."

"A tragedy. Thank God women don't have *that* curse, at least." She inhaled deeply on her Gitane. "I tried it once from sunrise to sundown, if you can believe it."

His heart started racing, images flowing by in his mind. "That's impressive. Why did you stop?"

"I was afraid I'd become addicted. Funny, I've never met a man who made me feel as good." She let out a laugh. "Sorry, I just wanted to shock you. But you seem to be unshockable, though you look like a nice man."

"I can act."

"Oh? Are you acting like a nice man or acting as if you're not shocked? Either way, it's wonderful. Most men take themselves so seriously, such silly boys."

She dropped her cigarette on the ground and stamped it out with her stiletto . . . which he suddenly had the urge to drop down and kiss. She stepped closer to him and said, "I need a small favor."

"Name it." His throat was suddenly swollen.

"Small for you, but for me it would mean a lot. I . . . don't want to run into McGillam again. Could you walk me home?"

Be still my heart.

"Of course. Which dorm are you in?"

"I live off campus, an apartment not far from here. Thank you."

She led the way through the back gate onto Mt. Auburn Street, and they started walking side by side without touching. He felt curiously drawn to her, not only by her sexuality, but by an immediate feeling of familiarity. Perhaps it was her French way of saying yes by drawing in her breath as he'd seen his Francophile Romanian expats do, or the upward raising of her chin to mean no. At some point she turned onto a side street he didn't know.

"This is fine. Thank you."

"But you're not home yet," he said. "I can't just leave you here."

"You're a gentleman, but really . . . I'm very private. I don't want people to know where I live. I hope you don't take it as an insult for I don't mean it that way."

"Not if you tell me not to." He suddenly didn't want to let her go. "Can I see you again?"

"Of course, silly. I chose you to walk me home, didn't I? I'll pick you up in front of the Fly Club tomorrow at six. I'm taking you to dinner."

With that she melted into the darkness, an apparition. He stumbled back to Lowell House, his knees barely holding him up.

✳   ✳   ✳

She appeared in a black sedan, an antique Jaguar from the late '50s, the kind you see in old British spy movies. As she slid out of the car, he barely recognized her. She was dressed in a black mink stole and black silk dress that reached down almost to her stiletto heels. And she was now a blonde.

He stood transfixed, trying to decide whether to flee or stay and be made a fool.

"Is this yours?" was all he could say, referring to the car.

"It's a 1959 Mark 2," she said. "I got it for my birthday last year." She tossed him the keys. "You drive."

The inside was beautifully restored, all leather and wood. It even had that rich leather smell. As he slid into the seat, he felt a different nostalgia now, a sense of the passage of a time he never knew, would never know. He slid the manual shift into first and slowly let go of the clutch. The Jaguar handled exquisitely. Soon he was revving the engine down Mt. Auburn Street.

"You drive a stick well," she said as she lit a Gitane. "Most American boys don't."

"I decided to leave my Ferrari at home." Better a joke than to tell her that he'd learned to drive a stick on his cousin's old Dodge Dart. "You change your hair color often?"

"Depends on my mood. Which do you prefer?"

"I'll always think of you the way you were when we first met last night," he said.

"How do you know that was my real color?" she said. "Don't be swayed too much by a first image."

He followed her directions to a French restaurant in Boston's elegant Beacon Hill neighborhood, where the maître d' escorted them to a quiet corner. The lights were low, the tables lit by candlelight. He grew nervous when he saw there were no prices on the menu.

"I'm taking you out tonight," she said, seeming to sense his unease.

"I'm not used to being taken out by a woman."

"By a stroke of luck, I grew up in a wealthy family," she said, her hand waving away the fact. "There's no reason for both of us to suffer from your temporary economic circumstances."

He was taken aback. "What do you know about my economic circumstances?"

"You're wearing the same suit you wore last night."

A wave of shame spread over him. "It's the only suit I brought to college," he said, then regretted it. "But I have an entire wardrobe at home."

"I didn't mean it as an insult. Neither of us chose our parents. I was poor once, or so they tell me, a long time ago. I barely remember."

She ordered a bottle of wine.

"Historically, few children of the wealthy have accomplished great things, with rare exceptions," she said. "In any event, you're at Harvard. Your struggles are over."

When the wine arrived, the waiter poured first into her glass for her to taste, adding to Hefflin's awkwardness, and when she nodded her approval the waiter filled his. The wine was like nothing he'd ever tasted. It was deep and smooth and it left his palate a bit dry at the end.

"A St-Emilion, '57. Do you like it?"

"It's . . . wonderful."

"Let me order the food for us both, just this once, so you can feel what it's like to be treated like a feckless bimbo, as I have so often been." She turned to the waiter. "We'll start with the *fois gras chaud,* then follow with *medallions de veau, sauce aux morcilles,* rare. We'll decide on dessert later."

"*Oui, madame.*" The waiter glanced at Hefflin as he left.

"You feel like a gigolo yet?" she murmured. "You have the looks, for sure—reasonably tall, lean, dark haired, a Mediterranean complexion, with that sexy curl falling over your forehead. You even have some of the suave mannerisms—the way you move, your gentlemanly gestures—like someone out of a classy old movie."

"Why an old movie? I could have been raised this way."

"No, the kids who are born with a silver spoon up their arse act differently, with a reckless self-assurance, a laissez-fair insolence, a sense of entitlement. Your appearance of ease requires a great deal of effort."

He remained silent, disturbed; surely this woman was seeing too much inside him.

"It's not so hard to observe if you know what you're looking for," she said. "I know you're a right-handed tennis player, for example?"

His brows rose. "How?"

"The calluses. I also know that you don't play much anymore since they aren't as noticeable as mine." She showed him her open palm. "You're also not used to wearing a suit, since you still keep your wallet in your rear pants pocket rather than in your breast pocket. And by the way you blink, I know you're wearing contact lenses. Oh, and somewhere in your film studies you learned that a man should go through a revolving door first, like you did when we entered, something rich boys always get wrong."

"Where did you learn all this?"

"You learn how to observe people if you're an ambassador's daughter who is always being followed."

"You mean spycraft?"

She smirked. "That term is so film noir. You can learn so much about people without having to engage in cloak-and-dagger histrionics, though that, too, is fun." She lit a cigarette. "For example, see that man at the bar?"

He followed her gaze to a young man dressed in khakis and a herringbone jacket.

"He's been following me all day." She waved her cigarette.

"What?"

"The problem is that I'm not supposed to notice him." She rose and walked over to the young man. After speaking a few words to him, the man rose and left, obviously embarrassed.

When she sat back down, she lifted her wine glass and sipped. "It's just a game some of us play. But he's not very good at it."

A game? His silence must have encouraged her to add, "It's an art form, you know, knowing how to follow someone. I can teach you if you like, at another time, if we're still friends."

"Was your father involved in intelligence?"

"What do you think ambassadors do? They go to some God-forsaken country in order to get firsthand knowledge of the society, the people, not only the leaders of industry but the lower echelon government employees who might be dissatisfied, the rug merchant in the souk who loves to talk."

"But isn't that the CIA's job?"

"*They* do the clandestine work—recruitment, break-ins, stealing secrets, the dark deeds. The diplomats gather information in broad daylight, and they have diplomatic immunity."

Their appetizers arrived—warm *fois gras* that melted in his mouth, leaving a rich, buttery taste. The waiter refilled their glasses. The candlelight had acquired a dazzling aura.

"Why did you invite me to dinner?" he dared ask, the wine supplying the courage.

"You're different from most of the boys I meet at Harvard," she said, studying him openly across the café table. "You have an aura about you, like you're floating through life untouched and untouchable. A ghost."

Her words hit home. *Is my ungrounded spirit so obvious? Or is she just a perspicacious observer?*

"You saw all that in a few minutes last evening?" he asked. "Why is that even appealing? I see it as a tragedy of sorts, the result of a real unrooted gypsy childhood, unlike what you might have had." Again, he'd said too much. He reminded himself that he needed to be Bill Hefflin, to stay in character.

"A real gypsy childhood?"

"My father is a doctor with the World Health Organization," he said, trying to recover by reverting to his legend. "We traveled a great deal, all over the world. After a while you feel as if you have no home, no base, like a true gypsy."

"We're not that different," she said. "I've lived for various periods of time in five different countries in the first eighteen years of my life, always following my father's next posting. But I've learned to see it as an advantage—a cauldron of knowledge of various cultures, languages, religions, and sexual mores. We have nothing to tie us down, you and I. No country to call home, no religion that's any better than any other, no prejudices ingrained in us by generations of bigotry, whispers, and innuendos. We're citizens of the world, traveling light."

Citizens of the world, traveling light. The words made him melt. He tried to look at his life through her eyes, but the disparity in their experiences was obvious.

"I wasn't so happy during those years," he said. "Every time we moved, I had to attend a different school, learn a new language, new social norms, new culture. After a while you don't know who you are."

"That's how I used to feel," she said, "but I learned to create my own self. I'm not my parents, and they are not me. And I don't hold a grudge against them, like you seem to."

How did she pick up that little Freudian morsel?

"My parents did what they had to," she went on. "I decided to make the best of a life that few children have. I took what I liked from every culture and made it my own. I became the center of my own universe." She sipped more wine. "So, I've saved you countless years on a psychiatrist's couch."

Her words made him catch his breath. *The center of her own universe.* The words dug deep into his heart.

"Where did you get all this wisdom?" he asked.

"Can't it just be my thoughts?" She brushed the air with her hand, a rhetorical question. "Here comes our veal."

The veal, so tender you could cut it with a fork, was smothered in a thick mushroom and cognac sauce, which he would have scooped up with a crust of bread and called a meal. He watched her take only small morsels at a time, like a bird, and adjusted his own portions accordingly. A second bottle of wine appeared. She started recounting her time in Bangkok when she was fifteen, then her six months in Phnom Penh after that. Her stories revolved around her parents and nannies and a few childhood friends, the offspring of expats who never stayed long. He sensed it had been a lonely life, but there was no sense of sadness or self-pity in her words or tone. The young girl learned early on to be self-sufficient, and she had created an internal world that seemed to require few others.

"I'd walk for hours through the narrow, crowded streets of Phnom Penh watching how the people lived, or I'd take a rickshaw to the Silver Pagoda where I'd sit and dream. My parents would take me to the Angkor Temple and we'd lie in a boat on the Tonle Sap Lake, where you find one of the largest floating villages in the world called Konpong Phluk. Those people live on the water, rarely setting foot on land."

She had spent several years in Paris where she attended high school while her father served in Beirut. Her parents decided she needed a stable home so she and her mother, who came from a wealthy French family, settled in one of her family's apartments in the 6th Arrondissement.

"No matter how strange and exciting all the other countries were, Paris is where I felt most at home," she said. "But that's for another night. It's late. We've finished the second bottle, and I've rambled on. Next time you have to tell me your stories."

What stories could he tell her? About his childhood in communist Bucharest or about his year in a refugee camp in Athens where they were receiving CARE packages? Or perhaps he should tell her about his years among the immigrants of Worcester, all huddling together, terrified of the world, hoping it would go away. No, all of that belonged in a black box securely sealed and hidden in some dark recess of his mind. He was Bill Hefflin, the son of a World Health Organization doctor with hints of royal blood. His job in the next few days was to remember the legend he'd created and the stories that filled in the background of his new identity.

"My tales aren't as colorful as yours," he said.

"Then just make them up. Create whatever history you want. But you've already done that, haven't you?"

He felt the hairs on the back of his head stand up. "What do you mean?"

"When we met, I thought you were Greek, but Hefflin isn't a Greek name, it's German. I looked it up. It has a long pedigree, coat of arms and everything."

He didn't remember ever telling her his last name.

"You assumed I was Greek," he said. "It happens that I just lived in Greece for a couple of years in my childhood."

She eyed him for a long moment, then, "Have it your way. From now on I'll think of you as Bill Hefflin, the man with no past. I like that."

She paid the bill, then whispered to the waiter and slipped some money into his pocket.

"We've both had too much to drink," she said to Hefflin. "He'll drive us back, then take the Metro."

They were chauffeured back to campus, the two of them sitting in the back of the Jaguar like royalty, not speaking, preferring instead to watch the lights of Boston go by, then the shimmering reflections on the Charles River as they crossed into Cambridge. He was dropped off in front of Lowell House with a quick kiss on the cheek that mostly caught the air, and the car drove off.

CHAPTER SEVEN

Bucharest
December 1989

OUTSIDE HEFFLIN'S WINDOW, soldiers in green uniforms carrying automatic rifles stood rigid, motionless, spread out over the barren airfield like chess pieces. There was only one other plane on the tarmac, silent, dead, a Russian make with "Aeroflot" stamped on the fuselage in Cyrillic letters.

"Welcome to Bucharest," the captain said in Romanian over the intercom, then repeated it in English.

The passengers disembarked onto the tarmac, and the soldiers herded them toward the terminal, which was eerily empty except for more armed soldiers standing in the corners like caryatids. The total silence was unnerving, a stark contrast to the frenetic activity of JFK, which he'd left behind only a few hours before.

He joined the line for the passport check—the passports having been handed back to them before landing—and when his turn came, he passed his passport through the grating to the uniformed soldier.

"Don't you have anything for me?" the young soldier said in Romanian, a brazen cold stare fixed on him. *God, even the soldiers?* He was an attaché with a diplomatic passport, for Christ's sake. He stared back pretending not to understand, the stupid American who knew nothing of official corruption, until he felt a tap on his shoulder. The stout, middle-aged matron behind him, dragging a large suitcase no doubt stuffed with presents for her relatives, handed him a pack of Kents and motioned with her chin toward the soldier. He shrugged and passed the Kents through the iron grating. The soldier dropped the pack into a large sack, its mouth agape to reveal it nearly full of packs of cigarettes, then stamped his passport. Hefflin opened his carry-on and handed the lady behind him a pack to repay her.

"Keep it," she said in English. "Don't you know how things work in this country?"

"My first time here," he said.

"God help you." She waved him away.

At the customs booth a man in plain clothes and a uniformed soldier rummaged through his carry-on.

"You are allowed one carton of cigarettes," the plain-clothed official said in English. Hefflin knew he was allowed three cartons. He'd done his homework. But the man didn't seem to want to argue.

"I didn't know," he said. "Please help yourself to some."

"Which carton do I take from?" the official asked. They looked at each other for a moment, two actors in a comic scene, both of them about to burst into laughter but for the shame that held them back.

"The open one, there." He pointed. The man took two packs—only two, my God, he wasn't such a bad guy after all!—threw one to his uniformed buddy, then waved him on.

He followed the general movement toward the exit of the arrivals terminal, to where a crowd of people behind a rope line were calling out excitedly to gain the attention of the disembarked passengers. He swallowed down the wave of emotion that swept over him at hearing his childhood language spoken all around him, no longer a cause for whispers between exiles in dark corners. Here it was public, legitimate, shouted out loud without shame.

He perused the crowd until he spotted a sign with his name written in bold black letters. The man holding it was tall, lanky, no more than twenty-five, he estimated, with dirty blond hair and sincere blue eyes—probably straight from the Farm. Both farms, in fact, for in the first five minutes they were together the young man told him he was from Iowa. His name was Henry. He had been in Bucharest for six months.

"A crazy place," Henry said as he toted Hefflin's carry-on and led him through the small crowd. "I've picked up a few words here and there, not so difficult if you know some Spanish. These Romance languages are all pretty similar."

"It's got some Serbo-Croatian in it, which makes it tricky," Hefflin said.

"Yeah?"

"With some Turkish sprinkled in, a remnant of the Ottoman Empire."

"No kidding. You studied the country, then?"

"Yes. Haven't you?"

"Yeah, sure, I read the syllabus they gave me, but it's all pretty alien, if you know what I mean."

"Yes, pretty alien," he said. "But in our line of business, we have to become as familiar with it as if it were our home."

They passed by the shouting crowd and more uniformed guards and finally exited the terminal where he had another revelation: The parking lot was a sea of identical cars, the Romanian Dacia, in either black or white, the only two colors available. The one car that stood out was the shiny black Mercedes parked to one side, the embassy car with a driver, waiting for him. Henry dropped the bag in the trunk while Hefflin slid into the back seat.

"Welcome to Bucharest, Mr. Hefflin," the man behind the wheel said. "I'm Tom. I'll be your driver while you're here."

"Hi, Tom. You know where I'm going?"

"To the Athénée Palace Hotel, then later to the embassy."

Henry got in beside him in the back seat, and they drove off.

"First time here, Mr. Hefflin?" Henry asked.

He nodded. "So how do you like it here, Henry?"

"It's pretty dismal, if you ask me," Henry said.

"I'm asking."

"Pretty dismal. The locals stand in line all day for bread, eggs, milk, shoes, whatever is being sold. They drink like fish this home-brewed crap—"

"*Tsuika*, plum brandy."

"That's it, and survive on these skinny chickens from Czechoslovakia, if they can find even those, along with this corn mush, similar to grits."

"*Mamaliga*."

"Yeah. Can't stand the stuff. Haven't had a decent steak since I've been here."

"If you ever do, make sure you know what kind of meat it is," he said with a smirk. "You may have an unpleasant surprise."

Henry laughed. "Don't worry, I've been warned. Still, you can't help feeling for the poor bastards. Forty-odd years of communism and what do they have to show for it? This son-of-a-bitch Ceausescu has dug one big hole for himself."

Not for himself, Henry—he lives like a prince—but for his people.

They passed a familiar building, a huge monstrosity built in the style of Soviet Socialist Realism resembling the Moscow State University: *Casa Scinteii*, the home of *Scinteia*, The Spark, the Party newspaper. This was the first building he recognized, and it gave him a chill. It was the symbol of everything he hated about the communists, their propaganda machine that published a rag full of lies about the West and weekly reports of Romanian accomplishments that never materialized. He was in Bucharest, no doubt about that now.

They drove down Avenue Kiseleff and past the Arch of Triumph, modeled after the French version. He saw other street signs that brought familiar echoes: Herestreu Park, Piatsa Victoriei, Piatsa Romana. He had memorized the layout of the city and many of its main avenues, but he would still need a map.

The Athénée Palace Hotel was a classic structure located in the heart of the city. It had a colorful history. Built in 1914, this grand hotel quickly became the center of fashionable society, and a cauldron of intrigue, rumors, false information, and top-secret intelligence. It had been a place where diplomats, black marketeers, spies, and prostitutes mingled naturally, spilling their tales over martinis and whiskey. Bucharest society was built on easy graft and the easy virtue of women—professional prostitutes interspersed with faded royalty and desperate housewives. The Athénée Bar had been the place where all these elements fed off each other, much like Rick's Café in *Casablanca*, though he suspected that under the communists it had lost much of its luster.

"Here." Tom handed him a bag as he got out of the car. Inside were several rolls of toilet paper.

"You're kidding," Hefflin said. "This is the Athénée Palace."

"This is Romania under Ceausescu," Tom said. "I'll pick you up in an hour."

CHAPTER EIGHT

Bucharest
December 1989

THE LOBBY OF the Athénée had little in common with the pre-War photos in the CIA archives. The place had the feel of an excavation of an ancient civilization that had been brutally defaced by a more recent and primitive one. A faded purple carpet covered its once-beautiful parquet floor. Cheap tables and chairs now stood, like embarrassed poseurs, in place of the elegant Louis XIV settees where ambassadors and statesmen had once discussed world politics. The marble Corinthian columns, still trying to retain their grandeur, stood witness, like ancient patriarchs, to the deterioration of their once-celebrated home.

The young man behind the reception desk greeted him with, "May I help you, sir?" in English. He had already been pegged as an American. He told the man his name.

"Mr. Hefflin, cultural attaché at the American Embassy, welcome," the man said breezily. "Your room is ready. Your passport, please."

He handed his passport, which the man opened and studied, taking notes in a large notebook, then handed back to him.

"Please carry your passport on you at all times in case an official requests to see it."

The man handed him the key to his room, then leaned toward him. "You will need local currency, yes? I can exchange at twice the official rate."

He knew the man was either a Securitate agent or an informant, as was every employee in the hotel. He also knew that every room in the hotel, public or private, was bugged. The offer was thus either allowed by the authorities or a way of compromising the guests.

He decided to establish his image as a naïve American, a young attaché new to the country. He took out his wallet and slowly counted out two hundred dollars. The man's eyes widened as he stared at the green bills. Was he giving him too much? What did two hundred dollars buy in Romania? He calculated the local *lei* at double the exchange rate and realized it was more than several months of a laborer's salary.

"A moment, please. I have to go to the safe." The man took the dollars, disappeared into a back room, then returned a few minutes later with a bundle of Romanian currency, which Hefflin shoved into his pocket.

"You don't want to count?" the man asked.

"I trust you."

"Ah, this must be your first time in Bucharest," the man said with a harsh laugh.

"Yes, first time. From the little I've seen, it's a gorgeous city."

The man leaned closer to him. "Would you like a woman for tonight? Any type you want: blonde, brunette, blue eyes, young, very young. I can arrange everything."

More kompromat. *So soon.*

"Not right now, thank you," he said. "But I'll keep it in mind."

"Or two women together."

"No, thanks."

"Oh, you prefer boys? I can arrange that, too, a nice boy, very clean."

"Just show me to my room, please."

The man grunted in disappointment, then banged the bell on his desk. A bellboy dressed in a shabby gray uniform appeared out of nowhere.

"You can have a drink at the bar—whiskey perhaps—while the boy brings up your valise," the man said. "You had a long flight, no?"

The boy lifted the carry-on, but Hefflin stayed his arm.

"I can carry it myself, thank you. Just the key, please."

He didn't care that they would rummage through his bag while he sipped his watered-down whiskey. There was nothing compromising for them to find. He just didn't want his cartons of Kents to disappear.

The man's face drooped in disappointment, then he pointed with his chin as he handed over the key. "Second floor, up the stairs."

As Hefflin trudged up the steps, he noticed two young women sitting in the chairs behind one of the columns. One of them hurried after him, a platinum blonde wearing a red dress and high heels. She caught up with him and gave him what she obviously considered to be a sexy smile.

"Company, mister?" she said in English.

"Not right now, thank you."

"Maybe later? Just one pack of Kents for the night."

Only one pack? Has the price dropped so much?

"No, thank you."

"Coffee. I'll stay the night for a bag of real coffee."

He knew coffee was scarce in Bucharest and that she could probably get a high price for it, but the offer shocked him nonetheless. Were times that desperate? He walked on, reached his room, and inserted the key. As he entered and turned to close the door, he saw she was still standing there. She had slipped the spaghetti straps off her shoulders and was showing him her naked breasts.

"I am very good in bed. The best you ever have."

"I'm married." He showed her his finger bearing a wedding band, which he'd placed there for just such an occasion.

"So? Your wife not here, no?"

"My wife is in here." He pointed to his heart.

As he closed the door, he heard her mumble in Romanian, "Stupid American romantic."

Jack Stanton, the station chief in Bucharest, had called the Athénée a factory for spying. Everyone, from the young man at the reception desk to the bartenders, waiters, cleaning ladies, and prostitutes, worked for the Securitate. All hotel phones and rooms were bugged, as were most of the pay phones in central Bucharest. The cleaning ladies were known to photograph all the papers left in the room, including those in the wastebasket. The same was true for the InterContinental and several other hotels where foreigners stayed.

None of that concerned him. He wasn't carrying any classified papers, and he didn't intend to say anything of importance on the phone. He was only worried about the remaining packs of Kents, which he suspected wouldn't be there when he returned. He stuffed his coat and jacket pockets with all the packs except one, which he left for the taking. On his way out, he peeked into the bathroom. Tom had been right. He placed the bag of toilet paper on the floor and prayed it would still be there when he returned.

CHAPTER NINE

Bucharest
December 1989

THE AMERICAN EMBASSY was a splendid Neo-Renaissance structure surrounded by a lush, overgrown garden. The original home of Maurice Blank, a celebrated banker and financier of Romania's War of Independence, it stood one hundred meters from the InterContinental Hotel. Long-range cameras and listening devices protruded from the top floor of the hotel, trained directly on the American Embassy. Apparently, the Securitate felt no need to hide them.

The inside was replete with marble floors, crystal chandeliers, and high ceilings painted with bucolic scenes. A man in a suit escorted him up the long staircase to the office of the chief of station inside the secure Operations room.

Jack Stanton, the chief of station for the past three years, was an overweight, balding, forty-something guy from Brooklyn. Hefflin found him sitting behind his desk holding a cigarette in one hand and popping M&M's with the other. He had dealt with Stanton over the phone and through wire messages, but this was the first time he was meeting him face-to-face.

Before he was allowed to step inside the Operations room, two men scanned his body with an electronic device, then his overcoat. At the bottom corner of his coat, the scanner buzzed. They examined the coat, tore apart the lining, and removed a round metal object the size of a quarter. They handed it to Stanton who held it up for Hefflin to see, then casually dropped it into his glass of whiskey.

"The TAROM flight attendant offered to hang up your coat, didn't he?" Stanton said.

Hefflin nodded.

Stanton chuckled. "They plant bugs all the time. I found one in my hat once, which I had stored in the overhead bin. They probably bugged it while I was in the can." Stanton put his feet up on his desk and looked him up and down. "So, Boris told you to come here, did he? He thinks there's something brewing?"

Stanton was one of the few who knew about Boris and that it had gained Hefflin a certain cachet with the Agency heads.

"The whole Evil Empire is coming apart," Hefflin said.

"Not here. Ceausescu's got the place tighter than a duck's ass," Stanton said. "They say that one in four locals is either an operative or an informant of the Securitate. Our guess is more like one in twenty. Still, you never know who it might be, that's the beauty of it. It could be your neighbor, your uncle, your brother. He's kept the people paranoid for decades."

"All good things must come to an end," Hefflin said as he sat in the chair across from Stanton.

"And there's his son, Nicu, an alcoholic, cocaine-sniffing playboy who spends more time in European casinos than at home," Stanton continued. "He's supposed to be the heir apparent."

"I doubt he'll get the chance."

"Don't be so sure"—Stanton snorted—"Ceausescu's a very wily guy. I can see him making some minor changes and loosening up the system just enough to appease the masses. The

Romanians are just dumb enough to fall for it. So"—he chewed on his M&M's—"what do you have for me?"

Hefflin stared at him, confused. "Have for you?"

"Yeah, they gave you something for me—new orders, intel—where is it?"

"They didn't give me anything."

"Then what are you doing here?" Stanton demanded.

He bristled at Stanton's tone but said nothing.

"Why are you here?" Stanton repeated more loudly, then let his feet drop to the floor with a thud.

"Boris wants me here," he said. "And so does Avery."

Stanton found another glass and poured from an open bottle of Johnny Walker Black. "Boris wants you here? And Avery just put you on a plane? To do what?"

"Whatever it takes."

"Christ! The Agency is going to shit," Stanton burst out. "Since when do assets dictate the actions of their handlers? Not that you actually handle anything, from what I gather. Boris just sends you intel. You don't even know who he is."

"I know he's never been wrong," Hefflin said. "Look, I don't want to be here any more than you want me to. I was ordered to come to Bucharest, against my objections, to meet Boris and see what he wants. Everyone is assuming Romania is going down, despite your doubts. Maybe Boris has a higher opinion of analysts than you do."

"American analysts?" Stanton laughed. "He'll pick your brain—and your pockets—before the first vodka. One of my men will have to go with you."

"Nobody is coming with me," Hefflin said. "Boris won't meet with anyone else."

Stanton came around his desk and loomed over him. "Look, there are rules all field agents need to follow. No fraternizing with locals. Any contacts, even casual ones, must be reported to me—date, time, a description of the contact, and what exactly was said. And an analyst, untrained in field work, certainly can't meet a Soviet asset alone."

"You should have received orders from Langley," Hefflin said, meeting his eyes. "Look them up."

Stanton searched through his mountain of papers on his desk and found the right one. "God almighty. 'Allowed to meet contacts without surveillance. Free rein to mingle with locals.' It says that here, in fucking black and white. You must be some hot shit." He gulped down his whiskey and poured another. "So, how is Boris supposed to contact you?"

"No need to know." Hefflin smiled. "Now, do you have a map of Bucharest handy? I want to walk around and get a feel for this city."

Stanton cursed, then rummaged through his drawer until he found a map, which he flung across his desk. "Don't let your status go to your head. You'll be approached by all sorts, including the Securitate and agents from other countries. Don't discuss anything of importance with anyone, and don't drink with any of them. And, most importantly, don't let any gypsies get close to you or you'll find yourself without a wallet or passport. The cute little girls are the worst."

After the meeting, Tom drove him to Cismigiu Park where he wanted to begin his pilgrimage. From there it was only a short walk to Strada Sirenelor, if he found the courage.

CHAPTER TEN

Bucharest
December 1989

THE MOMENT HE stepped into Cismigiu Park, he caught the faint aroma: a peaty, spicy smell, with a sweet, sappy tinge. Immediate images flashed in his mind: springtime, kids on bicycles, a man selling balloons, Sunday morning walks with Pusha along the gravel paths. The smell was everywhere, the air suffused with it. It instantly melted his chest, bathing it with a warmth that he hadn't felt since childhood. He searched for the source. A powder of snow covered the ground. The chestnut and walnut trees were but brittle skeletons, the flowerbeds barren. But there were many evergreens. He rushed to one of them, grabbed a handful of pine needles and brought them up to his nose. That wasn't it. Something else. He started walking.

The air was cold, the sun a faint beacon barely visible through a gray haze. At a row of cement tables, pensioners in heavy overcoats were playing chess while observers stood around them, silently pondering the boards. Women with children were milling about, a man with a cart was selling candy. Hefflin moved on, still searching. The smell was growing fainter, so he doubled back, took another path.

It was more intense now. It was there, somewhere close. The paint on the bench? No, it was old and peeling. He noticed a wall of shrubbery. Despite the calendar, their leaves were still clinging on like desperate castaways. Could they be the source? He brought his face close to a bush and took a deep breath. Yes, there it was, that heavenly fragrance. He pinched the leaves and breathed in until his lungs and brain were suffused with that divine aroma. How silly. Just some shrubbery. And yet it caused such an overwhelming sense of well-being, of childhood joy, which he had craved for so long.

He sat on a bench holding the crushed leaves next to his face, relishing the memories. He saw the pond in the distance, rowboats stacked on its banks, all covered with a thin layer of snow, the same pond but not the same.

It had been one of those long Bucharest falls. His mother was gently pulling on the oars, careful not to make the boat rock. Pusha was holding a bag of berries and popping them into her mouth.

"It's for good, isn't it?" she asked.

"It's Greece. Of course it's for good," he answered.

"Can you come back and visit?"

"Not for a while, I think. Not until I'm old enough."

They both remained silent, a chasm slowly growing between them.

"I don't want to leave," he whispered. "Maybe we can run away."

She smiled sadly. "You're such a silly boy."

"I'll write every day, I promise."

"Once a month, if you can," she said.

"Once a month? But I'll have so much to say. It won't all fit in one letter."

"Just tell me how much you love me."

"I'll fill the entire page with 'I love you. I love you,'" he said.

"And that you haven't found another girl."

"Another girl? What other girl? I promise to love only you, forever and ever."

"And I you, forever and ever."

A tear formed at the corner of her eye and rolled down her cheek.

Pusha, his first love, the deepest, the template. But she had abruptly stopped writing after a year, while he was still in the refugee camp in Greece. No explanations, no good-byes. He had wallowed in his misery for months, betrayed, abandoned. Yet he could not rid himself of her, and over the years she had become a symbol of not just lost love, but a lost childhood. Paradise lost. Love gradually morphed into worship, even prayer. It was not until much later in college, when he met Catherine, that he broke his own side of the promise, and that infidelity hurt him even now, ridiculous as it was.

The frigid wind was picking up, and he could see even the chess players were gathering up their pieces. He couldn't stay there any longer reveling in memories. He charted a path on his map toward Strada Sirenelor and rose to go. His pulse suddenly pounded in his chest. Would it still be there or had they demolished it? Maybe it was too late. Maybe he had come for nothing. His panic choked him. He started running, faces turning to gaze at the crazy man. It was only a few blocks away, but he had to traverse a thousand years to get there.

＊　＊　＊

He walked in the middle of the street, the uneven cobblestones under his feet helping his body remember. It was on this street that he used to play soccer with the neighborhood boys. But either the place had greatly deteriorated since he'd left or his memory was playing tricks. Gray stucco houses, once covered with lush ivy, were now dry and crumbling; fences stood broken, like toothless grins; sidewalks were cracked, collapsing. Most of the houses looked empty. *Perhaps it's too late, perhaps my house, too, is now deserted, and there's nobody left to tell me where to find her, or who I am.* Surely Tanti Bobo was still there. He started running down the street, his body suddenly light in its despair. The dark windows were agape, laughing at him; the cobblestones echoed his panic. All this may have been for nothing.

He stopped before a wrought-iron fence. Could this be it? But it was too small, much too small. The gate squeaked as he pushed it open. As he stepped into the narrow courtyard, he recognized his house on the right, still there, the only two-story structure in the courtyard. The windows and doors were now barricaded with rotting planks, long fissures cut the face of the building, and the small balcony on which Tanti Bobo used to read his mother's fortune in the coffee grounds now tilted, barely holding on. It was like seeing an old friend on his deathbed. The nausea rose up and almost choked him.

On the left of the courtyard the other houses stood in a row, single-story buildings that had been part of his mother's dowry. They had been occupied, in order, by Mr. and Mrs. Chiobanescu, Tanti Bobo, and Mr. and Mrs. Adrianu. The last one was where Pusha's family lived. But now the houses looked deserted, the roofs crumbling, the walls exposing large areas of bare brick.

He stood before the barricaded door to his house, unsure of whether to try to enter. Perhaps it was better to live with the memories rather than pollute them with images of decay, which he would never be able to erase from his mind. Yet something urged him on, a perverse desire to suffer and make himself feel it all. His hands, as if acting on their own, pulled off the rotten planks. He pushed on the door with his shoulder and it flew open, inviting him to enter.

The hallway was dark and smelled of mold. After his eyes adjusted, he saw an oil lamp in the corner of the floor. It still had some oil in it. Once he lit it, he could make out the stairs, rising up to their apartment on the second floor. The house had belonged to his family before the War, along with the other buildings in the courtyard. But after the War, as the story went, the new communist regime nationalized all private property. The house was deemed too decadent for one family, so they ordered another family to inhabit the first floor: Mr. Trent, a lawyer who wore a monocle, along with his wife.

He placed his hand on the banister on which, as a child, he would slide down every morning. It was now chipped, with several of its balusters missing. The wooden stairs creaked as he climbed. On the top landing he remembered an icebox near the window, which the iceman would fill with a block of ice each week, holding it with large tongs. To the right were the doors to the bathroom and kitchen, to the left the French doors leading to the rest of the apartment, which he now pushed open. He found himself in his old bedroom, and an old familiar memory suddenly hovered like a balloon above the floor where his old bed used to be.

It was in the middle of winter. Outside it was snowing heavily and the wind was howling. He remembered tucking himself under the heavy quilt and waiting for his father to start.

"Are you ready?" his father asked.

He nodded, his heart pounding with excitement.

"So, which story do you want to hear tonight?"

"The one with the hunter in the forest," he said.

"Ah, yes, that's a good story. So . . ." His father sat in a chair by his bed, cleared his throat, and began. "Once upon a time there was a hunter. He wasn't a very good hunter, as hunters go. The reason was that he didn't like killing anything."

"How can he be a hunter, then?" he asked.

"Well, that was the problem. He did it because he had to, like so many things in life. He was forced to hunt so his family could survive, but he didn't like it just the same. Anyway, one day he is in the forest. It is a bitterly cold winter day, and it is snowing heavily, with big, fat snowflakes, just like tonight. The sky is covered with dark clouds and there isn't even an inkling of the sun. The snow is so deep that his legs keep sinking up to his knees. His feet and hands are frozen, and he can barely walk, but he plods on, because he has to. Still, after several hours, he finds no prey—no rabbits, no foxes, no deer."

"Where are they?"

"Home with their families, like you are tonight. It's too cold to be outside. So, after several hours of walking, he decides to give up and go home. It is then that he realizes he's lost."

"Uh-oh."

"Yes, it's easy to get lost in the forest. The trees all look the same. And since he can't see the sun, he doesn't know east from west."

"What about his compass?"

"Well, I was getting to that," his father said. "He searches for his compass but realizes that he must have dropped it along the way."

"He's a clumsy hunter." He giggled.

"Yes, well, I did say he wasn't a very good hunter. So, what does he do?"

"He tries to retrace his steps in the snow."

"That's right. But after doing so for a little while, he finds that the heavy snowfall has covered his tracks. Still, he marches on, even though he knows he might be walking even deeper into the forest."

"Is he scared?"

"Of course he's scared. But even so, he doesn't lose hope. He knows he has to return to his family because they depend on him. So, on he goes, step by step. Soon he sees the daylight dwindling and knows that if he doesn't get out of the forest before nightfall he may freeze to death."

"Oooh."

"Just then he hears a noise."

"What kind of noise?"

"At first it's just the sound of movement of the brush. Then he hears a low growl."

"Oooh."

"He can't tell which direction the growl is coming from because of the howling wind. So, he raises his gun and slowly continues on."

"He's brave."

"Yes, I guess he is. Even though he hates killing, he knows he has to defend himself. Just as he passes by a big tree, he sees it: a big Russian bear."

"Are they the biggest?"

"They are certainly the fiercest. They can eat a man with just one swallow."

"One swallow?"

"Yes, believe me when I tell you. But this bear is lying down by the tree. He growls a few times, but the hunter can see that his heart isn't into it. Then he realizes why. The bear is wounded. The snow around him is red with his blood."

"What does the hunter do?"

"Well, at first he thinks he must kill it, because he knows there is nothing more fierce than a wounded animal. So, he raises his rifle, says a prayer for the bear, and is about to shoot when the bear starts talking to him."

He giggled again. "Bears can't talk."

"How do you know? In any case, this bear can."

"What does he say?"

"The bear says, 'It's no sport shooting a defenseless bear. I am wounded. I can't hurt you.' The hunter is surprised, to say the least. He's never heard a bear talk before. But he believes the bear."

"Why?"

"First, because the bear has an honest face. And second, because he sees how weak the bear is because of the blood he has lost. So, the hunter comes a little closer and sees that the bear's front leg is bleeding badly, probably from a shot by another hunter."

"What does he do?"

"He says to the bear, 'I can help you. I can place a tourniquet on your leg to make it stop the bleeding. You will die otherwise.' 'You want to help *me*?' the bear says in surprise. 'I am your natural enemy, though I have never eaten a man. Just little animals, poor things.' The hunter sees that this bear is like him. He hates to hunt and only does it to survive. So he says to the bear, 'I hate to see anyone suffering, especially a wonderful bear like you. But you must promise me that you won't eat me once I put on the tourniquet.' 'I promise,' says the bear. 'I don't have an appetite anyway.' 'And also, I am lost and need directions to get out of the forest and back home,' the hunter says. The bear agrees to that, too. So, the hunter uses his scarf to tie a tourniquet around the bear's leg and the bleeding stops immediately. The hunter tells him that he must bite off the tourniquet in an hour or so. By then there should be a clot, so he won't bleed anymore. The bear says he'll follow the hunter's directions. Already he is beginning to feel better, and he stands up. The hunter is suddenly awestruck by the enormous size of the bear and is afraid the bear will eat him."

"But he's an honorable bear, isn't he?" he asked.

"Yes, he is. The bear points with his nose and says, 'Walk that way, and in an hour or so you will be out of the forest. And thank you for saving my life. We will be friends forever.' He then gives the hunter a big hug."

"A hug?"

"Sure. Haven't you heard of a bear hug? So, the hunter follows the bear's directions and arrives home to his family in time for dinner."

"Does he ever see the bear again?"

"You know he does. For the rest of their lives the hunter and the bear remain the best of friends. They meet in the forest every week or so and discuss world events over tea with honey. So, are you ready for sleep?"

"I think so."

"Good night, then, and dream of the great friendship between the Russian bear and the reluctant hunter, and how they saved each other's lives."

Memories, like spirits, hid in the nooks and crannies of the apartment, pouncing to frighten or melt the heart of the returning child, now an adult. In the dining room, which was now empty, a mahogany dining table once stood, under which a memory was now waiting to ambush him. It was on that same table that he used to play chess with his father every night.

He remembered a particular evening during which his father was playing without a queen. He had his queen bearing down on one of his father's pawns protecting the king, with his knight and rook threatening the same pawn. His father's pawn was protected by his king and knight, while the other pieces were on the other side of the board doing God-knows what.

"I think I have you," he said, then took the pawn with his knight. His father took the knight with his knight, then he took his father's knight with his queen.

"Checkmate," he said, his excitement ready to explode.

"Not so fast." His father pointed to a bishop on the other side of the board whose path had suddenly opened up by the movement of the cursed knight. It now took his queen.

"Where did that bishop come from?" he cried.

His father raised his index finger, a teaching moment. "Always beware the hidden bishop. In life as well as in chess, the unexpected, the unseen element, that's the hidden bishop."

But there was another memory, a more recent one, lying adjacent to the old memory because of that damnable chess piece. It was at Harvard, very early in their relationship. Catherine had challenged him to a friendly game of chess. But a friendly game was not what she had in mind.

CHAPTER ELEVEN

Harvard University, Cambridge, Massachusetts
January 1980

SHE HAD GIVEN him directions to her off-campus residence—a large, one-bedroom apartment furnished with what looked like real antique pieces from some Louis-the-something period. When she opened the door, he gasped. She was dressed in a black dress that reached just above her knees, sheer black stockings, black heels, and a pair of black opera gloves that stretched up to her elbows. Edith Piaf was singing *C'est l'amour* in the background.

There was a bottle of red wine already opened and "breathing." He wondered what his parents would say if he told them to let their gallon bottle of Gallo breathe before mixing it with seltzer water. The chess set was waiting for them on a small table near a lamp with a pink shade. The pieces were beautifully carved out of mahogany and, as he lifted one up, he noticed they were weighted.

She poured the wine and they clinked glasses.

"A Saint-Estèphe," she said. "By now you must realize that I love Bordeaux wine."

"I just thought you like wines named after saints."

She smirked. "Now, the rules: for every piece we lose, we take off an item of clothing."

His pulse began to race. A faint hint of nausea. "Now I understand the opera gloves."

"A lady has to plan ahead." She pursed her lips.

"A lady doesn't play strip chess," he said.

"Oh, you do have a lot to learn."

She played white, lady's privilege. Her attack began with pawn to D4, which he countered with pawn to D5. The game proceeded with no pieces taken by either of them. He castled. She moved bishop to E2. He took her pawn with his, DxC4. She slowly removed one of her gloves like a stripper, all the while her eyes never leaving his, and draped it over the couch. He was trembling inside, not daring to face where this was leading. She took his knight with her bishop. He removed his jacket. He took her bishop with his knight and she removed her other glove. They played on. By the end of a half hour, he was barefoot with his shirt off and she was in her stocking feet and black slip. Edith was singing *Non, Je Ne Regrette Rien.*

"You work out." She eyed his chest. "And you're tanned."

No, just Greek. "What does the winner get?" he dared to ask.

"The winner chooses what *she* will do with the naked body before her."

He pushed down the panic that was urging him to flee. "You mean *he*," he said, taking one of her knights. She wiggled the spaghetti straps off her shoulders and let the slip drop to the floor. Underneath she was wearing a black corset with black garter belts tethering her black stockings.

"Not fair," he protested, though not convincingly, for she was a sight that stole his breath.

Her taking his knight two moves later forced him to stand, unbuckle his belt and drop it to the floor.

"A belt? Isn't that part of your pants?" she objected.

"Not unless your garter belts are part of your stockings."

"Very well, you'll still lose." She blew him a kiss.

Two moves later he took one of her rooks. She stood, placed a stocking foot on his armrest, and slowly pulled down her garter belt. "I'll even give you a bonus, since you're losing." She unrolled her stocking inch by inch, slipped it off her foot revealing dark red nail polish, then wrapped the stocking around his neck. His head was swimming. It was too late to back away now, not if he wanted to see her again, or retain his dignity. She lost another piece a move later and repeated the tease with her other stocking. She had only her corset and panties left—black silk, edged with lace. He, too, had only two pieces of clothing left, his pants and underpants.

He lost a bishop next and stood on uncertain legs to unbuckle his pants.

"Let me do it," she whispered. She knelt before him and began fumbling with his top button, no doubt purposefully, for she must have seen his erection. She pulled down the zipper, then let the pants drop.

"Black shorts, just as I thought." She laughed. "Most American men wear boxers, like my father. How silly." She brushed her hand against his bulging penis. "Someone seems to like this game."

He stepped out of his pants and pulled her up. "You don't want to end this game prematurely."

"Certainly not, though I suspect it would only be a short delay before resuming the game." She giggled.

They sat back down before the field of battle. He was ahead in pieces but suspected it was only by her connivance, to even out their initial imbalance in the number of items of clothing.

"Another bottle is in order," she declared, "for the endgame."

As she rose, he watched her lithe body move like a panther to the small wine rack on the kitchen counter. She pulled out a bottle and handed it to him to open. It was a different wine now with a name he didn't recognize: Châteauneuf-du-Pape. He pulled out the cork with the corkscrew and poured. Neither of them touched their glasses.

It was his chess move. Though on the surface his position looked good, he didn't trust the gleam in her eyes. She watched his face, then his hand as it moved the queen to check her unprotected king. She moved her knight to block. It was a desperate move, one answered by simply taking her knight with his queen, which he did, though nervously. She stood and with slow, teasing movements, unclasped her corset and swung it to the floor. Her breasts were firm, beautifully shaped, with pale nipples fully erect. The bulge in his underwear felt like it was about to burst. He took deep breaths and tried to control his passion by counting backward from one hundred. He remembered having read that in France women sunned themselves topless on the beach, so maybe this was no great concession on her part. Yet, for an immigrant in America, the image was magical.

"Now we're even," he said. "We each have only one item left."

She was sporting a mischievous smile, perhaps foreshadowing a secret trick that she was about to spring on him. She moved her king out of check. It was then he realized that this move opened the channel for a lone bishop on the other side of the board, which he had totally forgotten about. His king was now in check.

"Where did you learn that move?" he asked, stunned.

"The hidden bishop," she gleamed. "You didn't see it, did you?"

The goddamn hidden bishop that his father had warned him about. His panic caused him to scramble for an escape. His king had only one possible move, for her rook blocked the other file.

He reluctantly moved the king, sensing a catastrophe in the making. Her cold eyes pierced his while her hand hovered above her pieces, finally settling on her queen. She picked it up in those slim fingers with the red nail polish, and floated it above the board. His eyes followed like a condemned man watching the falling blade of the guillotine, until the queen settled on a square across from his king.

"Checkmate."

He was numb, his mind frazzled by his undeniable annihilation. Her hand motioned for him to stand and she led him to the bedroom.

The only light in the room was a flickering candle in the corner, which cast trembling shadows over the bed. As she pulled him onto the bed, the kindness in her voice, soft, even maternal, "I'm your first, aren't I?" tamed his trembling body and the terror it revealed so treasonously. He had feigned his way to this point, an impostor impersonating a man of the world, suave, urbane. But now his act had come to an end, the poseur revealed. She took his silence as an affirmation. His instinct was to flee, to save whatever was left of his dignity. But the kindness in her voice kept him there, along with a feeling of being safe, of a warmth that penetrated his spirit, a feeling he hadn't experienced since childhood.

She pulled him on top of her, her tongue teasing open his mouth, her hands gently pulling down his shorts. And then a warmth, moist and inviting, and he realized she'd already discarded her remaining item of clothing without his noticing and that he was now inside her, safe and yet so vulnerable. Her soft whispers, "You're wonderful, so wonderful," urged him on and he found that his body knew how to make love, his hands tenderly touching her where they produced pleasurable moans, his hips engaged in a slow dance with hers, until she gripped him tightly, her legs wrapped around his waist, and they both entered into convulsions that seemed to suspend all time.

That evening was to be followed by countless other magical nights during which she slowly brought him along, carefully, tenderly, until he had let go of his inhibitions. She had been his teacher in love as well as in spycraft. And, in his mind, the game of chess had forever become infused with her sexuality.

✳   ✳   ✳

He now brushed away the memories of Catherine and exited the remains of what had once been his house. As he sat on the outdoor steps, he tried to let the memories of a sweeter, more innocent life suffuse his mind, their remoteness and simplicity forming a safe island to which he could return for comfort. He remembered summer days lying with Pusha under the apple tree, she feeding him a berry for every kiss; evenings with Tanti Bobo reading their fortunes in their palms. Images, long buried, of a young boy named Fili and a girl named Pusha who were once inseparable.

He brushed aside those memories also. He reminded himself that, sadly, life moved on. Time marched only in one direction. Even if he found her, the girl with golden hair would now be a total stranger.

CHAPTER TWELVE

Bucharest
December 1989

As HE WALKED down the brick path of the courtyard, he felt something hit his shoulder. He realized it was bird droppings, an omen of good luck. A crow was circling up above. The part of him that still believed in magic was encouraged, expecting Pusha to come skipping out of her house and jump into his arms. But when he reached the spot where Pusha's house had once stood, all that was left was a shell of a building overgrown with weeds. There was a deep silence in the old *maidan*, the barren field where they had once kept chickens, broken only by the cawing of the crow circling high above. In the corner of the field stood their old apple tree, not as tall as he remembered it, but still retaining much of its majesty. He now noticed a figure was sitting on a stool underneath it, silently watching him: a gray-haired woman with a deeply wrinkled face, dark eyes, and a lit pipe hanging in the corner of her mouth. Though the long black hair had turned gray, the black eyes were the same, sharp and untrusting, gypsy eyes that pierced a man's soul.

"Come here, boy," she said in a hoarse voice.

He stared at her without moving, savoring the moment when he was still a stranger. It wasn't too late; he could still turn and run without her knowing.

"Come closer, boy. I've been expecting you. How lucky I am to see my little Fili again." She rose and opened her arms to embrace him. He hesitated, then buried his head in her bosom, as he had done so many times before.

"How did you know I was coming?" he asked.

"The crow told me." She pointed to the black bird that was now perched high up in the apple tree. "I've lost track of time. You have grown big and handsome." She crossed herself. "The crow also told me about your parents' passing. God bless them both. I loved them more than my own family. Come." She pulled him toward the same one-room house in which she had always lived, now much smaller than he remembered.

Inside it was dark and warm. Red embers in the open fireplace still radiated heat. He remembered the red embroidered peasant rug, faded and worn now, the oak chest in the corner that held all her gypsy clothes that Pusha loved to try on, the wind-up Russian phonograph on which she would play old gypsy ballads. But what was most familiar was her smell of dry smoke that he had grown to love and identify as his own.

She opened a drawer and took out an old tin box tied with a yellow ribbon, then sank into a faded red chair that he now recognized as the chair whose arm he would straddle as a little boy and pretend it was a horse.

"I've been forgetting things," she said as her trembling hands untied the yellow bow. Out of the tin box she took a bundle of photographs, which she set in her lap. "If one loses her memory, there's not much reason to go on living."

She sifted through old photographs, faded and yellow, then lifted one up to the light and looked at it, her eyes trying to push back the veil of time, to see the picture with her memory, to remember the particular day when she had sat on a stool under the apple tree with a dark, smiling little boy on her lap to have her picture taken. For it was a picture of him she was looking at, dressed in his gray knit *spilhozne* and white shirt, barefoot, sitting on the knee of a younger Tanti Bobo. He remembered her colorful gypsy dress, which in the old black-and-white picture translated into shades of white and gray. Her face was wrinkled even then, the wind and dust of her gypsy country life having left their mark early. But she looked happy, smiling, showing a golden tooth. Her bearing, straight-backed, tall, had the undeniable mark of pride. The camera had caught her heel raised off the ground in the act of bouncing the laughing little boy on her knee.

Then the picture went back into the pile and another one appeared, this one of a group. His mother, father, and Tanti Bobo were standing together and, in front of them, a seven-year-old boy. Tanti Bobo had her hands on his shoulders, as if protecting him, declaring and displaying, and at once laying claim.

And then that, too, disappeared, and after a little rummaging through the pile, a third photograph, the most fantastic of all, for it pulled him into it and had him feel and taste and smell what he'd craved for over twenty years, what he remembered without knowing. The picture, faded and cracked, showed the proud gypsy woman with her golden tooth nursing a baby at her breast.

"I was your wet nurse," she said, still holding the picture, her hand trembling more now, her eyes becoming moist. "I had just lost my own, and I still needed to feel a baby on my breast, so your mama let me nurse you, bless her soul."

"You had a baby?"

"It was taken from me very soon after it was born. I hardly had time to get to know it. But that is a long story." She waved at the air, shooing away the hovering memories. She put the pictures back in the box and then looked at him once more, trying to fit this new, adult Fili into her scheme of things. He suddenly felt ashamed at his stubbly face, and his abandonment of childhood, and thus of her, to time and old age.

"May I take these pictures?" he asked.

"Of course, you must take them. They are for you." She wrapped several pictures in an old scarf and handed him the little bundle.

"Most people are gone," she said, her head shaking. "They're going to tear down the entire neighborhood. There are a few families left but they, too, will leave soon. As for me, I asked them to let me stay as long as possible. I don't know if I can survive moving again, after living here so many years."

"A gypsy who doesn't like to move?" he said.

She smiled, her golden tooth showing. "No longer a true gypsy," she said. "I've lived too long apart from my people. The gypsy blood leaves you if you don't feed it." She put her pipe down on the table with a curious violence. Another displaced person.

She placed the tin box back in the drawer with care, as if storing a basket of food for the winter, and then leaned back in her chair, relieved, perhaps, that it was safely tucked away, able to feed her memory at a later time.

She began listing the boys in the neighborhood. "Little Mugur became a policeman, of all things. I haven't seen him in years. He married a Moldavian girl, but where they're living and what they're doing, I don't know. Mihai is a famous soccer player. He plays for Dynamo. Ninel has become a mechanic, and Luca, may God have mercy on his soul, Luca is one of *them*." Her face grew grim.

"Luca?"

"Luca Soryn, you remember him, the neighborhood bully. He joined the evil ones, the Securitate. High up. I never see him, but I hear stories. You never know what to believe."

Hefflin remembered him now. He had been a tall kid even then, always angry, beating up the neighborhood kids, even Hefflin a few times. He sighed. His friends, Pusha, all of it gone, irretrievable, leaving only remnants of memories.

"You have suffered. I can see it in your face," she said. "You still hold a grudge against your parents for taking you away. But theirs was a selfless act. It was much harder for them than for you to adjust to the new country."

"Maybe." He sighed. "But they only had to take their scars to their graves, while I still have a lifetime to live with mine. We became people without a country, like—"

"Like gypsies," she finished his sentence.

"I'm sorry."

"No, you're right. It's not a happy life. But Romania was never your country. You're not Romanian and would never have been accepted as one. The Romanians like to make distinctions. Your parents were always referred to as 'the Greeks,'—next to Gypsies and Jews, the most despised."

"And in Greece, where we lived in a refugee camp, we were known as 'the Romanians,'" he said. "In America, among other Romanians, we became 'the Greeks' again. It never ends."

"Yes, the gypsy analogy is an apt one." She nodded. "It's a condition you inherited from your parents, and they from theirs. If blame you must, blame your grandfathers who left their mountain villages in Greece before the War to seek a better life in Romania. But, of course, you can't blame ancestors long dead, so you blame those you can." She sighed. "But your parents left for you. They always acted unselfishly. I wouldn't be alive today if it hadn't been for them. Did they ever tell you the story?"

"No."

"No, they wouldn't. Let me tell you, then."

CHAPTER THIRTEEN

Bucharest
December 1989

"I FIRST MET your father after the War," Tanti Bobo began. "I was a true gypsy then. I belonged to the *Kaldaresh* tribe. My father was the *voivode*, the leader, of the *Mandale* clan. But I made the mistake of falling in love with a *gadjo*, a white man."

That was a real tragedy for a gypsy, he knew, because a gypsy could not marry a *gadjo* and still remain part of the tribe.

"He was a lieutenant in the Romanian army. Funny thing, I met him when he brought his men to drive us out of a prohibited area where we had camped," she said, her eyes far away. "I used to be pretty in my youth, and I caught his eye with my dancing. He didn't drive us away, but merely watched me dance. The next night he came and took me with him. I was going to say stole, but he didn't have to steal me. My heart leaped out to him. We became lovers that first night. I was brought back before dawn, and the clan knew nothing about it. It went on the same way for months. It was the happiest time of my life. He used to call me his gypsy queen and show me off to his men. I was proud and happy to be with him because, you see, I was in love."

But one day, she said, she found out she was pregnant with his child. To be pregnant and unmarried, and by a *gadjo*, no less, was unforgivable for a gypsy. As her belly grew, she piled on more clothes. Finally, it became too big to hide, and she had to confess. She was brought before the *Kris*, the assembly of elders who were the judges of the tribe. She confessed to everything, cried, and declared her love for the young lieutenant. But she had brought shame to her family and her people. They didn't take long to decide her guilt. She was banished from the tribe, as was the gypsy law. All the clothes and possessions that she couldn't carry with her were burned, like a leper's. Her name could no longer be spoken in the tribe. Their memory of her was erased.

That was the hardest thing for her to accept, she said. She no longer had a mother or father, or home, or past. And when the lieutenant found out she was pregnant, he disappeared. She was alone, desperate. She no longer wanted to live. Without her people, she was nothing, adrift in the world.

"So one night I broke into a pharmacy, stole some sleeping pills, and swallowed them all. I was in such a state that I didn't even think of the baby, God forgive me." She crossed herself. "I was lost, my soul destroyed. Your father found me on the street, half dead, and took me home with him. He pumped my stomach and kept me alive, bless the man. He let me live with your mama and him until I delivered my baby. Your mama was only a year younger than me but your father was ten years older. Still, we got along famously. They were angels, both of them. Then they moved me into this little house that was empty at the time, and I started earning a living telling fortunes and cleaning other people's homes."

"And your baby?" he asked.

"My baby. Yes, he was a wonderful baby." Her expression changed to deeper sorrow. "When my father found out he was a boy, he sent two men in the middle of the night to take him from me. I was the only child, you see. I suppose my father's desire for a grandson, even though the child was illegitimate and only half gypsy, was stronger than his hatred."

She never saw the baby again. Her parents and tribe moved on. She never heard from them.

"The reason I tell you this story is to make it clear that I still love my father, even after he banished me," she declared. "Because, you see, it was he, as the *voivode*, who had to pronounce the final orders, he who had to declare me a *gadje*, a non-gypsy. He had the power to override the decision of the *Kris*. But he didn't. He acted like a true *voivode*, even though it broke his heart to do so, because it was in the interest of the gypsy family as a whole. Your parents, too, acted in the interest of your family by leaving this country. It would have been easier for them to stay. Your children, and your children's children, will benefit the most."

"What if I don't have any children?" He asked her the same question he'd once put to his father. "Then who will have benefited from our leaving?"

She looked at him with her black, moist eyes. "Do you hate your poor parents that much that you would punish them posthumously by ending your family line?"

He did not answer.

"You were too young to understand then," she said, feeling his silence. "Now you're no longer too young. But your sorrow has a deeper cause. So, tell me the real reason you returned. You came back to find someone in particular."

His heart leapt. "Yes, I came to find Pusha."

Her cracked face opened up into a smile. "Yes, I know. I've always known. I just wanted to hear it from your own lips."

"You remember her?"

"Remember her? How can I not? You two . . . were always together. I've never seen such love, though I've heard of it, love that grows over many lifetimes."

The gnawing pain in his stomach rushed up to his throat. He felt his eyes tear up and he turned away.

"You must find her," she said, "or your life will never live out its purpose."

"But where is she?" He sat up, wiping his tears. "What happened to her?"

She shook her head, her face cast in dark shadows. "Her parents died a little over a year after you left. The word was that they were struck by a trolley as they were crossing the street. A drunk driver. It's no different today. Trolley and bus drivers are drunk before lunchtime. You will find them carrying their own bottles of homemade *tsuika* inside their coats and taking drinks while they're driving. No one dares say anything. You don't know how things are here." She waved her hand. "Pusha had no other relatives, so she was placed in an orphanage. The closest one, I think. St. Bartholomew's. I never saw her again. That is all I know."

"An orphanage." He let the news sink in.

An orphanage. Pusha. A year after I left, when I was in the refugee camp in Greece, and her letters stopped coming. She didn't stop writing because she forgot me.

"She must have been in shock, poor girl, how could she not be?" Tanti Bobo went on. "Alone in one of those horrible institutions."

He had read reports of Romanian orphanages where thousands of children were warehoused under terrible conditions. He could not bring himself to imagine Pusha there.

"How do I go about finding her?" he asked, his heart in his throat. "She must have left the orphanage years ago."

"Go to the orphanage," she said. "They always keep records."

The crow was still perched high in the apple tree when he left Tanti Bobo and made his way down the brick walkway past his old house. Strada Sirenelor was deserted. The cold wind had picked up, and the clouds had moved in.

He was still reveling in his memories as he turned the corner, so at first, he didn't notice the figure coming toward him. It was only when he heard a car pull up behind him that he saw the man with the dark overcoat and fur hat that was almost upon him, his head down, as if watching the slippery sidewalk. Hefflin turned to see a black Dacia with two men inside screech to a halt next to him. As one of the men got out and opened the back door, the man in front of him suddenly looked up at him and was about to push him into the car when he froze, his gaze focused on something behind Hefflin. As Hefflin followed the man's gaze, he saw a fat man in a heavy tan overcoat walking quickly toward them, his arm stiff by his side, his hand holding something long. Then Hefflin realized what it was: a pistol with a silencer. The fat man quickened his pace and raised the pistol. The man in front of him let out a swear word, then both he and his comrade scrambled into the car and sped off. The fat man stopped, looked at Hefflin for a moment, then turned back the way he came.

He listed against the wall of a building and remained frozen for several minutes, unable to breathe, his hands trembling. He fought off shock as he tried to put it all together.

The men in the car must have been Securitate, surprising, since he had barely just arrived in Bucharest. But who was the fat man with the gun, and why had he intervened? All these people had obviously been following him, and he hadn't even noticed.

He was just a stupid analyst after all, unaware of the environment around him.

What had happened to the skills he had honed at Harvard, the skills that Catherine had taught him, even before his training at the Agency? Even though his memories had been suffused with Pusha's story, it was the image of Catherine, his first teacher, that once more came to the fore.

CHAPTER FOURTEEN

Harvard University, Cambridge, Massachusetts
1980

BY THE TIME he arrived at the Fly Club, a little past eight, she was already there. She gave him one of her air kisses on the cheek—a single one this time—and led him to Tyler.

"A word with you, Hefflin," Tyler said. "Upstairs in the Green Room, if you'll indulge us."

He glanced at Catherine, a brunette again ever since their dinner together. She smiled and nodded as if to say, "It's all right, nothing bad."

The Green Room was a quaint sitting room with several leather chairs arranged around a coffee table and a roaring fire in the open fireplace. He'd never been in this room before, didn't even know it existed. It was located on the far side of the building, around a corner, beyond the three bedrooms. They each took a chair while Tyler handed out tumblers of Lagavulin.

"Mr. Hefflin, as you will no doubt recall, your method of admission to this venerable club was a bit unique," Tyler began.

"You're being quite formal today, aren't you, Tyler?" he said. "Is there something amiss?"

"Nothing amiss, dear fellow. We still love you like a brother, and the formality is only in line with the seriousness of the topic at hand."

Catherine was looking at him, though no longer smiling.

"As you will recall, your admission was influenced by an important supporter interested in your success at Harvard. I must say, you've turned out to be a most auspicious find, and a nice guy to boot."

"Thank you," he said, though he sensed a "but" coming.

"You've done very well in your studies—you have a 3.7 GPA, if I'm not mistaken," Tyler went on.

How does he know my GPA?

"It'll be 3.8 by the end of the term," Hefflin said.

"Excellent. I wish mine were close to that. What, if I may ask, are your plans after Harvard?"

"My father still hopes that I'll be applying to medical school," he said, "but I'm leaning toward grad school in economics."

"Excellent. Now, what I'm about to tell you requires discretion on your part. My words may not leave this room."

Hefflin felt his interest pique and leaned forward ever so slightly. "Very well."

"It will not seem too extreme, I hope, if you confirm your acceptance of these terms with your signature."

"My signature?" He was a little taken aback.

Tyler handed him a piece of paper. "It's simply an agreement that states the obvious, that you won't discuss with anyone what I'm about to tell you."

The document was similar to the nondisclosure agreements he'd studied in one of his economics classes. The only peculiar thing about it was that at the top it had the seal of the government of the United States. His name was typed at the bottom.

"Why am I signing a government document?"

"That will be obvious once you've heard my recitation."

"What are you getting me into, Tyler?"

"Nothing nefarious, dear fellow, I assure you. Ms. Nash can attest to that."

"Just a game." Catherine winked.

Hefflin signed the document and handed it back.

"Excellent. Now, we are here to formally invite you into a society whose existence no one, including the school's administration, is aware of. This society is composed of a select group of like-minded individuals consisting mostly of undergraduates, with some graduate students and a couple of professors mixed in. The purpose of the society is to see if certain students are suited for, and would consider a career in, the clandestine services."

"The CIA?" he gasped.

"That's one of the services, but not the only one. What we do is play games. Spy games. This way you can see if you like it, and they can see if you have a talent for it."

Hefflin sat silent for a moment, unsure of whether to take this seriously or treat it as a prank. "What do the games involve?"

"They vary. Sometimes you will be assigned a student at random, and you'll have to follow him or her without being detected. Or you may be asked to discover as much as you can about a person. You can use any means you can think of: research, direct observation, discreetly interviewing friends or relatives, anything that your imagination can conjure up. You might look into such things as their friends, casual acquaintances, lovers, business associates, anything you can find. You will be judged on your thoroughness and creativity. If the quality of the intel is good, you get bonuses. Monetary bonuses. They can run anywhere from hundreds to thousands."

He couldn't believe what he was hearing. "Who will be doing the judging?"

"*They* will."

"I suppose I won't ever know who *they* are?"

"You may. It depends on *them*. Does something like this interest you?"

"It sounds intriguing, like living in a spy thriller," he said. "What happens to the information I gather?"

"It all gets destroyed. We certainly don't want to compromise the privacy of any person. This is simply an exercise in cunning, social skills, wit, bravery, and bravado. Even if you decide this isn't for you, you'll have honed observational skills that will come in handy for the rest of your life."

Hefflin glanced at Catherine but she was looking down at her hands.

"As long as it doesn't interfere with my studies, I'm in," he said, partly for the possible income, which he desperately needed, but mostly because Catherine was a part of it.

"Excellent." They all rose and clinked glasses. "To Hefflin, our new player." The three of them gulped their Lagavulins, then Tyler and Catherine threw their crystal glasses into the fireplace. He did the same. The crystal exploded like fireworks.

"Come." Catherine took him by the arm. "I have a surprise for you."

She pulled him outside where her Jaguar was now parked in front of the entrance.

"Where are we going?"

She gave him a catlike grin. "For me to know and for you to find out."

*　　*　　*

They drove into Boston, all the while Catherine refusing his entreaties to reveal their destination. Charles Aznavour was singing on a tape, and she even sang along with some of her favorite songs. Her mood was festive. He, too, was ebullient, as if he'd just passed a test.

"The guy following you at our first dinner was part of the game, I assume," he said.

"He's no longer in the game," she said. "He flunked out."

"Because you spotted him?"

"I was his third failure. Normally they don't assign a player to follow another player, but after failing twice they assigned him to follow me so I could see what his problem was."

"And?"

She shrugged. "He didn't have the feel for it. Followed too closely at times, allowing me to spot him, too far at others and thus losing me. He tried to ask one of my professors questions about me in such a clumsy manner that she became concerned and told me about it. And when he found out I was an ambassador's daughter he called the State Department to get information about me. Can you imagine? The State Department immediately informed me, and I had to reassure them he was harmless. That was the last straw."

"I'll try to be more discreet."

"I know you will be." She smiled.

She took him to a Beacon Hill townhouse that belonged to a Saudi prince, who apparently never used it, where she introduced him to a different set of people than he was used to. They were all in their twenties, wearing expensive clothes and drinking cocktails while swaying to soft jazz.

"Who are all these people?" he asked.

"They're all children of wealthy families," she said. "Some are from Harvard, others from colleges around here. The very rich pretty much all know each other, either from private schools or tennis camps or vacations in the Alps or charity balls. They don't distinguish between new or old fortunes, as they used to, just the size of them." She laughed. "Ah, here he is."

"Who?"

"The man I want you to meet."

He looked to where she was pointing with her chin, a young man with a dark complexion, black curly hair, and black mustache who reminded him of Omar Sharif. He had just entered the room with three other young men who were carrying bottles of Johnny Walker Black.

"His name is Abdullah bin Sultan," she said, "the son of the Saudi defense minister, and a junior at Harvard. He lives in Kirkland House. He is your first assignment."

*   *   *

He waited outside Kirkland House until midnight for two consecutive evenings but didn't see anything out of the ordinary. On the first evening he was dressed as a homeless person and was carrying a large garbage bag, while on the second he had bought a blond wig. On the third evening, while sporting a false beard, which he picked up at the Drama department, he spotted a Harvard freshman he'd seen at the party enter Abdullah's apartment a little before eleven. Hefflin waited outside for several hours but did not see the young man leave.

For the rest of the week, he simply followed Abdullah in the evening. On one of those evenings the Harvard freshman brought along two other young men to Abdullah's apartment and by one in the morning they still hadn't left, at which point Hefflin went home. On another evening Abdullah and two different male friends drove to a nightclub in Boston, and Hefflin followed in a taxi. They stayed until half past one in the morning while he sat drinking coffee across the street in an all-night diner. Then they all drove to the Copley Plaza Hotel and took a room, at which point he returned to his dorm room.

At the end of his week, they met in the Green Room of the Fly Club, where Tyler and Catherine listened to his report. When he finished, they sat quietly, digesting the findings.

"How much of this did you know, Catherine?" Tyler asked.

"I suspected he preferred boys, but certainly didn't know anything about his orgies," she said. "I'm sure his father would be mortified."

"Homosexuality among Arabs is definitely frowned upon," Tyler said. "Well, Hefflin, you've certainly proven yourself, especially with the photographs you took. I'm quite confident that our game sponsors will be impressed."

Catherine smiled proudly.

Two days later, he found an envelope sitting on his desk in his dorm room. Inside was a note: "Congratulations on quality work." Behind the note lay ten one-hundred-dollar bills. The CIA? The NSA? He didn't much care. This was real money.

During the next several months, he was given three other assignments: the son of an American general who was into cocaine, the daughter of a conservative rabbi who engaged in nightly trysts with goyim, and an assistant professor of Polish literature who was having an affair with a secretary at the Polish Consulate of Boston. For his efforts he received a total of five thousand dollars. His spending money was certainly in better shape than it had ever been, so he didn't question it any further. His investigative skills had dramatically improved. Though he initially felt a twinge of guilt over invading other people's privacy, the fact that it was only a game and the reassurance that the information he had gathered would all be destroyed put his mind at ease. With the new money he was even able to take Catherine to the opera. Her pride at his success was evident, and his carnal rewards from her were at an all-time high.

One day Pincus approached Hefflin to say that he was one of the small number of professors who took part in the spy games. This did not surprise Hefflin, for he already suspected that Pincus was somehow responsible for his receiving that invitation to join the Fly Club. The initial meeting with Pincus, during which Pincus had drilled him on his knowledge of world affairs, had seemed like a job interview at the time, which now led Hefflin to suspect that Pincus had connections to government intelligence.

Pincus said that he was proud of Hefflin's achievements in the games and that he thought Hefflin was ready for the next level. He began teaching Hefflin intricate ways of passing on information using dead drops, handoffs in subway stations or along city streets, and coded writing. It was still just a game, Pincus insisted, but Hefflin suspected he was being groomed for a more clandestine profession. Hefflin told Catherine of Pincus's new role, and she did not seem surprised, but was rather proud that Pincus had taken him under his wing. Hefflin felt ebullient in his new role as master spy.

CHAPTER FIFTEEN

Bucharest
December 1989

St. Bartholomew's Orphanage was situated in an old institutional building in the outskirts of Bucharest, a three-story structure with a cracked stucco exterior, small windows with bars on the first floor, and a red tile roof, much of it broken. It was apparently still operating.

He asked the taxi driver to wait for him and climbed up the cement front stairs that led into a small hallway, where a middle-aged woman in a winter coat and hat sat at a desk reading a book. He didn't feel any difference between the temperature outside and inside the building.

He asked in English about a girl who was brought there years before. He wrote down the name: Pusha Pantelimon.

"Pusha? That's not a real name, just a nickname, short for 'doll,'" the woman said in Romanian.

He realized he had never known Pusha's actual first name. He resisted the urge to speak to the woman in Romanian.

He repeated the last name in English and pointed to the paper.

The woman shook her head. "Records that old are in the basement, and I'm very busy," she continued in Romanian.

There was no one else in the reception area, no sounds of children playing, nothing to break the silence except for the ticking of the wall clock. He took a pack of Kents out of his coat pocket and dropped it on the desk. She looked at him with insolent eyes, waiting. He dropped a second pack. Without expression and with a casual efficiency, she pulled out the middle drawer, swept the two packs into it, and stood.

"Wait here," she said in English.

She was gone for over a half hour, during which time he saw no other person enter or leave. And he neither saw nor heard any children. When she returned, her head was shaking.

"No, not here," she said in English.

"Not here? Why?"

"Maybe you make mistake. Another orphanage."

"No, this is the correct orphanage."

"Then too many years now. Dossiers get lost, taken. Who knows?" She shrugged.

He thanked her and walked out, disgusted with her attitude, with the country, even though he'd barely arrived. He had held the hope that someone had adopted Pusha and that he could track down the family. But in Romania few wanted to have children of their own, and even fewer cared to adopt. The birth rate under communism had dropped to such low levels that tax laws had been passed punishing couples without children. But who would want to bring up a child in this country, even if they could afford to?

His heart sank at the thought of Pusha spending her entire childhood in that bleak, battered orphanage. What had it done to her? What kind of person had she become? And once the children reached the age of eighteen, he knew, the orphanages released them out into the world with minimal education and few job skills, unprepared for life.

What was he to do now? He had reached a dead end.

He was grateful that at least the taxi was still waiting for him. He didn't know if he could find another one in that neighborhood. He told the driver to take him to the hotel, then leaned back, trying to erase the images that were forming in his mind. His Pusha was nowhere to be found, an orphan adrift in the morass of that communist hellhole. And if he ever found her, she would not be his Pusha anymore.

At some point he noticed the driver looking into his rearview mirror and thought that he was looking at him. But then the driver's glance switched to the side mirror, and it was obvious he was looking at something behind them. Hefflin turned to look out the rear window. A black Dacia was trailing some fifty feet behind them, the only other car on that secluded street.

"You American, yes?" the driver asked.

He said he was.

The driver breathed a sigh of relief. "That explain it. I was thinking they are after me."

"Who?"

"The Securitate behind us."

Hefflin turned to look again. He could make out two men inside.

"Can you do something to lose them?" he asked.

"Lose them?" The driver laughed. "You do not lose Securitate. You lose them, they find you at home. You just get used to them. They are everywhere, like rats."

✳   ✳   ✳

At the Athénée he skipped the bar scene and trudged up directly to his room. When he opened the door, he stopped. The scene was too absurd, even for Romania. A naked woman was sleeping in his bed. She couldn't have been twenty, if that. She was a beautiful redhead, not the same one who had approached him before. Upon hearing him enter she raised her head off the pillow.

"Hello. I think maybe you are lonely, yes?" she said in English.

He saw a silky yellow dress draped neatly over the chair and a pair of black high-heeled shoes underneath it. The dress was in good condition but dated. He examined the label and found that it was French and real silk.

"It belong to my grandmother." Her eyes lit up. "You like? I put it on for you." She hurried out of bed and slipped the dress over her head. It looked good on her. He handed her the shoes. She slipped them on and posed. "Better with high heels, no? It makes breasts and ass stand up."

"Please go."

"But why?" she said in Romanian. "I'm more beautiful than any girl in the hotel. Just ask anyone."

He knew she had switched to Romanian to see if he had lost his cool and would respond in the same language, after which she would report it to the Securitate. But he only motioned with his chin toward the door.

"Only a small bottle of real vodka, that's all," she continued in Romanian, "for the whole day and night."

"I don't understand anything you're saying, and I don't care," he said in English. "Now go."

She held her chin high in an attempt to salvage whatever was left of her honor as she walked out the door. On checking his bag, he saw that the pack of Kents was gone, probably taken by the cleaning lady since this young woman had nowhere to hide it. He glanced into the bathroom and was relieved to see that at least the toilet paper was still there.

He lay on his bed, more dejected than ever, for once the flame of hope is lit, the wind that extinguishes it makes the darkness seem even deeper than before. Pusha and Catherine, the two loves of his life, both gone. They were quite different—his love for Pusha was that of childhood innocence, idealized, while his love for Catherine was passionate, adult. Yet they were similar in one respect: both had abruptly ended the relationship without warning or explanation. He questioned whether either of them had ever loved him, or if love existed at all. It had felt like love then, and they had both said the word a few times, but other women had said similar words to him since then, and he'd learned to ignore them. One eventually learned from one's mistakes.

It exasperated him, the knowledge that he had no way of changing anything, other than to wait for another life in which things turned out better. Or perhaps the quantum physicists had it right: There were an infinite number of universes in which various permutations of him got the girl—Pusha, Catherine, or both. Both? Perhaps in one universe he was a Muslim, married to both Pusha and Catherine. He tried to imagine how that would work. Would he be able to divide his love between the two of them? Would they be able to share him? Would his love for each be half of what it would be with one alone, or was love infinite in its capacity?

He surrendered in frustration, reminding himself that in this universe he had neither.

He removed the scarf that Tanti Bobo had given him containing the old pictures. As he unwound the scarf, the pictures fell out and spread on the bed. Among them he noticed one he hadn't seen before. He held the picture up to the light. Three young men standing next to each other. The picture was blurred, cracked, yet he recognized the first man to be a much younger version of his father. It was taken in the summer, in a park among bushes and trees, the men in short-sleeved shirts. On the reverse side was a date: 1947. *Right after the War. Why did Tanti Bobo include this picture?*

As Hefflin peered closer, the second man next to his father looked vaguely familiar. For a moment he thought it resembled Professor Pincus. But that was absurd. How could his father have known Pincus in Romania in 1947? Pincus had told him he had fled Romania in 1938. He focused on the third man, tall, thin, clean-shaven, towering over the other two. Hefflin didn't recognize him. The picture was too blurred and faded for him to be sure of any of them.

He put the pictures away and focused again on finding Pusha. He still had one slim hope: Luca, the former neighborhood bully. Tanti Bobo had said he was a high official in the Securitate, so he would know how to track her down. But where to find him and how to approach him without divulging his own past? There was even the chance that Luca might recognize him. Still, he was desperate. He hadn't yet heard from Boris, so he had a little free time. He decided he'd ask Stanton to help him find Luca. Tanti Bobo had mentioned his last name: Soryn.

✻   ✻   ✻

"Are you nuts? What the hell are you doing wanting to talk to the Securitate?" Stanton fumed. They were sitting in Stanton's office the next morning, the ashtray already filled with butts.

"It's a personal m-matter," Hefflin stammered. "A friend of mine asked me to find an old childhood friend of his. Nothing to do with spying or geopolitics."

"A personal matter?" Stanton looked at him incredulously. "There's no such thing with the Securitate. Any information they gather they'll use to their advantage. Just by walking into the office of the Securitate marks you, either as a naïve idiot or a spy trying to do who knows what."

"It's just an innocent request to find a little girl from twenty years ago. Expats do this all the time."

"Not by going to the Securitate."

"This man, Luca Soryn, lived on the same street as that little girl, apparently," he said. "She was sent to an orphanage after her parents died, but they have no record of her. I got this from an old woman I visited yesterday. I just need him to look into any files they might have on her in some archive or other. It's the only lead I have. Besides, Boris hasn't contacted me yet. I'm just using my time to do someone some good."

Stanton sighed in disgust. "At the very least, someone should go with you."

"No, then it would look like an official visit, and that's not what this is. Look, there's no way I could be compromised. This is just an innocent request to track down a childhood friend."

"There are a hundred ways you could be compromised, and the fact that you don't see it worries me even more," Stanton said. "What the hell does Boris want with you here, anyway?"

After searching through the database on his computer, Stanton wrote something on a piece of paper, crumpled it up, and threw it at him. "He's a fucking colonel in the Securitate. A colonel! He'll milk you for information, then open a dossier on you the moment you leave. Don't say anything stupid."

Hefflin called right away and was given an appointment that afternoon.

*   *   *

Luca Soryn was a tall, fat man in his thirties wearing a tight gray suit that he'd obviously bought at a time when he was much thinner. Despite the appointment, Hefflin was made to wait for over a half hour outside the office in a straight-backed wooden chair especially created for making one uncomfortable. He wondered how many less fortunate souls had sat in that same chair, trembling at the thought of a Securitate interrogation.

As Hefflin now stood across from the colonel, he tried to catch a glimpse of the young boy—tall, lean, dark haired—an image that only vaguely resembled the porcine apparatchik before him. He recognized the eyes, perhaps, and maybe the nose, though both were perverted by the fat cheeks dotted with spider veins, the telltale sign of chronic alcoholism.

"Mr. Hefflin, please take seat," Soryn said in heavily accented English, then leaned back in his chair behind his massive desk, his position of power, and assumed his somber Securitate tone. "What can I do for the American cultural attaché? A strange time to come to Bucharest, no?"

"Is it?"

"There are fascist hooligans trying to stir up trouble. I am sure you have heard. Nothing we cannot handle, of course. But the times are—how do you say?—delicate."

"Actually, I came to see you on a more private matter," Hefflin said.

"Oh?" Soryn leaned forward, perhaps smelling an opportunity.

"I have a friend in America who was born here. He asked me to look up a childhood friend of his, a girl, that he knew when they were young."

Soryn's body relaxed. He sank back into the chair, patted his pockets, then spotted the pack of Carpati on the desk. Hefflin offered him a Kent.

"Don't mind if I take." Soryn reached for the pack.

"Keep it," he said. "I have plenty more."

"Thank you." Soryn lit up and inhaled deeply. "What is friend's name?"

"Vasili Argyris. His girlfriend's name is Pusha Pantelimon. They used to live on Strada Sirenelor."

He saw a flash of recognition pass over the man's face, then the eyes veering to the left as he searched his memory.

"Strada Sirenelor? That is where I grow up."

"Yes, I went there," he said. "An old gypsy woman mentioned your name. She thought you might be able to help."

"Ah, that explains it." Soryn let a smile pass over his lips as he inhaled the cigarette. "Yes, I do remember a gypsy. Is she still alive? She must be very old now. And I vaguely remember a boy, the son of a doctor."

"Yes, his father was a doctor, I believe."

"And there was a girl, cute thing, more mature than her age. They were always together." Soryn's face took on a dreamy expression. "Ah, childhood. Things were much simpler then, yes?"

For a moment, Hefflin saw the years melt away, along with all the unspeakable acts that a Securitate agent had to perform, and felt a passing sadness for the man. Then Soryn's expression changed.

"Pusha, yes, that is what everyone calls her, I remember now. I never know her real name. Sad case. Her parents died in bus accident, I believe, or something like that. She was instituted in orphanage."

"I've been there, St. Bartholomew's," Hefflin said, "but the woman there couldn't find her records."

"Really? That is unusual. We keep very good records in this country."

"Yes, I know. That's why I came to appeal to you. I thought you, being an important official and an old acquaintance, might be able to help find her."

"Yes, perhaps." The compliment seemed to inflate the man. "But if the dossier is missing, it may be impossible. It was such a long time ago."

"I understand. I just thought I'd try one last person, my last hope."

"Yes, of course. Where are you staying, in case I find something?"

"At the Athénée Palace," he answered, though he was sure the man had already found that out before seeing him.

"Very well." Soryn looked at him as he rose to shake his hand. "*Nu vorbits Romineste?*"

"Sorry, I don't speak the language," Hefflin said.

"You will not have much success as cultural attaché." Soryn laughed.

"I hope to learn it, in time."

"Let us hope you are here long enough, Mr. Hefflin," Soryn said as he showed him out.

CHAPTER SIXTEEN

Bucharest
December 1989

THE BAR AT the Athénée Palace was crowded. A group of mostly men had arrived from the InterContinental Hotel where there had been a row. One of a group of German businessmen discussing world politics over dinner had asked a waiter not to hover near their table. The waiter became offended. Several "guests" suddenly intervened, identifying themselves as Securitate, and the businessmen got up and left. Others followed. Among them were some low-level diplomats and the few Western journalists that were in the country, intermingled with the usual prostitutes, vultures who had followed their prey to the Athénée. The Athénée of old, which had been the center of intrigue for so many years, was now promising to become so again.

Hefflin squeezed to the bar and asked for a *Stoli* on the rocks, not bothering with the lime. He knew they hadn't seen any in years. Next to him were two reporters speaking American English.

"When the hell is something going to happen around here?" one asked. "I've been here almost a month, and it's as if nothing has changed. Ceausescu looks as comfortable as ever."

"Still, the news is filtering in," the other said. "The people know that communism is on its last legs."

A man sidled up next to Hefflin and ordered a whiskey.

"Which country are you from?" the man asked him in Romanian. The man was young, good looking. Behind him stood what looked to be his wife, smiling at the room.

He hesitated long enough to remember not to answer in Romanian.

"Excuse me?" he said in English.

"Oh, sorry, I thought you spoke the language," the man said in English. "Many businessmen do. You a journalist?"

"State Department. You?" he said, trying to turn the conversation toward the stranger.

"We live in Chicago, me and my wife," the man said. "Every couple of years or so we come back here to see our parents. They're getting old now. Sometimes we don't tell anyone we're coming just to avoid obligations." The man let out a laugh. "I know it's bad form, but really, we'd need several crates if we bought presents for everyone. What do you do at the State Department?"

"I'm a cultural attaché."

The man laughed. "I suppose that's not an easy job if you don't know the language."

Here it was again. "I specialize in official etiquette," he said, "like who sits where at a state dinner, how you're supposed to address an official, that sort of thing. We have translators for the rest of it."

"It should be easy in Romania," the man said. "Just address them as Crook Number 1, Crook Number 2, and so on."

Is this guy for real? Doesn't he know there are microphones everywhere? He put on his diplomatic smile. "My job is to make things run smoothly."

"Of course. You're a diplomat. Still, it can't be easy to keep a straight face when you have to show respect for the hoodlums running this country."

Is this guy a plant intended to draw me out? Is everyone in this bar an informant?

"Work, work, work, that is the American motto," the man continued. "The saying—it was originally about Russians but it applies just as well to the Romanians—'We pretend to work—'"

"'—and they pretend to pay us,'" Hefflin finished the sentence.

"You've heard it. Well, at least we didn't have to work our asses off in this country. And what's it all for? We'll all end up in the same place in the end."

"Hard work is what made America great," Hefflin said, hoping that banalities would bore the man enough to drift away.

"We should have gone to Germany or France," the man said. "You know, Europeans work to live—"

"—while Americans live to work. Yes, I've heard them all."

"There's truth in that." The man slapped the bar. Apparently, he had had a few drinks before he got there. "In America I work, eat, and sleep. That's it. Oh, and I watch TV. I'm too tired to even pay attention to my wife, if you know what I mean."

Hefflin glanced at the man's wife who was pretending not to listen. "There's no perfect system," he said with a shrug of the shoulders.

"A diplomat to the end," the man said and, to his relief, turned his back to him.

"Mr. Hefflin, I believe?" One of the reporters was now staring at him. "John Evans, AP News."

He was taken aback. How did this guy know him? As if sensing his thoughts, Evans said, "We check airline rosters every day to see who is coming in. You're the new face on the block."

Great. He had hoped to slide in and out without anyone noticing the faceless bureaucrat. But this was a small town when it came to foreigners, he reminded himself. New faces were a curiosity, at least for a few days.

"I thought they closed the borders to foreign media," Hefflin said.

"They have. We got in a month ago. This is Archie Zinwald, *Herald Tribune*." The man pointed with his chin to his buddy.

Hefflin nodded to both men. "You have IDs?"

The men both took out their official press IDs and showed him.

"Sorry, but you know the routine," Hefflin said.

"No insult taken," Evans said. "Securitate is everywhere. So, can I ask you what you think of the changes happening all over the Soviet Bloc?"

"I'm the State Department cultural attaché," Hefflin said, then turned to pick up his drink. "Anyway, I suggest such discussions take place somewhere other than here."

"Oh, we know this place is crawling with bugs," Evans said. "Same with the bar at the InterContinental. But it doesn't matter. We're the press. And you're a diplomat. They can't do anything to any of us."

"Don't be so sure," Hefflin said. "There have been foreign reporters killed in many parts of the world."

"For sure, but here everyone knows what's going on," Evans said. "Romania is the last holdout. We're all asking the same questions."

"Well, then, I think we're witnessing the inevitable march of history," Hefflin said. "People all over the world want freedom, a basic right. Sooner or later, they'll get it." He sipped his drink trying to determine how he was going to escape these journalists.

Evans leaned closer. "When do you think that will be?"

"Hard to say." He shrugged. "The Romanian people have certainly suffered enough." He gulped his drink, then ordered another.

"How the hell are you going to convince Ceausescu to step down?" Zinwald whispered. "He's pretty entrenched."

Hefflin picked up his second drink and tried to step away from the bar and the ears of the bartender. But the journalist tugged at his sleeve.

"What's the U.S. going to do if he refuses?" Zinwald insisted. "I mean, you must have a plan, right?"

Evans pulled him away from the bar toward a corner, as if there were any place in that hotel that wasn't bugged. "A cultural attaché, well, that's code for an Agency man. And you coming here now, just when the rumors are flying. What message are you carrying?"

"I'm just here to ease diplomacy," he said. "That's what a cultural attaché does."

"So, you're here to ease him out?" Zinwald said. "How do you plan to do that? Off the record, of course."

"Maybe we'll just make him an offer he can't refuse." Hefflin laughed. "Off the record, of course." The drink was getting to him. "Now, gentlemen, you know I'm only jesting. The people of Romania will decide their own future."

"Sure, sure, but you must have contingency plans," Zinwald kept on.

"There are always contingency plans, a whole dossier of contingency plans." He waved his arm. "That's what government bureaucrats are paid to do. Few are ever used."

He regretted saying that the moment it left his mouth, especially using the local "dossier," which had recently come into his lingo. He spotted a free table and excused himself.

He sipped his second *Stoli* as he took in the room. Most people were standing, wanting to hobnob, to hear and spread the news, or, at least, the rumors. It wasn't much different than New York cocktail parties except for one thing: it was quiet. Everyone was whispering, wanting to avoid the eavesdropping waiters and hidden microphones.

A man sat next to him, middle aged, wearing a worn suit. His face was unremarkable, a blur, the face of a bureaucrat. The most dangerous kind.

"Excuse me, Mr. Hefflin, just a word with you, if you'll be so kind." The man's English was good, the best he'd heard since the Securitate agent on the plane.

"Who are you?" Hefflin asked.

"My name is unimportant. Just think of me as a civil servant. A poor one, I might add."

"Aren't they all. What do you want?"

"I have something that might be of interest to you." The man pulled out several photographs from his pocket and passed them to him. One showed him standing next to a naked girl, the girl he had found in his room. The other showed her next to him putting on her yellow dress.

Hefflin broke into laughter.

The man looked at him with obvious surprise. "Surely, they are embarrassing, are they not?"

"If I had a wife, or a boss who knew nothing about this miserable country, perhaps," Hefflin said. "As it is, I'll frame them and hang them in my office."

The man gathered the pictures and replaced them in his pocket. "You Americans," he spat. "One moment you act the Puritan, the next the playboy." He stood and hurried out of the bar.

Securitate. So now they are actively trying to compromise me. This first attempt was amateurish, but the next one may not be. He wondered how they had taken the pictures.

He noticed a man staring at him from across the room. He recognized him immediately, a face he'd seen in his files, the Bucharest chief of station of the Hungarian intelligence service. The man was sitting at a corner table with two women whose hands were all over him, annoyed that his attention had been diverted. The Hungarian stood, ignoring the women trying to pull him back, and started walking toward him. Did the man know him? He certainly didn't want to talk to him, not in this place.

The Hungarian walked by him, set his drink on the bar, then turned and gave him a subtle sign with his eyes toward the exit. As the Hungarian walked out, Hefflin wondered how the station chief of Hungarian intelligence knew him, a faceless analyst who had never been in this country, at least not as an adult. Still, if the journalists were aware of him, an intelligence service would be as well. Curiosity getting the better of him, he swallowed his drink and followed.

A black Mercedes with its motor running was waiting outside. The rear window rolled down and the Hungarian's face appeared.

"Let's take a ride," the Hungarian said in perfect English. "It's too cold to stand outside."

Hefflin hesitated. He wondered if this was normal. The station chief of a foreign country, until recently a part of the Soviet Empire, had just asked an American cultural attaché to enter his car. Though he wasn't a field agent, he *was* an agent, and any information he could gather was welcome, wasn't it? He didn't know whether it was the drinks, or that he just felt adventurous, but despite loud protestations from a little voice inside his head, he got in.

The Hungarian poured two glasses of vodka and handed one to Hefflin. The car started moving. He noticed that the window separating them from the driver was closed.

"*Noroc*, as the Romanians say," the Hungarian toasted. "It means luck. They certainly need it."

"*Noroc*," Hefflin repeated and tasted the vodka. It was not Stoli but an equally good brand, probably Hungarian.

"So, what is a CIA analyst doing in Bucharest?" the Hungarian asked.

How the hell did the man know him?

"I'm a cultural attaché at the State Department," Hefflin said, trying to keep up the charade.

"You're Bill Hefflin, the top CIA analyst on Eastern Europe," the Hungarian said. "You arrived a few days ago and have been roaming the city like a tourist. You're obviously not a field agent. Otherwise, you'd have noticed my two guys in Cismigiu Park, or the chess-playing Bulgarian agent with a mustache, or the fat man in the tan overcoat who eventually scared away the Securitate. I don't yet know who he is."

Hefflin stared at the man for a moment trying to decide which tack to take, then figured it wasn't worth the effort.

"You're Adorjan Balzary, Hungarian chief of station," Hefflin said.

"That's better. No more bullshit."

"So why are all these people trailing me?"

"You're a new face, an American cultural attaché, a spy until proven otherwise." Balzary downed his vodka and poured another. "Don't worry, they already figured out you're not a real player, so most of them will be assigned to other tasks."

"But how do you know so much about me?"

"I've been following your career," Balzary said, "along with the other guys at Harvard."

Harvard?

"I was a student there, during the same time as you," Balzary continued. "I actually remember you. Lowell House, wasn't it?"

Despite his effort, he knew his mouth was hanging open. So that's how Balzary knew him. The Hungarian chief of station was a Harvard alum.

"I was in Dunster House," Balzary said. "Loved every minute, though I had very little money for girls. My parents were refugees, practically penniless. If it weren't for the scholarship . . . well, you're wondering what I'm doing back here."

"The question crossed my mind."

"Nostalgia, pure and simple," Balzary declared. "My childhood memories, my friends, my native tongue, I missed it all."

Christ, another unanchored spirit. Is the world full of them?

"So, after Harvard, I came back here. Everyone, including my parents, thought I was crazy. People escape Hungary to come to America, they said, not the other way around."

"They were right," Hefflin said. "So how did you feel returning to your childhood home?"

"Well, to tell the truth, I didn't like it at first," Balzary said. "I thought I could just fit back in, you know, find all my old friends, pick up the old ways, the language. But I'd become more American than I realized. Everyone in my old country was so afraid, paranoid. They treated me like an American spy. They said I had an accent and they wouldn't even talk to me. All the things I'd heard about communism, which I thought were just propaganda, were actually true. The State controlled everything. Everyone was spied on, no one dared say anything against the government, lines everywhere—for food, clothing, toilet paper." He waved his hand. "But I was a patriot, still am. Hungary has a great history. Soon after I arrived, the intelligence service recruited me and, after an extensive vetting process to make sure I wasn't a CIA plant, invited me to join. To them I was very valuable—a Harvard-educated guy who spoke both perfect English and Hungarian and who knew the American system. I quickly became one of their favorites."

"I'm sure."

Balzary eyed him suspiciously. "You think I'm ungrateful. After all, America gave me freedom, a good education, a better life than my family ever had in Hungary. All of that is true. But my soul, it still begged to be back among my people, even those miserable suckers who stood in line for hours to buy a pair of shoes that didn't fit. Just hearing the language was enough for me. And being in the secret service brought all sorts of benefits. I didn't suffer like most of the population. Still, did I believe in the communist system?" He groaned. "I didn't even know what communism was, not the way it worked on the ground. The great lie the State kept repeating was that we were still in the revolutionary stages; that, once perfected, communism would become that paradise of equality we all dreamed about. Of course, it never happened. Never will happen. But I was too naïve then, too young, and too full of my special status."

Balzary became silent, perhaps realizing he was doing all the talking.

"So, is this an alumni get-together?" Hefflin asked.

"Some of that, but I also wanted to pick the brain of the CIA's best analyst." He searched for cigarettes, found a pack, and lit one. "How is America going to play this? Is Ceausescu on his way out or what?"

Hefflin was surprised at the respect Balzary seemed to have for American power, as if the Americans could decide who was in or out, which government survived and which fell. It reminded him of the expectation that the Romanians still held decades after the War that at any moment America was going to liberate them from the Soviets.

"You live next door," Hefflin said. "You should know more about it than I do."

"Our country is undergoing its own changes as we speak, nonviolent, civilized," Balzary said. "But the Romanians are not that way. They cower for decades and then have a bloody revolt. This asshole, Ceausescu, is bent on staying come hell or high water."

"And?"

"Well, Romania has a large Hungarian population, as you well know, so we care what happens. We're becoming a democracy, like everyone else. We can't have a Stalinist state next door and not care."

"So there may be some uprisings here among the ethnic Hungarians?" Hefflin asked.

"Not out of the realm of possibility." Balzary smiled.

"Perhaps somewhere in Transylvania?"

"Timisoara, more likely. There has been a problem there recently, with a priest. I assumed you knew." Balzary stared at him for a long moment.

"Yes, but will it go anywhere?" Hefflin said, trying to hide his ignorance.

Balzary leaned closer. "We are all on the same side now. You're obviously here for a reason. You're the only American who has arrived in the past month. Maybe you have some message from Bush, some plans. If you do, I should know about it. The CIA has a way of betting on the wrong horse. You guys always want a thoroughbred to replace the old nag, while here we only have old nags."

"Sorry to disappoint you, but I have no plans," Hefflin said. "I'm just here to observe."

Balzary leaned back and lit a cigarette, his eyes never leaving his, as if trying to gauge what this analyst knew. It was a long time before he spoke again. "Okay. I'll accept that, for now. History is moving forward on its own. It doesn't need any help from us."

"You expect a change, then?" he probed.

Balzary shrugged. "All men are mortal. Ceausescu is a man." A haze had settled over Balzary's face, the blank expression of a spy. He seemed to have decided the conversation was over. "So, I used to see you walking with this hot chick back at Harvard. You still with her?"

Catherine? He'd seen him with Catherine? The question put him off balance.

"No, that was just a fling," he said.

"Too bad. You guys looked good together. Hey, after this is all done, maybe we can have a real drink, shoot the bull."

They pulled back up to the Athénée just as they were both finishing their vodkas.

"Be careful with your new government," Hefflin said. "They may want to clean house."

"Nah, whatever regime is in power, they'll always need spies. That never changes. Besides, we know where all the skeletons are buried."

As he was about to open the door, Balzary held his arm.

"One more thing: Ceausescu's offshore accounts."

"His what?"

"The Swiss accounts he stashed for his old age," Balzary said. "The rumor is that they are substantial. Which means everyone is after them."

"So?"

"A friendly warning. Be careful. When it comes to vast sums of money, the old rule may not apply."

"What old rule?"

"That spies don't kill other spies."

The crowd at the bar had only grown louder. He waved off two women and climbed up to his room. It was empty, for a change, and he lay down on the bed to review his unexpected meeting with Balzary. A Harvard man, a kindred spirit who, like himself, had pined for his homeland. Not a communist but an ally now. And, yet, he was holding something back.

He heard a knock and climbed wearily from the bed. When he opened the door, he saw a tall man in a cashmere overcoat and, as the man raised his hand in greeting, a gold Rolex watch.

CHAPTER SEVENTEEN

Bucharest
December 1989

"Harold Mayfield, from Chicago." The man extended a manicured hand.

"An American. Lucky coincidence," Hefflin said.

"There are no coincidences in this town, Mr. Hefflin. May I come in, just for a moment?"

"Of course." He stepped aside to let the man in.

Mayfield entered the room and perused the furniture. "Nothing close to a Western hotel, is it?" He chuckled, then removed his overcoat and settled himself in one of the two chairs. Hefflin sat in the other.

"I'm afraid I have no drink to offer you," Hefflin said.

Mayfield shook his head. "I'm staying at the InterContinental. Same stale communist rooms. Spies everywhere. You can't even leave a bottle of soda around. It'll be gone by the time you get back."

"What can I do for you, Mr. Mayfield?"

"You're . . . what should we call you . . . a diplomat?"

"A cultural attaché."

"Ah, yes. Such euphemisms. But you came at the perfect time, and bearing gifts, I gather."

"Gifts?"

"Come, come, Mr. Hefflin, I was at the bar when you were talking to the journalists. And then I saw you walking out after Balzary. You know, once this country opens up, I mean becomes some bastardized version of democracy, the business opportunities will be enormous."

"Really. How? The people are poor. They can't afford Western goods."

"Not yet, but wait five years." Mayfield's eyes widened. "In the meantime, they'll need infrastructure, a wireless telephone system, banks—real banks, that can actually lend to people to buy goods. They'll need credit cards, a food distribution system, privatized agriculture, new factories. After wages rise, then will come the Western stores and goods, hotels, theaters, the works. There are fortunes to be made here, Mr. Hefflin."

"I never focused on that, Mr. Mayfield. I'm a State Department employee."

"If you insist." Mayfield smiled. "But your role is the first essential step. Nothing can be done with the system as is. You are the linchpin, Mr. Hefflin. So?"

"So what?"

Mayfield flicked on the radio by the bedside, turned up the volume, and whispered into Hefflin's ear. "How will you get rid of Ceausescu? And what is the time frame? We need to know to make plans. What tricks do you have in that dossier you brought from Washington?"

He felt a cold sweat roll down his back. "What dossier?"

"The dossier I heard you mention to the journalists." Mayfield leaned back. "No need to demur, Mr. Hefflin. We're both Americans, and we need to give American industry a leg up."

"I was only joking with them, Mr. Mayfield. There is no dossier."

"I understand." Mayfield patted Hefflin's knee. "Secrecy is essential. But not from your own compatriots. There can be something in it for you, you know. You're not going to be a government employee forever, are you? Private industry needs people like you who know the terrain."

"I think you have the wrong guy." Hefflin stood.

"You have a bonus in the six figures and a secure job waiting for you, Mr. Hefflin. Information is what we need."

"Please, Mr. Mayfield. I need to rest."

Mayfield stood and took his coat. As he moved toward the door, he handed Hefflin a business card. "One more thing: Once Ceausescu goes, there will be a race to find his offshore treasure. We know it's significant. Everyone is salivating. A man in your position . . . well, you must have inside information. A large percentage can be yours, with no further effort on your part." He slipped the card into Hefflin's pocket. "You can contact me at the InterContinental."

When Mayfield had gone, he looked at the card: "International Investment Group, Harold Mayfield, VP of Development." The telephone number had a Chicago area code. He tore it up and flushed it down the toilet. He turned off the radio, kicked off his shoes, and stretched out on the bed fully clothed. He thought about how frustrated the Securitate must be listening to blaring music and knowing that a private conversation was taking place.

Just as he was dozing off, the phone rang. He picked it up and said, "Hello."

A man's voice: "Let's get together for a vodka."

"Usual place?"

"Yes."

He hung up and let out a satisfied sigh. The words he'd been waiting for. Boris had finally made contact.

CHAPTER EIGHTEEN

Bucharest
December 1989

A BITTER EVENING wind was blowing from the north with hardly any snow on the ground. Despite the cold, people were gathered on street corners in the center of the city, talking, arguing, behavior that had been unheard of in the past. There was something stirring in the air, Hefflin could feel it, a sense that fate had finally arrived in Romania.

He lifted his coat collar and continued walking on Calea Victoriei, then abruptly turned onto Strada Piatsa Amzei and entered the front door of a building. After a few minutes, he exited through the back door onto the adjacent street. He followed this routine several times, until he was sure he wasn't tailed. He was honing his field skills, and it felt good. Perhaps Balzary was right—over the past few days, the Securitate and the other intelligence agencies had realized he was just a feckless analyst, not a field agent, and had decided they had better ways to allocate their manpower.

The streetlamps were unlit—the government's effort to save on fuel. The moon was hidden behind a gray shroud. Even the shadows had decided it was too cold to be outside. Most buildings were dark except for one faint light at the end of the block, the ground floor, his destination. A sign above the door read

The Red Barrel. But that light, too, was flickering, as if unsure of itself. He heard noises coming from inside, male voices. *Why meet here? Couldn't Boris find a more secluded place, a private apartment, a dark alley, perhaps?*

He took a deep breath and entered. Inside, a half dozen men huddled in their winter coats were sitting around rough wooden tables. On each table was an oil lamp and bottles of clear liquid—either plum brandy or vodka. The moment he stepped inside, the conversations stopped and all eyes—suspicious, threatening—turned to him. A waiter came over and motioned with his chin for him to follow. The conversations resumed.

The waiter escorted him to a dark corner table where a man was sitting alone. The table had no oil lamp, just a bottle and two glasses. He pulled out the chair and sat down. He could make out a white beard, dark eyebrows, a black Astrakhan hat with a few strands of dark hair escaping on the sides. He felt a little disappointed. He had secretly hoped that Boris would turn out to be a beautiful Natasha wearing spiked heels.

"So you received my message, Vasili."

A deep, raspy voice, reminiscent of his father's, spoke in English. Boris lit a cigarette and for a moment Hefflin saw the eyes: dark blue with wrinkles at the edges that placed him in his sixties, perhaps older.

"Is the beard real?" Hefflin asked.

Boris chuckled. "Of course not," then handed him a piece of paper with a telephone number on it. "In case we get interrupted, memorize the number. If you need to meet, call and let it ring once. That means we meet on the number four trolley at one in the afternoon. If twice, at two, and so on."

"You will always be there waiting for my call?"

"One of my men will be," Boris said. "He knows nothing about us, just tells me the number of rings. So"—he leaned back—"tell me, Vasili, why do your people call me Boris?"

How did Boris know his internal CIA alias?

"I named you . . . after *Boris Godunov*," he said, "the opera where you first made contact with me. Your inventiveness has fascinated me over the years."

"Good spycraft is an art, like writing a novel," Boris said. "You know something about that."

Hefflin's brows shot up. "How—?"

"Yes, I know you published a novel as a young man," Boris said. "*Pusha*, under your childhood name, *Fili*. I even read it."

How did this Russian know about an obscure novel he'd published under a pseudonym? The Agency had created an entire legend for William Hefflin, erasing any connection to his old identity.

"Fili was what came out of my mouth when I first tried to pronounce Vasili as a small child," he said. "It stuck. Everyone called me Fili afterward. I'm impressed at your thoroughness."

Boris shrugged. "I am a spy; that is my job. I will keep it between us."

"So, what did you think of it?" The words left his mouth before he could prevent them. He felt disgust at his ego, which sought admiration wherever it could find it for his meager teenage effort at fiction, even from this Russian spy.

Boris tilted his head, pondering. "A promising first attempt. Passionate. Full of nostalgia for your childhood and your little Pusha."

"Easy to ridicule," he said, a bit hurt.

"No, no ridicule," Boris said. "I wish I had a love like that in my youth. Maybe I would have done other things with my life."

Boris filled Hefflin's shot glass and topped his own. They touched glasses, then each threw back his head and emptied it, as was the Russian custom. The vodka was fine, not the kind they usually served in Bucharest.

"I carry my own bottle of Stolichnaya," Boris said, reading his reaction. "I cannot drink the Polish piss they have in this shithole of a country. Soon to be remedied, I think."

"You *think*?"

"Something is brewing." Boris smiled.

"You're not being exactly clairvoyant. The entire Eastern Bloc is denouncing communism."

"Yes, but they have all done it relatively peacefully."

"And?"

"And I don't think the Americans understand the Romanians. If you start a revolution here, it will not be a velvet one."

Hefflin poured a second round of vodka. "Some of our people think Ceausescu is strong enough to withstand a few demonstrations. He may make some changes, give the people some false hope, anything to stay in power."

Boris leaned forward close enough for Hefflin to smell the tobacco on his breath. "And you? You are their best analyst. What do you think?"

"I think history is not on his side," Hefflin said. "Communism is finished. One way or another, Ceausescu must go."

Boris nodded. "And what does your president believe?"

"Like any politician, he hedges his bets."

Boris's face blossomed into a forced smile. "Maybe he wants to help history along, start some brushfires, rile up the population, make them promises he cannot keep, like you have done in so many other places."

Hefflin shrugged. "It hasn't been a stellar history, that's for sure."

Boris lit a cigarette, then let the smoke out slowly, letting it drift up his face, which now looked like a demon raised from hell. "Does your president want Romanian blood on his hands? Look at history. Romanians do not have peaceful revolutions. They like bodies in the streets, executions. They want to know that they have gotten their money's worth. I do not want them to later see their butchery has the CIA's fingerprints on it and blame the Americans again."

A strange fellow, this Boris. Hefflin asked him why he cared so much about the Americans.

Boris smirked. "I care about these miserable Romanians. I am afraid you are going to fuck it up again. So I am here to give you a message, from Gorbachev to Bush. It is this: 'No need to soil your hands in Romania. Mother Russia will clean up its own mess.' Got that?"

"A threat?"

"A friendly suggestion. We are no longer in a position to threaten."

"Ceausescu won't leave quietly," Hefflin said. "He feels safe, safe enough to go to Iran on a state visit in a few days."

"Yes, he is a megalomaniac," Boris said. "He cannot imagine anyone rising up against him. But at the same time, he is also paranoid. He has doubles, look-alikes, that attend public celebrations, and people that taste his food before he eats it."

"So, what are you talking about, then? A coup?"

Boris nodded. "It will begin with some demonstrations, peaceful ones. They will spread. The situation will become progressively worse. At some point the army will declare a state of emergency.

They will claim that the population has turned against the leadership, so they have no choice but to act to avoid violence."

"So you have the army with you."

"The important part," Boris said.

"Where will these demonstrations start?" Hefflin asked.

Boris thought for a moment, perhaps deciding how much to say.

"Timisoara."

Timisoara, again. The same city Balzary mentioned.

"What will happen to Ceausescu?"

"He will be flown to Russia or some African country, or maybe he will just rot in Iran," Boris said with a dismissive wave of the hand.

"So, it will happen while he's in Iran?"

Boris shrugged. "It will happen when it will happen."

Hefflin considered what Boris was saying. The Russians were going to take out Ceausescu with a coup. Gorbachev was going to do the West's business for them. Why? Part of him did not believe it. But this was Boris speaking, the asset who had never been wrong. Boris had to have solid sources, not only in the military but also within the political power structure.

Hefflin asked about the new government that would take over.

"A transitional government first, followed by elections in six months," Boris said.

"Democracy? All done by Gorbachev? Why?"

"Gorbachev is a pragmatist. He thinks neither pure communism nor pure capitalism works for the common man. He trusts that the people will choose socialism, a middle ground. And he hates Ceausescu, a pig in a long line of pigs that got fat on communism. It is time to bring this pig to slaughter." Boris spat on the floor in disgust, his face red, his eyes full of hatred. "You know, the worst mistake Marx ever made was to reject religion. Yes, I know, the 'opiate of the masses' and all that. But communism, at its core, is a Christian belief system. Each man labors according to his means and receives according to his needs. All for the common good. What can be more Christian than that? The problem is that man is not like that. Communism failed for the same reason religion is failing." Boris settled back in his chair and poured another drink. "We are all fallen angels, my friend. We all try to get the better of our neighbor. That is reality. Tell Bush to let this play out. Do not interfere."

"So this is why you brought me here? To give me this message?"

"You do not think that turning the last remaining Soviet state into a democracy is important enough for you to come to Bucharest?"

"A dead drop would have sufficed."

"No, you are right and very perceptive." Boris's eyes twinkled. "I have much more for you, even more important."

CHAPTER NINETEEN

Bucharest
December 1989

"WHAT DO THE Americans know about Ceausescu's offshore accounts?" Boris asked.

The offshore accounts again.

"Not much," Hefflin said. "We've tracked moneys transferred out of Romanian state banks into Swiss and Luxembourg banks. We know some of that money is used for legitimate purposes, like funding embassies, paying Western companies that trade with Romania, and so on. But part of it is siphoned off, wired to other offshore accounts several times over, until it disappears. You know the game."

"You are telling me that the mighty NSA cannot follow the money?" Boris smiled.

Hefflin felt his face twitch. Boris was taunting him. "Swiss secrecy laws are a major obstacle," he said. "The Swiss have also reinforced their computer security systems, making them almost hack proof."

"Almost?" Boris's eyebrow rose.

"I believe you are the asset here," Hefflin said.

"Ha, very good, Vasili. Never volunteer information. But you already told me too much."

Hefflin was feeling like a pupil. This Russian acted like he was his mentor. "The short answer is no; we don't know where Ceausescu hid his money."

Boris played with his false beard. "It would be a crime to leave all that money in those offshore accounts, no? When Ceausescu goes down, who will be left to collect it? His three children? Or maybe someone in the Securitate who has access to those accounts? And if they are all dead or in jail, the banks will keep all of it."

"Maybe you can get him to return it," Hefflin said, "in exchange for a secure future in some Third World country."

"A deal, with Ceausescu?" Boris let out a laugh. "No, he thinks he will live in his palace forever. Which brings me to my plan. The idea is a little crazy, but all good ideas are crazy, no?"

"I'm afraid to ask."

"You have a cousin in Bucharest by the name of Irina."

"How the hell do you know about my cousin?" Hefflin stammered.

"I am a spy, Vasili, I told you. If I know about your book, I know everything about you."

The thought sent chills down his back. *Are all Soviet spies that good, or is Boris a special case?*

"Who the hell are you?" Hefflin asked. "What's your real name?"

"Ah, not so fast, Vasili . . . we are just getting to know each other."

"Why did you choose me as your contact? Who is the cutout that brings the intel into the U.S.?"

Boris raised his hands in a sign of surrender. "I will tell you everything, I promise, in time. You just arrived. Patience is an art that every spy must cultivate." Boris lit another cigarette from the one he was smoking. "Now, your cousin, your first cousin, the daughter of Uncle Ion, your father's brother, both dead now, may God have mercy on their souls." Boris crossed himself. "Irina is a great stage actress. She is in a play right now at the Odeon. You should be very proud of her."

"I am," he said. "I've followed her career, though I haven't spoken to her since . . ."

"Since you left," Boris finished his sentence. "Yes, I know. She has a lover."

"I'm sure she's had many lovers."

"This one is special." Boris's eyes twinkled again. "He is an important man in the government, a very important man."

"Is he?" Hefflin didn't like where this was going.

"Victor Vulcan. His official title is Minister of Agriculture, but he is more than that. He is Ceausescu's money man. That is, he manages his illegal offshore accounts. He knows where all the money is buried."

"And?"

"Don't act stupid," Boris started. "What kind of spy are you?"

"I'm an analyst. And I'm not going to involve my cousin in your crazy schemes."

"We are talking about maybe a billion dollars or more that Ceausescu stole. She can help us return it to these miserable people. Help give them a new start."

"Why don't you just bribe or threaten this money man. Once the government falls, he'll spill everything."

"By then it may be too late," Boris said. "Everyone is after this money, and not to return it, either. Whoever gets to him first will walk away with it."

"Who is 'everybody'?"

"Everybody: high-ranking members in the Securitate, the Russians, the French, the British, not to speak of private parties, industrialists with security connections to America, Germany, and other places. This place is swarming with vultures. A billion dollars, maybe more, is not pocket change. People will do anything to get their dirty little hands on it."

"More reason not to put Irina in danger," Hefflin said.

"No more danger than she is already in," Boris said. "You think I am the only one who knows she is his lover? I am smart, yes, but it does not take a lot of smarts to figure out that she may be a way of getting to him."

The more Hefflin thought about it, the worse it sounded. "Doesn't Vulcan have a family?" he asked. He was reaching for straws.

"A wife and two children," Boris said. "Yes, someone might use them for leverage. But if I know this guy, he does not care much about them. He is still relatively young, in his early fifties, and has been screwing around practically since his honeymoon. He has put away his own little nest egg in Swiss accounts. The life that he imagines in the West as a rich bachelor is too much to pass up. He will just disappear and deal with his family problem later, if ever." Boris shrugged.

Hefflin felt a hollowness forming in his stomach, a place of decay. He hadn't spoken or written to Irina in twenty years. Now Boris wanted him to involve her in spying.

"So, let's say, hypothetically, I talk to Irina," Hefflin said. "How do you propose she go about it?"

"Well, you see, this guy still thinks Ceausescu will survive. He will not make a deal until—how you say—the manure hits the fan."

"Close enough."

"So, the timing has to be right. There will come a point when he will see that the people have turned, that his situation has become—how you say—"

"Untenable."

"That is when Irina will approach him."

"And?"

"She will say that she has a close relative, a high official in the American government, who will guarantee him asylum in the United States. Maybe a big house in California, with a swimming pool. He can keep his own offshore money, but he has to give up Ceausescu's. If he refuses, he risks being arrested, maybe even assassinated, who knows? Like I say, many people are after this money. And they will not be so nice as us." Boris sat back. "Do not give me that look. I said the plan is a little crazy, but not that crazy, no?"

"So, you brought me here to convince my cousin to get to the money man?"

"Vasili, if we find this money, my loyalty to the Americans will become secure. I am not getting any younger. A time will come when I will have to defect. This will guarantee my—how you say—golden years in sunny Florida or somewhere equally warm and pleasant. And you will become an even greater star in the Agency." Boris paused, seeming to gauge the effect of his proposal. "Look, if I thought I could convince her myself I would."

Hefflin downed his vodka and poured another. Even though he had just met this Russian asset, he was beginning to like him. But he didn't even know what kind of woman Irina had become. A stage star, perhaps as corrupt as her lover. This wretched country corrupted everyone.

"I don't know how she would respond," he said. "She may turn me in to protect herself."

"Her own cousin? No. If she is as smart as the rest of her family, she knows this country is on the edge of a big change. And she knows that when that change comes, she will be vulnerable."

"Vulnerable? How?"

"Vasili," Boris said patiently, "she is the mistress of a corrupt communist apparatchik, a criminal who has stolen millions of dollars for himself and Ceausescu while the people starved. And he is the architect of some very bad policies. Ask Stanton, he will tell you. Only a few people know about the affair now, but if it becomes public, well, how is her career going to do then?"

"You want me to blackmail her?"

"Blackmail? Did you hear me say blackmail?" Boris made a long face. "No, but her affair has to be buried. The few people who know about it have to be bribed to keep silent, another affair has to be started, and so on. In the new regime, she has to look clean."

He thought about what Boris was saying. Perhaps the Russian was right. Irina may need help to hide her history. Who knew what his cousin had done to reach stardom in this communist state.

"All right, I'll make contact and then decide if I want to ask her," he finally said. "But I can't promise anything."

"That is fair." Boris nodded. "And do not tell Stanton about this, not yet. If Vulcan agrees, and you have to get him out, then you can tell Stanton. He will arrange everything if he thinks he is getting Ceausescu's treasure."

The word caught his ear. He was about to follow up but there was a sudden hush in the room. He turned to see two men in black coats who had just entered. Several men at the tables stood, blocking the view of Boris's table.

"Securitate," Boris said. "You were followed."

Before he realized it, Boris had melted into the darkness at the back of the bar. The waiter pulled Hefflin by the arm and pushed him into the back, then through a door into the kitchen. A big man who looked like the cook pulled him through another door that led to a back alley.

"That way, then left, then left again." The cook pointed, then shut the door.

He followed the directions and arrived on a dark street corner where a lone taxi was idling. The driver leaned out the window and yelled in English: "Inside. Quick."

Hefflin got in and the taxi drove off. They drove for several minutes, taking abrupt turns onto side streets, finally ending up a few blocks from his hotel.

"Your hotel is there." The man pointed.

Hefflin got out and was about to pay the man, but the taxi drove off. As he walked back to his hotel, he felt the wind had shifted. It was now blowing from Timisoara.

*   *   *

"He said Mother Russia will clean up its own mess?" Stanton let out a laugh. "Why? Because Gorbachev is such a good guy?"

They were sitting in Stanton's office, where Hefflin had returned immediately after his meeting with Boris.

"Gorbachev comes from a new breed," Hefflin said. "He knows Ceausescu is a relic, a Stalinist who has caused the death and suffering of millions of his people. And we know there's no love lost between Gorbachev and Ceausescu. When Gorbachev visited Romania in May of '87, Ceausescu humiliated him by reprimanding him for loosening his grip on Soviet society. He did this both privately and publicly. Gorbachev is reported to have left livid."

"So, you're telling me this is personal?"

"Both. Gorbachev hates the guy, yes, but also regards him as a tyrant with too much blood on his hands to survive. Gorbachev believes in a kinder, gentler socialism."

Stanton grunted. "What, then? Are we supposed to just sit on our asses and watch as a coup unfolds? Is Boris on the level or is Gorbachev just playing us?"

"Gorbachev doesn't have any cards to play. He has his own problems," Hefflin said. "Look, Boris hasn't steered us wrong yet. Just pass the message along."

"All right. I'll pass the message to Langley without any commentary. But it smells to high heaven."

He left Stanton's office with an uneasy feeling. He had followed Boris's request and not told Stanton about Ceausescu's money, or Irina and Minister Vulcan. This wasn't the first time since arriving in Bucharest that he had kept something from the Agency, and he suspected it wouldn't be the last.

CHAPTER TWENTY

Bucharest
December 1989

THE ODEON THEATRE was located on Calea Victoriei, not far from the InterContinental and the university. It was a historical monument built in the neo-Romanian style, with Greek columns majestically guarding its entrance. The marquee banners announced *The Three Sisters* by Anton Chekhov, starring two actresses he didn't know and one he did: Irina Argyris. He had followed his cousin's career over the years, reading the reviews in Romanian newspapers, but he'd never had any contact with her, though his parents and she had corresponded. Knowing that most letters arriving from America were read by the authorities and that all trans-Atlantic phone calls were monitored, he had decided before leaving the States not to let her know he was coming. He would just appear unannounced, an apparition, a lost relative from the distant past. Maybe the shock would make her more amenable to Boris's plan, but he doubted it.

It was a half hour before curtain time and a line had formed at the ticket booth. He hadn't noticed anyone following him, but that didn't mean anything. He was no field agent. It didn't matter, anyway. He was just going to the theater. He bought a ticket in the orchestra section, last row corner seat, and followed the people inside.

The theater had been built in 1911, he remembered reading somewhere, by the architect Grigore Cerchez, and modeled after the famous Odeon Theatre in Paris. Today it was an amalgamation of Old-World elegance and communist-era neglect. Two stories featuring a row of white columns flanked the main orchestra seating. The curtain was a dusty purple, frayed at the bottom, a remnant from a more opulent era. The seats were a dark red velvet, worn, yet stubbornly insisting on being recognized for their previous regal pedigree.

He settled in and watched the people file by. The cost of a ticket was minimal, even by Romanian standards, subsidized by the government to provide one of the few remaining venues of culture for a population deprived of Western films or books. The people were dressed in their finest—dark overcoats now peeling off to reveal Old World suits and outdated evening dresses. They took their seats quietly—with none of the bustle and loud conversations of a Broadway production—and, despite, or because, of the misery outside its walls, the hall slowly filled to capacity.

The lights dimmed, then went completely dark. The curtain rose. The titular three sisters sat in a drawing room, Olga, the eldest, recalling their father's death a year ago, Masha whistling a tune, Irina dreaming of returning to Moscow. Irina. He hardly recognized her. Irina playing Irina, the youngest, the romantic, the dreamer. He watched in awe as his cousin, blood of his blood, wearing a white dress, spoke the immortal words of Chekhov as if they were her own. She is fantasizing about one day escaping the drudgery of a decadent, privileged life and finding meaning in work. It is her name day today, Chekhov's Irina, and friends arrive with presents and talk of romance. But there is a pall of anticipated disappointment hovering over the entire scene.

As the play progressed, he began to sink into the depression Chekhov's Irina is feeling at life's meaninglessness, at an empty existence of eat, sleep, and work that can only be relieved by death. He immediately saw how this play, written in Russia in 1910, spoke to a Romanian audience in 1989, worn down by the drudgery of a structured, sterile life. The curtain came down with Chebutykin's fatalistic words referring to the mystery of life: "It doesn't matter, it doesn't matter," and Olga's, "If we only knew, if we only knew."

The lights went up. The audience sat quiet, almost stunned, then the curtain rose once more and the actors appeared onstage holding hands, smiling, themselves again, just a play, a dream, we're all awake now. There was vigorous applause, the actors bowing, then the applause trailing off as the curtain fell once more. People filed out even more quietly than they'd entered, dejected, perhaps, at the hopelessness of the last scene, of life.

Hefflin approached one of the ushers and slipped a hundred *lei* bill into the man's vest pocket.

"I'm supposed to meet one of the actors," he said in Romanian. "How can I go backstage?"

The usher hesitated, then took out the bill and his eyes grew wide. "That door—" he pointed—"but they may not let you in."

He made his way to the door marked by a gold star and pushed it open. He found himself in a corridor, people hurrying by, paying him no attention. He heard high-pitched laughter coming from behind a door and he was sure it was Irina's, a memory from the past. As he was about to knock, the door abruptly opened and out came one of the male actors, turning inside again to say, "I'll see you at the party. Don't be late." He excused himself as he passed by Hefflin, who proceeded into the dressing room unannounced.

Before him sat Irina pulling at her face in front of a mirror, taking off her makeup. She looked even more beautiful up close than onstage. She had last seen him as a boy of eight. Would she recognize him? He fought the sudden urge to flee. Perhaps he was placing her in danger, a State Department official carrying a Russian asset's crazy plan. But how could he come back to Romania without seeing his cousin?

When she saw his reflection, she spoke into the mirror without turning.

"Can I help you?" she asked in Romanian.

He closed the door behind him, extending the mystery for a moment longer. Irina. Memory.

❋   ❋   ❋

He was sitting next to her on the red couch in the middle of the living room. He was eight years old or so. She was ten years old and was wearing a yellow dress with thin straps and smelling of roses.

"So how is your sweetheart, Pusha?" she asked. He said he had already promised to marry her. Irina asked when the wedding would be.

"Papa told me I'm too young to marry, even though I'm already eight," he said. "I have to get a job first."

She laughed, then took a book from the shelf and sat beside him. She opened the book and showed him a painting. It had three framed parts to it. The first showed a man dressed in robes with two naked figures on either side.

"This painting is called *The Garden of Earthly Delights*," she said. "This first one shows God introducing Eve to Adam."

He had never seen a naked woman before and stared at the figure. His heart was pounding.

The next painting showed naked figures and fantastic animals. Some figures seemed to be dancing, others were shown in strange poses, doing things he didn't understand. He felt dizzy, and yet the bizarreness attracted him.

When Irina turned to the next painting, his throat tightened. It depicted a dark, scary place with terrifying creatures and naked men and women, some being eaten alive, others being tortured, their faces in agony. Nausea oozed up from his stomach.

"This is hell," she said.

"Tanti Bobo told me there is no h-hell," he stammered.

"Oh, yes there is. Papa says it is the hell we make for ourselves."

"Irina, what are you doing showing him those pictures?" Uncle Ion shouted from across the room.

The book snapped shut. Uncle Ion grabbed the book from Irina's hands and placed it on the top shelf.

Meanwhile, little Fili ran to the balcony just in time, his stomach convulsing, and started retching.

*　　*　　*

From inside his bag, Hefflin now removed his gift, wrapped in Christmas paper, tied with a red bow.

"I have a present from one of your longtime admirers," he said in Romanian as he placed the package on the vanity.

Without turning—a diva used to receiving presents from admirers—she pulled on the bow and slowly unwrapped the gift. A book. She stared at it for a moment, then lifted her eyes to his reflection.

"Hieronymus Bosch. *The Garden of Earthly Delights,*" she uttered, her face a question mark.

"You once showed a little boy these images, and it made a great impression on him," he said.

"A little boy?" She turned and looked directly at him. "I remember. He was so upset at the grotesque images that he got sick. I was a mischievous child. For years I regretted what I did to him."

"No lasting harm," he said. "You told him there was no hell, other than the one we create ourselves. A good lesson to learn . . . and live by."

She rose and opened her arms. "Fili? Is it really you?"

"Yes. Unfortunately, I've grown up."

They embraced, then stood apart again, each trying to gauge how time had changed the other. She had become a real beauty and was now at the height of her career. Even under communism, the Romanian theater had thrived, and she had become one of its leading actresses.

"Why didn't you write to tell me you were coming?" she burst out. "How long are you staying? Oh, we have so much to talk about."

"I don't want to take up your time now," he said. "I heard that fellow say you're to meet him later. I don't want to impose."

"Don't be ridiculous. You can come with me. Tonight was our last performance and we're having a small celebration. A lot of people will be there, actors, directors. Only if you're up to it."

She explained that the party was at the apartment of Mircea Gabor, a legend, the Romanian version of Olivier.

"He'd love to meet you, to pick your brain about America." She beamed. "What did you think of the play? I know it doesn't compare to Broadway, but . . ."

"You were magnificent," he said, "and the play was very much at the level of a serious Broadway production, though much of Broadway these days is musicals, comedies, and fluffy romances, for tourists."

She scrunched up her face. "We do tend to be morose here, but what do you expect, this miserable situation we're in, living in a cage?" She pursed her lips. "Let me change, and I'll be out in a few minutes."

"Wait. If I'm going to come to this party, I have to bring something. Wine?"

"Whiskey," she burst out. "Real whiskey one can only buy at the Tourist Shops. But at this hour they're closed."

He thought for a second, then said, "I know where I can get some. Two bottles?"

"With two bottles of whiskey, you'll be the life of the party."

"Then I'll get three."

Twenty minutes later, a black Mercedes pulled up in front of the Odeon Theatre, which was dark now. He and Irina had been waiting under the marquee.

"Is this car for us?" Irina marveled. "Who is your friend?"

Hefflin led her into the back seat without answering.

"Good evening, sir," Tom said in English.

A bag resting on the floor contained three bottles of Johnnie Walker Black.

Irina's eyes grew wide with wonder. "Fili, where did you get all this whiskey?"

"A private source. No questions. Let's not spoil the fantasy."

Hefflin winked. He knew it had been no trouble for Tom to get the whiskey. The embassy liquor closets were fully stocked with cases of Johnnie Walker Black, Stanton's private stash.

CHAPTER TWENTY-ONE

Bucharest
December 1989

THE MASSIVE STRUCTURE rose out of nowhere, a neoclassical behemoth lit by innumerable spotlights, a towering flame in the middle of a fuel shortage, a beacon in a city shrouded in darkness.

"Ceausescu's palace," he muttered.

"*Casa Republicii.* The Tyrant's monstrosity," Irina spat. "The people are starving and he spends billions on this abomination."

He had read reports, seen pictures, but had never focused much on it, just another monument that tyrants build to themselves. Ozymandias. Though as yet unfinished, it was supposedly the world's second largest government building, after the Pentagon. Practically one-fifth of Bucharest's most historic area had been razed, not only to accommodate the structure itself but the surrounding apartment buildings designed to complement it. Seven hundred architects and twenty thousand laborers in three shifts had supposedly worked on it, a monument to the greatness of socialism.

"Where are we, exactly?" he asked. "I've lost my bearings."

"We're in central Bucharest," Irina said. "This used to be called Spirit Hill, also known as Uranus Hill."

"Uranus?" He suddenly lit up. "There's a street with that name near our old house on Strada Sirenelor."

"That's right. This is the Uranus Quarter. Strada Sirenelor is only a few blocks away."

"But I've been to our old house, and I didn't see this huge palace," he said.

She explained that Ceausescu had built tall apartment buildings to surround his palace so that he wouldn't have to look at the crumbling city beyond it. The apartments were given to the most privileged. One of them was Gabor.

"They regard actors that highly?" he asked.

"Yes. Don't they in America? Besides being the most celebrated actor in our history, he is also a member of the Central Committee, so be careful what you say around him."

Mircea Gabor, a member of the Central Committee, something the analyst in him should have known, and perhaps had known without taking notice.

"Listen." He took her hand. "At the party you're not to introduce me as your cousin. My name is Bill Hefflin, State Department attaché, just arrived. I saw the play and wanted to meet you, an admirer. I learned Romanian from government courses, so it'll sound broken, with a heavy accent. You invited me to the party on the spur of the moment, to increase cultural understanding, that sort of thing."

"Bill Hefflin?" She laughed. "Why the secrecy?"

"I don't want any complications," he said.

"What sort of complications?"

He marveled at her naivete. Had she been that cloistered in her theater life?

"Look, the situation here is tense," he said. "I'm an American official. I don't want the government to use my relative as leverage against me. Do you understand?"

She thought for a moment. "You mean blackmail you to do something on my account?"

He nodded.

"It's not beyond them, I suppose, a State Department official. But you don't have to worry about me. I have protection."

Protection, a mafia word. But she wasn't smiling.

"What kind of protection?"

"I'm good friends with an important man, high up in the government." Her eyes looked deeply into his to make sure he understood. "It's been quite a few years. He's married, of course, but no one knows about us. Just a couple of close friends." She looked at him again and, no doubt, saw his disapproval. "It's accepted here. Everyone has lovers. Isn't it the same in America?"

"It's certainly not accepted, but people do have affairs, until they're caught. Then there's a scandal."

"A scandal? But Kennedy had many lovers, no?"

"Yes, he did. A different time. Things have changed since then, still changing."

"American Puritanism. I've read about it." She nodded. "And yet, American movies are full of sex. I saw some when I was in East Germany two years ago at a film festival."

"Yes, there's a lot of hypocrisy about sex," he said, "and other things."

She crossed her arms and thought for some time. "If you want to be Bill Hefflin then that's how I'll introduce you, but the rest of the story doesn't work," she said. "No one would invite a perfect stranger to a party, especially an American official. Maybe if I say that you are a personal friend of my cousin in America and he wanted you to meet me, to see how I am doing and give me a present. That would be more believable."

Tom followed Irina's street directions and stopped in front of one of the new apartment buildings facing the palace. Hefflin told Tom he'd call if he wanted to be picked up.

The apartment was on the second floor, facing away from the palace. The door was answered by Mircea Gabor himself—a tall, elegant patrician, with graying hair.

"Irina, darling." Gabor smiled and kissed the air beside both her cheeks, Hollywood style. Irina introduced Bill Hefflin, a friend of her cousin in New York.

"New York? Well, then, we have a lot to talk about," Gabor said. "And what's this? Gifts?" He took the bottles of whiskey and raised them in the air. "Look, friends, countrymen, manna from America."

There was a roar from the crowd inside. Thirty or so people now gathered around them, marveling at the whiskey bottles.

"Real whiskey, Johnnie Walker Black," one middle-aged man exclaimed. "Who is this demigod you've brought among us, Irina?"

As Hefflin made the round of handshakes, the bottles were being opened and the nectar poured. Among the group were several well-known directors, the rest actors and actresses, some from the play he'd seen that evening. Soon everyone was holding a glass of whiskey, some having first gulped down their cheap vodka to empty their glasses, others just pouring it into the sink. He instantly became the toast of the party.

At first his Romanian, with its intentionally heavy accent and grammatical errors, brought genial corrections. But as the whiskey continued to flow, fewer of the revelers seemed to care about his mangling the Romanian language. Everyone wanted to know about New York—how exciting was it, how tall were the buildings, what Broadway plays had he seen, did he know any actors?

His responses, relatively honest at first, soon grew into fictional accounts of cocktail parties at which Frank Sinatra showed up, or where Jack Nicholson did a five-minute bit from *One Flew Over the Cuckoo's Nest*. He could see in their faces that that was just what they wanted to hear, so he did his best to provide it to them. It was an opulent, even decadent America that they envisioned, one in which the literati attended black-tie soirées and famous actresses bathed in champagne. Then, at one point, a well-known director, a man in his sixties with white hair and a bow tie, asked what he did for a living.

"I'm the cultural attaché at the American Embassy," he answered.

The director's face dropped, then he put his drink down. "Really. And Irina invited you here?" He stood, excused himself, then walked over to others, his arms raised in agitation. Gabor placed a hand around the man's shoulders and said something at which everyone laughed. A joke, to settle the nerves. Then Gabor walked over to Hefflin.

"You must forgive Cornel, he's afraid of his own shadow," Gabor said.

"Is there a problem?"

"You told him you are an American official, and he thinks your presence will place him in jeopardy with the Securitate. A silly man, really."

"I'm sorry. I never thought about that."

"He's in the minority, I assure you. Things are not as bad as all that."

He noticed Cornel and two other men gather their coats and walk out.

"See? Only a couple. The rest are laughing at their expense. Now, to more serious business." Gabor pulled him to a corner.

"I wanted to ask you a question. It is quite personal to me, so forgive my directness."

"If I can answer it," he said.

"Do you go to Broadway plays?"

"Of course. I live in New York."

"How lucky you are. So, there was a play, *Tribute*, starring Jack Lemmon, several years ago now. Did you see it by any chance?"

Luckily enough he had seen the play and told him so.

Gabor hesitated, looking embarrassed, a man of delicate manners.

"Is it true," Gabor whispered, "that they wrote the play especially for Jack Lemmon?" The man's eyes were sparkling, the expression conveying that he wanted the answer to be yes, that a play had been written especially for an actor and that, had Gabor been living in America, the land of miracles, one would have been written for him. Here was the preeminent actor of Romania, at the height of his profession and adulation, begging him, at the risk of betraying his insecurities, to confirm his deepest narcissism.

"Yes, I heard the same thing," he said with a somber face. "A great honor, of course, but not so unusual for an eminent actor in America."

Gabor let out a satisfied sigh, as if this affirmation had fulfilled his dreams. "In another life," he said, then downed his whiskey.

"I'd like to ask you something in return," Hefflin said. "How free are you to choose the plays you put on?"

Gabor eyed him cautiously. "It depends. We put on mostly European and British classics—Shakespeare, Chekhov, Ibsen—but every so often we are allowed an American play, Tennessee Williams or Arthur Miller, for example, as long as it gets by the censor." He winked. "Some plays we obviously can't put on."

"It must be difficult for an artist to thrive under these conditions," he ventured, the whiskey giving him courage.

"Yes, and no," Gabor said. "Boundaries exist everywhere. An actor, by definition, must always live within the boundaries of the words on the page. One can view this as a limitation, but it would be a mistake. In actuality, the actor needs these restrictions. It is exactly the restrictions the words impose that force the actor to fully explore the role. Too much freedom is poison."

"To an actor, perhaps," he said. "But when the performance is over and the curtain goes down, your boundaries remain."

Gabor smiled. An actor's smile. "We all live under life's restrictions. You do, too, albeit different ones than mine. You think you are free because you vote, you can go anywhere you please, you can say anything you want. But your freedom is illusory. You can't go anywhere unless you have the money to do so; you have a vote, but the millionaire who contributes to his candidate can pick up the phone and call him whenever he wants a favor, while you can't. Yes, you can say anything you want, but does your voice matter as much as the owner of a newspaper or a television station, or the rich who buy commercials? Freedom is a subtle thing. In America, you have the freedom to be successful and wealthy, but you also have the freedom to be poor, even homeless. Still"—he leaned closer—"I do prefer your system, but that may only be because I imagine I'd be successful. I may be wrong. Here I'm a big fish in a small pond. In New York, I could be a starving actor waiting on tables."

He refreshed both their glasses from a whiskey bottle that Hefflin now saw Gabor had purloined for himself.

"Let me tell you a secret." Gabor's face drew close to his. "There are more communists in New York than there are in all of Romania." He frowned to place accent on his words. "The

New York liberals are the idealists, the real communists. What we have here is a bunch of crooks."

Hefflin was taken aback by Gabor's candor. Was it the whiskey talking, or did Gabor feel so secure in his position that he could say anything, even to an American official?

"What about The Man, himself?" Hefflin asked.

"He, especially, God bless him. He's the biggest crook of all." Gabor laughed a stage laugh, an actor in the Central Committee.

"What will happen to your own situation, if things change?"

"You mean *when*," Gabor said. "I'm an actor, my position among them is only honorary. I'm tolerated, a propaganda pawn. I'll go on acting, whatever fate has in store for this country that I love so much. The bigger question is what will happen to the rest of the crooks. And the answer is probably nothing. You can't go after one without going after them all. And whose hands are clean enough to start pointing fingers?" He gave another stage laugh, then turned to talk to other guests passing by. The two men then drifted apart, but Hefflin was left with a different view of the life of the powerful in Romania. All yes-men, including Ceausescu, himself. No one believed in communism, just going along to get along, surviving within life's boundaries.

"How do you people put on plays and go to parties while the world outside is about to crumble?" he later asked Irina.

"What do you want us to do, stop breathing?" she said. "Our life is on the stage. The rest is just a nightmare from which we hope to awaken one day."

The party broke up around one in the morning when all of the whiskey was gone. After such a rarity, no one wanted to sully their palates with cheap vodka or homemade plum brandy. One of the actors offered to drive him and Irina to their respective destinations—the least he could do for an American who had brought them Johnnie Walker.

They drove toward Irina's house first, which was located on Strada Docentilor, just off Kiseleff. The streets were dark, deserted, no one following them, an advantage of not using the embassy car. As they turned onto Docentilor, Hefflin saw a black sedan parked in front of Irina's house, motor running. Irina stiffened.

The actor stepped on the brakes. "What do you want me to do, Irina?"

"It's all right, he already saw us," she said. "Who knows how long he's been waiting."

Their car picked up speed again, then pulled up behind the black sedan. Irina gave Hefflin a quick kiss on the cheek, then a smile and a shrug. That's life. What can one do?

As she stepped out of their car and into the back of the black sedan, he noticed the license plate: 1-B-125. He knew that any number starting with 1-B belonged to an important official. The lower the number following it, the higher the official. Ceausescu's Aro Jeep had the plate 1-B-111.

CHAPTER TWENTY-TWO

Bucharest
December 1989

"IT BELONGS TO Victor Vulcan, the minister of agriculture," Stanton said the next morning, checking his list of official license plates. "Otherwise known as the minister of manure. Why do you want to know?"

"I spotted his car last night in front of the house of a certain actress."

"That must be Irina Argyris, his longtime mistress. What were you doing there?"

So Stanton knew about Irina's lover. He wondered who else knew and why he hadn't heard about it.

"I don't remember you including that little morsel in any of your reports," Hefflin said, a bit perturbed.

"If I reported on all the lovers of government officials, I'd be writing a novel," Stanton said. "So, what were you doing there?"

"I happened to be in the same car with her," Hefflin said. "One of the actors offered to drive us home from a party."

Stanton's eyes widened. "We do get around, don't we? In town for a few days and you're already attending parties with leading actresses. You should be a field agent. You're a natural. How did you swing it?"

"She's the cousin of a friend of mine in the States," he lied. He knew Stanton didn't know his real name. Only a few people in the Agency did. "He asked me to look her up. I had a free evening and decided to see Chekhov's *The Three Sisters* at the Odeon, one of my favorites. I was impressed. So, I went backstage to meet her. I am the cultural attaché, after all."

"Of etiquette," Stanton said, then burst out laughing.

"I view my portfolio in wider terms."

"No doubt. So what, she just invited you?"

"We started talking, I with my stilted Romanian, and one thing led to another. She wanted to know how her cousin was doing, then our conversation turned to the theater scene in New York and she said she was sure that Mircea Gabor would like to meet me."

"Gabor. Well, well. A member of the Central Committee. What did he have to say?"

"Quite a lot, actually." Hefflin told him about Gabor's obsession with the play *Tribute* being written especially for Jack Lemmon, causing Stanton to burst once more into raucous laughter.

"I also brought them a couple of bottles of Johnnie Walker Black," Hefflin added.

"You what?" Stanton practically jumped out of his seat. "From my private stash?"

"Paid for by taxpayer dollars," he reminded him. "It was for a good cause, to loosen tongues."

"Great, so you decided to play spy on my account. What did my precious nectar reveal?"

"Gabor is no communist, for one thing. He says there aren't any communists left, in fact, certainly not in the higher echelons of power. He calls them all crooks, including Ceausescu."

"Christ!" Stanton slapped the table. "That son-of-a-bitch better learn to hold his liquor. Who else was there? Who overheard him?"

Hefflin was taken aback by Stanton's anger. "There were about twenty or thirty people, directors and actors. And nobody heard him. We were whispering in a corner. What's the problem?"

"The problem, my dear Hefflin, analyst that you are, not a field operative, I must remind you, is that Gabor is *our* asset, our eyes and ears in the Central Committee, has been for years. I don't want him blowing it by drunkenly mouthing off to a stranger."

Gabor? A CIA asset? He remembered reading reports from a source inside the Romanian Central Committee but never knew who it was.

"Maybe you should have told me," he grumbled.

"You're a fucking analyst." Stanton's jaw muscles tightened. "You don't need to know the identity of sources. I'm only telling you now because you had contact with him, and you might again."

"No harm done," he said. "He wasn't talking to a stranger, after all, but an American State Department official."

"How did he know that? You could have been a Securitate plant."

"Irina vouched for me as a friend of her cousin in America. Besides, he's just an actor." Hefflin waived his hand dismissively. "No one takes actors seriously. Aren't there regular parties at our embassy for Romanian artists?"

"There were, in the past. No longer. Ceausescu has clamped down on contacts with Westerners as his paranoia has grown. And as to whether or not they take actors seriously, I'd like to remind you that an actor was our previous president."

He had forgotten about that, or had tried to. The most powerful nation on earth with an actor at the helm. If it were a movie script no one would buy it.

"Tell me more about this minister of agriculture," Hefflin said.

"It's not pretty." Stanton poured himself a glass of Scotch as he recounted how Ceausescu, in order to finance his multimillion-dollar palace as well as other ill-conceived projects like oil refining, which never worked out, had to borrow heavily from the West. Over the past few years, he'd gotten it into his head that he wanted to pay off all those loans at any price. Since Romania produced no real products the West wanted, he was exporting mainly raw minerals and grain. He had been selling practically all of the grain produced, leaving only enough for Bucharest and a few other major cities. The peasants on the collective farms were starving. There had been a weekly influx of them into Bucharest to buy bread.

Hefflin had read the reports. The government had even instituted an internal visa system to deal with the problem, preventing the peasants from entering Bucharest.

"And do you know who's been in charge of all this, doing Ceausescu's bidding?" Stanton asked.

"Let me guess: our minister of agriculture."

"None other," Stanton groaned. "And he's been especially zealous about it, sending the Securitate to collective farms to clean out any grain or livestock the peasants saved for their own survival. Millions of peasants are living on the edge of starvation, choosing to feed their children and relegating themselves to eating roots and grasses, which they boil into soup. Communism is supposed to be the peasants' party and they're the worst off."

"The peasants have always borne the brunt of famines, ever since Romania's collectivization in 1946," Hefflin said. "Stalin set the example for Ceausescu."

"All this while the communist intelligentsia lives fat and happy, shopping at their well-stocked Party stores."

"Irina Argyris is aware of this; they all are," Hefflin said. "She hates them all, the fake communist apparatchiks, but she's just like the rest of them. She survives. I don't blame her for seeking protection, as she put it. I'd have done the same."

He stopped, afraid that he was defending her too much. But he sensed that somewhere inside he did blame her, for what he wasn't sure. For not suffering more? For hiding behind her playacting while others starved? She had retreated into her own world onstage, a survivalist mode, knowing she couldn't do anything to change the system. This form of individualism was the opposite of what communism taught and more akin to capitalism. Everyone for him- or herself.

He wondered if this were the natural order of things. Both capitalism and communism had evolved into basically similar systems: individual struggle for survival, damn your neighbor. It was just that capitalism had been more successful, allowing more scraps to fall off the table down to the poor. Trickle-down economics, Reagan had called it.

"What will happen to Vulcan when Ceausescu falls?" Hefflin asked.

Stanton shrugged. "He'll either be shot or made a minister in the new government. Depending on how the wind is blowing ..."

Hefflin stood. "Thanks for the info."

"Where are you going?"

"I'll be having lunch with a beautiful actress," he said as he walked out.

"Don't do anything stupid," Stanton yelled after him. "He may only be the minister of manure, but he'll bury you in it if you mess with his mistress."

CHAPTER TWENTY-THREE

Bucharest
December 1989

HE DECIDED TO spend the time before his lunch date with Irina walking the streets. Along the way he passed long lines of people waiting outside butcher shops and grocery stores. In Piatsa Amzei there were lines for eggs and milk. He walked into a store that had no line, only to find the shelves bare, save for a row of canned beets. Outside a clothing store there was a line for men's shoes, size 38, according to an old man who had been standing in line for several hours.

"But not everyone here is size 38," Hefflin said in Romanian.

"Your ignorance tells me you're a foreigner, but your accent tells me you were born here," the old man said. "So you must have left when you were young."

He felt foolish having spoken in his native tongue. Perhaps the old man was a Securitate informant. *Christ.*

The man leaned closer. "You see, we stand in line to buy whatever they bring—size 44 dresses, size 40 galoshes, size 42 pants—then we exchange it among ourselves for what we need. We are an example of reverse evolution, back to the barter system." The old man gave him a toothless smile. "Go back home. You don't belong here."

He wanted to tell the old man that he was already home, but it would have been a lie. At that moment Romania felt like an alien world. He had been in Bucharest for several days yet he still felt he hadn't quite arrived. The innocence of his childhood was nowhere to be captured. The city was barely recognizable, the people tired, defeated. It was one thing to hear stories from his parents or relatives, or from intel that crossed his desk, and another to experience it firsthand. A miasma of dejection had settled over the city and it permeated every aspect of daily life, from the endless lines for food, to the petty bribes demanded by anyone in the minutest position of power, to the loss of common politeness. Some forms of speech from a more civilized age still remained, especially in the older generations. The plural form of addressing a stranger was still practiced, though not always by the authorities. One might still see a man kiss the hand of a woman, as he had seen several men do at Gabor's party, though the younger generation usually laughed at such an anachronism.

The saving grace was the language. For him it was suffused with personal memories and collective allusions, with facial expressions and hand gestures, with turns of a phrase that captured just the right meaning or emotion, often in ways inexpressible in English. He loved to bathe in it, to let it awaken those parts of his mind long dormant and hidden. But the language took on a different flavor altogether when spoken by a party apparatchik or an insolent store clerk—creating new, less sanguine associations, marring its essence, adding a layer of desolation to the language.

He missed New York. He craved a walk down Fifth Avenue to gaze at the posh windows of Bergdorf Goodman and Saks Fifth

Avenue and forget about this misery. He was about to leave when a little girl approached him. Her entire left arm was in a cast.

"Please, sir, I am starving. A little money for milk, a piece of bread. Please, sir." She held out her good hand. She was pretty, perhaps ten or eleven, with dark eyes and skin, like his.

"Shoo, get away from here," the same old man in line said. "Don't give her anything. She's a gypsy."

"She has a broken arm." He couldn't understand the old man's cruelty.

"That's a fake cast," the old man said. "There's nothing wrong with her arm. They do that to appeal to your heart. Shoo, get out of here. Go back to your mother."

The little girl looked at the old man, then at Hefflin, and, seeing that her scam had been revealed, raised her nose up in proud defiance and walked off.

"They're a nuisance," the man spat. "They'll do anything, including sending their children out to beg."

Hefflin walked away, riled by the encounter, noting that the child looked well fed, better than some of the other children he'd seen. But what did he know about the gypsy life? Everywhere they went they were considered outcasts, an annoyance.

He asked for directions to a Tourist Shop and found one a few blocks away. At the door, the woman asked to see his passport before admitting him. No locals allowed. Inside, the scene was bizarre. Items that the locals would never have dreamed of affording were displayed in a poor parody of a Western store: a wall of liquor bottles from America and Western Europe stood next to kitchen appliances from Germany; a mountain of American cigarette cartons was stacked next to leather jackets from Italy; French perfume was displayed adjacent to Italian soap;

bottles of Romanian Murfatlar wine, made only for export, were lined up next to crates of Spam and sardines.

The place was nearly empty—only a young Western couple shopping for gifts for their relatives. He bought a bottle of French champagne, paid with dollars, and left.

*   *   *

Irina's home was a beautifully restored, two-story traditional Moldovan house, the type one saw in postcards, reserved only for the privileged.

The moment Irina opened the door, he noticed her red eyes, her drawn face.

"A hard night?" He handed her the bottle of champagne.

"Don't judge me," she said, her eyes avoiding his. "You don't live here."

The house was beautifully furnished with heavy, antique furniture. Among them he recognized the red couch she'd inherited from her parents, long deceased. There was a black cord going from the wall into a desk drawer.

"The telephone," she said, noticing his gaze. "Victor promised me this house hasn't any listening devices, but the telephones come with a microphone already installed at the factory. All they have to do is flip a switch and hear everything in the apartment. So, everyone just puts the phone in a drawer or closet." She shrugged.

"Victor Vulcan. Minister of Agriculture."

"You know him?"

"The embassy does. You've been an item for years, they tell me."

"So, the spies know about us." She sighed. "He's not a bad man, you know. Quite intelligent, handsome, funny at times."

He sat on the red couch, the one on which she'd shown him the Hieronymus Bosch pictures of hell twenty-odd years before, and she sat across from him.

"You didn't marry, have a family," he said. "A woman like you must have plenty of admirers."

"Children? In this miserable place?" She waved an arm. "Nobody wants to have children anymore. Oh, some still do, the peasants, the apparatchiks, and the optimists who think things will change."

"And you don't?"

"Not in my lifetime. Yes, communism will fall at some point— it's happening all around us. But then what? It will take a generation or two to undo all the damage in the people's mentality, and that's if we have an honest government, which we've never had, not even before the communists. Besides, I'm an actress. What would I do with children?"

She went into the kitchen and returned with plates of various cheeses and salamis, along with a loaf of bread. Then she came back with a plate of quiche. She seemed to have no problem getting food, though he couldn't imagine her standing in those lines.

"I pay the butcher to save me meat, which he delivers in the evening," she said, reading his mind. "Same for the grocer. And Victor brings certain delicacies from the Party market."

A system based on *baksheesh* and privilege. "At least you haven't suffered as much as others," he said.

Her back stiffened. "I'm a great actress. Two years ago, I received the award for best leading role in a drama, the Romanian version of the Tony. In America I'd be a millionaire. Here I'm on a State salary, equivalent to that of a postal worker."

He said nothing. He felt her sense of injustice, her efforts to be a success in a country where individuality was discouraged.

But he also saw the spoiled child in her. She was part of the privileged class, protected, admired, and barricaded from the suffering of the millions around her. And it still wasn't enough.

"In America actors don't have it easy," he said. "You only see the successful ones, but the rest, the young and not-so-young who only get an occasional part, if that, struggle to survive. Ninety percent of actors in their union, the Screen Actors Guild, can't make a living as an actor. There's no State salary for them. New York is full of aspiring actors and writers who work as waiters and bartenders. Most of them don't ever make it big."

"I'd be the talk of Broadway and Hollywood." Irina's eyes glistened now. "I have ambition, and I'm a fighter. And—judge me if you must—I know how to make use of people in power."

"Men, you mean."

"Yes, men, since they're the ones who have the power. But if Romania were run by lesbians, I'd learn to be that, too."

He thought of Pusha and what she had had to go through to survive. He brushed the thought aside as he saw Irina bring out a bottle of *tsuika* and two glasses.

"Isn't it a bit early for *tsuika*?" he asked as she poured.

"The hair of the dog, as you Americans say." She smiled. "Many of us start the day with a shot of *tsuika* or vodka. At least it's past noon, and I don't have a performance tonight. The play is over. Everyone is just waiting now, to see what happens."

They toasted Broadway, Hollywood, America, Marlon Brando, Elizabeth Taylor, Gregory Peck, Marilyn Monroe, Anthony Quinn, Burt Lancaster, in no particular order. Then she put on a record of Charles Aznavour, and they toasted him, too.

"What do you think, would I be a big star in America?" she asked, a bit tipsy now.

"Eventually, maybe. But how would you survive in the meantime? I don't see you waiting tables."

"I'd find a rich man and make him most extraordinarily, most indisputably, happy." She slurred her words. "New York is full of rich men, isn't it?"

"Rich men? Sure, New York is crawling with rich men. But they travel in their own circles. Not easy to meet. And they're not always the nicest guys."

She shrugged. "Rich men are the same everywhere." Her eyes settled on some far distance. "Hollywood, then. The lens is kind to me. I did two films, Russian productions, and got great reviews from the local press, whatever that means." She let out a deep sigh and waved her arm in disgust. "Better a big fish in a small pond, is that what you're telling me?"

"I think Gabor arrived at the same conclusion."

"Yes." She nodded. "He had many chances to defect. He's been allowed to travel to the West many times—Italy, Israel, West Germany, even England. He has always returned. Of course, his family remained behind for insurance—the way the State always does it—but his reasons for returning go deeper. He loves the Romanian language, the Romanian culture. He says he couldn't survive anywhere else."

She let her gaze wander, taking in her house, her belongings. "He's probably right. I'd never be as good an actress in English. Language has nuance, layers of meaning. An actor working in another language loses something. In the end, it's the work that counts. Everything else, fame, money, all of this—" she waived her arm— "doesn't matter." She smiled, a sad, accepting smile. "You must forgive me. I'm just a stupid girl dreaming of what might have been, in another life. I've achieved everything—more than everything—I've ever dreamed of. And now I want more. That's how people are. We're never satisfied." She crossed herself, then drank the rest of her *tsuika*. "I must be grateful to God for what he gave me."

"And I want to help you keep what you've achieved," he said, his eyes settling on hers.

"Help me keep it?" Her hand went up to her cheek. "Why? Am I in danger of losing it?"

"Perhaps." He hesitated, reminding himself to tread lightly. "You know how long it takes for an actress to build a reputation, a following, and how quickly it can be destroyed."

"And who would want to destroy it?"

"Irina, things are changing. Soon there will be a new government, a democracy, hopefully. The people who are now in power will fall. And those whom they associated with will be dragged down with them."

She stared at him, then at the distance beyond him. "You're talking about Victor."

"You've been with him for a long time. No matter what you think of him, he's done some very bad things. Among them is that he has stolen millions of dollars for Ceausescu and has hidden it in offshore accounts."

She leaned back in her chair, her eyes unfocused, her face now drained of its animation. "He stole millions for that tyrant while the people are starving?"

"And he's the only one, other than Ceausescu, who knows where the money is hidden," he said.

Her expression changed; her facial lines now drawn tightly in a manifestation of resolve.

"You, Americans, have all the power. Why can't you find it?"

"We're trying," he said gently. "But they are all numbered accounts. Difficult to find. We need to convince Victor to give them to us."

"Convince him? Ah, I see." She suddenly broke into jagged laughter. "Are you crazy? Just because I sleep with him you think he'll give me Ceausescu's dossier? You've been watching too many of your spy movies."

He waited for her laughter to die down, regretting having approached her after so much drinking. "When the time comes, and he sees he has few options, you can tell him that you have a close relative who is an important man in the U.S. government."

She suddenly stopped laughing and stared at him. "Are you? An important man?" Her hand went up to her throat. "Oh my God, you're a spy. I should have known when you told me your fake name. My cousin is a spy."

"I can make this deal with him," he said, trying to push beyond her question. "Asylum in the West, a new identity. You need to convince him it's the only way he can save himself."

She leaned back, thinking, her face drawn in fear.

"He won't believe me," she said. "I'm an actress, a woman. I'm nothing important in his eyes. And if he does believe me, he may just have me shot as a traitor for having anything to do with the CIA."

"You've been with him for a long time. He must have feelings for you."

She twisted her face. "He says he loves me. In bed, when he's drunk. But this is different. Something like this, spying, risking his life."

"There are many people after that money, Irina. And they know he is Ceausescu's money man. If things pan out badly for the current government, his only chance is with us."

"But what if Ceausescu survives? Did you consider that?"

He hesitated, realizing that his belief in Boris was so complete, he hadn't really doubted Boris's plan.

"Ceausescu will be gone, one way or another," he said. "Then you will be left with the consequences of the public finding out about your affair."

There it was, Boris's not-so-subtle blackmail.

"Yes, I'd be left exposed. How will the public react?" She shrugged. "Everyone in this wretched country has had to compromise. We are forced to do it every day. If they go after me, they'll first go after Gabor, who is on the Central Committee, and after many others who have played the game to stay alive. After so many years and so much misery, we're all stained to one degree or another." She sighed. "I'm not trying to excuse my actions, only to explain them. My art is all that is important to me. I was ambitious, yes, I admit it. I used all means at my disposal to help me succeed, may God forgive me." She crossed herself three times.

"You have a chance at atonement, of a sort." He began to feel nauseated. This was his cousin he was manipulating. But he went on. "We can make your affair with him disappear—or at least bury it."

"I've been with him for four years," she said. "Several of my friends know, your spies know, and the Securitate surely knows. They must have a fat dossier on me."

"We can make all of that disappear," he said. Finally, the last card left to play. "I can even bring you to America, if you want."

Her eyes dulled as she stared at him. "Shame on you." She stood, walked around the room, then turned to face him. "I won't help you to save my reputation or my career or for the chance of going to America, which you should have offered me without any strings attached. But I've already decided I'm not leaving Romania, so you can relax about that."

He sank into the couch, his face suddenly burning with shame.

"But I *will* help you because, for better or for worse, this is still my country. For once I have a chance to do something."

CHAPTER TWENTY-FOUR

Bucharest
December 1989

HE DECIDED TO walk back to his hotel to give himself time to digest all the alcohol along with the shame he felt at trying to bribe and blackmail Irina, when all he had to do was appeal to her moral nature. They had spent the entire afternoon drinking *tsuika* and it had left him quite drunk. He was grateful that it was now past seven in the evening, and the streets were empty and dark. He didn't relish the idea of the police having to deliver a drunk diplomat to the embassy in a paddy wagon.

He kept to the shadows and the dark side streets. The night was cold but there was no wind. The silence accentuated the echo of his footsteps, which reminded him of the narrow, stone-paved streets of Siena, in Italy, which common folklore said had been made narrow so that a lone pedestrian could hear the approaching footsteps of an assassin or thief. It was that memory that now made him suddenly aware of the irregular rhythm of the sound of his footsteps. He stopped walking and heard the sound of an extra step before the silence returned. He began walking again and the rhythm of the sound of his footsteps was first regular, then irregular again.

He turned at the first corner, hid in a building entryway, and continued stomping his feet, making them grow fainter. Soon he heard the other footsteps growing louder. A moment later, a man dressed in a dark overcoat and wool hat passed by his hideout. With one fluid motion Hefflin stepped out of the entryway and hit the back of the man's head with a knife blow he had learned in his martial arts training. As he was doing this, he realized it was a stupid thing to do, for he didn't know the man's identity or intentions, but the alcohol had relieved him of any inhibitions. The man groaned and sprawled onto the cobblestones. Hefflin straddled him and delivered two punches to the man's face, then frisked him and found a Beretta in a shoulder holster.

The man was young, in his twenties. The overcoat was of a higher quality than those the local population wore.

"Who the fuck are you?" Hefflin asked, pushing the pistol barrel deep into the man's neck.

"CIA, like you," the man stammered. "Get the fuck off me."

He relaxed his grip. "CIA? Why are you following me?"

The man groaned, trying to regain his wits.

"Who ordered you to follow me?" Hefflin repeated. "Was it Stanton?"

"Langley," the man said. "They told me you're just a fucking analyst. I'll never live this down."

"Look, asshole, I don't know if you're CIA or Securitate or KGB," Hefflin said. "I'll put you down if you don't give me an answer. Why were you ordered to follow me?"

"Boris," the man said. "They're tired of you being the only guy handling Boris. I've been trying to follow you since you got here, but haven't been able to identify Boris yet. Langley is pissed."

"Does Stanton know about you?"

"No. This is direct from Avery."

Avery. The director of operations wanted to know Boris's identity to take over his handling, to control him. *Fucking Avery.*

"Well, now you'll look like a real hero when you explain to Avery how you were taken down by an analyst."

The man stood, rubbing the back of his head. "They won't like this."

"Yeah? Well, you can tell Avery that I don't like his stupid games."

"Who the hell is this actress, Irina Argyris? Why have you been seeing her?" the man asked. "Give me a break, all right? I gotta tell Avery something."

Through the alcohol haze, Hefflin remembered that Avery knew his real name, and thus must know that Irina was a relative.

"Just tell him her name. He'll know who she is," he said. "And here, take this back." He removed the magazine from the Beretta, ejected the bullet in the chamber, then tossed the gun back. "Nothing looks worse than a field agent having his gun taken from him."

The man walked away with a muttered "Thanks," and faded into the darkness.

The thought occurred to Hefflin that the guy might be waiting around the corner to knock his teeth out just for revenge, so he took off in the opposite direction, turned into a dark alley and onto another narrow street. After a few more turns, he knew he was lost.

He stopped to retrace his steps. He didn't see the punch coming, just felt a blow to the side of his head. His body hit the cobblestones hard, then he felt a kick to his stomach. He lay on the ground curled up, unable to breathe, to think. Several figures were hovering around him, speaking a language he didn't recognize. Czech? Hungarian? One of the figures knelt beside him and a face wearing a balaclava came close to his.

"Mr. Hefflin, what is American diplomat doing with lover of Ceausescu's accountant? You must be after offshore accounts, no? What has the actress told you?"

Hefflin coughed, then tasted blood in his mouth. "What off-shore accounts?"

He felt a kick to his kidney delivered by one of the other men. He curled in agony.

"Come now, we saw you fighting with the other man. Who was he? He probably wants the same thing we do. You surprise him and hit him from behind, like a coward. You are obviously not a field agent. You are drunk. I do not think CIA agents get so drunk, no?"

"I'm a cultural attaché." Hefflin let out a groan.

Hefflin heard laughter. *Who are these guys?*

"Miss Argyris is just a friend," Hefflin spat. "I know nothing of any offshore accounts."

"So, you are just a diplomat. Maybe you come with plans for change of government," the man said. "You are last American to come to Bucharest, so you must have reason to be here." The man clinched Hefflin's face and twisted it up toward him. "What do you know of Lazlo Tokes?"

"Never heard of him," Hefflin muttered.

"Timisoara?"

"A city in Romania."

The man let go of his face and sighed. "Either you are very low-level diplomat or very good liar. Either way, do not think diplomatic status means anything in this country. I can kill you right now and nobody will find your body, but I think you are not worth the trouble."

The man stood. Hefflin heard footsteps walking away, then the silence returned once more.

When he arrived at his room in the Athénée, he dropped into bed without even removing his clothes and passed out.

CHAPTER TWENTY-FIVE

Bucharest
December 1989

HE SPENT THE next morning in his hotel room nursing his pains and his hangover. Every part of his body hurt and a headache pounded in his temples. He hung over the toilet dry retching for an hour, then sank onto the cold tile floor and drifted back to sleep. When he awoke it was early afternoon. He took a long bath, letting his mind clear and allowing his memories of the previous evening to spill onto the pages of his notebook.

The man had asked about the offshore accounts, and the language he had heard whispered in the background was not Romanian. They were not Securitate, as he had initially thought. These were the other forces searching for Ceausescu's money that Balzary had warned him about. They had also mentioned Timisoara and had asked about a man. What was the name? Tokes. Laszlo Tokes. The name didn't mean anything to him. He thought of asking Stanton, but then he'd have to tell him about being attacked and interrogated. Stanton would go ape-shit and probably petition Avery to send him back to the States. He was tired of Stanton trying to restrict his actions, constantly reminding him that he was just an analyst. And he was tired of being followed by everyone, of walking the streets like a dumb tourist, of being pushed around. He had to raise his game.

By midafternoon he was feeling better. He ate a quick lunch of *mamaliga,* the soft polenta with butter that the hotel served, then headed for the embassy.

Stanton wasn't in, for which he was grateful. He settled himself before the computer screen and typed in Laszlo Tokes's name. There was a file on him, albeit sparse. What there was, however, was enough to raise his pulse. Tokes was a Hungarian assistant pastor in the city of Timisoara who had been a critic of the communist regime for years, going back to articles he had written in an underground journal while a pastor in the town of Dej. After being transferred to Timisoara, he continued his anti-government activities with seminars and other actions, culminating in a secretly taped interview with a Canadian news crew that had been shown on Hungarian State TV in July. As a result, in October he had been officially transferred to another city and ordered to vacate his apartment by the fifteenth of December. Hefflin looked at the calendar on the wall: it was the sixteenth.

He logged out and left the Operations room. It was already early evening and the place was practically deserted except for the night Control on duty. He was a middle-aged man, gray-haired, experienced. Hefflin asked for Stanton but Control said Stanton was still out.

"I need a firearm," Hefflin said. "What do you have?"

The man looked at him through thick, wire-framed glasses. "You're not allowed a firearm. You're not a field agent."

"Check with Stanton. I'm allowed anything I want," Hefflin said.

Control went into another room. Through the glass door, Hefflin could see him talking on the phone, nodding a few times, then replacing the receiver. When he returned, his face displayed a dour expression.

"Stanton said, and I quote, 'Why the fuck does he need a gun?'"

"For protection, why else? I'm being followed."

"Of course you are. Everyone is. That doesn't mean you need a firearm. But the situation is getting tense, I give you that." Control shook his head and let out a long sigh. "According to Stanton, you have carte blanche here. Why, I can't imagine. So, how much training have you received?"

"Same as field agents."

The man looked impressed. "Follow me, then."

Control led the way down the stairs to the basement, used a combination lock to open a steel door, and turned on the light. The room was composed of steel racks full of various firearms, from scoped sniper rifles to handguns.

"I suggest a small Beretta." Control handed him a pistol similar to the one the Agency man had carried. "Easily concealed, rarely jams, lethal at close range, carries ten in the magazine and one in the chamber. We're not going to get into any prolonged gunfights, are we?"

Hefflin ignored the sarcasm and signed out the Beretta with an extra magazine. On his way out, he decided to pass by Stanton's office to leave him a note telling him he was going to be gone for a few days. Stanton's office was unlocked, as usual. Since the office was inside the Operations room, Stanton apparently didn't feel he needed to lock it. Stanton's desk was the usual mess, with files piled high and papers spread all over the place. Hefflin couldn't imagine how Stanton could keep track of them all.

He wrote the note and placed it on the desk, then noticed a file labeled "Pincus" placed on top of a tall stack of files. When he opened the file, he found several pictures, which he spread out on the desk. They were dark, grainy photographs of a man dressed in civilian clothes standing before a house. As he looked closer, he realized he was looking at Pincus's house, and the man was the assassin who was about to enter it. Unlike the pictures Avery had shown him, however, one picture had been taken with the man facing the camera. He studied the face for a moment, hoping to imprint the man's image in his memory. Maybe he would run into him in Bucharest, though it was a long shot. He pushed down the thoughts of revenge. He was in a hurry. As he left the embassy, he wondered why Stanton had a file on Pincus and where he had obtained that picture.

Three streets down from the embassy, he spotted a taxi and hailed it.

"Gara de Nord," he told the driver.

At the train station he bought a one-way second-class ticket on the night train to Timisoara.

CHAPTER TWENTY-SIX

Night Train to Timisoara
December 1989

THE SECOND-CLASS COMPARTMENT was nearly full, mostly with workers traveling to nearby factories for the night shift. He had chosen a second-class ticket in the hope of blending in, but now realized that had been a mistake. His American clothes immediately set him apart from the worn overcoats and dirty uniforms around him.

He sat in the back seat next to the window and tried to make himself small. The men were quiet, absorbed in their own lives. Whatever talking was done occurred in whispers, as were all conversations in Romania. From early childhood the people knew to express themselves in vague allusions, a raising of the eyebrows, the flick of a finger. No names were ever mentioned. "How is the guy you told me about?" "What happened to that friend of yours?" "How did that matter resolve?" And so on.

The trip to Timisoara was scheduled to take ten hours, long enough for a good nap. The regular tick-tock, tick-tock of the iron wheels quickly brought on the desired drowsiness and he melted into the warmth of oblivion.

＊　　＊　　＊

The sound of a door slamming roused him into consciousness. He found the train almost empty, the workers having disembarked at local stops. His watch told him he had slept for five hours. He felt refreshed.

There were four men left in the carriage. He noticed two of them were dressed differently than the other two workers. These men wore jeans, leather jackets, and Russian fur hats, a common uniform of the Securitate. He felt for his gun in his coat pocket.

Though the Securitate agents were not looking at him, he was sure they had spotted his foreign clothes. Had they been following him from the beginning or had they boarded the train sometime later?

He could feel the train moving rapidly. Outside it was still dark. The two men stood and walked over to the two workers.

"Move to the first-class compartment," one of them ordered, flashing his Securitate ID.

The two workers scrambled out of their seats and hurried out of the cabin. Hefflin was left alone with the Securitate agents now. They turned toward him and approached.

"Your papers," one of them said in English.

Hefflin removed his passport from his jacket pocket and handed it to him.

"You are diplomat," the agent said. "Where are you going?"

"Timisoara," he said.

"Why? And on a night train?"

"I've never been to Timisoara," he said with a smile. "I thought the night train would be less crowded."

The man gave him a half smile. "You are sightseeing, then?"

"You could call it that."

"But why today?"

He shrugged. "Why not?"

The man tapped the passport in his palm, as if considering what to do.

"There is a curfew in Timisoara. The city borders are closed. You will disembark at the next station and return to Bucharest." The man's voice had turned to ice.

"This train is going to Timisoara, so the city borders can't be closed," Hefflin said. "As a diplomat, I have a right to go anywhere I please."

"You are a guest in this country, Mr. Hefflin. You have no rights; except those we give you. Now get up. A station will be approaching in a few minutes."

Hefflin didn't move. The man motioned to his partner, an ape in man's clothing, who swooped down and lifted Hefflin off his seat, then dragged him into the aisle. Hefflin was about to object when he felt a hard blow to his stomach. He doubled over, unable to breathe, the pain swelling up into his throat. He coughed and tasted some bile.

"You don't seem to get the message, Mr. Hefflin. We don't put up with foreign provocateurs trying to stir up counterrevolutionary forces."

He didn't know where the anger came from that made him respond with, "I'm going to Timisoara, and you can't stop me."

"Really? We will see."

They dragged him down the aisle then propped him against the exit door. The gorilla bitch-slapped him twice, then slipped a knife out of his jacket pocket.

"Maybe you have a reason for going to Timisoara today," the smaller man said. "Maybe you want to start trouble. Who else knows you are going to Timisoara?"

"I phoned your wife," Hefflin said.

The gorilla suddenly yanked open the door on which Hefflin was leaning. For a moment Hefflin felt himself teetering on the edge, about to fall into the darkness, when a frigid gust of wind lifted him up. As he was swept back inside the cabin, he grabbed the gorilla's knife-wielding right hand with his left. The man started swinging with a left hook, but Hefflin stepped into the punch and knuckle punched him in the trachea. The man started coughing and choking. He didn't know it yet, but he had a crushed trachea. He would never take another breath. Still holding the knife-wielding hand, Hefflin dropped to one knee, twisted his body, and pulled the man over his shoulder through the open doorway into the darkness below. There was no scream.

Seeing Hefflin's combat abilities, the smaller man reached for his gun, which was inside his holster. Hefflin rolled to one side while inserting his hand into his coat pocket. Just as the man managed to pull out his gun and aim, Hefflin pulled the trigger twice. The bullets exited through his coat pocket and hit the man in the chest.

It had all come back to Hefflin. His body had remembered, one movement flowing into another. He heard his instructor's words: A fight has to end in six seconds.

He sank to the floor, the pain slowly returning. He had just killed two men, but he felt no remorse. They were trying to kill him. And yet, he thought he should do something, say a prayer perhaps. He crossed himself as his mother used to do, then patted down the dead man's pockets and found a wallet. From inside he removed the man's Securitate ID and placed it in his pocket. He then pulled the body toward the open door and pushed it into the swiftly moving darkness below.

CHAPTER TWENTY-SEVEN

Timisoara
December 1989

TIMISOARA, NICKNAMED LITTLE Vienna, was the country's third most populous city, and one with an illustrious past. The city had been under Ottoman rule for nearly one hundred and sixty years, then under Austrian rule. Its architecture reflected Turkish, Austrian, German, and Serbian influences. It was the first European city and the second in the world, after New York City, to use electric street lamps; the first city in the Hapsburg Empire to have a public lending library; the first European city to introduce horse-drawn trams; and it was the birthplace of Johnny Weissmuller, the most famous film Tarzan.

The sun was just coming up as the train pulled into Timisoara's Gara de Nord. The trip had taken a little over eleven hours. The train had remained practically empty until it approached the outskirts of Timisoara, where it began to fill up with people of all types—men, women, children, young and old. These people were now speaking loudly, excitedly asking each other questions: Could the Securitate evict him from his apartment? Drag him to jail? What would the people do? Then he heard the name Tokes. He realized they were all coming to see what would happen to Laszlo Tokes.

At the station the people spilled out onto the platform, hundreds of them from several train cars. He followed along with them as they walked en masse through the city streets. Other people joined them along the way, the procession growing even larger as it moved toward the center of the city. Some people were in a festive mood, others walked quietly, their somber faces betraying fear. Many held bottles of *tsuika* from which they took a swig every so often, then passed it along to others.

The city was mostly made up of older buildings, which seemed well kept, unlike parts of Bucharest. After some time, the crowd turned a corner and he saw an even larger mass of people spread out across several streets. Some were singing hymns, others stood quietly, seeming to wait for something. He made his way closer to what seemed to be the focus of activity.

"What is everyone waiting for?" he asked a young man in Romanian.

"Tokes refuses to leave his house," the young man said. "The mayor is inside trying to convince him to leave."

"He's been a thorn in the government's side for years," another man said. "Now they want to transfer him to another parish to silence him." The man spat on the ground.

Hefflin now saw that a human chain had formed around the entrance of a building. Uniformed militia were trying to push their way through the crowd, but the chain of linked hands grew deeper, refusing to let them pass. More voices joined in the chorus of hymns, and the defiance grew louder. This went on for some time, a standoff, then the crowd suddenly stopped singing. A quiet descended over the entire scene. Hefflin spotted a man standing outside the entrance of the building, speaking to the crowd. But he was too far away to hear what he was saying. Word of mouth began to filter among the people.

"Tokes is asking us to leave, to avoid conflict with the authorities," a woman up ahead said.

The crowd shouted, "No! No!" And, "The people have a voice!"

Tokes went back inside, and the hymns returned. Several hours passed, the throng growing larger, more impatient. Hefflin tried to make his way through the crowd, but it had become so thick that he could hardly move. Another man appeared at the entrance. He was holding a megaphone.

"Comrades, I ask you to disperse and go home. You have until seventeen hundred hours at which time we will have no choice but to bring in the water cannon."

The crowd roared, some brandishing fists. Tokes again appeared to plead for the people to go home but, once more, they refused.

"The Securitate pigs are forcing him to say these things," one man cried out.

Five o'clock came and went without the water cannon appearing. By seven o'clock the crowd had grown to over a hundred thousand, extending for several blocks in all directions. From one section a new song sprang up: "*Awaken, Romanian!*" It was an old patriotic song that had been banned since 1945, when the communists had taken over. The song was taken up by everyone who still remembered the words. Others started chanting, "Down with Ceausescu!" and "Down with communism!" Thousands of people were shouting words that, until now, they had not dared utter even in their sleep. Hefflin's heart leapt into his throat and tears filled his eyes. He felt a surge of pride at the courage these miserable people were now showing, and he suddenly found himself chanting along with the crowd, "Down with Ceausescu! Down with communism!"

The mob marched toward the center of the city. When they reached the Communist Party Headquarters, thousands of people, young and old, continued to chant, "Down with communism!" and "Down with the thieves!" Hefflin sensed a line had been crossed. The people were no longer afraid.

"What more can they do to us?" one woman said to him. "Let them mow us down and be done with it."

The cause was no longer Tokes's. Everyone had forgotten the priest. They had gathered in front of the Party Headquarters to chant for themselves and for their children. Suddenly, there was a commotion. Hefflin saw some demonstrators throw stones and bricks through the Headquarters windows. The crowd roared with approval. The militia, which surrounded the building, drove the crowd back temporarily, but eventually lost control and gave up. Some demonstrators broke into the building but were soon chased out by the militia. When the water cannons finally appeared, the demonstrators attacked them, climbed the trucks, and dismantled the hoses. They dragged the broken parts and threw them into the river. The militia just stood by and watched, seemingly confused. No one had ever seen this happen in Romania. Securitate members dressed in civilian clothes started beating people with batons but only succeeded in angering them more. Then the military trucks arrived filled with soldiers. The crowd withdrew, but soon reformed in other parts of the city and continued their marching and chanting.

Hefflin found a public phone, dialed a code, then the number to the Operations room. He heard a young voice answer.

"This is Hefflin," he told him. "I need to speak to Stanton."

"He is in the field, sir," the young voice said. He sounded excited. Hefflin could hear voices shouting in the background.

"Look, I'm in Timisoara," Hefflin said. "There's something important happening here. Demonstrations. Thousands on the streets. The army is out in force. I need to get a hold of Stanton."

"You're in Timisoara?" The young man sounded surprised. "That's where Stanton is."

Stanton in Timisoara? What the hell is he doing here?

"He's at our safe house, sir." The man gave him the address.

Hefflin hung up, returned to the streets, and asked a young boy for directions.

"Down two blocks," the boy said and pointed.

He gave the boy a coin and started walking, wondering what the hell Stanton was up to in Timisoara.

CHAPTER TWENTY-EIGHT

Timisoara
December 1989

THE CIA SAFE house was a nondescript three-story stucco house on a side street. The entrance had an intercom and a camera next to the door. He pressed the button and looked into the camera. A voice on the intercom said, "Yes?"

"I am Bill Hefflin, cultural attacheé to Bucharest Embassy."

The door buzzed open and he entered. Two men were standing in the entrance, one holding a gun. The other man patted him down and found the Beretta.

"What are you doing here?" one of the men asked. "We received no word to expect you."

"No, this is unscheduled," he said. "I need to talk to Stanton. Bucharest office told me he's here."

The man's eyes narrowed. "They shouldn't have done that. Come with me."

The man led him up the steps to the second-floor hallway, then into a side room. "He's in a meeting. Wait here." The man closed the door and left him alone in the room.

Through the door he could hear hurried footsteps, a sense of agitation. The demonstrations had placed the station on high alert, no doubt scrambling to get information on casualties, how far the crowds would dare go, and what the government response would be. He heard faint voices. At first, he thought they were also coming from the hallway, but then he traced them to an old enclosed fireplace rising up in one corner of the room. Those old fireplaces, no longer in use, were made of ceramic tile, which heated up as the wood or coal fuel burned at the bottom. There was usually an identical one in the adjacent room, which shared the same chimney to the roof.

He opened the metal door at the bottom of the fireplace where the wood or charcoal normally burned. The voices became clearer. There were two men arguing. He recognized Stanton's voice. He could only make out a few words, which Stanton kept repeating: "army," "tourists," and "snipers." The meeting ended abruptly with "tomorrow" being repeated a few times.

He rushed to the door and opened it a crack. He saw Stanton exiting the adjacent room with another man, taller, more erect, dressed in a suit. At first, he didn't recognize him; the suit threw him off. Then he realized it was General Stanculescu, the deputy defense minister. What was Stanculescu doing talking to Stanton? It had the flavor of a secret meeting, for Stanculescu was out of uniform, perhaps traveling incognito.

The two men shook hands, and the general was escorted down the stairs to the exit. The same man that had brought him to this room now informed Stanton that Hefflin was waiting for him.

"What? Here?" Stanton cried.

Hefflin closed the door and quickly sat in one of the chairs. He heard the stomping of Stanton's boots, the opening of the door, then Stanton's aggravated voice.

"What the hell are you doing in Timisoara?"

"Probably the same thing you are," he said. "Trying to find out what's happening with these demonstrations."

"That's not your mission," Stanton snapped. "You're supposed to be concentrating on Boris."

"My mission was to assess the entire situation in the country," he said. "Who was that man you were talking to?"

Stanton's head snapped back. He stared at him, then said, "Who?"

"The man who just left."

"Oh, him? That was the mayor," Stanton said. "I told him to show restraint, to have a peaceful resolution to the Tokes affair."

Why was Stanton lying to him? Hefflin knew what Stanculescu looked like. He had seen multiple pictures of him in the files. And what was this about the Tokes affair? A few days ago, nobody had ever heard of the priest. Now Tokes's situation had taken on the importance of an affair, like the Dreyfus affair, the famous nineteenth-century scandal in France, depicting the miscarriage of justice and anti-Semitism.

"I think it's late for a peaceful resolution," Hefflin said. "The Securitate are already beating civilians with batons and water cannon."

"It can get a lot worse than that if they don't stand down," Stanton spat.

He wondered what Stanton was holding back. Stanton, no doubt, had intel of which Hefflin was ignorant. But then he reminded himself that in the CIA only a few operatives ever knew the entire picture.

"What did you want to see me about?" Stanton asked, annoyed.

"I wanted to report the demonstrations, but obviously you're on top of it." He got up to go.

"Where are you staying?"

"I was going to find a hotel."

"That's crazy. There are bedrooms upstairs." Stanton indicated with his chin. "You can spend the night, with the understanding that you're on the train back to Bucharest in the morning."

Hefflin nodded, then climbed the stairs and entered one of the bedrooms. As he stretched out on the bed, he wondered what the hell Stanton was doing talking to General Stanculescu about tourists and snipers. And what did they know was going to happen tomorrow?

CHAPTER TWENTY-NINE

Timisoara
December 1989

THE NEXT MORNING Hefflin left the safe house without seeing Stanton. On the way out, he was handed back his Beretta. The sky was overcast, but the temperature was warmer than previous days.

He had no intention of immediately returning to Bucharest. As he approached the square, he saw that the demonstrations were already in full force. The crowd had grown even larger than the day before, filling the square and side streets near the Communist Party Headquarters. Army personnel carriers were stationed in front of the Party Headquarters building and on street corners. Militia and plain-clothed Securitate forces carrying machine guns were spread throughout the square. In order not to be trapped by the crowd, Hefflin planted himself in an alcove at a far corner of the square and waited for events to unfold.

During the next several hours, the crowd continued to grow, Romanians and Hungarians joining to chant "Down with Ceausescu! Down with communism!" He knew that Hungarians and Romanians didn't always get along, but now they had apparently joined in a common cause. The military announced through megaphones that the square had to be cleared. The crowd responded with chants of "The army is with us," and "Join us, boys." The standoff continued for several hours more.

Civilian trucks were now trying to make their way through the crowd. When they reached the square, workmen started pouring out of them carrying large sacks. There was a roar from the crowd as the men opened their sacks and started passing out their gifts. Hefflin heard people screaming, "Fresh bread! Fresh bread!" The men started throwing the loaves into the crowd.

"Who are they?" he asked a woman next to him.

"They're workers from the bread factories nearby," she said. "They bake fresh, quality bread for export, while we stand in line for three-day-old bricks made from cattle grain."

There was a sudden rush of people in front of the Communist Party Headquarters. They ran through the phalanx of soldiers who had been caught off guard and burst into the Headquarters building. The soldiers just stood watching, unsure of what to do. Soon papers and files came flying out the windows. Portraits of Nicolae and Elena Ceausescu were cast down onto the street and trampled. Then dark smoke started billowing out of the windows. Everyone was suddenly running out of the building. The Headquarters was on fire.

Crackling sounds rang out, like fireworks. At first the people didn't move, unsure of what to make of it. Then several in the crowd fell to the ground. People turned to run but the crowd was too dense and massive for anyone to run anywhere. More shots rang out. Hefflin saw two women collapse. The square was now filled with screams, the people panicking, a stampede beginning. People were pointing up at rooftops. Hefflin spotted a man in civilian clothes on one rooftop aiming a rifle into the crowd, then firing. A man fell. Another sniper on an adjacent rooftop was now firing at the line of soldiers. Two soldiers fell, wounded.

Snipers. Just what Hefflin had heard Stanton say to Stanculescu. And they were shooting at both civilians and soldiers.

The soldiers panicked and started shooting into the crowd. People were now collapsing by the dozens, men, women, and children. Others, wide-eyed, hysterical, were scrambling to find shelter, breaking down doors to enter buildings or hiding behind parked cars. Hefflin observed the massacre from his protected alcove, his mind trying to deny what his eyes were witnessing. But it was happening now, he had to remind himself. History was repeating itself.

Tanks appeared from somewhere along the flanks of the crowd and started rolling at full speed toward the protesters. He saw one tank plow right into the people massed in the square, running over fleeing bodies. The metal treads of a tank ran over a woman and two children. He heard rapid gunfire. The Securitate with machine guns were now spraying bullets into the jostling crowd. People fell by the dozens.

Hefflin buckled over and started retching.

✳ ✳ ✳

Hefflin walked the streets along with the Romanian people. Some were crying, others were swearing revenge. Most were just walking like zombies, in shock and disbelief. He heard that demonstrations had resumed in other parts of the city, the crowds moving like herds from one square to another to avoid the military and the snipers. Who were these snipers, everyone was asking, for they seemed not to discriminate between civilians and military. The military were so confused that they were firing at everyone, including other military.

Hefflin roamed the streets, dazed, like the rest of the people, unable to take in everything he had witnessed. At some point he passed by a coffee shop on a side street and stopped to go inside. The place was empty. The waitress, a woman in her sixties, brought him a cup of steaming coffee. She saw the look on his face as he tasted it.

"It's real coffee," she said. "We're lucky to be living next door to Hungary."

He knew the people in the area lived better than in the rest of the country because they were able to smuggle goods across the border. If demonstrations could happen in Timisoara, therefore, they could happen anywhere in Romania.

"What happened with the marches?" the woman asked. "No one has come in here to tell me anything. My children were going to join them." Her face was dark, her wrinkles tightened into deep valleys.

"First snipers started firing from rooftops, then the army panicked and started firing into the crowd," he said in Romanian. "There was a massacre. I'm sorry. I hope your children are all right."

"Oh, God." She crossed herself several times. "Why don't they just kill us all and be done with it?"

He left and resumed his walk. By nightfall the streets were relatively quiet. There was a curfew but no one was paying any attention to it. He returned to the Communist Party Headquarters where he found the square empty except for the bodies piled on top of each other like firewood. Soldiers were slowly loading them into trucks.

He couldn't take his eyes off the mangled torsos, the puddles of blood, the abnormal angles of arms and legs. He no longer felt ill. He didn't feel anything. The images no longer had any effect on him. It was as if his mind had overloaded and had just given up.

Whatever happened to Boris's quiet coup? He thought of Stanculescu, who was in charge of the military in Timisoara. Did he order the massacre or had events just gotten out of control? Who were those snipers in civilian clothes, and did Stanculescu know about them beforehand?

As he was about to leave, he spotted a figure taking pictures of the stacked bodies. A woman. She was standing at a street corner about a hundred feet from him, her face obscured by the camera. She was wearing a dark parka and jeans. Long brown hair. He looked over to the soldiers to see if they had noticed her. Someone taking pictures of the massacre was not something they would like. He wanted to yell to her to get away, but thought that would only alert the soldiers.

He started moving through the shadows toward her, to warn her. He heard one of the soldiers yell at her to halt. She didn't move, just kept taking pictures. When he heard a shot, he started running toward her, ducking down between cars, unsure where the shot came from or who the target was. When he looked up at her again, she was gone.

He heard two more shots, then saw the wall of the building next to him burst open as the bullets hit it. He turned onto the side street into which she had disappeared and started running. From the square came shouts to find the photographer. He hoped the woman had entered a building, her home, perhaps. Documenting an atrocity would earn her an arrest, perhaps a bullet. He didn't know what he would do if he found her, perhaps get her to the safe house or use his diplomatic passport, if that meant anything anymore.

When he reached a corner he stopped, out of breath. He had been walking the streets all day, witnessing the atrocities, and his legs were sore, as was his spirit.

He heard men talking, then a woman's voice. It was coming from around the corner. He peered around the edge of the building and saw several soldiers interrogating the photographer. She had her back to him. The soldiers were speaking Romanian while the woman was answering in French. His years of high school French weren't enough for him to understand her deep-throated burbling, except for a few words: *journaliste*, *Le Monde*, *atrocités*.

He took out his Beretta, held it by his side pointing down, then turned the corner and walked toward them. When the soldiers saw him, then his gun, they raised their rifles and ordered him to stop. He held up his left hand with the Securitate badge he'd taken from the agent on the train.

"You finally found her, good job," he said in native Romanian. "I've been running after her for a half hour. I'll take it from here."

The soldiers let their guns slide back down. The Securitate held rank over all of them.

It was then, just as the journalist turned to look at him, that the world burst into a thousand lights.

"Catherine?"

CHAPTER THIRTY

Harvard, Cambridge, Massachusetts
June 1982

IT WAS THE week after exams and his heart was singing. He'd aced his finals and his GPA was now 3.88. He had decided that in the fall he would apply to all the best graduate programs in the country. Although his years at Harvard had been paid by a full scholarship, he couldn't rely on receiving another one for graduate school. He was hoping that between student loans and a job he would be able to make ends meet.

One afternoon at the end of that week, he saw a man dressed in a dark suit loitering outside his dorm room. The man came forward and identified himself as André Vodin, an official in the State Department. Vodin invited him for a cup of coffee, which Hefflin accepted despite his reservations. At the Casablanca Café, over cups of latté, the man began by apologizing. He was not really State Department, he said. He was there on Professor Pincus's recommendation to consider Hefflin for a challenging field.

"And it's been a real treat to follow your Harvard career," Vodin said in Romanian.

Hefflin did not attempt to hide his surprise. "You're Romanian? And you've been following my career?"

"Just from a distance, without any intrusion, I assure you."

"Who are you? Other than Professor Pincus, no one at Harvard knows about my past, and I'd like to keep it that way."

"Yes, I know, Vasili. But, still, the sweet memories of childhood, surely you haven't lost those?"

He didn't say anything, though he could feel his face growing warm.

"Of course you haven't. Even if they took place under a vile communist regime. But what does a boy know of such things? He only remembers the happy times of childhood, his mother cooking *mamaliga* or *mititei*."

"I don't particularly like to reminisce about old times," he said.

"But oh"—Vodin's face grew dark—"the country now is in worse shape than ever. Ceausescu has his foot on the people's throats. Everything Romania produces is sold to acquire hard currency, while the people are starving. And the Securitate roams the streets uncontrolled."

Hefflin thought of Pusha and how she must be suffering.

"It's been going on for a long time," Hefflin said. "What can one do about it?"

"A great deal, if you have the mind and heart for it." Vodin looked at him for a long time, waiting for him to understand something he wasn't quite saying.

"Clandestine work?" Hefflin asked.

Vodin nodded.

"You work for the CIA?"

"Quite right, Mr. Hefflin, or should I say Mr. Argyris."

His throat tightened. The CIA had taken the trouble to find his real family name.

"You already seem to like aliases, and you did quite well in our little spy games at the Fly Club." Vodin smiled, then took another sip of his latté.

"The Harvard scholarship, the Fly Club. You're the mysterious sponsor?"

"Let's just say the Agency likes to encourage promising prospects. We have a small cadre of recruits in these select gentlemen's clubs. And what better place to hobnob with tomorrow's leaders? All in all, we think you're the perfect person for that type of career."

"Why?"

"Because you're stateless, in the psychological sense, with no real identity. You don't feel as if you're Romanian or Greek, or even American. You're a drifter, my dear Vasili. You need a home. We can be that home for you. And you'd be helping in the crucial work of toppling that regime, and that ideology, once and for all."

"I want to study economics," he said. "I'll be applying to graduate schools in the fall."

"Yes, I know, so much the better. Economics is what will collapse the communist system in the end. With your knowledge of the language and the people, you'd be an immediate asset. Of course, we can't promise the remuneration you'd receive in the private sector, but we can match that of an academician, even top it." Vodin leaned forward like a negotiator who is about to make his pitch. "You know, a career in economics is not an easy one, even if you're talented. If you go the academic route, which I don't advise, you'll be struggling to climb the ladder toward a tenured professorship, with all the in-house backstabbing and the need to publish. If you join the private sector, a Wall Street firm, you'll face the cutthroat world of money-manipulation. What I'm offering is a safe home, free of all that, a secure career where you'll be part of an elite team of men and women like yourself, from Harvard, MIT, Yale, Stanford, all focused on one thing: creating history."

Vodin's pitch sounded appealing. But the image of James Bond drinking vodka martinis in chic bars was not for him. He'd read enough spy novels and seen enough movies to know that he couldn't live a life of constant danger, one in which he might have to kill or be killed. Nor could he imagine himself living in another country again, further perpetuating his statelessness. But Vodin was right in one respect: he craved stability, a home, as Vodin put it, where he wouldn't have to join the dog-eat-dog world of the private marketplace and in which he could make a difference. The idea of being a part of history intrigued him. He saw himself as an analyst, dissecting his old country and planning the demise of the regime, though he wasn't so naïve as to believe that communism would fall any time soon.

"My first choice is Wharton," Hefflin said.

"Wharton's a great school, no doubt about that, and, coming from Harvard with your grades, you're sure to get in," Vodin said. "But there are other great schools, Columbia for one. And it has the advantage of being in New York City, the center of the universe."

"Columbia is on my list," Hefflin said.

"No need for a list." Vodin stared at him.

"You're certain I'll get in?"

"As certain as I am that Ceausescu will one day die a horrible death."

The letter came a week later. Columbia University had accepted him into their economics graduate program with a full scholarship, room and board, and a two-thousand-dollar-per-month stipend for living expenses. He hadn't even applied.

His future seemed to be set. Only one thing remained: Catherine. She was graduating that year with a degree in French literature and had decided to take a year off before applying to any graduate programs. Even her summer plans seemed to be unformed. He asked about their future a few days later as they were walking toward her apartment.

"I can't commit to anything right now," she said. "My life is . . . complicated. I have a lot of thinking I must do. I lo—" She tried to say the word—he could almost see it on her tongue, in her eyes—the L word she'd said during lovemaking. But now, in bright sunlight, she couldn't quite get it out. She kissed him softly, then said, "Don't be angry at your family. In the end, they're all you have."

He tried to take her words to heart, but he had drifted so much from his family and the expats he had grown up with that they seemed like a relic from a bygone era. Who among the immigrants in Worcester could tell the difference between a Bordeaux and a Beaujolais, or between an impressionist or expressionist painting, or between Hegel and Herder? Who among them had been to the opera in the past twenty years?—he and Catherine had been to several that year alone. It occurred to him, not for the first time, that Catherine had brought out the man in him, and his love for her was intertwined with immense gratitude. What had she seen in him that had caused her to invest so much time and effort into his social education?

He asked her this question as they walked.

"Do you still need me to pump up your ego?" she asked without looking at him. "I consider you a kindred spirit. We're the same, you and I, though you may not see it."

"How?"

"You're a lost soul craving for his other half. You may not believe it, but underneath all this bravado, so am I. And since I met you, that craving has resurfaced."

"Will I ever know this mysterious past of yours?"

"Yes, I hope so, but first I have some thinking to do." She stopped walking and turned to look at him directly. "You're so close to my heart I could scream. I know I'll never find anyone like you again."

"Why do you have to? I'm right here."

She started walking again without answering, her eyes focused on the ground. He didn't want to push her, so he tried to change the subject. "I've been accepted to the Columbia graduate school in economics," he said. "On a full scholarship."

"Congratulations."

"It's all due to you," he said. "You've introduced me to another world. I don't know how to even begin to repay you."

"Then don't. Sometimes you just have to accept a gift and simply say thank you." She left him standing on the street with a wave of the hand.

The next day he found a letter delivered via in-house mail.

Mon cheri,

I'm off to Paris for a few weeks, then traveling wherever the wind takes me. Sorry we can't be together. It was a wonderful time, never forget that. You'll be forever close to my heart.

Adieu

P.S. Don't be a silly boy and try to find me.

A few days later, he happened to run across an announcement in the *International Herald Tribune*—a paper that he'd accustomed himself to buying religiously at the kiosk in

Harvard Square. His eye caught her picture standing next to a tall, good-looking man. The announcement stated that Catherine J. Nash, daughter of John Nash, ambassador to Sweden, and wife Monique, had become engaged to be married to Jacques Molinaire, son of the renowned banker Etienne Molinaire and wife Celine. The wedding was expected to take place in the fall.

CHAPTER THIRTY-ONE

Timisoara
December 1989

THE SOLDIERS WERE all staring at him, waiting for an answer.

"You know this woman?" the soldier asked again.

"A reporter for a French rag," Hefflin said, trying to control his emotions. "She's been a pain in the ass for years." He pointed the gun at her. "I'll take the camera. This will be enough evidence to detain you for some time."

He held her gaze for a long moment, assessing the minor changes the years had wrought—perhaps a few new wrinkles around the eyes, a more worn look, but she was still as radiant as he remembered. His heart was throbbing in his throat. He noticed there was no ring on her finger.

She suddenly turned and began walking in front of him. As they reached the corner, he heard whistles, then a few rowdy remarks from the soldiers.

"An old lay, hey? Lucky dog."

"I'd like to be a fly on the wall when he interrogates her."

They turned onto a side street and kept walking in silence. When they had reached another street and they could no longer hear the soldiers, she stopped and turned to face him. A tear was rolling down her cheek. Without a word she embraced him, gently, warily.

"What on earth are you doing in Romania?" she asked against his shoulder.

"I can ask you the same question."

"I'm a reporter for *Le Monde* covering the events here," she said.

"The borders have been closed to reporters for weeks."

"I've been in Bucharest for over a month," she said.

A month? All this time she'd been in Bucharest without his knowing. He took her by the arm and hurried her along. "We need to get you off the streets."

"But you didn't tell me why you're here," she said.

"I'm a State Department attaché."

"An attaché? For what?"

"Etiquette."

She burst into laughter. "That's ridiculous. No one will believe you." She laughed some more. When the laughter finally stopped, she said, "So you did join the Agency after all."

He pulled her along.

"Where did you learn Romanian so well?" she asked. "Your accent was practically native."

He shrugged. "Intensive course at the Agency."

"You must have a real ear for languages."

How does she know a native accent, anyway?

"And that Securitate badge," she went on.

"I took it off an agent on the train. A long story. Now, where do we go?"

"*Le Monde* has an office near here. I'll be all right there. It's not far."

She led him down several streets until they reached an old house in a secluded corner of an alley. There were no signs on it.

"This doesn't look like a newspaper office," he said.

"It's a private home. The newspaper leases it for journalists to stay in when here."

They looked at each other, neither able to traverse the divide between them.

"What have you been doing since . . . you left Harvard?" he finally asked. His gaze drifted down to her left hand. "You never married, I see."

"No. I go by the name Catherine Devereaux now."

"Your mother's maiden name."

"You've been doing some research, I see."

"But I saw in the *Herald Tribune*—"

"That was my parents' idea, but I couldn't go through with it. Or be with you. Not in the state I was in. So I ran off, traveled around for months, worked with *Medicins Sans Frontieres* for a year, then joined *Le Monde*."

"You ran out on him, too? A double-header." He swallowed down his anger.

She took his hand. "I'm not proud of what I did. That was me at my weakest. I knew that I was not ready for marriage or even a committed relationship. All I could do was run. I needed a clean break."

"From me?"

"From myself." She pulled him closer, their lips almost touching.

"What does that even mean?" he asked.

She pulled him inside the building and embraced him, their lips locking, their hands suddenly tearing at each other's clothes.

"Why didn't you come after me?" she gasped between kisses.

"I thought you got married."

"You should have made sure. What kind of spy are you?"

They sprawled onto the floor, their hands clutching at each other's bodies, his mouth hungry for the feel and taste of her mouth, for her essence of which he had been deprived for so long. Her legs, long and shapely as he remembered them, wrapped around him and clutched him tightly as they entered into that age-old dance of life and death. His lungs breathed in her breath, her body glistened as it slid and swirled against his, urging him on, daring him to dare while she whispered "I'm sorry, so sorry." He swore he would never lose her again. When the dance came to its climax and he felt the little death, a voice whispered in his ear, *"You can never catch a bird in flight!"*

They lay entwined, neither of them wanting to let go, to be alone again. Hefflin felt his world slowly contracting from the boundless expanse he had just experienced to that of a nondescript building in Timisoara on a dark night in December during a revolution.

"Why did you leave me?" he asked.

She waved her hand, keeping her eyes closed.

"If I could, I would have gone with you anywhere in the world. But I couldn't be with you or anyone. Still can't."

"But why?"

"It's a long story and I'm not sure I can tell you. Not just yet. It will sound silly to you and you'll think me a fool, or worse." She turned and kissed him on the cheek.

"So, then what?" he said. "We just meet every few years during a revolution?"

She slipped a card out of her coat pocket and handed it to him. Below the *Le Monde* logo were the words "Catherine Devereaux, *Journaliste*," and a telephone number.

"My office in Paris," she said. "They'll know where I am."

"I don't want to lose you again," he said.

"When this is over, I'll tell you everything, I promise."

They embraced for a long moment, the silence between them deeper than ever. Then she stood, gathered her clothes, and climbed up the stairs.

When he was back out on the street, he inhaled deeply to regain his mental balance. He had a train to catch.

CHAPTER THIRTY-TWO

Bucharest
December 1989

THEY WERE RIDING in a black Dacia, not an official Securitate car, Soryn at the wheel. Hefflin sat next to him, only adrenaline keeping him awake after the long overnight train ride back to Bucharest.

Just as his head had hit the pillow in his hotel room, Soryn had called. "I found the girl," he yelled, the *dog*, the *heifer*. An object to him. Apparently Soryn was no longer concerned about Hefflin's phone being tapped.

"You found Pusha?" His heart was pounding at this sudden turn of events.

"Yes, Pusha, who else? I will pick you up in twenty minutes."

He was looking at the man's face now to catch signs of deceit. But Soryn was Securitate, he reminded himself. He lied for a living.

"Are you sure it's her?" he asked for the third time.

"I tell you it is her," Soryn said. "It took a lot of doing. The dossier in archives had blacked out name of man who adopted her. I knew he had to be high up to arrange that kind of secrecy. I also knew there had to be another dossier, more classified. And I found it."

"Who is he?" he asked, trying to control the impulse to shake the man.

Soryn glanced at him with a strange look, then a slight smile appeared on his face as he returned to his driving.

Did he suspect how much this meant to him? Hefflin told himself he needed to calm down. He was supposed to be doing a favor for a friend.

"She is now daughter of assistant to deputy minister of finance," Soryn said. "Very privileged. And very nervous that a revolution will take away her privileges, like all of us."

The assistant to the deputy minister of finance. How lucky she is.

"You know her?" he asked.

"I met her once at Party function, but I never suspect she was same little girl from Strada Sirenelor."

Hefflin did all he could to keep from screaming. Was Soryn telling him the truth? Why would he lie? "My friend will be glad she's doing well," he said. "But why would a man so high up adopt a nine-year-old from an orphanage?"

"Well, she is very pretty, for one thing. Maybe he fell in love with her. You know, there are many privileged couples in Romania who cannot have children, and most of children in orphanages are—how you say—damaged." Soryn turned to give him a twisted smile. "She grew to be very beautiful woman, you know. A little spoiled, a little wild, like all children of privileged. They grow up differently than regular children. Family has dacha in country, they belong to tennis club, she wears European clothes and drives a little Mercedes. You understand?"

He nodded, his heart aching, the image of his little Pusha coming into a not-so-pretty focus. The communist system changed everyone, usually for the worse. The vast majority of the population had sunk into despair—the humiliating petty bribes to get a loaf of bread or a cut of meat, the fear of being overheard cursing the government, the loss of dignity in walking around with torn shoes. But she had escaped all that. Did she feel any guilt in living a life of luxury while the rest of the people starved? Why was he so disappointed by this news?

"She will fit well in America, no?" Soryn smiled. "She already knows how to be rich."

"In America?" Soryn's words startled him. "I never said anything about America."

"I know, but she has dreams, like rest of us, of escaping this place and living in—how did Reagan put it?—in shining city on hill."

There it was, the fables that never died. American streets paved with gold. But how many people lived in poverty in America, or were homeless, while the rest went about their business as if the poor didn't exist, having learned from a young age how to be blind to the suffering around them? Was Pusha so different from the privileged Americans?

"You spoke to her?"

"Yes, very quickly. I follow her to Party store where I know she shops. She was very surprised that Vasili asked about her."

"She remembers him, then?"

Be still my heart.

"Of course. She remembers Vasili very well. She says she was hoping for many years that he will come back for her one day."

"Really? Did she actually say that?"

"Yes, and more, how much she was thinking of him every day. You know, from way she talks about him, I think she loved him very much. Still loves him." Soryn glanced at him before he could turn his face to hide his watering eyes.

"I think she wants to go to America to be with him," Soryn added.

"But you said she lives a privileged life here. She certainly wouldn't live that way in America."

Soryn waived his arm in disgust. "Privilege in Romania is one thing—shopping for food at Party markets, sending for clothes from Europe—but it does not compare with West. Our Party stores are poor imitation of your regular stores in America."

His mind was swirling. Pusha, the spoiled adopted daughter of an apparatchik.

"But it is not just about privilege," Soryn went on. "This girl has heart, I can see that, underneath that hard surface we all have in this country. I think Vasili holds special place in her soul."

Her soul? Soryn could see into her soul in the few minutes he had spent with her? *Bullshit.* And yet, what if Soryn, this childhood bully turned Securitate agent, was telling the truth for once in his life? Could he afford dismissing him out of hand? Pusha. The strings, long buried, were once more tugging at his heart. Had she really thought of him all these years? Did she still love him? How could he find the truth?

"I have to meet her myself," he said, "to hear from her own lips her feelings for Vasili. He would want that."

"Ah, that will be difficult. She is always with people, watched," Soryn said.

"You were able to speak to her."

"I am Securitate. But if someone sees her talking to American official, she will be in much trouble, even if her father is important. The way things are, everyone is suspect."

"You can arrange a secret meeting somewhere, in this car, for instance," he said

"Maybe. But I would be risking my neck for this friend of yours. Besides, how would she get away, even for an hour? No, no, this would put us all in danger."

What, then? They were silent, Soryn watching the road, Hefflin contemplating yet another brush with fate.

"Let me ask you something," Soryn broke the silence. "Does Vasili love her?"

The directness of the question caught him off guard. *Love? Worship? Why does this Securitate agent want to know? Leverage?*

"I don't know," he demurred. "It's been a long time."

"Is Vasili married? Children?"

"No, none of that, still single," he said.

"Ah, then maybe he is still waiting for her, no? They are same, perhaps. Each waiting. Real love, like in books. How can you keep them apart? It is tragedy."

"It's not up to me," he said.

"Then contact Vasili and ask him if he wants Pusha to come to America to be with him."

"They haven't seen each other in over twenty years," he said. "People change."

Especially under communism.

"Yes, true, but how will he know unless he sees her again?" Soryn insisted. "He must still hold candle for her, as you Americans say, even after twenty years. Sounds like true love to me."

"The expression is 'carry a torch,' but close enough. And what if it doesn't work out?"

Soryn shrugged. "Then she will still live free in America. Look, she is afraid. We all are. She knows her situation here can disappear overnight. It only takes spark for country to catch fire, and that spark already light fire in Timisoara. Who knows what will happen next?"

This Securitate man took Timisoara seriously. No longer just a demonstration.

"Even if all you say is true, no one is allowed to leave Romania, you know that," Hefflin said.

"You are cultural attaché, a spy by another name, do not bother to deny it," Soryn said. "Even if you are not, your embassy is full of them. They know how to get people out."

Was the man insane? An extraction operation for someone's girlfriend? What was he doing talking spycraft with this Securitate agent? Was the car bugged? Would they try to use all this to blackmail him?

"I have no idea what they can or can't do," Hefflin said, "but even if they could, they wouldn't be crazy enough to do it for someone's childhood sweetheart."

"No, but they do it for important information."

He turned to look at Soryn who was staring ahead, ostensibly concentrating on the road, but he could see the man was about to spring something on him, an ace up his sleeve.

"What kind of information?" he asked.

"Information on how system works," Soryn said, "who real criminals are in Securitate, the thieves in government. Dossiers, entire suitcase of dossiers, on how Tyrant starved population so he can pay off foreign debt, on political prisoners rotting in jails, on assassinations."

"The West knows most of that," he said.

Soryn let out a sigh. The man was obviously struggling to bring up something else.

"What about Tyrant's offshore accounts?" Soryn said.

Hefflin's ears pricked up.

"I know where important dossiers are kept," Soryn pressed on. "If there is going to be chaos, which I think will happen soon, that is when I can get to most sensitive Securitate dossiers. But timing has to be right."

"You can get a dossier listing Ceausescu's offshore accounts?" He felt a shiver run up his spine. "Does such a dossier exist?"

"Of course. There is dossier for everything in this country. Offshore accounts is complicated business. What do you think, Ceausescu just memorized numbers in his head?" Soryn let out a laugh.

"And what do you get out of it?" he asked, but he already knew the answer.

"I come with you and Pusha to America," Soryn blurted out.

"You want to defect?"

"Yes, defect. When time is right, you can put us both on your American plane."

"What fucking American plane?"

"If revolution is real, and even more bloody, your government will send one of their planes to evacuate your embassy."

Soryn pulled onto the side of the road and turned to him, a different expression on his face now, the cold Securitate.

"Look, I am Securitate. People despise us, for good reason. If country goes up in flames, I will be first to burn. I am no genius, but even I can see this play has to end."

"So, this was all about you? Is any of the Pusha story true?"

"Yes, all of it, I swear to God. I just see opportunity, and I take it. Pusha and Ceausescu's money in exchange for asylum, a package deal. A good deal, no? Not so hard to convince your station chief, Mr. Stanton."

He knew the man was probably lying, inflating his importance. And yet, if Soryn could get information on Ceausescu's offshore accounts, he could convince Stanton this Securitate colonel was worth the trouble of getting him out. And he could spare Irina from having to approach her lover, Ceausescu's money man. Even if the CIA didn't send one of their planes, Stanton had other means of exfiltration.

He suddenly saw his career flashing before his eyes— smuggling a Securitate colonel out of Romania with his Pusha, then the information on the offshore accounts turning out to be bogus, a ruse. And yet, and yet, this was his Pusha they were talking about. She was worth risking his career. His life. If she still loved him. Then he thought of Catherine. Meeting her again had brought back all the old emotions. He knew he loved her and felt she loved him. How could he compare his feelings for her with memories of a childhood love that had crystallized inside his heart? He didn't even know if any part of Soryn's story was true.

"I need proof that Pusha is real," he said.

"Proof? But I told you, she cannot come to meet you."

"I want you to ask her a question, something Vasili told me. Ask her where their favorite place was."

"Their favorite place? What kind of question is that? Maybe she cannot remember. Twenty years!"

"Just ask her."

"All right, I ask her. But you are putting everything at risk for one stupid question."

"Even if she can answer it, I still need proof that you have Ceausescu's offshore accounts. That's the deal."

*   *   *

Later that evening he lay on the bed in his room at the Athénée, unable to sleep, conflicted about what he was doing. It was clear that Soryn had been dangling the prize of Pusha while planning his own escape. But could he really walk away from the possibility that this was his Pusha? All this time as an adult he'd avoided thinking of her. He had even sworn that he'd never bring her to America to end up as yet another displaced immigrant. But now, could he risk the possibility of her being harmed if the regime fell? And what if Soryn's tale was true and all this time she had been waiting for him to return to find her? Would he bring her to America? Suddenly he was faced with the possibility of having two women who loved him and having to choose between them. Perhaps he was living in a universe in which he could have both. The idea at first enchanted his fantasies, but then roiled him into a frenzy of dread. The whole thing was too absurd. He was sure he would end up with neither of them.

He waited by the phone for Soryn to contact him with the answer to his question. If she were the real Pusha, she'd remember. And if she did, he knew he had to act, whether or not Soryn had the offshore accounts. But he would not mention anything to Stanton, not until he was sure.

In the morning he was awakened by the ringing of the telephone. He recognized Soryn's voice pronouncing the words that would decide his fate.

"Under apple tree."

CHAPTER THIRTY-THREE

Bucharest
December 1989

IT WAS LATE morning and the sun shone brightly but without giving off any heat. Hefflin was standing at a street corner near Piatsa Amzei, pacing back and forth to keep himself warm. He had left the Athénée by the employee door and had taken several buses around the city. When he was certain he wasn't being followed, he walked to the rendezvous point. Irina had followed his instructions and had used one of the pay phones on the outskirts of Bucharest, which were not usually monitored, to leave a one-word message on the secure embassy line: "Fili."

A few minutes later, a black Dacia stopped in front of him and he got into the passenger seat.

"Whose car is this?" he asked.

"I borrowed it from one of my colleagues," Irina said. "I told him mine was in the shop. I even covered the license plate with snow." She laughed nervously. "I don't know why we need this secrecy. If they've been following you, they already know you came to my house."

"Just a precaution," he said. "I don't think the Securitate has time to bother with me anymore, or you. They've got other things to worry about."

She drove through the back streets and parked among other cars on the side of an alley. She shut off the motor and they sat silent for a moment.

"Is it really happening?" she finally asked. "Are we finally going to be rid of the Tyrant?"

"It depends on what the army does," he said.

"Victor is afraid. He doesn't know what will happen to him if the regime falls."

He didn't know what to tell her. Vulcan, the minister of manure, had the blood of countless lives on his hands.

"Depends on how vindictive the people are," he said. "You know them better than I."

"He was just a cog in a big machine."

"Just following orders." He finished her thought.

"He is very agitated. There haven't been demonstrations like these before. When the factory workers joined the marches in Timisoara, something broke in him. He knows this is different, that it may be the end."

"Did you broach the subject?"

"Last night, I asked him what would happen if the government fell." Her hand went up to her throat.

"And?"

"He told me not to worry, that Ceausescu was returning from Iran, and he would set everything straight. I pointed out that we're the only country left, that even Gorbachev was changing Russia. He said nothing for a while, just sat and drank. That is when I got up the courage. I said that there might be a way for him to make an arrangement, in exchange for what he knows. He got angry. He asked me who I had been talking to. I blurted it all out. I said I knew someone who could make a deal with him. An American official, a close relative. Ceausescu's offshore accounts for a secure life in the West." She sat silent for a moment, her eyes glistening. "That's when he slapped me."

"What?"

"He became furious. He started shaking me, demanding to know what spy I was talking to, and so on. I told him your name, that you were a cousin and a highly placed American official, and that you could arrange for him to flee to the West."

"What did he say?"

"He became quiet, slumped into a chair, and thought for a long time. Then he just got up and left." Her tears were rolling down her cheeks now. "Then this morning he just showed up at my house with a bouquet of flowers, apologized, and said he wanted to meet you, tomorrow, at seven in the morning in Cismigiu Park, at the chess tables."

His mind started racing. He had to contact Boris, but there was little time. He recalled the telephone number Boris had given him at their first meeting. One ring meant they were to meet on the number four trolley at one in the afternoon, two rings at two, and so forth.

"Who do you think will take over if Ceausescu falls?" Irina asked. "Some of the same people who are in the Party now, perhaps, the same clique, with different hats?" There was hope in her voice, the same thieves taking over, nothing changed. Saving her lover, and her. "He's afraid he'll be shot. He's got a wife and children."

"You care about him?" he said.

"How can I not? It's been years. He's not a bad man, even after all that he's had to do. Full of guilt, now. Afraid to show his face in public."

"We all have to face ourselves in the end," he said.

"Yes." She sighed, looked away, then started to cry. "What should I do?"

"Just go home and wait," he said. "Things will soon take care of themselves."

CHAPTER THIRTY-FOUR

Bucharest
December 1989

BUCHAREST TROLLEY CARS, one of his dearest memories from his childhood.

As a child they had always intrigued him, the fact that they turned and twisted throughout the streets of the city without there being a steering wheel, that they knew which tracks to follow when several of them intersected, that they seemed to go on forever.

It was in one of these trolley cars, more haggard than he remembered, that he now found himself, looking out through a grimy window at the city going by. It was only early afternoon but the people were already returning from their jobs to stand in line for whatever was being sold, filing in silently, their heads low, their faces grim. Sitting next to him was an elderly woman carrying a bag in which he spotted a half-rotten tomato, a jar of beets, and several carrots. Part of the evening dinner.

At a stop she rose and hobbled off. An old man with a full white beard wearing a torn fur hat took her place. The man was dressed in peasant clothes and smelled of farm animals. Hefflin turned away to avoid the smell, though he reminded himself that people in the city often raised chickens and pigs in their backyards to supplement the meager meats found in the market.

The trolley continued on and it soon filled with people as it made its stops every couple of blocks. At some point the old man rose, then pulled on his sleeve. It was only then that he looked closely at the man's face and recognized Boris.

They made their way to the exit and got off at the next stop. Boris led the way down several side streets to an ornate pre-war building. Hefflin followed him inside and up the staircase to the second floor.

The apartment was spacious, with a baby grand piano in one corner, heavy Italianate furniture throughout the living room, and Tiffany-style lamps. A Persian rug partially covered the parquet floor. Several original oil paintings hung on the walls.

"Nice apartment," he said. "All this elegant, antique furniture, the piano, the paintings. Where did you get them?"

"It took me many years to collect these little treasures," Boris said. "People have nice things from before the War, which they sometimes have to sell. The parents die, and the children need money, or they somehow escape the country and leave it behind. Come, see the dining room."

He opened a set of French doors to reveal a formal dining room with a mahogany table with eight chairs and an ornate vitrine filled with china. Hefflin approached the table to run a hand along its shiny wood. An overwhelming feeling swept over him—of evening dinners with his family, of hiding under the table behind his mother's embroidered tablecloth, of painted toenails.

"You are getting emotional," Boris said.

"It's nothing," Hefflin said. "This furniture reminds me of my childhood. We had something similar."

"Yes, it is beautiful, isn't it? I bought it from an old friend many years ago." Boris took off his coat and brought out a bottle of Stoli from an aged wooden bar in the corner. "They still let me keep this apartment even though I do not live in Bucharest full-time. I had one in Budapest, also, but now, with their new democratic government, they took it back. Never mind. All for the best." He chose two shot glasses and poured the vodka. "To a new Romania. May they take this apartment, too."

They each raised their glasses, then tilted back their heads and gulped them down.

"So, Vasili, we have many things to discuss," Boris said. "But you contacted me, so you begin."

"Irina approached Vulcan last night with the offer," he said.

"Good. So?"

"At first, he got angry, even violent. But this morning he changed his mind. I assume it was after hearing about the events in Timisoara. He wants to meet me."

"Wonderful, Vasili. See, what did I tell you? Sometimes the crazy plans are the best. So, when and where?"

"Tomorrow, seven in the morning, in Cismigiu Park, at the chess tables."

"Good. You know the place, it is outdoors, and has many avenues for exit. I like it."

"I haven't told Stanton yet," he said. "But if Vulcan agrees to the terms, I'll need the Agency to get him out."

"No need to involve Stanton," Boris said. "Leave exfiltration to me and my people."

Hefflin was confused. Boris was changing the plan. "You're going to involve the KGB?"

"No KGB. I have my own local people who I have developed over many years. I trust them. It will be much easier for me to get him out of the country. And they do not need days or weeks to put the plan in action. They can be ready in one day."

"But how will you get him to the States?" he asked.

"I will get him to Western Europe, then you can take over and present him to the Agency. You will be a big hero, no?"

Boris found a pad of paper and started writing. After a few minutes, he tore off the sheet and handed it to him.

"Give these instructions to Vulcan and tell him to follow them exactly."

Hefflin read the instructions, then folded the paper and placed it in his wallet. He wasn't quite fine with Boris doing the exfiltration but decided he had no choice.

"The second item is Timisoara," Hefflin said.

"That was *my* first item," Boris barked. "What the fuck is happening in Timisoara?"

"That's what I want to know. You said there would be peaceful demonstrations, followed by a quiet coup."

"Not my fault!" Boris yelled. "The army went crazy. It was not part of the plan."

"There were snipers," Hefflin said sharply, "shooting at both civilians and soldiers."

"Snipers? How do you know this?"

"I was there. I saw them. They were dressed in civilian clothes."

"You went to Timisoara? Without telling me?" Boris paced the floor in agitation. "When?"

Hefflin recounted the events in Timisoara, leaving out the incident with the Securitate on the train and his meeting Catherine. He did tell him he saw General Stanculescu dressed in civilian clothes coming out of the CIA office with Stanton.

After hearing the story, Boris thought for a moment, then rushed into another room and returned with an enlarged photograph, which he handed to Hefflin. It was a black-and-white picture of two men dressed in civilian clothes sitting at a table in what looked like a bar. Hefflin recognized both men. One of them was General Stanculescu, the other was the assassin that murdered Pincus whose picture he had seen on Stanton's desk.

"Where was this taken?" Hefflin asked.

"In East Germany, three years ago, taken by one of our agents," Boris said. "Stanculescu was there for a military conference of Warsaw Pact nations. Do you know the other man?"

Pincus's assassin. What the hell was he doing meeting with Stanculescu?

Hefflin lied and said he never saw him before.

"I know the CIA is widespread, and you are an analyst, so you would not know a field agent," Boris said.

"He's CIA?"

"He used to be Securitate, but then he fled Romania and became a free agent. After that we think he became a black ops operative for the CIA. So Stanculescu may be on the CIA payroll." Boris glared at him expectantly.

"You don't sound too sure. Maybe the assassin is still working for the Securitate," Hefflin said.

"No, I have many friends in the Securitate. They tell me he is no longer one of them. And one of our KGB operatives swears this man killed one of our assets in Bulgaria."

Hefflin was confused. If the assassin was CIA, on whose orders did he kill Pincus? He felt the ground shifting under him. Avery had told him he thought the assassin was a Securitate agent. The tape of the dialogue in Pincus's house seemed to confirm it. But the pictures Avery had shown him did not have the one Hefflin had found in Stanton's office, which showed the face of the assassin. Didn't Avery have that photograph? Where did Stanton get it? And then there was Stanton's meeting with Stanculescu in the safe house in Timisoara during which Stanton seemed to know ahead of time about the snipers that would show up the next day.

Boris rubbed his beard again. "So, I ask myself, Vasili, what was Stanculescu doing in Timisoara? Who started the shooting? Who were these snipers? Something is not right here, Vasili."

Hefflin nodded in agreement. Something was definitely not right here.

There was a knock at the door, and both men froze.

CHAPTER THIRTY-FIVE

Bucharest
December 1989

BORIS REMOVED A pistol from his pocket and slowly opened the door. Before him stood an old woman wearing a scarf around her head and a heavy winter coat.

"Mrs. Pitescu—" Boris smiled, hiding the gun behind his back. He turned to Hefflin. "Mrs. Pitescu is the building superintendent. So, what can I do—" But Boris didn't finish the sentence, for as he turned back toward the old woman, he saw that she was no longer there. In her place was the fat man, whom Hefflin recognized as the stranger that had scared away the Securitate agents who had tried to shove him into the car when he first arrived in Bucharest. The fat man was holding a gun with silencer aimed at Boris. He spoke in Russian as he motioned for Boris to drop his gun.

"Ah, one of my compatriots," Boris said, letting his gun drop to the floor. "You speak any English? My friend here does not speak Russian." Boris pointed to Hefflin.

"I am sorry to interrupt such festive occasion, tovarisch," the fat man said in heavily accented English, then spotted the bottle of Stoli on the table. "Russian vodka. Well, well, guest must be very special."

"He is," Boris said. "The American State Department attaché, but you already know that."

"Yes, I have been following him since he come to Bucharest," the fat man said. "And I have seen you meet together."

"You have? And we have not spotted you?" Boris chuckled. "Well, that does not say much for our friend, or me. So, tovarisch, why did Moscow send you here without my knowledge?"

"Simply put, to catch traitor," the fat man said, then closed the door behind him. "And now I have."

There was a momentary silence, then Boris burst out laughing. "Oh, really? I am the traitor? My dear . . . what should I call you? Your alias will do."

"Anton."

"Well, Anton, I know how much this means to your career, and I will put in a good word for you, for effort. But as for your intellect, I am afraid you will get a failing grade."

"You are in no position to give grades," the fat man said. "It is clear you have been meeting with this CIA agent in Bucharest for purpose of passing State secrets. For some time we have suspected traitor exists. But even I did not think a man of your accomplishments over so many years, a hero of Stalingrad, would be that traitor."

Boris sat on the couch and crossed his legs nonchalantly.

"You must know, tovarisch, that in our line of work, nothing is as it seems," Boris said calmly. "Take Vasili, here. He was born in Bucharest, left at the age of eight, studied economics at Harvard and Columbia, and was recruited into the CIA straight out of college. You would never think that a man like that would join our socialist cause. And yet, here he is."

"What are you saying?"

"I am saying that you have things backward, my dear Anton. It is he who has been passing information to us. For years."

"You are trying to trick me, tovarisch."

"He is telling the truth," Hefflin said. "America is a capitalist cancer, a cruel worshipping of wealth by an elite few at the expense of the masses. Socialism, in whatever form, is infinitely superior to capitalism. Here, see for yourself." He motioned to the picture on the coffee table. "That is a photograph of General Stanculescu, taken in East Berlin three years ago. The man next to him is one of our CIA agents. That was the meeting when Stanculescu was recruited. I brought the picture here tonight so my friend can know who to trust, and not."

The fat man picked up the picture and studied it. "Stanculescu is CIA? For three years, you say?"

"So, now you can join us for some Stolichnaya." Boris went to the bar and brought over another shot glass. The fat man sat down still holding his gun in one hand and the picture in the other. As Boris filled the glass, the fat man stared at it suspiciously.

"It is good vodka, Anton." Boris refilled his own glass, then Hefflin's. "Look, we will drink first, so you can be reassured." Both Boris and Hefflin downed their drinks.

The fat man seemed to relax. "Well, in that case I will have just one, though I am not totally convinced." He emptied the glass with one swallow and set it back on the table with a satisfied sigh. "Our country does make excellent vodka."

Boris poured another round, but before anyone could touch his drink again, the fat man's face started to grow blotchy. His eyes grew wide, his hands dropped the gun and picture, and he started choking. A moment later his chin dropped to his chest and he fell forward—dead.

"Fifteen seconds," Boris said, looking at his watch. "It is supposed to be ten." He felt for the pulse on the fat man's neck and was satisfied.

"Poison?" Hefflin asked. "But how did you slip it in?"

"I did not have to," Boris said. "The glass was coated with it. I keep one on my bar for just such an occasion."

"I hope you don't ever forget which glass it is," Hefflin said.

Boris disappeared into his study and returned a moment later with some papers. "Our friend, here, will be found with evidence incriminating someone else as the traitor," Boris said as he handed him the papers. One of them was a statement from a numbered account in a Luxembourg bank containing five hundred thousand dollars.

"The account also has the name attached to it on the bank's records," Boris said. "More difficult to find, but I am confident that my KGB comrades will be able to get it."

"Who does it belong to?" Hefflin asked.

Boris handed him a picture of a man entering a private house. Hefflin recognized him.

"Mikhail Drikov? The Soviet Deputy Ambassador to Romania?"

"That is the home of Maria Minulescu, a well-known Romanian singer," Boris said. "She has been his lover for the past two years."

The third item was a picture of the singer with a man at a party in a private home.

"This man is one of Stanton's operatives," Boris said. "He was trying to recruit her."

"Did he succeed?"

"No, but just seeing them together is enough." Boris smiled.

"You're setting up the Soviet Deputy Ambassador as the traitor?" he asked.

"Why not? He is as corrupt as they come. That is his real bank account in Luxembourg. I found it last year. I just did not know how I was going to use it, until now." Boris placed the items in the inside pocket of the fat man's coat.

Together they struggled to carry the body to Boris's car, a Scoda parked on a side street, and lifted him into the passenger seat.

"What's your plan?" Hefflin asked.

"I am going to drive to another part of the city and park on a dark street," Boris said. "Then I am going to call my KGB operatives at the embassy to come pick him up. My story will be that he contacted me to give me intel on the traitor. Before he could say much, other than that the traitor was the Deputy Ambassador, he died of a heart attack. The man is fat, probably smoked three packs a day, and ate pork. He was due for a heart attack anyway. The good thing is that the poison mimics a heart attack. It is also untraceable. The papers on his body will be taken by the KGB with my orders to send them directly to Moscow. So, now go to your hotel and make sure no one else follows. As for Vulcan, I will assume that our operation is for the day after tomorrow, unless I hear from you otherwise. Oh, by the way, your powers of observation need to be improved."

"Yes, I'm sorry for not spotting the fat man following me."

"Yes, that, too."

Hefflin returned to his room at the Athénée more agitated than ever. If the man in the bar with Stanculescu in East Germany had been both a CIA operative and an independent contractor, then on whose orders did he kill Professor Pincus?

The convoluted machinations, lies, and violence that field agents were routinely involved with both intrigued and repulsed him. It was obvious by Boris's jovial demeanor that the fat man was not the first person he had killed. To him the man had been just a chess piece, a pawn that needed to be sacrificed. Whether the man had a wife and children, or liked vodka or blinis, was irrelevant. Hefflin had not gotten over his own violent encounter with the Securitate agents on the train, about which he had avoided telling Boris. Of course, he knew such things occurred in the dirty world of espionage, but seeing it up close and personal left him craving his quiet desk where he analyzed sanitized intel like parts of a jigsaw puzzle.

As he tried to calm his mind, he began to review several more questions. First, if Stanculescu was a CIA asset, what was he doing in Timisoara? Stanculescu was obviously not part of the quiet coup that Boris had planned. And why had Stanculescu and Stanton discussed snipers in the CIA safe house in Timisoara before the snipers appeared the next day?

The other item was the fat man. It was apparent that the KGB knew there was a traitor in their midst who was passing information to the CIA. That bothered him more personally, since it placed Boris in danger. Perhaps Boris had averted a catastrophe this time, but how long would the diversion last? Suddenly, Boris's days seemed to be numbered.

For now, he had to concentrate on the meeting with Vulcan in the morning. Did he trust Boris with the exfiltration? He reassured himself that Boris was a man of extraordinary means, and yet the planned silent coup had gone awry. Things were happening about which Boris had no knowledge. Boris was not perfect, after all.

As he tried to will himself to sleep, he thought about Boris's comment regarding his powers of observation. If Boris wasn't referring to his not spotting the fat man following him, what then? It was this last question that finally brought on his restless sleep.

CHAPTER THIRTY-SIX

Bucharest
December 1989

THE SKIES WERE gray, the morning sun was nowhere to be seen. The chess tables in Cismingiu Park were empty, the severe cold having driven away even the most hard-core players.

Hefflin stood by a tree and waited. The park was deserted except for a worker pushing a wheelbarrow full of dried branches, probably taking them home to heat his house. He watched the man slowly make his way to the chess tables and stop to light a cigarette. The worker was dressed in a green uniform and hat, but the shoes, Hefflin noticed, were of high quality. The man had forgotten about disguising his shoes.

Hefflin approached the small table and sat across from the workman to light his own cigarette. "Minister Vulcan."

Vulcan continued to stare down at the chess table. "Do you play, Mr. Hefflin?"

"I used to. Not for a long time."

"I think you play chess all the time, even now." Vulcan smiled and looked up at him.

"What can I do for you, Minister?"

"You should not have involved Irina. She knows nothing about my world or yours. She has tried to keep her life in the clouds, like so many artists. But—"he waived his cigarette—"since you have already done so, is your offer serious?"

Hefflin nodded. "Provided you have the dossier with Ceausescu's offshore accounts. All of them."

Vulcan gave him a tired look. "I have everything you want. Will I be allowed to keep my own little nest egg?"

"Yes. We'll even throw in a house and car, wherever in America you wish to settle. Along with a new identity."

Vulcan looked at him for a long time. "How can I trust you, Mr. Hefflin? What guarantees do I have?"

"The CIA keeps its word, Minister. Otherwise, no one would take us up on our offers of safety or sanctuary. Word gets around if our promises are broken. But how do we trust that you have the goods?"

"I will be in your hands," Vulcan stated. "If I don't produce the accounts, you can always bring me back here to face my fate. Or put a bullet in my head."

Hefflin had to admit that the man was obviously quite intelligent, even ready to face the worst, if it came to that.

"Tell me, Minister, why does a man like you become involved with such a tyrant?"

Vulcan gave him a wry smile. "Why do any of us do stupid things? Life is short, so we want to make the best of it, I suppose. You see it as black and white, but from my perspective, it was all gray, a slippery slope, as you say. You perform a little favor here, another one there, all to please your immediate superior in the grand pecking order. Before you know it, you're in it up to your neck, and you're too scared to back out. Eventually you get to the top and, of course, now you want to reap the rewards to justify all those years of groveling." He shrugged. "My original degree from the university was in biochemistry. I graduated first in my class. I had the dream of one day finding the cure for aging." He laughed. "Then I was tapped to join the government, which was the beginning of the end of my dreams. I ended up as the Minister of Agriculture. Ridiculous." He lit another cigarette from the one he held. "I ask you the same question. Why did you choose to waste your time over these petty squabbles we humans engage in? You could have used your life for something grander."

The question hit him hard and left him without an answer. It was a question he had asked himself for years.

"When are you ready to do this, Minister?"

"As soon as you can arrange it," Vulcan said. "I think time is quickly running out."

"And your family?"

"My family will remain here," Vulcan said. "Whatever happens, they will be fine."

"And Irina?"

"Irina will have an account waiting for her in a Luxembourg bank." He removed a piece of paper from his pocket and handed it to him. "You can give her the information, for I fear I will not be seeing her again."

Hefflin placed the paper in his pocket and handed Vulcan the sheet with the directions from Boris. "Memorize it, then burn it."

Vulcan read it over once, then handed it back to him.

"If for whatever reason you can't proceed tomorrow, follow the same instructions the next day," Hefflin said.

Vulcan stood and threw away his cigarette. "Nice doing business with you, Mr. Hefflin. Good luck to both of us."

Hefflin watched as the man slowly pushed the wheelbarrow toward the exit, then lower it next to a shed and walk out of the park.

CHAPTER THIRTY-SEVEN

Bucharest
December 1989

FROM HIS MEETING with Vulcan, Hefflin went directly to the embassy to search the CIA computers for whatever they had on General Stanculescu. It wasn't much. He skimmed through a short biography but saw no mention of the general either being an asset or having been approached. He wasn't surprised. Analysts didn't usually have access to the identity of CIA assets. He signed off. The thought occurred to him to ask Stanton to help him gain higher access but he thought the better of it. Stanton would probably refuse, pulling the "need to know" excuse.

He thought for a while, trying to decide what he should do, and a plan soon began to take shape. The only way to find out what was going on was to bypass normal CIA regulations, but it would be risky.

He sauntered into Stanton's office where he found the chief of station busy chewing out one of the agents for losing a Securitate colonel he had been following. Hefflin waited outside until the yelling was done, then entered and asked Stanton to look up General Militaru on the computer.

"Why can't you do it yourself?" Stanton asked.

"They gave me a temporary password while here, and it isn't working," he said.

"Christ, the fuckups around here are monumental. What do you want to know?"

"Just need to refresh myself on his biography," he said. "We know he's paid by the KGB. He may be involved in the coup."

Stanton let out a disgusted sigh. "I'll print it out for you."

Hefflin eased around to the side of the desk to observe Stanton type in his password. General Militaru's file appeared on the screen, then Stanton hit the PRINT button.

"I hope I don't have to tell you that this can't leave the building," Stanton intoned. "Shred it when you're done."

"Thanks. Sorry to bother you."

He retrieved the printout material and returned to his desk. He waited until Stanton left his office for lunch, then entered it and signed in on the computer using Stanton's password. If the shit hit the fan, the records would show that Stanton signed in on his own computer.

He brought up Stanculescu's file. At the bottom there appeared a box labeled "Restricted Access," which opened with Stanton's password. The first page had a description of the general's activities during the past several years. He skimmed down until his eyes stopped at one sentence: "Since his recruitment in East Berlin in 1986, General Stanculescu has provided valuable intel on military and security matters, as well as the political factions inside the military establishment." References were attached to other documents.

So Boris's suspicions were right. Stanculescu was a CIA asset. That explained why Stanton had been talking to him at the safe house, but it did not explain why Stanculescu, who was in charge of the military in Timisoara, would allow all the bloodshed. Had the situation simply gotten out of hand? It wasn't difficult to see how demonstrations could incite violence. But another thing still didn't make sense: How had Stanton and Stanculescu known about the snipers before the demonstrations had even taken place?

He next brought up Professor Pincus's file. As he skimmed through the biography, he paused to reread a section. Pincus had converted to Christianity in 1935, fearing the rise of anti-Semitism in Germany and Romania. He had fought in the Romanian army during the War and had escaped Romania along with his wife under unexplained circumstances in 1948, not in 1938, as Pincus had told him when they first met. After a few years in Paris, he and his wife immigrated to the U.S., where he became a professor at Harvard. So Pincus's story about joining the Air Force and bombing the Ploesti oil fields was all fluff. Pincus joined the CIA in 1955 and served primarily as a recruiter of Harvard students during the decades afterward, though at times he was used for other purposes. Several references to other documents followed, along with a list of his academic publications. The final paragraph stated that Pincus had been assassinated by an agent of the Securitate on Ceausescu's orders.

Underneath were several pictures showing the assassin entering Pincus's house. Beside the one Avery had shown him, in which the assassin's face was not visible, there was one with the assassin's face in full view, the same picture he had seen on Stanton's desk. He enlarged the picture and studied the face more closely. Even considering the passage of time and the grainy pictures, he was convinced that the man entering Pincus's house was the same man that had met Stanculescu in East Berlin. So, why hadn't Avery shown him this picture? Was the man really working for the Securitate, or as a free agent when he assassinated Pincus?

Hefflin felt a growing anger. He knew he had to get to the bottom of this, if for nothing else than for the sake of Pincus's memory.

He printed the pictures, signed out, shredded Militaru's file, and left Stanton's office.

* * *

Defense Minister Milea read the reports on his desk and sighed deeply.

On December 20th, a general strike had been called in Timisoara. Certain units of the military in Timisoara had suddenly turned on the government, refusing to fire. Crowds were reported climbing the tanks in solidarity with the "People's Army," placing flowers inside the barrels of the tank guns. The snipers had suddenly disappeared. The mood was festive, everyone sensing Romania was turning a corner.

Milea turned to look through the windows of the Central Committee building at the crowd below. It had grown to extend beyond Palace Square. Hundreds of thousands of people, he was told, were roaming the streets of Bucharest. Unheard of. Reports were coming in from across the country. The army was incapable of controlling the crowds with just water cannon and tear gas, and they had been given live ammunition. There had been many civilian deaths in several cities where army units were still loyal to the government.

Milea sat behind his desk and tried to think things through. Until now his role as defense minister had been to protect the country from outside aggression. The military interventions in Timisoara and other cities had been ordered by Elena Ceausescu while her husband had been in Iran. Now that Ceausescu was back, Milea was being asked to personally take charge of the military against the Romanian people inside the capital. Knowing how furious Ceausescu was at his resistance, he didn't know how long he could hold out. He also feared the troops would panic, as they had done in Timisoara, and start shooting wildly, even at their fellow soldiers.

He leaned back in his chair and lit a cigarette, then put it out. He remembered he had promised his wife to quit smoking. He then let out a dry laugh and lit another one. He would probably face a firing squad when this was over or be imprisoned for twenty years. He might as well enjoy a last cigarette. And the hell with Ceausescu, he decided. Let them do what they wanted to him, he was not going to murder for the Party. And certainly not for this president, whose days were numbered.

He heard a knock, then saw the door open. Gulescu, part of his personal Securitate guard, walked in without looking up at him. The man was holding a piece of paper, some other bad news, no doubt. Gulescu quickly closed the door behind him, then took short, efficient steps toward the minister.

"What is it?" Milea asked.

Gulescu came around behind the desk without answering. As he bent over to show Minister Milea the document, he removed a pistol from his pocket and placed it against Milea's temple. Before Milea could utter another word, Gulescu pulled the trigger. A tinny gunshot, like a cap pistol, sounded, followed by blood splattering across the room. Milea's head slumped over the desk. Gulescu wiped down the gun and placed it in the dead man's hand. He then walked out in the same efficient manner in which he had entered so that he could report the suicide to his superiors.

CHAPTER THIRTY-EIGHT

Bucharest
December 1989

MINISTER VULCAN DRIFTED in and out of sleep, his body unable to lie still. The dreams had tormented him for months, ever since the dominoes began to fall: Poland, Hungary, East Germany, Czechoslovakia, Bulgaria. In his recurring dreams he suffered through all the possible outcomes: arrest, prison, torture, execution. Each morning he awoke with a new layer of fear weighing upon his soul. He was grateful that guilt had not yet begun to insinuate itself, for guilt implied having made the wrong choices, and he didn't believe he had had any choice in the actions he had taken. Survival was the prime directive of any organism. All his deeds could be justified by invoking the prime directive.

Still, there were things worse than death. He was an Orthodox Christian, a believer, so in the middle of the night he thought of God and the afterlife. He had already formulated various versions of a response when God, or Saint Peter, or whoever was in charge of such duties, asked him to justify his actions in life. His answers were all variations on the same theme: "What else could I have done? It was either follow orders or perish."

He also knew the comeback: "Yes, but did you have to be so eager, so creative? Did you have to drain those poor peasants of every kernel of grain? And what about the money you stole for yourself and the Tyrant? That money could have fed many people."

"They should have revolted," would be his answer. "Sheep are made for shearing."

He knew that last statement would probably earn him a place in hell, but he couldn't come up with a better one. Gluttony was a sin, there was no way around it. He would try to change the subject by listing his good deeds as a father and husband, but that, too, was dangerous territory. He had not been a faithful husband, far from it. The actress, Irina, was only the latest in a long string of mistresses.

So he had tried to accustom himself to the idea of hell. Perhaps hell wasn't as bad as the priests made it out. There was no description of hell in the Bible, after all. Hell was a concept created by the church to keep the masses in line, much like the fear instilled by the Securitate. Hell, if it did exist, might actually be more to his liking. All of his friends would be there, no doubt.

He turned again, this time toward his wife, and found her staring at him.

"You're awake," he said.

"You talk in your sleep," she whispered. "You should be more careful what you say."

"More careful? In my sleep?"

"You talk of being shot or hanged. One time you called The Man a blithering idiot."

"Good God! Was I loud?"

"Loud enough for microphones."

"There are no microphones, I keep telling you. My men sweep the house every week."

"So you say. But walls have ears nevertheless. They always have."

They lay silent for a while.

"What will happen to us, Victor?" she finally asked. "I mean, when the whole thing comes tumbling down."

"Nothing will come tumbling down, darling, not for a long time," he said.

"Are you deaf and blind?" she asked. "Because I am not. We've made a deal with the devil, and I fear he will soon come to collect."

"Don't be silly," he said, though he was surprised at her show of a conscience. She had never asked him where all their money came from or what he actually did in his job as minister of agriculture. "Besides, you and the children will be well taken care of, no matter what."

"And you?"

"I always end up on my feet, like a cat, you know that." He tried to smile.

The silence between them grew wider, creating a chasm that both seemed to feel.

"I don't want you leaving without us," she said.

"Leaving? Where?"

"Abroad. To escape whoever and whatever comes next."

"Darling . . ."

"I don't want you taking that actress with you and deserting your family."

He had to admit he was surprised. How long had she known about Irina? No, he wouldn't be taking Irina or his family. There was no place for any of them in his plans.

"Don't mention her again," he said. "She is not and has never been important. Just a stupid diversion. You know how stressful my job has been."

She reached out and squeezed his hand. "You have been a good father, at least. The children love you."

"And you?"

She let go of his hand and turned her face away from him. "I am your wife. Of course I love you. But you've brought so much between us. So much."

He turned his body away from her. Two individuals, each lying on their own side of the bed. That had been their life for years. Too late to fix now.

✳   ✳   ✳

He made sure he followed his morning routine without deviation. He rose from bed at seven, showered and shaved and drank the French coffee procured from the Party store, which his wife prepared for him. The one exception was his wife's *cozonac*, the sumptuous sweet bread with the ground walnuts swirling inside, which he avoided due to his weight but which he now indulged in, knowing he would never taste it again. Even more out of character was his comment on how good it was, which made his wife smile.

"It's the little things that make life worth living," he said, then cursed himself for going too far.

He kissed his children as they rushed off to school, then gathered his briefcase and coat.

"I forgot. We won't be having lunch together today," he said, as if just remembering. "I'm going to the Tourist Shop to look for an expensive present for you."

"For me? But why?"

"Don't pretend you forgot." He smiled. "Our anniversary is in a week. Twenty years is a milestone to celebrate. And it will come with a sincere promise to be a better husband."

She looked at him for a long moment, her eyes shining with tears, and embraced him. "Nothing too extravagant."

"What's money and privilege for if not to enjoy them?" He took one last look at his wife, his living room, and left.

His Securitate entourage was waiting in the black Dacia outside his house. He arrived at the ministry a little before nine, his usual time.

At one in the afternoon, he exited the ministry building accompanied by his two-man Securitate detail and was driven to the Tourist Shop a few blocks away. During the short drive he saw people gathered in large groups in the streets, talking loudly, no longer whispering. He was glad he was leaving all that behind. May God curse them all.

He allowed himself to dream of the life that awaited him in the West as a way of controlling his nerves. The thought of leaving his wife and children behind temporarily derailed his fantasy but he pushed it aside. He felt no remorse. They would be fine without him. His life would not be constrained by the past. He was still relatively young, after all, and still had a full head of hair, with graying temples that added distinction. He would have to lose some weight, but that would be easily accomplished with the healthy foods he would find in the Southern European countries. No, he would not settle in sterile America. He pictured himself in a villa overlooking the Mediterranean, Monte Carlo perhaps, with a new identity, lying on a chaise longue by a pool with several bikinied women nearby sipping daiquiris or piña coladas, or whatever they drank in those very decadent, very marvelous countries. At night he would visit one of the casinos, a woman on each arm, and hobnob with royalty. And then there would be the parties on his yacht, rubbing elbows with the wealthy and powerful. Oh my. Life could be so beautiful.

When he reached the Tourist Shop, he was sorry the ride had been so short, for his fantasies seemed to have no bounds. The

Securitate officers remained with the car while he entered the building. The entryway was deserted. The door to the shop was made of solid wood so no Romanians could glimpse the Western goods they were forbidden to buy. Vulcan did not enter the shop but continued down the corridor and exited through the back door into an alley where a utility van was waiting. The rear door was open. Vulcan climbed inside, the door closed, and the van drove off.

Inside the windowless space, it was dark. He could make out a woman. As his eyes adjusted, he further saw, to his delight, that she was young, pretty, and blonde, just the way he liked them. She handed him a bundle.

"Change into these clothes. Quickly," she said in Romanian.

"Right here? In front of you?"

"Surely, Minister, this isn't the first time you've taken off your clothes before a woman not your wife."

He could feel his face flare up, but he did as told. Within a few minutes he was dressed in workmen's clothes.

She handed him a passport and papers.

"You will be driven to the first train station outside of Bucharest, where no one will recognize you. You will get on the next train to Constanta. Here is your ticket."

"Alone? I thought someone would accompany me."

"There will be people on the train who will look after you. You won't know them. They will come to your aid if there is a problem, but we don't expect any. The Securitate has enough on its plate. In Constanta you will be met by a woman named Marika. She is also a blonde. She will approach you outside the station and take you to the ship."

The van stopped. The woman opened the back door and jumped out. She helped him climb in front with the driver, and the van took off. As it disappeared around the corner, she removed the blond wig and stuffed it in a garbage can. She then found the nearest public telephone, dialed a number, and spoke when she heard the gruff voice answer. "Yes, Uncle, he just left."

The train trip to Constanta took a little over six hours. Since it was winter, there were few passengers traveling to the port city. Vulcan tried to spot the men supposedly looking out for him but saw mostly laborers and farmers traveling short distances. Perhaps there were no such men protecting him. It was only a ruse, to console him. But the trip was uneventful, and for that he was grateful. He spent his time deciding how he would manage the Americans. Once on Western European soil, he had operatives who were ready to help him escape the Americans' clutches. But the Americans were like bloodhounds: they wouldn't rest until they found him again. He didn't want to spend the rest of his life hiding in some godforsaken African country. He knew the Americans were pragmatists. They loved to make deals. And they had no idea of the vast amount of money that existed in Ceausescu's many accounts. The Americans were silly people, after all. All this talk about Ceausescu's dossier. There was no dossier. The dossier was all in his head. He had long ago memorized all the account numbers, and he recited them now, just to be sure.

He disembarked in Constanta around eight in the evening. The train station was nearly empty. He slowly walked toward the exit, barely able to contain his excitement. He was almost there. Just meet up with this Marika blonde and get on the ship. A merchant vessel, no doubt. He'd have to share quarters with sailors who hadn't bathed in a month, but never mind. A wondrous life awaited him. Just a little more patience, the same patience he had developed over so many years of squirreling away all those millions.

Outside the station he stopped and took a deep breath. The smell of freedom was already in the air. He spotted a figure across the street standing under a lamppost. A woman, blonde. *Marika, darling. How wonderful you look.* He started walking toward her when he felt a hand fall hard on his shoulder. Upon turning, he saw two men in leather jackets standing behind him.

Where the devil did they come from?

"Minister Vulcan, please come with us," one of them said.

"You are making a mistake," he stammered. "My name is—" What the hell was it? He looked down at his passport to find the name.

"There is no mistake, Minister. Your wife informed us you might be fleeing the country."

"My wife?" Vulcan couldn't imagine his dear wife doing such a thing. How could she even have known? He cursed. It was that damned *cozonac* that he had complimented her on. That was it. But she had suspected him, even before that. She had warned him not to leave without her. He should have listened. Where were the men to help him?

As the Securitate pulled him into the car, he glanced across the street, but the blonde was gone.

CHAPTER THIRTY-NINE

Bucharest
December 1989

THE NEXT DAY Ceausescu spoke from his balcony in Palace Square to a staged crowd of over one hundred thousand pro-government workers organized by the Securitate. He was a relatively short man with a peasant face and an equally peasant accent that the locals always made fun of. He wore his usual black winter coat and black Astrakhan hat. His wife, Elena, stood by his side, as usual, ready to remind him where in his grand oration he had left off after being interrupted by the usual loud applause. The speech was televised live nationally. Stanton and Hefflin, along with the rest of the Agency crew, were huddled around the television set in the Operations room. Several CIA field operatives had been sent to mingle among the crowd, and were reporting back through shortwave radios.

Ceausescu began in his usual way, addressing the crowd as loyal citizens who should not allow the fascist terrorist forces to derail the socialist cause. The front rows of the audience, the most loyal, applauded with fervor, often interrupting the speech at the appointed phrases. But eight minutes into the speech, part of the crowd in the back started chanting "Timisoara! Timisoara!"

Ceausescu stopped his speech and looked confused. Then what sounded like gunshots rang out. The crowd in the back started breaking up, people running for cover. A visibly shaken Ceausescu tried to quiet the people by raising his arms and ordering them to settle down. He was joined by his wife, Elena, who kept yelling for the people to be quiet. But what was clear to all was that for the first time in his long reign, Ceausescu had lost control.

Stanton sat transfixed. No one in Romania had ever seen the leader falter like this, and it was being transmitted on live television for the entire country to observe.

"I never thought I'd see this day," Stanton said gruffly.

Ceausescu tried to appease the crowd with ad hoc promises of increases in salaries and other benefits. But it was too late. The crowd had already turned. Ceausescu and his wife were visibly panicked, and Securitate forces rushed them back into the building.

After that debacle, the riots spread throughout the capital.

Reports came in of elite anti-terrorist squads, who had no compunction at firing on civilians, and Securitate forces fanning throughout the city. Snipers on rooftops were seen shooting at anything that moved. Dead soldiers and civilians lay unattended on the streets. The snipers were labeled "terrorists" but no one knew their identities or their true aims. By nightfall the city was quiet again, but everyone dreaded the next day.

*　　*　　*

It was a little past two in the morning when General Stanculescu's military plane landed in Bucharest. He had nothing but bad news to report from Timisoara and wasn't sure of his reception by his superior, Defense Minister Milea. Many people had been killed and wounded, certainly more than expected. It had begun with the snipers, but at some point, it had spread. The army units panicked and began to fire indiscriminately into the crowd. But the demonstrators hadn't backed down. The people had passed a point of no return, he was convinced. They no longer demanded better conditions, but roared in unison, "Down with Ceausescu!"

The revolution had begun.

Reports claimed it had already spread to other cities and protests were now beginning in the capital. Ceausescu's televised speech had been a disaster. For the first time, the people had seen a confused, frightened leader. The remnants of the Securitate would put up some resistance in a last-ditch effort to protect the regime, but it would be futile. Then they would fight simply to save their own necks. If he had known it would be this easy, he would have agreed to this years ago, and saved his people all the misery.

From the airport he called his wife to tell her he had arrived and that he would be going directly to the Central Committee.

"No, under no circumstances are you to go there," she said. "There were demonstrations everywhere, people dead in the streets. Ceausescu is bent on trying to crush them. Whatever he decides, you don't want to be seen as being a part of it."

"But I received orders before leaving Timisoara to report there as soon as I landed," he said.

"From whom?"

"Milea, through his assistant."

"Milea is dead. They say he committed suicide, refusing to give troops live ammunition."

Stanculescu was stunned. Suicide? Milea? Why hadn't he been notified? No, Ceausescu must have shot him, plain and simple, for refusing his orders.

He told his wife he'd see what he could do.

He hung up and called the military hospital. The doctor on call was an old friend. Stanculescu told him what he needed.

An hour later, Stanculescu was lying in a hospital bed, one leg wearing a full cast.

"I hope this will be enough to excuse me from attending the Central Committee," Stanculescu said. "Call and tell them of my condition. But what if they take an X-ray and find out it's not broken?"

"We'll just say that you have a meniscal tear in your knee, which you can't see on X-ray." The doctor winked. "They're not doctors. By the time someone figures it out, it will all be over."

But at a little past nine in the morning, a car appeared in front of the hospital. The driver hurried inside and found General Stanculescu lying in bed, his leg in a cast.

"General, I have been ordered to drive you to the Central Committee," the man said.

"You can see I can't be moved," Stanculescu said.

"Sir, my orders are to inform you that, as defense minister, your presence is urgently needed."

"Defense minister?"

"Yes, sir. We have been trying to contact you. Six hours ago, following Minister Milea's suicide, you were named defense minister."

Damn it. What kind of joke is life playing now? He turned to the doctor who raised his arms in a gesture that said, "There's nothing more I can do."

CHAPTER FORTY

Bucharest
December 1989

GENERAL STANCULESCU HOBBLED on his crutches as he entered the Central Committee building where he was met by Colonel Natsu, whom he knew well: a middle-aged career soldier with two teenage sons, a wife, and a mistress.

"What is the situation, Colonel?"

"The demonstrations are growing, Defense Minister. There are reportedly hundreds of thousands of people on the streets throughout the city. Factories are on strike. The Special Forces and Securitate units are inadequate to regain control of the situation. The president has ordered two army units, one mechanized and one tank unit, to come from Oltenita to assist. They have not yet reached the city limits."

Stanculescu turned to the colonel. "Natsu, do you want to survive this day?"

Colonel Natsu stared at him, then stammered, "Of c-course, sir."

"Then do as I say. First, order the two military units to stop at the outskirts of the city and not enter under any circumstances. Second, order the military units already in the city not to fire on unarmed civilians. Third, order four helicopters to land in front of the building, in the middle of the square."

Colonel Natsu hesitated, no doubt calculating his options. After a moment his expression cleared, having arrived at a decision. He clicked his heels and saluted. "Right away, sir."

Stanculescu turned toward the conference room where he knew the Central Committee was meeting. He slowly thudded his way on the crutches, cursing the damned leg cast, which had failed to fulfill its function. As he was about to enter the room, the doors opened and out came President Ceausescu himself.

"I thought I heard your voice. What the hell happened to you? And at such a critical moment?"

"An injury in Timisoara, Mr. President."

"Where are the army units I ordered from Oltenita?"

"On their way, sir. They have encountered heavy traffic on the highway. People leaving the city."

"Leaving the city? But I ordered the city closed."

"There aren't enough troops to block all exits from the city, Mr. President."

"We need overwhelming force." Ceausescu clenched his fist. "A tank on every corner. These terrorists have to be crushed."

"Mr. President—" Stanculescu's voice grew softer. "The situation is graver than Defense Minister Milea may have understood."

"That traitor!"

"Sir, the crowd has become unpredictable. Your personal safety must be the prime objective. I've taken the precaution of ordering helicopters to land in the square outside the building. It is my professional opinion that the Central Committee must immediately evacuate and regroup at another location."

"What are you saying? Are you mad? Leave the seat of government at this crucial moment? No, I will speak to the people again. They won't be fooled by these terrorists."

Ceausescu reentered the conference room and ordered the members of the Central Committee to join him on the balcony to address the people.

*   *   *

The crowd that had been gathering all morning now had mushroomed to several hundred thousand in and around Palace Square. Hefflin marched alongside the people and entered the square as the chanting began, slogans no one would ever have imagined uttering even to him- or herself: "Down with Ceausescu!" and "Down with communism!" The people, subjugated and terrorized for decades, had now lost their fear. Everyone was aware of the uprisings that had begun in other major cities throughout the country, and they were now tasting blood.

"Our time has come!" a man next to him shouted. A woman yelled, "Down with the thieves!"

Part of the crowd started singing the old national anthem, "*Awaken, Romanian!*" while others continued with curses and raised fists. There were no soldiers or police that he could see. Hefflin heard the faint sound of helicopters, barely audible above the roar of the crowd. Four helicopters were hovering high above the square, as if unsure of their orders. After a few minutes, three of them flew off while the fourth started descending. The crowd did not seem to notice, continuing to yell obscenities and slogans.

The helicopter approached the Central Committee building and slowly descended onto the rooftop. Was its mission to bring in forces or for evacuation?

The crowd suddenly grew even more agitated. Ceausescu now appeared on the balcony, accompanied by his wife and surrounded by members of the Central Committee. The president held up his arms to plead for quiet. The people responded with boos and curses. As Ceausescu tried to speak, the roar of the crowd grew louder, some throwing rotten tomatoes and potatoes at him. A mob rushed toward the entrance of the building, overpowered the guards, and entered. The Securitate whisked Ceausescu and his wife back from the balcony into the building.

Hefflin used his binoculars to focus on the rooftop. After a few minutes he spotted figures scurrying toward the helicopter and boarding it. A moment later, the helicopter began to lift, then hesitated, bobbing sideways. It finally started climbing again, then flew over the rooftops out of the city.

*   *   *

Securitate agents pulled the Ceausescus back into the building and hurried them toward the elevators.

"To the roof, Mr. President. A helicopter is waiting," Stanculescu called out.

"The roof? You said they would land in the square," Ceausescu cried.

"You saw the crowd, Mr. President. There was no room for them to land. But one has landed on the rooftop. I suggest you use it."

"The mob has broken into the building," a Securitate agent called out.

Curses and screams could be heard emanating from the floor below.

"Quickly, Mr. President," Stanculescu urged. "There is little time. You can fly to another location and reorganize the army to put down these terrorists."

"I go to regroup!" Ceausescu cried, then pulled his wife into the elevator. Two of his staunch loyalists joined them, along with two Securitate agents.

Stanculescu waited patiently for the crowd to appear on the stairwell. When they reached him, he pointed to the elevator. "They're going up to the roof."

The mob continued up the stairs, yelling invectives.

Inside the elevator, the Ceausescus were huddled in a corner.

"Can't this damned elevator go any faster?" Elena Ceausescu cursed.

The elevator climbed slowly, old and bronchitic as it was, and before reaching the top floor, it exhaled its last breath.

"Why aren't the doors opening?" Ceausescu screamed, scratching at them with his fingernails.

"Cursed elevator," Elena spat.

"It has stopped between floors, Mr. President," one of the agents said. The two agents then pried the doors open. The floor stood three feet above them. The agents lifted Elena and Nicolae Ceausescu up to the floor, then helped the other two men. The crowd could be heard yelling from the floors below.

"Up the stairs to the roof, Mr. President!" one of the Securitate agents yelled.

The men half-carried the Ceausescus upward to the rooftop where a helicopter stood, its blades spinning. The Ceausescus were panting like rabid dogs, barely able to lurch across the rooftop. Elena clutched her purse as she was lifted into the helicopter, followed by Nicolae. The other four men squeezed inside.

"There are too many people," the pilot yelled above the noise of the engine. "We're too heavy!"

Ceausescu ordered him to take off.

The pilot revved the motor and the helicopter slowly lifted a few feet above the rooftop. The mob burst through the rooftop door and rushed toward them.

"We're too heavy!" the pilot yelled again. The helicopter rocked sideways, then slowly started to climb. The people on the rooftop raised their fists and roared. The Ceausescus clutched each other in terror as they watched the hundreds of thousands of angry people on the streets below yelling and cursing, willing the helicopter to crash down.

They were soon flying beyond the city, over the outskirts, where Ceausescu now saw the tanks and personnel carriers parked in the fields, the ones from Oltenita that were supposed to put down the rebellion.

"Why are they just sitting there?" Ceausescu cried. "Look, the soldiers are just standing around, smoking. Stanculescu said they were coming into the city."

No one in the helicopter said anything.

Only Elena said aloud what they were all thinking. "They betrayed us. Traitors, all of them."

*   *   *

They were flying over the countryside, the roar of the engine filling the cabin, silencing all. A few minutes before, they had landed in Snagov, where Ceausescu had tried unsuccessfully to get in touch with his generals. Desperate, Ceausescu then ordered the pilot to fly to Târgoviște. The pilot considered escaping, but was terrified he would be shot by the two Securitate agents. In the helicopter again, flying as slowly as he could, he waited for an opportunity. When he saw his chance, he furtively pressed a button on the console. An alarm went off inside the cabin, which caused Elena to scream and slap her palms to her ears.

"Surface to air missile radars have locked onto us, Mr. President," the pilot yelled. He began taking evasive maneuvers, the helicopter diving and curving, everyone in the cabin screaming.

"Put us down!" Ceausescu cried. "In the field, anywhere."

The pilot did as ordered. Within minutes they had landed in an open field beside a road. Everyone rushed out, leaving the pilot behind.

The Securitate men flagged down the first car they saw and the Ceausescus got in, followed by the two Securitate agents. The other two men were left behind to fend for themselves.

After traveling a few miles, the driver, a doctor, pretended his car had a mechanical problem and stopped. The Securitate agents requisitioned a second car belonging to a bicycle repairman, who drove them and the Ceausescus to a farm cooperative. When the manager of the cooperative realized the identity of his guests, he called the local police who soon arrived and arrested the Ceausescus and the two Securitate agents.

Romania's forty-four-year reign of terror was apparently over.

CHAPTER FORTY-ONE

Bucharest/Târgoviște
December 1989

A BLACK DACIA was waiting outside the American Embassy. Hefflin got in next to the driver, a clean-shaven man with gray hair sporting a Russian fur hat and a lit cigarette between his teeth.

"So, I finally get to see the real Boris," Hefflin said. "Christ, you have more disguises than Sherlock Holmes."

"Sherlock Holmes? I love the guy. Read all the stories." Boris chuckled. "Yes, this is the real me. They have to recognize my face."

Hefflin examined Boris more closely. The clean-shaven face looked vaguely familiar, somehow.

"Where are you taking me?"

"To a trial," Boris said. "Here, put this on." It was a Romanian army uniform.

"You must be kidding."

"Do I look like I kid? Okay, I do kid a lot, but not this time. They will assume you are my military attaché," Boris said. "No one will ask any questions. By the way, the Securitate caught Vulcan in Constanta. His wife betrayed him. Do you believe it?"

"His wife turned him in? Did they find the dossier on him?"

"There was no dossier." Boris frowned. "Maybe he has a copy in Europe. Maybe he was just fooling us."

"So, after all this, we have nothing," Hefflin said.

They drove to a military base on the outskirts of Bucharest. Boris flashed an ID card to the sentry who waved them in.

"They know you," Hefflin said.

"Of course. I'm a colonel in the KGB. I used to be Chief of Station here, before I was promoted. In this country, I can go anywhere. For how long, though, who knows?"

They pulled up to a military helicopter sitting alone on the tarmac, its blades spinning.

"We must hurry. We do not want to miss the show," Boris yelled above the noise of the rotors. "Truth is, the show cannot start without us." He chuckled. Within minutes they were flying above the dark streets of Bucharest.

❊   ❊   ❊

They were huddled together in a small room, an elderly couple who reminded Hefflin of pictures of immigrants on Ellis Island. Elena Ceausescu wore a light-colored winter coat with a dark fur collar and was clutching a leather handbag. Nicolae Ceausescu had on his usual black winter coat and Astrakhan hat and was patting his wife's hand as if to say, "It's all right. Nothing bad will happen here." Several soldiers were standing in the room looking out of place, almost embarrassed. Hefflin was dressed in the uniform of a Romanian army lieutenant. No one paid any attention to him. As he and Boris entered the room, Boris snapped his fingers and the soldiers immediately left, locking the door behind them.

"Finally, you've arrived, tovarisch," Ceausescu said to Boris in Romanian. "Why haven't you put a stop to this madness? You've had your joke; you made your point. I'll follow Moscow's orders from now on."

"It's a bit late for that," Boris said, also in Romanian. Hefflin was impressed at how well Boris spoke it. "There was a chance that all this drama could have been avoided, but you chose to fire on your own people rather than talk to them."

"I never ordered them to use live bullets!" Ceausescu cried.

Boris shook his head. "Your army and your Securitate killed thousands of civilians. Now you have a revolution on your hands."

"Lies, all lies!" Ceausescu cried. "This is no revolution. It's a coup d'état, pure and simple. The people love me. It's those ungrateful beasts. You think you have loyal generals around you, then they turn out to be traitors. Traitors to the socialist cause."

"You're wasting your breath," Elena said to her husband. "He's no better."

"Hush, my dear." Ceausescu patted his wife's hand again. "He can be reasoned with, not like the others."

"He's in on it, can't you tell?" she insisted. "And who is this other person?" She motioned with her chin to Hefflin. "I've never seen him before."

"He's with me," Boris said. "Now, have the soldiers searched you yet?"

"They don't dare touch us," Elena blurted out. "At least they have that decency."

"Well, I need to do that now," Boris said. "We don't want State secrets to fall into the wrong hands."

"We're not carrying any State secrets," Elena said. "What do you think we are?"

Boris smiled. "Like Churchill said, 'Madam, we have already established that. Now we are just haggling over price.'"

Ceausescu removed his wallet from the inside jacket pocket and threw it on the table. "There, that's all I have on me." Ceausescu stood and spread his arms for Boris to pat him down. Boris looked through the wallet and threw it back on the table.

"You don't have the indecency to touch me," Elena said.

"Madam, I can do it nicely . . . or by force," Boris said. "It's up to you. Please stand."

Elena cursed, then stood. As Boris patted her down, she cried, "Pig! How dare you!"

"Now the purse," Boris said.

"You have no right to rummage among my personal items with your filthy hands."

"Now, now, my dear, let him play his little games," Ceausescu said.

"No, he can't have it. He has no right." Elena clutched her handbag to her chest.

With one quick movement Boris pulled the bag from her hands.

"Animal! Thief!" she screamed.

A knock at the door sounded. A male voice called, "Is everything all right, Colonel?"

"Everything is fine. No cause for concern," Boris yelled back.

"You have no right," Elena repeated.

Boris opened the purse and looked inside, then inserted his hand. Hefflin heard the sound of plastic and metal as Boris rummaged through her personal items. When Boris removed his hand, Hefflin spotted a piece of paper, which was instantly palmed as by a card sharp. Boris handed the bag back to Elena.

"My apologies, but it had to be done." Boris turned to Ceausescu. "I salute you, tovarisch. Have no worries. There will have to be a little show, just to appease the masses, after which all will be well."

"That's what I wanted to hear." Ceausescu smiled. "And make sure those fanatics get what they deserve."

When Boris and Hefflin were back out in the corridor, one of the soldiers whispered in Boris's ear.

"Very well. Proceed," Boris ordered.

They stood to one side as the soldiers brought Ceausescu and his wife out of the room.

"He took something out of my purse!" Elena cried, pointing to Boris. "Thief. Give it back to me."

"Just this." Boris showed the soldier a silver-plated pocket mirror. "A souvenir. She won't need it where she's going." Boris winked and the soldier laughed.

Hefflin hadn't noticed Boris slip the mirror out of the handbag. He decided not to ask about the piece of paper.

As the Ceausescus were ushered into another room, Hefflin saw Boris exit the building through a side door. Through the window of the door, he could see several men in military uniform standing outside in the courtyard, engaged in a heated discussion and pointing at various walls. He recognized one of them: General Stanculescu, the new defense minister. Boris raised his arms as if to quiet a neighborhood brawl, then pointed to one wall, and the discussion was over. Boris returned wearing a smile.

"What was that all about?" Hefflin asked.

"Just some technicalities. Nothing of importance."

"What sort of technicalities?"

"They could not make up their minds on the position of the firing squad. I had to step in and make that decision for them."

"The firing squad! But there hasn't even been a trial yet."

"There will be. It should not take long."

"The Nuremberg trials took months," Hefflin pointed out.

"They actually took years, if you count all of them," Boris said. "But there is no time for that, Vasili. There are rumors that Ceausescu loyalists might be trying to free him."

"But . . ."

"We are in the middle of a revolution, my young friend. You think Marie Antoinette got a fair trial?"

Hefflin wondered why Boris had brought him to witness this farce trial and planned execution.

A moment later they entered a room where the Ceausescus were now sitting at a table next to each other. About a dozen men filtered in, some in military uniform and others in civilian clothes. Among them was General Stanculescu. A film crew was taping the proceeding. Boris pulled Hefflin to the back of the room behind the camera so neither of them would appear on tape. No one asked about the identity of the soldier standing next to Boris. The uniform seemed to make him invisible.

A man in a gray suit who identified himself as the prosecutor cleared his throat. "Let the trial begin."

CHAPTER FORTY-TWO

Târgoviște
December 25, 1989

"I ONLY RECOGNIZE the Grand National Assembly," Nicolae Ceausescu declared even before the prosecutor had a chance to speak.

Hefflin stood quietly in the back and tried to take notes. His report to Langley was going to have as many quotes as he could scribble down.

"Let the record show that the accused refuses to speak with us," the prosecutor said disdainfully. He was holding papers that he was constantly shuffling. But even as he tried to find his place, he began with off-the-cuff remarks charging the Ceausescus with holding lavish parties and acquiring the most sumptuous foods and clothes from abroad. He continued to ramble on about the two defendants robbing the people and that they were now cowards for not even wanting to talk.

The generals, who were standing and observing, began to move about nervously. It was obvious the prosecutor was flustered.

"We also have evidence proving both of them committed high crimes," the prosecutor insisted, trying to regroup. He then turned in desperation to the chairman of the prosecutor's office to read the bill of indictment.

The chairman of the prosecutor's office began with a list of offenses. It started with degrading human dignity and acting like despots and continued with genocide, the destruction of State institutions, and destroying the national economy. The prosecutor asked if the defendants understood the charges.

Nicolae Ceausescu declared that he would only answer questions before the Grand National Assembly. He did not recognize this court.

The prosecutor noted that the people did not have medicines, which resulted in the deaths of countless children, that there was nothing to eat, little heating for the winter, and spotty electrical power. The prosecutor then repeatedly asked who ordered the shootings in Timisoara and Bucharest. Ceausescu denied there had been any shooting. The prosecutor insisted that there had been acts of genocide, with at least thirty-four shootings.

Hefflin looked at Boris, who shrugged. There had been thousands of deaths.

"And they call that genocide," Elena Ceausescu said to Nicolae.

The trial continued with accusations leveled by the prosecutor followed by denials from Nicolae and Elena Ceausescu, interspersed with outbursts from Nicolae that the court was illegal and that they were nothing but a bunch of putschists. Ceausescu recounted the schools and buildings he had built, the hospitals and roads, and declared that he had created the most decent and caring country in the world. What about the palaces in which they lived, the prosecutor asked. The palaces belonged to the people, Ceausescu answered. They asked him about his Swiss bank accounts. Elena demanded proof.

Asked if they would sign statements that any money found in Swiss bank accounts belonged to the people of Romania, both

Ceausescus refused. After some more back-and-forth, the prosecutor declared the investigation concluded.

In his closing statement the prosecutor declared that he found the two accused guilty, and demanded the death sentence and the impounding of their property. Apparently, he was both prosecutor and judge.

In a confused reordering of business, the defense attorney provided by the court then had a chance to speak. In a lengthy oratory, he listed even more comprehensively than the prosecutor the crimes committed by the two accused and repeatedly insisted that this was a legal proceeding. Hefflin thought that if this was the defense attorney, they had no need for a prosecutor. In the end, the defense attorney pled with the defendants to claim insanity as their only possible defense. The Ceausescus were incensed that such a prevarication would even be suggested. The proceedings ended with the prosecutor once more calling for the death sentence.

Hefflin was stunned at the ineptness of the proceedings, the *ad hoc* accusations without the introduction of any evidence or witnesses, the inadequate preparation. The verdict and punishment had already been decided before the trial had even begun. The repeated declarations that this was a legal military tribunal made it clear that no one there thought so. He could see by the expressions on the faces of the accusers that they felt shame at being there, forced to be the judges, jury members, and executioners. Balzary and Boris had been right: Romanians needed blood. He glanced at Boris now and saw the slight smirk, the perverse appreciation of the farce that had just been conducted.

The Ceausescus were ordered to stand, then the soldiers attempted to lead Nicolae out of the room.

"No, together, together," Elena cried. "We want to die together."

The request was granted. The soldiers brought twine and began to tie the hands of the accused behind their backs. "Shame! Shame! I brought you up like a mother!" Elena protested to the soldiers.

Nicolae did not resist.

CHAPTER FORTY-THREE

Târgoviște
December 25, 1989

THEY WERE LED down a corridor, allowing them a few seconds to think, perhaps to reflect on the finality of the situation. Elena complained that the rope on her wrists was hurting her, while Nicolae smiled at one of the soldiers, as if this were all a joke—*you've had your fun, it was a good gag, really, but now it's time to stop this foolishness.*

When they reached the end of the corridor, the soldiers pushed them out into the courtyard where three other soldiers stood brandishing rifles. Before Hefflin could reach the exit, automatic gunfire rang out.

The television news later that day showed the entire trial, which lasted less than an hour. Hefflin was relieved that the camera had not panned around to show his face. After the trial, the film immediately cut to the courtyard. The three-man firing squad had opened fire as soon as the Ceausescus had reached the wall, before even the cameraman could capture the moment. All that the film showed was a cloud of dust during the last burst of gunfire, then the mangled bodies of the Ceausescus on the ground. Nicolae had dropped to his knees, the upper part of his torso thrown backward. Elena was sprawled sideways, her purse beside her. The camera swooped in on the blood pooling around them, the still faces, the empty fish eyes—gory images that had to be shown to the people, who were all too eager to believe in conspiracies, in fake blood and fake bullet holes, in doppelgangers substituted at the last minute.

It was December 25, 1989. Christmas Day.

What the television cameras did not capture were the last words uttered by Elena Ceausescu: "You motherfuckers!" Nicolae Ceausescu reportedly began singing "*The Internationale*," a nineteenth-century socialist anthem, just before the bullets started flying. He didn't get to finish it.

Hefflin watched the television screen in the embassy as the image of the new leader appeared: Ion Iliescu.

"Where the hell did Iliescu come from?" Stanton muttered sourly.

The sudden surfacing of Iliescu was also a surprise to Hefflin. Iliescu had not been involved in any demonstrations and no one was aware he had any role in the revolution. Boris certainly hadn't mentioned him. Hefflin knew the man's career well. Iliescu had been a loyal communist. He had even served as the Central Committee's head of the Department of Propaganda and had been regarded as Ceausescu's heir apparent until the early 1980s, when he had been sidelined by Ceausescu, who felt threatened by his popularity. Iliescu had never denounced communism, having proposed instead a kinder, gentler, Gorbachev-style socialism.

And then Hefflin remembered. It all made sense. Iliescu had attended Moscow State University at the same time as Gorbachev. They had been classmates.

❋   ❋   ❋

Shooting in the capital continued for several days following Ceausescu's death. The entire army was now united on the side of the revolution, but sniper fire continued. The question on everyone's mind was who was doing the shooting? Conventional wisdom had it that the snipers were remnants of the Securitate, and yet no one could explain their purpose in these futile killings. Ceausescu was dead. A new government, calling itself the National Salvation Front, had taken power, with Iliescu at its head.

On the third day there was a report, buried under more important developments, that a fire had broken out in the Securitate headquarters. Because of continuing sniper gunfire, the fire department was slow to respond. Reportedly, many of the archived files in the basement had been damaged. Mobs of civilians took advantage of the mayhem to enter the building and rummage through the files.

That evening, Hefflin received a call at the embassy from Soryn. Throughout this bloody episode, he had barely thought about Soryn and Pusha. It now occurred to him that Soryn may have been caught up in the fighting, perhaps part of the Securitate that was still resisting.

"I have the dossier!" Soryn yelled into the phone.

"The offshore accounts?"

"Yes, it's all here, the banks, the account numbers, the sums in each. Everything. The pig stole even more than anyone imagined."

"And Pusha?"

"She is ready. Our deal is still good, no? The girl and the dossier for asylum in America."

"I still haven't met Pusha," Hefflin said.

"The revolution has interfered with my plans," Soryn explained. "You can understand that she is terrified. But she agrees. Are your plans ready?"

"Yes, but I have to verify both her identity and the dossier," he said, trying to hide his excitement.

"Once we are in the American Embassy, you can verify both," Soryn said. "I do not think the CIA will go back on its word once we are on American soil. That is the deal, yes?"

He reluctantly agreed.

"I will contact you with the time and place for the meeting."

CHAPTER FORTY-FOUR

Bucharest
December 1989

THE STREETS WERE alive with the sound of gunfire. The National Salvation Front reported that forces loyal to the old order, referred to as "terrorists," were still resisting.

Hefflin left the Athénée to make his way toward the rendez-vous point. Soryn had called at his hotel, shouting the location where he would be waiting with Pusha. The man was obviously panicking.

Hefflin tried to stick to the dark side streets, his hand in his coat pocket over the pistol. He was no longer worried that the Securitate was following him. They now had their own skins to worry about. But he was concerned that he might run into a crazed Securitate agent or foreign "terrorist" fleeing for his life and shooting at anything that moved.

Armored personnel carriers rumbled down the streets, while pockets of civilians were huddled in doorways, some holding a bottle of *tsuika* or vodka, eager to celebrate the mopping-up operation. Every so often a shot rang out, a sniper somewhere on a rooftop. Between the eruptions of gunfire, there was an eerie quiet. On a dark street that looked deserted, he passed by a wide doorway where a dozen or so people were huddling.

"Hey, where are you going?" a man asked in Romanian.

"Look at his clothes. He looks American," a woman remarked.

"God bless America," the man yelled out in English, raising a bottle.

Hefflin nodded and pressed on. At the corner he took a left onto another dark street, their meeting point. But it was deserted. Where were they? He checked his watch and realized he was a few minutes late. Had they already come by and left? Had they been detained? Had Pusha not been able to get away?

A figure wearing a military uniform emerged out of a dark doorway.

"Mr. Hefflin, over here. . ." The man waved at him.

"Soryn? What are you doing in that uniform?"

"I also hold the rank of lieutenant colonel in the army," Soryn said. "The uniform will get us through the checkpoints. Is the airplane ready?"

"It's too late for an airplane," Hefflin said. "All nonessential personnel have already been evacuated. Stanton has arranged other means, by ship from Constanta."

"By ship? During this chaos? There is fighting in the streets, for Christ's sake. The army has closed all exits out of the city."

"Not to worry. We have our people. We do this all the time."

"I am, *was*, a colonel in the Securitate," Soryn cried. "A colonel! Do you know what that means? I will be hunted down like a mad dog."

"You'll be housed in the embassy for a few days, until everything quiets down," Hefflin said calmly. "Then you'll be driven to Constanta in an embassy car, carrying a diplomatic passport, which the CIA will provide for you. Do you have the dossier?"

Soryn sat on the curb, took off his military cap, rubbed his face. He looked conflicted, unhinged. "I think you are not telling me the truth."

"Stanton is ready for you," Hefflin said.

Soryn moaned, then looked up at him. "I am married, you know. One child, a boy."

"No, I didn't know," Hefflin said. "I assumed . . . You're not wearing a wedding band."

"What a coward I am. Running with my tail between my legs to save my own skin. That is the kind of man they made me." Soryn let out a ragged laugh. "The lives I have destroyed, the innocent people I have put in jail, or worse. For what? For *them*, the apparatchiks. But you learn not to look at yourself. After so many years of doing these things, it all seems natural. That is how it is done, they tell you. Until one day it all comes to an end, and you have to answer for everything. You know—" he looked up at Hefflin, his eyes glistening— "I have not been to church since my mother last took me when I was ten. I refused to go. All I wanted was to join the Party and become Securitate, because they were the ones who had all the power."

Soryn thought for a moment longer, unable to decide. Then he stood. "There will not be any deathbed conversions for me. I am Securitate. Always have been. Yes, I have the dossier. I will give it to you when we are safe inside the embassy."

Hefflin didn't like the game Soryn was playing but let it go, since he was playing one, also. There was no ship in Constanta, no plan to get Soryn out. There had been no time for arrangements. Even though most CIA personnel had remained in Bucharest, the rest of the embassy staff had been reduced to a skeletal crew. Hefflin only had plans for one: Pusha. Now that the revolution had succeeded, the border would soon be open, at least for her.

"All right," Hefflin said. "Where is she?"

"Around the corner. Come."

He followed Soryn into an alleyway where he spotted a military vehicle parked in the shadows, the outline of a figure sitting in the back. *Is it really Pusha?* He stood frozen . . . All those years of yearning for her, and yet he wasn't ready to see her. He'd imagined this moment for over twenty years and thought he'd prepared himself for it, but a paralyzing terror had now overtaken him.

"Get in, we are in a hurry," Soryn ordered in a military voice, then pushed Hefflin toward the car.

Hefflin shook off his reverie and got in next to the young woman, not daring to look up, afraid of what he might see. There was a strong aroma of cheap perfume. Soryn slid into the driver's seat and turned on the ignition. The car started moving.

"Hello. You speak Romanian?" a woman's mellifluous voice asked in stilted English.

He forced himself to turn and look at her. It was too dark to see her face properly but he could make out long blond hair, a dark coat, black knee-high leather boots. As they drove, the moonlight momentarily illuminated her face—a flash of bright red lipstick, overdone blue eye shadow, large blue eyes, a pretty face—then darkness again. *Did Pusha have blue eyes?* He couldn't remember.

"No, very little," he said in English.

"I am Pusha. What is your name, please?"

"Do you remember Vasili?" he asked, his voice a trembling mess.

"Of course, my childhood sweetheart. I think of him many times every day. You are taking me to him?"

The longing to switch to Romanian, their common childhood language, urged him on until it overwhelmed him. What was the point of continuing this absurd charade? He had to make sure it was Pusha, and that she was truly returned to his life.

"Do you remember my childhood name?" he asked her in Romanian.

She drew in her breath, her hand up to her throat. A long moment during which she stared at him.

"You are Vasili?" she asked in Romanian.

"I thought so!" Soryn called out in Romanian. "I thought I recognized you but wasn't sure. It's the eyes. They don't change. You used to be called Fili. That's it. Fili."

She recovered from her surprise and reached for his hand. "I know I've changed, Fili. I've grown up, and so have you. We'll need time to get to know each other again."

Time. Twenty-odd years. But still, he had to ask, to be sure, his analyst's obsession. "Do you remember the old gypsy?"

"Tanti Bobo, of course," Soryn said with a laugh.

Hefflin wanted to shoot the man.

"The old gypsy," Pusha said. "I vaguely remember her. Is she still alive?"

"You haven't gone back to the old neighborhood?" he asked. "Yes, she's still alive. She told me to find you."

"She was sweet. A lovely woman, for a gypsy."

The car stopped for a group of men in military uniforms, a checkpoint. He heard Pusha draw in her breath. A soldier holding an automatic rifle approached, then saw Soryn's uniform and saluted. "Lieutenant Colonel."

"I'm taking these Americans to the embassy," Soryn said. "They're lost."

The soldier laughed, then waved them on.

Pusha let out a sigh of relief. "It was a wonderful love we had, wasn't it?" she said. "I know we can get it back." She squeezed his hand.

He detected a slight accent, a touch of . . . what? Though he hadn't been in Romania since his childhood, he'd been studying the various dialects and accents as part of his job. It helped to identify intercepted NSA recordings. Hers had a flavor of . . . the Banat region.

"Have you lived in Bucharest all your life?" he asked.

He felt her stiffen.

"I lived in Arad for a few years," she said quickly, "when I was younger, when my adopted father was transferred there to be the . . . local minister of finance."

"Arad. That explains the Banat accent," he said.

"You know Romanian accents?"

"Just a hobby of mine," he said.

"Are you really a State Department official or a spy?" She gave a nervous laugh, Soryn joining in.

"Does it matter?" he asked.

"No. I just want to know the man I'm going to America with, that's all. The man Vasili—Fili—has become."

He was about to question her further—the letters she'd written, their afternoons under the apple tree, her time in the orphanage—but the car suddenly stopped on a side street. Ahead lay a small square in which a group of soldiers were crouching behind an armored vehicle. Two soldiers approached them and saluted.

"Snipers on the rooftops, sir," one of them said. "You'd better back up, take another route."

Single gunshots, the soldiers in the square ducking behind their vehicle. One of them responded with automatic fire.

Soryn started backing up the car, but behind them, another armored vehicle was now entering the street. Soryn waved for it to back up, but it simply stopped and stood its ground.

"Damn them. I have to get out and order them back," Soryn said in Romanian. "Stay here."

He got out of the car and started walking toward the vehicle from which several soldiers were emerging. He started yelling at them to back up to let them pass, then stopped and stiffened. An officer had stepped out of the vehicle. Soryn saluted, removed papers from his pocket, and handed them over. The officer studied the papers then looked up at Soryn.

"Where are you taking these civilians?"

"To the American Embassy, sir," Soryn answered. "Special orders from the Ministry. An American diplomat and his assistant."

The officer stared at Soryn for a moment, then back at the papers. "I want to see their passports."

"Right away, sir."

The officer waved to his men and the armored vehicle started backing up while Soryn got back into their car.

"He's a damned full colonel," Soryn said, and started backing the car toward them. The armored vehicle had now retreated enough to give them room to go around it.

"How are you going to explain her Romanian passport?" Hefflin asked.

"I'm not."

The officer held up his hand for them to stop, but they drove right past him and onto the main street. Hefflin heard the gears grind, then felt the car surge forward. The officer yelled for them to stop. Soryn accelerated. The officer again yelled to stop, then ordered his men to fire. Bullets hit the back of the vehicle. Hefflin pulled Pusha to the floor of the car and covered her with his body. As they turned a corner, the back windshield exploded.

Pusha screamed. The car jolted onto the sidewalk, hit a fire hydrant, then crashed into the side of a building.

When he looked up, he saw Soryn trying to get out of the car. He was holding a leather dossier in one hand and a wooden case the size of a small valise in the other. As Soryn struggled to open the car door, Hefflin grabbed the dossier from his hand. Soryn cursed, then started running down the street carrying the wooden case. Pusha was screaming hysterically, her arms flailing. He grabbed hold of her wrists.

"Let me go! I didn't sign up for this, let me go!" she screamed.

"Pusha!"

"I'm not your stupid Pusha. He just paid me to pretend, to help him get out of the country."

"What?"

"He told me what to say, got me these clothes. He said it was my chance to get to America."

"But he knew about the apple tree," he said, not wanting to believe her.

"I don't know anything about no stupid apple tree. Now let me go!"

He let go of her wrists and she bolted out of the car. As she scrambled into a building, the soldiers appeared at the end of the street. *Stay or go? Diplomatic immunity.* But he already knew that during a revolution he couldn't count on such niceties.

He crawled out of the car carrying the dossier and started running. Behind him the soldiers were yelling for him to halt, then he heard gunfire just as he entered an open doorway. A dark corridor. He had to find another exit. At the end of the hall there were steps going down, then a door. He pushed down on the rusted handle, but it didn't budge. He kicked it and on the third try it clanked open.

He found himself in a dark alley between buildings. Two doors in the next building, one slightly ajar. He squeezed through it and he was now in another corridor, this one even gloomier than the previous one. He felt his way in the dark until he reached another corridor that led him to the main exit on another street. After peering out and finding the street empty, he started running, keeping in the shadows. He turned another corner and ran some more. He could no longer hear any gunshots or soldiers' voices.

Slow down, walk, he told himself.

Even if they found him now, he couldn't be connected to Soryn. Just an American diplomat observing the revolution, like the rest of the population. He placed the dossier inside his coat, entered another hallway, and sat on the steps. He needed to think. *Fucking Soryn. He would do anything to save his skin— abandon his family, take advantage of my nostalgia for a lost childhood, hire a stranger to pose as my Pusha. Christ, where did Soryn find her?* But he realized that couldn't have been too difficult. Any young woman would give her right arm to get out of the country and go to America.

Then he thought of the apple tree. Where could Soryn have found out about the apple tree?

He heard a heavy vehicle approaching. As he peered around the doorway, he spotted a personnel carrier entering the intersection ahead. It stopped, the soldiers scrambling out. The same officer, now shouting orders. The soldiers fanned out, some entering buildings. Were they still searching for him?

A single gunshot, an echo, the officer's head exploding in slow motion, the body toppling like a log.

Sniper. But where had the shot come from? The soldiers scrambled behind the armored vehicle. Another shot, a soldier going down clutching his chest, the others rearranging themselves. The sniper was a damned good shot. The soldiers opened fire, pointing up at the rooftop of the building in which Hefflin was hiding. Another single shot, this one bouncing off the armored vehicle, then single shots coming from other rooftops. Two more soldiers went down. More snipers. An ambush?

Across the street he saw movement inside a doorway. Civilians. One of them raised his camera. *Reporters? In the middle of a sniper ambush?* Several of them came out onto the sidewalk to take pictures. One of them, a female, started running across the street, to get a better angle, no doubt. *Is she insane?* And then he heard a single shot coming from the top of his building. The woman cried out, then her body sprawled forward onto the cobblestones. *Fucking guy. The sniper just shot a reporter. A woman.*

The soldiers started firing up at the roof of his building. *Fucking guy.* Hefflin took the stairs two at a time, not thinking, just going by instinct, the gun in his hand. On the four flights up, he realized he'd reached the top floor.

It was dark. He ignited his cigarette lighter and searched until he found a set of narrow stairs to the roof. He went up silently and reached a door, slightly ajar, enough for him to squeeze through. The rooftop was flat. He crouched down, trying to gauge the situation, a half-moon peering between the clouds. He couldn't see the sniper. He heard another shot, from the other side of the roof, behind the brick chimney. Automatic fire from the soldiers, some hitting the side of the building, others flying above his head. He peered around the chimney and spotted a figure in the shadows crouching behind the parapet. He stood and aimed his pistol, a thirty-foot shot. Unsure of his aiming skills, he started slowly walking toward the figure, the automatic gunfire obscuring the sound of his footsteps. The sniper, still unaware of his presence, peered over the parapet, aimed, and fired. As Hefflin approached, ten feet away now, he saw the military uniform, the lieutenant colonel's insignia, then the wooden case that had housed the sniper's rifle. He waited until the automatic fire ceased, then let out a soft whistle. Soryn turned and stared at him. Their eyes met.

"Fili?"

"Fucking Luca, you were always an asshole. Now you're a murderer."

As Luca Soryn swung toward him and raised his rifle, Hefflin pulled the trigger. Soryn's body danced against the parapet like a marionette until Hefflin heard nothing but the clicks of his empty gun. The body lay motionless, the head bent to one side, the chest riddled with bullet wounds. Hefflin spat. *No deathbed conversions.*

CHAPTER FORTY-FIVE

Bucharest
December 1989

His hands trembling, his knees wobbly, he made his way down the stairs and into the street. Sniper gunshots were still coming from multiple rooftop locations. The soldiers were being outflanked. The woman was still lying facedown on the street, but he could see her moving.

A loud boom, then a second—the armored personnel carrier firing two rounds of the small cannon, the top floor of a building exploding, the roof collapsing. This was his chance. He started running. A bullet hit the pavement, then a second one struck the street a few inches from him as he reached the woman. With one movement he lifted her onto his shoulder and started running toward the nearest open doorway. As he reached it, another bullet hit the side of the wall. He felt a wet warmth on his chest. He gently placed the woman on the floor of the hallway and checked himself for wounds. He found none. The blood was all hers. Her right pant leg was drenched with it. He tore the pant leg away and found a pulsating wound on her thigh. Christ. The bullet had hit an artery. He took her scarf and tied it around her thigh above the wound. The bleeding decreased, now just an ooze.

"Dankeschön," she moaned.

"I have to get you to a hospital."

"American? Thank you." She tried to sit up, then groaned and fell back down. "My camera, film."

"The camera is here." He showed her the camera, which was still hanging from her neck along with her leather bag. "I'll place it in your bag with your film. Lie still while I try to get help."

Outside, the shooting continued. As he tried to figure out how to get the reporter to a hospital, he heard a noise from inside the building. Footsteps. He immediately thought of his gun, then remembered he had used up all the bullets on Soryn. He dragged the wounded reporter behind the stairs, then realized the footsteps had stopped. He turned and stared at a young man brandishing a Kalashnikov. Middle Eastern. The man looked frightened, his hands shaking, making the Kalashnikov dance. A moment of indecision.

This is it.

As the thought flashed through Hefflin's mind, he started saying a prayer out loud. He didn't know why he did this—he wasn't particularly religious. The words just came out of his mouth: "Our Lord, who art in Heaven—"

"American?" the sniper blurted out, his face bursting into a broad smile. "You American? I love—"

A shot, followed closely by another. The man tumbled forward, the rifle clanging onto the stone floor, his body sprawling next to it, blood slowly pooling.

In the corner, standing on the steps rising from the basement, stood another man holding a pistol. As the man approached, Hefflin recognized him.

"Balzary!"

"What the hell are you doing? Trying to be a hero?" Balzary asked.

"How are you here?"

"I thought you needed some help," Balzary said. "One of my men spotted you and called to say you were in trouble. You're a fucking analyst, out of your depth."

"A sniper wounded a reporter," he blurted out. "I need to get her to a hospital."

"I saw the whole thing. Damned stupid of you to run out like that. Where is she?"

"Behind the stairwell. She's bleeding. We have to hurry."

Balzary leaned over the body of the gunman and quickly searched it. From the pants pocket he removed a passport. Hefflin caught a glimpse of it. Lebanese. What the hell was a Lebanese doing as a sniper in Romania?

Balzary slipped the passport into his pocket. "Let's get your reporter. I have a car in the back."

They carried the reporter down to the basement then out a service door. In the dark street was a black Dacia. They put the reporter in the back seat, unconscious now, blood still oozing into her clothes. They drove off.

"Where are we taking her?" Hefflin asked.

"Floreasca Hospital, the only decent one near here," Balzary said.

As Balzary drove through the back streets, avoiding the gun battles at major intersections, a nagging thought was creeping up in Hefflin. The Lebanese sniper had smiled when he realized Hefflin was American and was about to say more before Balzary shot him.

*　　*　　*

They drove onto Strada Polona, the most direct route. There were no cars on the road. The woman was still unconscious but the oozing seemed to have slowed down. He didn't know if this was good or bad. Maybe she'd lost so much blood that her blood pressure was very low.

Balzary supplied as much speed as the miserable Dacia could muster. After a few minutes they spotted a tank up ahead with several soldiers milling about. A checkpoint. As they approached at full speed, he could see them scrambling, their guns pointing at the car speeding toward them. One soldier held up his arms. As Balzary slowed down, Hefflin fished for his passport and held it open out the window.

"Emergency!" he yelled in Romanian. "We have a severely wounded foreign reporter. Going to Floreasca."

The soldier glanced at his passport, then smiled. "American? And your Romanian is so good?"

"Born here," he cried. "American diplomat now. Please, we're in a hurry."

"You're Romanian! God bless you, and God bless America. Follow me."

The soldier jumped into a military vehicle and turned on his siren. They were now traveling quickly, the siren blaring, the Dacia barely able to keep up with the soldier's vehicle. Two more checkpoints appeared but they were waved through without even slowing down.

"I didn't know you're Romanian," Balzary said as he was driving.

"Keep it to yourself," he said. "I don't need complications from the Securitate."

"Got it. You're just a dumb American." Balzary laughed. "You and I are in the same situation, it appears."

"No," Hefflin said. "I never wanted to return to this wretched country."

When they reached Floreasca Hospital, the soldier helped them carry the reporter inside.

"I must leave you here," Balzary said. "Stay out of trouble." With that he turned and drove off.

Upon entering the emergency room, Hefflin was confronted with controlled chaos, as his father had described it. Several members of the medical staff dressed in white gathered around the unconscious woman and began cutting off her clothes while others started an IV and sent off blood to be typed and crossed for transfusions.

"A bullet hit an artery in her right thigh," he told the doctor in Romanian. "I placed a tourniquet on it a half hour or so ago."

"Snipers?"

"Yes."

"Damn them. We have two of them here," the doctor said.

"Securitate?"

"No, that's the strange thing. Foreigners. Middle Eastern."

Middle Eastern again. Just like the Lebanese gunman Balzary had shot.

"Can I see them?" he asked.

"I don't know." The doctor hesitated. "Whoever they are, they're still patients. Privacy and all that."

Hefflin removed his State Department ID and showed it to the doctor.

"American State Department."

The doctor's eyes lit up. "And you speak Romanian like a native."

"I'm more than State Department." He stared into the doctor's eyes.

The doctor's face grew pale. "Ah, in that case, you should see them."

The doctor led him inside a long room where he now saw the sorry state of Romanian hospitals. The floors were grimy, the gurneys rusted, with missing wheels, the sheets dirty, some with caked blood that had obviously been there for some time. Bandages rolled up on the tables were soiled, though the doctor assured him that they would be boiled before being reused. There were few IV bags hanging above the beds, even for patients that had been wounded.

"We're short on antibiotics, morphine, medicines of every kind," the doctor said, obviously noticing his expression of distress. "Our instruments are rusted relics from fifty years ago. We have only one X-ray machine that is working. Our operating rooms are broken down—only two have functioning anesthesia machines, and they are decades old. It is a disgrace. I can't wait to go to Western Europe where I can practice real medicine."

"I thought Floreasca was supposed to be one of the better hospitals," Hefflin said.

"It is. You don't want to see the other ones," the doctor said.

They stopped in front of two gurneys on which lay two young, dark-skinned men. One had his right shoulder bandaged, the other had a bandage wrapped around his head.

"The shoulder wound was clear through, thank God," the doctor said. "If we needed to get the bullet out, I don't know if I could have found a surgeon willing to come in with all this shooting. The other man was hit over the head with a piece of wood by a civilian as he was fleeing. He has a concussion."

"Did they have papers on them?" he asked.

"Yes, here." The doctor removed two passports from envelopes attached to the beds. One of them was Libyan, the other Syrian. The stamps showed they had both entered Romania from Hungary on tourist visas several days before the Timisoara uprisings.

He remembered two of the words he had overheard Stanculescu say to Stanton: "tourists" and "snipers."

"They speak no Romanian," the doctor said.

Hefflin approached the man with the shoulder wound. "Who sent you to Romania?" he asked in English.

The man avoided his eyes and remained silent.

"We've tried English, French, and German," the doctor said. "If he understands, he won't say anything." The doctor waived his hand in disgust. "It's a shame to waste our IVs on him, but I figure the authorities will want to talk to him. Hell has a special place reserved for these snipers."

"One of them is already there," Hefflin said, "a Securitate officer who shot the journalist I brought in."

"God bless the one who got him."

"By the way, it just occurred to me," Hefflin said. "In case she needs to be transfused, do you test your blood supply for HIV?"

The doctor eyed him with a look of exasperation. "No. The idiot president didn't want to admit that HIV could exist in Romania. To him it was a Western disease due to Western debauchery. Can you imagine? In a country like ours, where the only amusement left is sex and where everyone, men and women alike, regard the vows of marriage as only a suggestion."

"Well, Ceausescu is gone now," Hefflin said.

"Thank God, and may the devil torture him like he tortured us," the doctor said. "We'll try to avoid giving her a transfusion, if at all possible."

Hefflin loitered in the emergency room as several wounded soldiers were brought in and the controlled chaos began again. He tried to imagine his father as he must have been in his youth, treating patients in a similar emergency room in Bucharest, perhaps even the same one, and felt that he was in the process of completing some circle of life.

He left the hospital feeling as if fateful forces were converging on him. It was obvious that Stanculescu had known about the snipers posing as tourists, and he had told Stanton about it. Did Stanculescu have prior intelligence? What had Stanton done with that information? Then he remembered the dossier inside his coat and resolved to focus on the job at hand. He had to verify its authenticity.

✻　✻　✻

"So, a Securitate guy actually gave you this?" Stanton said, rifling through the dossier. Hefflin had borrowed the doctor's car to bring it to the embassy straight from the hospital. "I'll get these accounts checked out. How the hell did you manage it?"

He recounted the events of that night, leaving out the girl posing as Pusha. The deal with Soryn had simply been the dossier in exchange for asylum in the U.S.

"And then you shot the guy?" Stanton marveled.

"He was a sniper. He had shot a woman reporter," he said. "I guess I just got angry."

"Remind me not to get you angry." Stanton handed the dossier to an assistant to have the offshore accounts confirmed. "Still, if Balzary hadn't been there, you'd be dead."

"The second sniper had a Lebanese passport," Hefflin said. "When he heard me pray in English he smiled. He was about to say he loves America when Balzary shot him."

"Lebanese?" Stanton rubbed his chin.

"Not only that, but in the hospital emergency room there were two other Middle Eastern snipers who were being treated for wounds."

"Are you sure about this?" Stanton asked.

"I saw the passports myself. They came in through Hungary on tourist visas."

Stanton reflected for a moment, then looked away dismissively. "Tourist visas, in the middle of winter? I'll check into it. In the meantime, keep it under wraps." He then stared directly into Hefflin's eyes. "The important thing is that you kept your cool. I take back everything I said earlier. You'd make a fucking good field agent."

Stanton found two glasses and poured some Johnny Walker Black. "You know, if this money's there, you'll probably get both of us a promotion. And I'll owe you." He clinked Hefflin's glass and swallowed the drink. "Ain't that a fucking irony?"

A technician returned within the hour with the report, which he handed to Stanton. As Stanton read it, his face grew grim. "They're old accounts. They were emptied out about two years ago."

Hefflin's stomach felt as if someone had kicked it. "You were able to verify that so quickly?"

"The NSA can do fucking wonders," Stanton said.

"I don't know how you guys do it," Hefflin said as he rose to go. "You go to all this trouble, even risk your lives, and then find out that your contact lied, or got you outdated information, or was just plain wrong."

"Welcome to field operations," Stanton said.

CHAPTER FORTY-SIX

Bucharest
December 1989

EVEN THOUGH IT was a sunny day, Hefflin felt a sense of fore-boding as he pushed open the wrought-iron gate and entered his old courtyard. There was no movement inside. Tanti Bobo's wooden stool under the apple tree stood empty. He approached her one-room apartment and knocked on her door. Hearing no answer, he entered. The room was desolate, the fireplace cold, a chair overturned.

"They took her to Coltea Hospital," a female voice said. A middle-aged woman, her head covered by a black kerchief, was standing at the open doorway. "There was a man who came to see her. A neighbor said he looked like Securitate." The woman spat. "When he left, the neighbor came by and found her on the floor. She was badly beaten."

A putrid taste rose up from his stomach. *What kind of man would beat an old woman?*

"When did this happen?" he asked.

"Several days ago. Such a pity. She didn't even get a chance to see the Tyrant dead." She crossed herself and walked away.

Several days ago? The apple tree. Soryn had beaten the informa-tion out of her. He gritted his teeth, biting down on the furious desire to kill Soryn a second time.

He caught up to the woman and asked for directions to Coltea Hospital, then started walking. It wasn't far, a half hour walk, she said. He looked for a taxi but couldn't find any. He pushed himself into a run. He followed her directions and reached as far as Piatsa Unirii where he found a taxi. He gave the driver ten dollars and told him to go to Coltea Hospital. The driver hesitated, then slipped the bill in his pocket. "For a moment I forgot that the Tyrant is dead," the driver said and then laughed. "Now I can own American dollars."

They took a left on E81 and within a couple of minutes Hefflin saw it, a majestic nineteenth-century stone building with red horizontal stripes, just as the woman had described it.

He rushed inside, a frenzy urging him toward panic, and prayed he wasn't too late. The receptionist directed him to the third floor, room 309.

The bed was empty, the room smelling of disinfectant.

"You looking for the old gypsy woman?" a male voice asked.

He turned to see a man wearing a white coat.

"Yes. The receptionist said she was in this room," he said.

"I guess her list hasn't been updated yet." The man shrugged. "Things move slowly here. I'm Doctor Batrinu. I was with her when they brought her in. She came in badly beaten, but the actual cause of death was a stroke."

Hefflin sank into the chair. Tanti Bobo. In his child's mind he thought she'd always be there, the same way he had thought of his parents, and of Pincus. Now she, too, was gone. His past seemed to be evaporating, one person at a time, like a dream that fades away as one awakens. And now he'd be forever carrying the guilt. It was his fault. If he hadn't asked Soryn the question, she would still be alive. He tried to hold back the torrent of tears.

"You knew her?" the doctor asked.

"Yes," he said, "from a long time ago."

"Any next of kin?"

"No. She was alone."

"How well did you know her?"

"She was practically my mother," he said, the idea suddenly taking shape, becoming solid, making him choke.

The doctor let out an embarrassed cough, as if he had crossed a line calling an old gypsy his second mother. "Well, then, perhaps I should give it to you." The doctor went to the nurses' station and returned holding a tin box. Hefflin immediately recognized it as Tanti Bobo's box containing the old pictures.

"She was clutching it when they brought her in. It took some effort to pry it from her fingers."

The magic box with all her memories. He took it and thanked him. "When is the funeral?"

"Well." The doctor looked away. "Since no one came for her, she was buried in a pauper's grave yesterday, at Ghencea Cemetery. But you won't be able to find it. It's an unmarked grave, one among many. We didn't know her name, you see. She had no papers on her or in her home. How did she live? Obviously, she wasn't getting any pension from the government."

"She told fortunes," he said. "She didn't need much."

The doctor shook his head. "What was her name?"

"I don't know. I only knew her as Tanti Bobo."

He thanked the doctor and walked away, fearing he'd break down in front of him. Ghencea Cemetery. It was only a stone's throw away from Strada Sirenelor, but there was no point in going there. An unmarked grave among many.

CHAPTER FORTY-SEVEN

Bucharest
December 1989

IT WAS A little past seven in the evening and the bar at the Athénée Palace was filled with journalists. Now that the borders were open again, all the major news outlets in the world had sent reporters to cover Romania's revolution. Hefflin recognized several languages: French, German, Czech, Finnish—or what he thought was Finnish. Everyone was in a celebratory mood. The snipers had all disappeared, and the city was left to gather its dead and begin the mourning process. He had been having breakfast at a café that morning when a waiter slipped him a note. It read: "The Athénée Bar at seven."

So here he was, waiting at the bar with his first vodka, mulling over the fact that he hadn't yet heard from Catherine. It had been a week since he had seen her in Timisoara. He had been waiting for her to get in touch with him, but he'd received no word. She had disappeared yet again. Their meeting in Bucharest in the middle of a revolution seemed absurd on its face, but then it wasn't all that unlikely, he told himself. She was a reporter covering the same revolution to which his own job had brought him.

He spotted a tall man walking through the door sporting a three-day-old graying beard, dark sunglasses, a full-length, black Astrakhan coat, and a bright smile.

"I just bought this coat this morning," Boris announced. "It is Russian. Very good quality. What do you think?"

"It looks good on you," Hefflin said, "but you didn't buy it, not in Bucharest. My guess is you took it from some official who is now shivering in some jail cell."

Boris chuckled. "The deputy minister of internal security, but it fits perfectly, as if it were made for me. I think it is fate."

"It is theft, but since you stole it from a thief, it is also justice."

They ordered vodka and toasted the revolution.

"So, now that the revolution is over, what will you do?" Boris asked.

"It depends on you, to some extent," Hefflin said. "You're the one who demanded I be here."

"I wanted you to witness history. To create history! Was I wrong?" Boris winked. "You can give your friends back home a firsthand account of the famous trial."

"They've already seen it on television," Hefflin said. "No, you wanted me here to get my cousin to convince Ceausescu's money man to give up the offshore accounts."

"That, too." Boris smiled. "Unfortunately, our efforts failed. I do not know if we will ever see that money. But who knows? Fate has a way of surprising you."

"What is going to happen to this country now that you've given it its revolution?"

"Not me. It was the people's revolution," Boris said with a straight face.

"With a little help from Gorbachev. And now he placed his old classmate in power."

Boris let out a deep sigh. He seemed worried, dissatisfied.

"Yes, Iliescu," Boris said, "another apparatchik, part of the same gang, but now a reformed capitalist. He has seen the light, as you Americans say." He chuckled. "His conversion is something Gorbachev did not plan on."

"Still, he's Gorbachev's man. That's why you wanted us to keep our hands off, so Gorbachev could put his own man in charge."

"I wanted to avoid a bloody revolution," Boris said, his face suddenly serious. "I knew that it would not matter in the end who came to power. The truth is, there are very few real communists left in the world, even in Russia. Everybody has been repeating the same lies all these years just to get along."

"Even Gorbachev?"

Boris waved his hand. "Gorbachev is a strange fellow. I think he really believes in a gentle socialism, a little bit like you, no?"

Hefflin shrugged. "I don't think I believe in anything anymore."

"Gorbachev will not last long," Boris said. "He will always be known as the man who brought down the Soviet Union. History may be more kind, but not the Russian people."

"That's too bad," Hefflin said. "I think he's a great man."

"Why? You think he saw all this coming? The destruction of the Soviet Empire?" Boris shook his head. "He is not a revolutionary. He wants *perestroika* and *glasnost*, remember? A slow unclenching of the fist, an evolution out of stagnation. But it is all getting away from him."

"Still, he planned *this* revolution." Hefflin waived his hand. "A quiet coup, you said. But you misled me. You brought in those foreign 'tourists,' the snipers you needed to make sure there was blood in the streets to anger the people, to push them to a revolution. An old Soviet technique. Just in case the army refused to fire or the people needed a little extra gore to get them to revolt. Those snipers have since disappeared, even the wounded in the hospitals."

"They were flown out two days ago," Boris said. "The only plane allowed to take off during this whole time of transition. But you are wrong, my friend. It was not us."

"Don't bullshit me, not now," Hefflin said. "It's all over. Tell me the truth."

"It was not our operation," Boris insisted. "And I found out about it too late."

He looked at Boris, then through him. "Then whose operation was it?"

"I think you know," Boris said.

Hefflin felt the bile rise up in his throat. "The snipers were ours?"

"Stanculescu was part of it," Boris said. "A CIA asset. He brought in the snipers through Hungary. Our quiet coup, led by General Militaru, never got off the ground. I give Bush high marks for outflanking Gorbachev. After all the blood, the people will never accept socialism in any form, even Gorbachev's kinder one."

Hefflin gulped down the vodka to keep the nausea from overwhelming him. All those dead civilians. Balzary must have been part of it, since the snipers came in through Hungary. That was why Balzary shot the Lebanese sniper before he could say he loved America. Balzary must have known Hefflin was not party to the plan.

"Christ. And I thought we were the good guys," Hefflin said.

"Don't be so naïve, Vasili. The Americans and the Russians have been starting revolutions for decades. Bush was once the CIA director, remember?"

"I know all that, but until now revolutions were just historical events for me. Seeing one up close, the blood, the bodies on the streets . . ."

"Still, Bush's plan was brilliant," Boris said. "Iliescu has now outlawed the communist party and proclaimed himself a capitalist. He is Gorbachev's man in name only."

"So, who is pulling the strings now, Bush or Gorbachev?" Hefflin asked.

Boris smiled. "Who do you think? America has all the money. The Soviet Union is bankrupt, about to fall. Gorbachev thinks he can save socialism from the ashes of communism, but he is deluded. The men behind him, the ones waiting to pick up the pieces, know better. Russia can become a wealthy country. It has oil, natural gas, minerals, as you well know. For the inspired, there are billions to be made when the time is right. In the end, Gorbachev is just an enlightened apparatchik. The men of vision are the ones who will come after him when the system finally falls. They will become our versions of the Carnegies and Rockefellers."

"You sound like you want to be one of them."

"Why not? You think I want to remain a salaried KGB colonel forever?" Boris winked. "So, I ask again, what are your plans?"

"I guess I'll be returning to the States," Hefflin said. "There's nothing keeping me here."

Boris smirked. "You sound dejected, Vasili. But you never really thought you would find your childhood again, did you? Oh, don't think I do not know what you have been going through, returning to your old house and finding everyone gone."

"You know about that?"

"I am a spy; I keep telling you. So, you have not found your little Pusha."

"You know about her, too?"

"I read your book, remember? I know everything."

"Do you know about Luca Soryn?" Hefflin asked.

"Who the devil is he?"

"Ha! You don't know everything."

He recounted his adventure with Soryn—the deal for asylum, the false Pusha, the female reporter, the shooting of Soryn, and the outdated dossier of Ceausescu's accounts.

Boris stared at him for a long time, his eyes betraying surprise, followed by admiration.

"I am impressed," Boris said. "You, an analyst who is used to sitting behind a desk. The dossier was outdated, yes, but still you got it. Maybe you should be a field agent."

"No, thank you," Hefflin said. "I like where I am, sitting in the last row corner seat watching the world go by."

Boris shook his head and made a "tsk, tsk" sound, like Hefflin's mother always did. "You did the right thing to shoot him. Men like that give us spies a bad name."

Hefflin downed his drink and ordered another round for both of them. "Still, I'm no closer to finding out what happened to Pusha." He didn't say anything about Catherine, his other love lost. It would have been too depressing, even for Boris.

"You never know. Life is full of surprises," Boris beamed. "You are still young. You will fall in love again."

"You are an eternal optimist."

"How else do you get through this fucking life? Besides, the world is better this morning: one more communist tyrant has fallen. That is something to be happy about."

Hefflin hesitated. "I have one more question to ask you. Something to show you, actually." He took out the old picture of his father alongside two other men from 1947 and showed it to Boris.

Boris's face lit up. "Where did you get this?"

"From Tanti Bobo, the old gypsy in my neighborhood. It belonged to my father. That's him, on the left. The next man is Professor Pincus, I think. And I'm going to go out on a limb and say that the third man is you."

Boris held the picture up to the light. "I was pretty good-looking when I was young, no? At least the ladies thought so. How did you recognize me?"

"When you picked me up to go to Ceausescu's trial, you were clean-shaven. You looked vaguely familiar. It took me a while to connect you to the third man in the picture."

Boris's face suddenly darkened. "Yes, and that is poor Pincus. They killed him like a dog in his own house. What for? The world is going crazy." He brushed the air with his cigarette.

"You know about his murder?"

"Of course." He sighed. "But now that you showed me this, I must tell you one other thing, the main reason I told you to come to Bucharest right after they killed old Pincus." He fiddled with his cigarette, then took another sip of the vodka. "You see, the way my packages arrived to you every few months was a little complicated. First, one of my people, a trusted person, traveled to Cambridge and gave it to Pincus. Then Pincus instructed one of his Harvard student recruits, as part of their spy games, to drive to New York and place the spike in Central Park. A different student each time. They thought it was all just a game. Pretty good, no? Two cutouts, the second always different. So, when Pincus was killed, my agent learned of it the next day and called me. I thought at first that my activities were blown and that the KGB killed Pincus. I was sure I was next. Then I thought of you, that you might also be in danger. So, I took the next flight to New York to place the message in Central Park myself, the message telling you to come to Bucharest. I was the homeless man with the beard I think you noticed and ignored. A mistake on your part, but you were only an analyst then." He smirked. "I thought I could protect you better here, in Bucharest, where I had some power."

"Protect me? Why is it your job to protect me?"

"Ha!" Boris waived an arm that almost hit the waiter going by. "All these questions. You are like one of those interrogators that drive prisoners crazy with their questions."

"So, you think it was the KGB that killed Pincus?" Hefflin asked.

"That is what I thought at the time, but I quickly found out it was not. The KGB knows nothing about Pincus, or my activities."

"Avery thought it was the Securitate. But then I came across the picture of the assassin." He told Boris that the assassin was the same man who was photographed with Stanculescu at a bar in East Germany.

"The same man?" Boris rubbed his beard. "And Avery thinks it was the Securitate?"

"Avery has audio from a bug in Pincus's house. The assassin spoke native Romanian with Pincus. I heard it myself. The man told Pincus that he had been found guilty of treason *in absentia* and that he was there to carry out the sentence."

Boris let out a guffaw. "The Securitate is mostly an internal organization, to suppress the people. They rarely murder anyone outside the country. But I intend to find who ordered the killing of Pincus before I leave this earth."

They were both quiet for a long time, pondering the situation.

Hefflin finally asked the obvious question. "How did you know my father and Pincus in Bucharest in 1947?"

Boris smiled. "A riddle wrapped in a mystery inside an enigma, that is what Churchill called Mother Russia."

"Is that it? Is that all you're going to tell me?"

Boris sighed. "It is a long story, one that I intended to tell you while you were here. But events caused our little tête-à-tête to be postponed. It will need to be postponed yet again, I am afraid, for I have to catch a plane in an hour. My story has to be told properly, an entire night with several bottles of vodka. But I will give you one hint so you have something to think about until we meet again: The story is based on a theme in many of your ancient Greek tragedies. The *Oresteia*, for example. Just turn the theme on its head."

With that, Boris downed the rest of his vodka and patted him on the back. "Expect more missives from me in the future. Our arrangement is still good, no?"

"Yes, if you want it."

"Of course. But you must not tell your superiors anything about me. That will remain between us. And be careful. The story with Pincus may not be finished yet. *Dasvidanya*."

Boris turned to go but then stopped and turned back. "Ah, I almost forgot. I have a little gift for you." Boris handed him a little blue bottle resembling a small perfume bottle.

"What's this?"

"This is what I coated my glass with," Boris said. "Who knows? Now that you have succeeded in making some enemies, it may come in handy. Use a Q-tip. Don't touch it."

Hefflin inserted the bottle into his jacket pocket. "I plan on returning to my boring analyst job, but thank you."

Hefflin watched as Boris sauntered out of the Athénée Bar like a demigod who still held the fate of Hefflin's life in his hands. *No, the story with Pincus is definitely not yet finished, but it soon will be.*

Hefflin finished his drink, then booked a seat on the morning flight to New York. He was done with Bucharest. Pusha would be almost impossible to find, if she were still in Bucharest, or in Romania, for that matter. Or if she were even alive.

He had one more task to complete before he left, his most difficult.

CHAPTER FORTY-EIGHT

Bucharest
December 1989

STANTON LIVED IN an apartment on Soseaua Nordului in a building used for mid-level diplomats and embassy functionaries. Hefflin arrived a little after ten in the evening and found Stanton in jogging pants and a T-shirt, his hair mussed, his feet bare.

"What the hell is the emergency?" Stanton asked.

As Hefflin moved past Stanton, he smelled the whiskey. The one-bedroom apartment was furnished with old, pre–communist era furniture. On the coffee table was an open bottle of Johnny Walker Black and one glass. The ashtray was filled with cigarette butts.

"Celebrating by yourself, Jack?" he asked, then took off his coat and threw it on the couch. He then poured some whiskey into another glass and drank. "You'll forgive me if I'm not in a celebrating mood, not after all the slaughter."

"Feeling betrayed, if you must know," Stanton said. "Not that it's any of your fucking business."

"I've been to the embassy looking for you. The place is deserted. New faces rummaging through the files. What's going on?"

"What's going, my dear analyst, is that I'm off the payroll, effective immediately, as per Avery."

"Fired?" He didn't understand. *Why would Avery fire him? Did Stanton overstep his orders?*

"It was the snipers, right, Jack?" Hefflin asked. "Balzary knew all about those tourists, didn't he? They entered Romania through Hungary. That's why he shot the one aiming the gun at me, so he wouldn't say he loved America, that America was paying him. Balzary realized I wasn't read in on the operation."

Stanton remained silent.

"It wasn't the Russians who sent those snipers. It was us," Hefflin continued. "Gorbachev wanted a quiet, bloodless coup. But you, and your Langley friends, weren't satisfied with that. You wanted a real revolution. Isn't that right, Jack?"

"I see you and your buddy Boris put your heads together." Stanton smirked. "Maybe you should figure out who you're working for."

"I thought I was working for the good guys," Hefflin said. "The ones with the white hats."

"You're a fucking Boy Scout!" Stanton shouted. "You don't know shit about the real world."

"Why don't you enlighten me?"

"Fuck you. Go back to your desk and let the adults do the real work."

Hefflin didn't know where the sudden rage came from, or how the whiskey in his glass splashed all over Stanton's face.

Stanton cried out as the alcohol burned his eyes. "You fucking—" But he didn't finish his sentence before Hefflin's fist caught the angle of his jaw. Stanton stumbled and landed hard on his back. He lay on the floor for a moment wiping his eyes, then rolled over and stood.

"All right, analyst boy." Stanton spat blood. "I'll show you what a real field agent can do." He feigned a punch, then swung his leg across Hefflin's knees, which brought Hefflin crashing over the coffee table, surprised that the overweight, chain-smoking slob had such effective moves.

"Get up, you soft piece of shit," Stanton growled, "or I'll kick you like a dog."

Hefflin staggered back to his feet just as Stanton landed a blow to his stomach. He doubled over, his gut burning, the pain swiftly rising into his chest and stealing his breath. He saw the shadow of another blow swing toward him but he stepped to one side in time, then backed away to catch his breath.

"There's no place to run, you coward," Stanton said, then took a step toward him and threw another punch, which Hefflin parried. Hefflin then swung the side of his foot onto Stanton's knee. He heard a crack. Stanton wailed in pain. Hefflin followed with a knuckle punch to the bridge of Stanton's nose, which brought the heavy man down.

"I got the same combat training as the field agents, Jack," Hefflin said. He pulled Stanton into a chair and slapped him across the face. "Now, tell me what's going on, or I'll break every bone in that fat body of yours."

"F-fuck you," Stanton stammered.

Hefflin slammed the side of Stanton's chest with his fist and felt a rib give way.

Stanton howled. "All right, all right, you moron, I'll spell it out for you. But don't blame me later for telling you. Give me a fucking drink first."

Hefflin picked up the whiskey bottle and filled Stanton's glass. Stanton gulped it down, coughed, then looked up at him.

"Yeah, the snipers were ours. All right? Boris had you wrapped around his little finger. Leave Romania to us, we'll take care of it, he said. A quiet coup, he said. And then what? Did you ask yourself that?"

"Thousands of people died, Jack."

"The Romanians needed to have a real revolution, a clean break with communism," Stanton said. "Gorbachev planned to install Iliescu, his university buddy. Langley couldn't have any of that. Once there were bodies on the streets, the people wouldn't stand for anything short of a clean break with the past. That's also why—" Stanton wiped his mouth as if trying to wipe away those last words.

"What, Jack? What else did you do?"

Stanton hesitated, taking another drink.

"I'll punch it out of you," Hefflin said, raising one fist.

"Milea," Stanton burst out.

Hefflin didn't understand at first, then didn't want to understand. "Milea, the defense minister?"

"You read the reports," Stanton said. "The people got really incensed when they were told he had committed suicide. Just as Langley predicted. They were convinced Ceausescu had killed him because he had refused to order the troops to fire on the people."

"And we murdered him?"

"He was a fucking criminal anyway," Stanton said. "They all were. We had a guy in the Securitate, Milea's private guard."

"Christ." Hefflin sank into a chair to take it all in. "The snipers, the dead civilians, and the minister of defense, all to incite the populace to revolution, to block Gorbachev's plan. But Iliescu still got the job."

"Yeah, but now he can't ever go back to communism or socialism or whatever Gorbachev planned. Did you hear Iliescu speak?

Communism is dead, he said. Democracy and capitalism are what he's preaching now. He knows the people would hang him otherwise."

"This is about business, isn't it, Jack?"

"Of course it's about business. The place is ripe with opportunity for American multinationals. Military equipment alone will be worth billions, never mind infrastructure, hotels, the rest of it. It took Bush a while to figure that out." He spat. "Another Boy Scout. You have no idea what it took to convince him to finally do something."

"I think I do, Jack," Hefflin said. "It took the murder of Pincus."

Stanton looked up, surprised. "Ah, shit. How do you know about that?"

"Avery showed me pictures of a man entering Pincus's house. He said the man was Securitate, but his face was turned away from the camera. But then I saw another picture on your desk of the same guy entering the house, this time with his face showing. Then Boris showed me a picture of Stanculescu, your asset, at a bar in East Berlin with the same guy who entered Pincus's house. Was he CIA, Jack? Boris thought so, but he said the guy was also a free agent at some point."

Stanton shrugged. "The CIA needed a Romanian expat. Because of the audio surveillance inside Pincus's house, they needed a guy who spoke native Romanian, who could pass as Securitate. They also needed a Romanian to pose as part of the Securitate detail in East Berlin so that he could approach Stanculescu. We don't have that many field agents that are native-born Romanians." Stanton let out a laugh. "Don't you get it? Fucking Bush needed to get angry, he needed a push. Otherwise, he'd have let Gorbachev have his way with this miserable country. Not that I give a rat's ass, but the higher-ups do."

"Which higher-ups?"

"The businesspeople, you moron; who do you think runs our country?"

"Who ordered Pincus's death?" Hefflin asked.

Stanton sighed, taking a long time to answer. "It was Avery all the way."

"Anyone higher up?"

"I get my orders from Avery," Stanton said. "Where he gets his, that's his business."

Hefflin drank directly from the whiskey bottle, then lit a cigarette. "All this for a few bucks."

"Not just a few bucks. Billions," Stanton said. "And a new member of NATO and the European Union. I guess it's all for the good. You can't make an omelet—"

"—without breaking eggs. Yes, I've heard them all. But why were you fired?"

Stanton let out a chuckle. "That's the irony. I was never a part of it. I only found out later."

"What?"

"I was following the official policy of the United States to lay off, to let the Romanian people decide. But your message from Boris lit a fire under the dons at Langley. The Russians weren't going to keep their dirty little hands off. Gorbachev was to create a quiet coup, you said. Langley concluded that Gorbachev intended to keep Romania in his sphere of influence. Boris's message, in addition to Pincus's assassination, finally pushed Bush over the edge. He authorized Avery to have a parallel operation, behind my back." He gulped more of his drink. "When I found out about the snipers from Balzary, I wired Avery for an explanation. Fucking idiotic thing to do. I got no response. Then I contacted Stanculescu and met him at the safe house in

Timisoara to try to convince him to scuttle the operation. But the snipers were already in place by then."

"When I saw you with Stanculescu, you were trying to convince him to drop the plan?"

"Yeah, another major fuckup on my part. Stanculescu contacted Avery to complain that I, the CIA station chief, was interfering with the plan." Stanton tried to smile. "You may think I'm an asshole, and in many ways I am, but slaughtering civilians crosses my line. The operation went ahead anyway, and I was in deep shit with Langley. Then I started digging and stumbled across the pictures of Pincus's assassin. I recognized the guy. He's a Securitate operative, recruited several years ago. He's done some wet work for the Agency over the years. So that's when I realized there was something else going on here. I started creating a file. That's what you saw on my desk, my work in progress. I had no further contact with Avery until he arrived in Bucharest."

"Avery is in Bucharest?"

"Arrived last night with his team. They're here to sanitize the office and return all Agency personnel back to the States. He's putting a new team in place and returning to Langley tonight."

"And your file?"

"They have it, everything. It will never see the light of day."

Hefflin sat stunned for a long time, then rose to leave. "Sorry, Jack. I had it all wrong."

"Of course you did. You're just a fucking analyst." Stanton gave him a bloody smile. "So what are you going to do with this information?"

Hefflin said nothing, just took his coat and headed for the door.

"If you start making wild accusations, you won't last twenty-four hours out there," Stanton called after him.

Hefflin stopped and faced Stanton. "Twenty-four hours is more than enough time to get Avery hanging by his balls."

As he turned to go, he saw that the front door was now open. In the doorway stood a man holding a pistol with a silencer. Both he and Stanton recognized him: Pincus's assassin.

Hefflin stared at the barrel of the silencer, waiting for the flash, the slight recoil, the glow of pain in his chest. He closed his eyes, accepting all that fate was going to deliver, just as he had with the sniper. Then he heard them, four muffled shots in succession. He waited for the pain, the shock that came with it, the last gasps of life. But nothing happened. He opened his eyes and saw Stanton's body crumpled on the floor, blood oozing through his shirt.

He stood stunned, unable to move.

The man quickly approached Stanton's body and fired the coup de grace.

"Why?" was all Hefflin could muster.

"Orders. To tie up loose ends," the man said.

"And me?"

"Not my orders. Get lost, before my orders change."

Hefflin left the apartment, his mind numb, and dissolved into the darkness of Bucharest. He thought of waiting for the assassin so he could take revenge for Pincus's death, but what was the point? The man was just doing his job.

✳   ✳   ✳

The next morning on his way to the airport, he drove by Irina's house to say goodbye. She seemed philosophical about the events taking place. "We never had an honest government before communism, so why expect one after?" she said. The news about Vulcan had reached her. She shrugged. "He's one rotten apple among many. Count me among them." When he handed her the piece of paper with the numbered account Vulcan had left her, she just crumpled it up and threw it back at him. "And don't bother trying to hide my history with him," she said. "Nobody cares. We all just want to forget." He kissed her goodbye and she promised to come to New York at some point, after things settled down. "We first have to learn how to act like civilized people," she said, "before we are allowed in public." She gave him a wry smile and embraced him.

When he boarded the plane to New York, he was grateful that he was returning to civilization, if that's what one called it.

CHAPTER FORTY-NINE

New York
January 1990

THE LONG FLIGHT back to New York felt like a slow process of depressurization from the depths of hell. Hefflin's sense of relief at returning to New York was mixed with a deep depression over the loss of his idealized childhood, his innocence, and the young love that he now knew was gone forever. The second love of his life, Catherine, who had resurfaced in Timisoara, was yet another wild card for which he had no explanation. He decided to set it aside for the time being. He had a more pressing task.

Upon landing at JFK, he took a taxi to the New York Public Library from where he sent two sets of anonymous faxes, one to the director of operations, Avery, and the other to the president's national security advisor. The faxes contained two pictures: one showing General Stanculescu meeting with a CIA operative in East Germany, the other showing the same CIA operative entering the home of Professor Pincus. Along with the pictures was a message: "Avery ordered the assassination of Professor Pincus and made it look like a Securitate hit to convince the president of the United States to start a bloody revolution in Romania. He also used the same agent to recruit Stanculescu to the CIA and to assassinate Jack Stanton, the CIA station chief in Bucharest, who discovered Avery's plan. The photos and other materials will be mailed to the *New York Times* in five days if no action is taken."

He had no other material. It was a bluff, but he hoped that the photos alone would at least start an investigation.

Three days passed with no word of any action on anyone's part. Hefflin was scheduled for the usual debriefing in a few days and his anxiety was mounting exponentially. Did the national security advisor not believe the photos were real, or was he also in on the plot to push the president to intervene in Romania? Some part of Hefflin started to fear that he was still the same naïve analyst he had been at the beginning of this adventure and that he had not learned a thing about the real world.

At midnight of the fourth day, he was awakened by the buzzer on his apartment intercom. Still in a daze from sleep, he pressed the intercom button.

"Yes?"

The doorman's voice said, "There is a gentleman here to see you, Mr. Hefflin. A Mr. Sullivan."

Hefflin tried to break through the fog of his somnolence. *Sullivan?* He didn't know anyone by that name. "Can you repeat the name, please?"

"Sullivan," the doorman said more loudly. "He says he works with you."

"I think you'll want to see me, Bill," a familiar voice said over the intercom.

A surge of adrenaline suddenly wired his brain and body. He rushed to the window and peered down at the street below. A black limousine was idling in front of the building.

His mind started panicking. He thought of escape routes, of the fact that he had no gun, then settled his nerves long enough to push the button. "Let him come up."

A few minutes later, he heard a knock on his door. When he opened it, he saw the sneering face of Avery with two large men in black overcoats standing behind him.

"Hello, Bill. I apologize for the late hour, but I thought a private tête-à-tête was in order before your debriefing. May I come in?"

Hefflin opened the door wide to let the director of operations enter the apartment. The two goons remained outside. Avery did not remove his coat but simply settled himself into the couch.

"This is certainly a surprise," Hefflin said, trying to inject sarcasm in his voice. "I was asleep, actually. May I offer you a drink?"

"A straight scotch will do fine," Avery said. "Will you join me?"

Hefflin went to the cabinet in the corner, removed two glasses, and poured from the open bottle of Johnny Walker Black. He handed one to Avery and sat in the chair across from him.

"It's funny how a brand of liquor makes its way throughout a department," Avery said after tasting the scotch. "I don't know who started the tradition. I believe that was Stanton's drink also. Poor soul. A shame what happened to him."

Hefflin was silent for a moment, unsure of whether he should acknowledge that he was present when the assassin shot Stanton. He decided that feigning ignorance was his best option.

"Stanton? What happened to him?"

"He was shot," Avery said, "right in his apartment in Bucharest. Probably someone settling old scores. Securitate, most likely. He must have made some powerful enemies while there."

Hefflin groaned. "Bad luck. A lot of old scores were settled during that chaos. He was a good man."

"A good field agent, that is undeniable," Avery said. "But his loyalty had come into question over the past few weeks."

"Oh?"

"Yes, well, it comes as quite a surprise to all of us. Apparently, he was involved in a convoluted plot to create a bloody revolution in Romania." Avery took another drink and crossed his legs.

"Really. How so?"

"Among other things, he hired snipers from some Middle Eastern countries to kill a few civilians and," Avery chuckled, "a few soldiers as well, just to get the revolution rolling. Quite brilliant, actually. He was quite an anti-communist. A fanatic, it turns out. He apparently believed that the Romanians would never have dared an uprising without first spilling some blood to get them riled up. All without the Agency's knowledge, of course. I only found out about it when I arrived in Bucharest after it was all over."

"You were in Bucharest?"

"Yes, just for a couple of days, to oversee a cleansing of our unit. It was a viper's nest, as it turns out. We found all sorts of evidence in his office. Quite a messy fellow he was. Papers everywhere—payments for a Lebanese charter plane to bring the snipers in and out, a list of their names and country of origin, requisitions from certain friendly Romanian army units for Kalashnikovs for the snipers, and so on."

Hefflin gulped his drink and tried to make sense of Avery's ranting. Where was Avery going with this? Did he think he could lay all the blame on Stanton? But the possibility suddenly did not seem that outlandish. Stanton was dead, unable to defend himself.

"It's hard to believe he did all this on his own," Hefflin said.

"I think so, too, as do my superiors." Avery stared at Hefflin for a long moment.

"Who else do you think was involved?" Hefflin asked.

Avery finished his drink and set the glass on the coffee table between them. "I think you know, Bill."

"How would I know?"

Avery leaned back in the couch, assessing him. "You were born in Bucharest and were taken away by your parents at a crucial age. It left you permanently scarred, unable to adjust to a new life in America, and yearning to return to your beloved country. You have been mourning the devastation that the communist regime has wrought on it all these years, eager to use your analytic skills to bring down the regime but frustrated that your efforts were not succeeding quickly enough. When Boris asked you to come to Bucharest to create history, as he put it, you saw your chance."

"What?" Hefflin's chest suddenly filled with a tight gnawing.

"Once there, you found a kindred spirit in Stanton, another extremist who couldn't just sit back and let the Russians install their own regime, as Boris demanded. So you and Stanton devised this plot, a bloody revolution, to ensure that the Romanian people would never stand for anything other than capitalism and democracy."

"None of this is true," Hefflin stammered.

"No? And when all was said and done, you tried to lay the blame on me. Was that Stanton's idea or yours?"

Hefflin couldn't speak. He could hardly breathe.

"I know you think you're a field agent now, after your experiences in Romania, but you're still just an amateur," Avery said. "The same day that you landed in New York, the faxes were sent from the New York Public Library. Did you think we wouldn't put two and two together?" Avery let out a laugh.

The two men remained silent, staring at each other.

"You'll never make it stick," Hefflin finally said.

"Oh, I think I will," Avery said. "Papers, notes, they can all be created and destroyed. That's what the Agency excels at; you should know that. We've toppled governments that way for decades. You don't think we can take care of an eccentric, disgruntled, neurotic analyst?" Avery picked up his glass but noticed it was empty and set it back down. "There is another option."

"Another option?"

"You see, Bill, I think you have the makings of a great field agent, if only you took a larger view of the terrain, a more realistic view. Realpolitik, a philosophy Kissinger ascribes to. You deal with the world as it is, not as you would like it to be. If you have to make deals with the devil, or bloody your hands a bit, so be it, as long as the outcome is favorable. As it turns out, Romania is now better off than it would have been without the revolution. Everyone has sworn off communism or socialism and has found an albeit late conversion to democracy. We'll have a new NATO partner and a new country in which to expand our business interests. How is that bad?"

"Thousands of innocent people were slaughtered," Hefflin said.

"Yes, unfortunate collateral damage, but considering the larger good, worth it. Don't you agree? Now, there is a solution, but for that I think we need a second round of drinks, don't you?"

"There is a solution?" Hefflin asked, ignoring the request for more drinks.

"There is always a solution, Bill. That's the fun part of the little games we play. For starters, let's say we just forget about those faxes you sent and you give me all the photographs and other material you claim to have."

"What about the national security advisor?"

"We don't have to worry about that." Avery waved his arm. "You think that an anonymous fax from a public library would go directly to the national security advisor? It first has to be vetted, researched, verified. Besides, it was all on paper, which is perishable. If it had been sent electronically, that would have been another matter."

"He never got to read it?" Hefflin asked.

"I'm afraid he's too busy to waste his time with crank faxes," Avery said. "Do you know how many crank calls and anonymous faxes we get every year? We have personnel dedicated just for the purpose of going through that slush pile to try to figure out if there is anything worth pushing up the chain of command, pushing up to you and your fellow analysts to spend your precious time to analyze. One of my people on the Security Council brought your little gift to my attention before anyone else saw it. I'm afraid it was all for naught."

Hefflin thought for a long time, dejected. He had underestimated Avery. The director of operations was playing chess while he was playing marbles. Avery had placed him in a no-win situation.

"So, what are my options?"

"You come under my wing where I can groom you to be the star field agent you were meant to be," Avery said jovially. "All this nonsense will remain a little secret between the two of us. Now, I think we need a second round of drinks to seal our deal, don't you?"

"And if I don't agree?"

Avery's eyebrows suddenly darkened. "Then you won't survive the next twenty-four hours."

Hefflin stood and felt his knees weaken as he went to the liquor cabinet. He pondered a moment, then chose two fresh glasses and poured the scotch. He then placed Avery's fresh glass next to the empty one.

"To our new arrangement, then," Avery said as he lifted his glass in a toast.

Hefflin hesitated, then raised his glass. "To our new arrangement."

They both swallowed their drinks and slammed their glasses on the coffee table.

"I'm glad we have arrived at a meeting of the minds," Avery said. "Now, I must—"

Avery did not get to finish his thought. His face suddenly became blotchy, his eyes bulged, his hands went up to his throat, then his head dropped onto his chest. Hefflin looked at his watch. Fifteen seconds, just as Boris had said. Boris had been right yet again. His little poison had come in handy.

Hefflin took Avery's second glass with the poison coated on its inside, along with his own second glass, and washed them in the kitchen sink. He then poured some scotch in the empty glasses to make it seem as if they were in the middle of their drinks, after which he took a deep breath to steady his nerves. A moment later, he rushed to the door, yanked it open, and cried out to the two men in the hall. "Come quickly! Something's wrong with the director!"

CHAPTER FIFTY

New York
January 1990

THE AUTOPSY ON Avery showed a probable cardiac arrhythmia as the cause of death, which was a conclusion that marched with an apparent cardiac condition for which he was being treated.

During the debriefing, Hefflin stated that the apparent reason for Avery's visit to his apartment was Avery's concern for Hefflin's personal security after Stanton's assassination in Bucharest. Avery wanted to know if Hefflin's activities in Bucharest might place him in danger from any remaining Securitate agents still active in the U.S. Hefflin stated that he did not think so.

The rest of the debriefing focused on his activities in Bucharest and his contacts with Boris. He mentioned nothing about Pusha or Catherine or his failed efforts at finding Ceausescu's offshore accounts. His assessment regarding the revolution was that it was a spontaneous uprising by the people, the result of decades of misery and oppression and Ceausescu's determination to stamp out any resistance with brutal military force.

By the end they seemed satisfied. They complimented him on his brave actions with the sniper, the subsequent saving of a journalist's life, and his valorous self-defense against the Securi-tate agents on the train to Timisoara. Someone muttered that he deserved a fucking commendation. He was patted on the back and told to take a few weeks off before returning to his analyst position.

He returned to his apartment in a daze, relieved that it was over. He had dreaded the possibility of being given a lie detector test, but nobody even mentioned it. After a shot of Johnny Walker Black, he was ready to focus on the other loose strings in his life.

Boris's relationship with Hefflin's father had left Hefflin perplexed. The Russian's hint that the reason for choosing Hefflin as the recipient of all the valuable intel could be found in the Greek tragedies both confused and intrigued him, and the suggestion to "just turn the theme on its head" added another wrinkle to the riddle.

He started digging into the themes of the Greek tragedies. He'd read several of them in college, including the *Oresteia*, which Boris had suggested. But that had been years before.

The *Oresteia*, a set of three plays, dealt with the curse on the House of Atreus. It described patricide, fratricide, even cannibalism caused by each succeeding generation in retribution for acts perpetrated by the previous one. As he reread the plays, his heart was repelled by the gore and brutality, and he couldn't imagine how he could have admired them so much in his youth. Now that he'd seen death and violence up close—even caused it—he could no longer idealize it in fiction. He was at a total loss as to how these themes could possibly have anything to do with him. He finally tossed the *Oresteia* aside and decided to forego trying to solve the riddle, at least for now.

During this time, he had also been thinking of Catherine, from whom he had not heard at all. A few days after his debriefing, he decided to call the number of the *Le Monde* headquarters in Paris that was on the card Catherine had given him. The

operator put him through to the assistant editor, a man named
Legarde, who told him that Mademoiselle Devereaux was out
of the country on assignment. The man would say no more. If
Monsieur would leave his name and number, he would make
sure to pass the information along to her when she called in.
Hefflin gave the man his home telephone number, which had
an answering machine attached.

He didn't receive any messages for the next ten days, but on
the eleventh he found a short one. Catherine's voice sounded
distant and crackly. She said she was in Tunisia on assignment
and didn't know how long she'd be there. His spirit was suddenly
in flight. Just hearing her voice made his chest ache with the
desire to see her again. Every day he checked his machine and
cursed it when he didn't find a message from her. As the days
went by, his spirit dropped to new lows. He placed several more
calls to the *Le Monde* headquarters and left messages with Monsieur Legarde who assured him his messages would be passed
on. How could she torment him like this, especially after their
night in Timisoara? Had she no heart? How could she say she
loved him and then treat him in this fashion? As he returned to
his analyst duties, he tried to put her out of his mind and concentrate on his work.

He didn't hear from her again until a month later. This time
she was calling from Poland, covering the Solidarity movement.
During the next few months, he received postcards from various
Eastern European countries culminating in an August voice
message saying she was in the Soviet Union covering its dis-
solution. He ran a search of *Le Monde* articles and found none
with her byline.

In September he flew to Paris on an assignment for the
Agency and dropped in at the headquarters of *Le Monde*. The

assistant editor knew of no one by the name of Catherine Devereaux or Catherine Nash. When he showed him a picture of Catherine he had photocopied from her Harvard yearbook, the man didn't recognize her.

"But I've been calling here and speaking to the assistant editor, a Monsieur Legarde."

"I am Monsieur Legarde," the surprised man said, "but I've never spoken to you."

Frustrated, Hefflin said, "Here, listen . . ." He picked up the telephone on the desk, put it on speaker, got an outside line, and called the number on Catherine's card. It was answered by a secretary who put him through to a Monsieur Legarde. On the phone, he told Monsieur Legarde his name and asked for Miss Devereaux.

"I'll give her your message," the voice on the line said.

"Don't bother," Hefflin said. "I'm standing next to you right now. I'll tell you in person."

The line went dead.

"Sorry for the misunderstanding," he said to the real Legarde, then walked out.

"Wait, *Monsieur*," the man called after him. "I need to know who has been using my name."

Hefflin just waved and left. He recognized the operation to be the work of a security agency. You call a specific number; the operator transfers you to some person who pretends to be the assistant editor of *Le Monde* and takes your message. The CIA used this procedure, too.

"So then, Catherine, or whoever you are," he muttered to himself, "who are you working for?"

CHAPTER FIFTY-ONE

New York
November 1990

OUTSIDE, THE WIND was howling, the winter sleet clattering on the windows of his new Upper West Side apartment, a large one-bedroom, third-floor walk-up. It had been a conscious choice, the result of his clandestine experiences in Romania. He had moved from his Upper East Side sixteenth-floor high-rise apartment into this nondescript brownstone on a quiet side street. It was still near Central Park, but its best feature was that it had no doorman. He no longer liked the idea of a doorman watching him come and go and knowing who visited him.

A few months after returning to New York, he had received an Agency medal for his bravery, an analyst who survived the assault of two Securitate agents, took out a sniper, and saved the life of a reporter. The medal, ensconced in a velvet case, was sitting on the mantlepiece above the fireplace.

In Romania, Iliescu had been democratically elected in the general elections that spring, and the country had begun its slow, drudging journey out of forty years of communism into some sort of democracy. But there were no heroes in the Romanian revolution, no Lech Walesa, no Vaclav Havel. Instead, some of the same apparatchiks took power under a different banner.

As for Catherine, she continued to send him postcards from various places around the globe, no longer mentioning anything about *Le Monde*. He assumed the man he'd spoken to on the phone had informed her that the jig was up. The missives were short, impersonal, without her name on them. "Took a dip in the ocean at Sharm-El-Sheikh. Off to the Czech Republic tomorrow," or, the latest one from just a few days ago, "Here to witness Lech Walesa's bid for the presidency."

What was she thinking? Feeling? Pusha and Catherine, the two loves of his life, one permanently gone, the other out of reach, her life a mystery. He was obviously cursed.

He hadn't heard from Boris since their last encounter at the Athénée Bar. That was almost a year ago. A lot had been happening in the Soviet Union and Hefflin's superiors were anxious to get Boris's take on it. The silence worried him. Had Boris been discovered? Was he even alive? As Hefflin had learned in Bucharest, life was cheap, especially during upheavals, like those now occurring in Russia.

On the way home from work he had bought a bottle of Châteauneuf-du-Pape for a private celebration, which he now opened and set on the coffee table to breathe. The occasion? He'd decided it was time to hang paintings on the walls of his apartment. He remembered the bare walls of his family home in Worcester, the result of his family always feeling like they were in temporary quarters, expecting to move again, like professional gypsies. He had carried this sense of impermanence throughout his life, until now. His return to Bucharest had cured him of it. For the first time since leaving Romania, he felt grounded enough to consider America his permanent home. Well, New York City, at least. So, no more bare walls. It was a major breakthrough and it required the proper commemoration. He had thought of inviting some friends over from the Agency, but that would have meant explaining the occasion of his celebration, then being obligated to dive into his past. What was the point

of creating a new name and legend if he was going to dash it all
with the truth? Better to leave his life an enigma.

Several framed lithographs were leaning against one wall,
impatient, eager to be displayed. He gathered the tape measure,
hammer, and hooks and began his work. On the wall above the
couch, he placed Renoir's *Dance at the Moulin De La Galette*,
a festive scene of late-nineteenth-century Paris. It gave him a
nostalgic feeling for a world long lost, which fit well with his own
lost childhood. He had decided to cure his nostalgia by facing it
every day, in the hope of becoming numb to it. On the opposite
wall he hung a Picasso depiction of a woman's face, her eyes
seeming to follow him wherever he went, much like his experience in Bucharest. This was followed by Matisse's *The Dance*,
in which nude women danced in a joyous circle, reminding him
of the hora, a dance popular in both Greece and Romania; and
then a Chagall, with a floating sheep's head evoking a dreamlike
state that alluded to his own surreal life. When he was finished,
he walked around the apartment with his glass of wine admiring
his achievement. For the first time there was life in his home,
and it felt complete.

The buzzer sounded. In his ebullience, he pressed the button
to open the downstairs door, a very un-CIA thing to do, but
he didn't think or care. The wine, and his joy at having passed
a hurdle of sorts by finally hanging up his paintings, made him
careless. When he heard the knock on the door, he swung it open
without even looking through the peephole.

Before him stood a tall man with a white beard and the long
white hair of a poet, wearing a full-length mink coat and mink
hat.

"Vasili, my boy!" The man spread his arms wide and hugged
him, almost lifting him off the floor. After three kisses on the

cheeks the man stomped inside, closed and locked the door behind him, and took off his hat.

"Boris?"

"You expect Santa Claus?" He was out of breath after walking up three flights. "What is this place? No elevator? No doorman? Are you hiding?"

"My new clandestine persona, a result of my field experience," Hefflin said. "What are you doing here? How did you find me?"

Boris sat heavily on the couch, still wearing his fur coat. "Let me catch my breath for a minute while you pour the drinks." He removed a bottle of Stoli from a deep pocket inside his coat and placed it on the coffee table. Hefflin brought two glasses and poured.

"To old friends." Boris raised his glass.

"To old friends," Hefflin echoed.

They emptied their glasses in one swallow then refilled them.

"You know, you are only one of five Western spies who have actually seen my real face." Boris smiled. "The other four are dead."

An uneasiness oozed into Hefflin's chest. "So, you're here to kill me?"

"No, my boy, they died of natural, or maybe unnatural, causes. I don't know, but not by my hand, at least. I am here on a different mission, a holy mission, to pay an old debt, a sacred debt."

Boris removed his coat and threw it onto a chair. Underneath he was wearing a three-piece gray pinstriped gray suit with red tie and matching handkerchief.

"It is a bespoke suit from Savile Row. See how it hugs my body? They measured me five times until it fit perfectly. Feel the material. Best money can buy," Boris crowed. "Of course, it will not fit perfectly for long. After a few months it will be too large."

Hefflin leaned forward slightly and gazed at him. "Why is that?"

Boris took out a pack of Dunhills and lit one.

"You know, in our business, we are most of the time alone," Boris said. "Yes, we have a woman here for a few weeks, there for a month, but in the end, we always have to go. That is the nature of our job. You did the right thing and became an analyst. For me, the only friends I can count on during cold winter nights are this—" he lifted the bottle of Stoli— "and this," he held up his cigarette. "Now even these friends have betrayed me." He started to cough, a deep hacking grind that brought up phlegm. He dug into his vest pocket for a handkerchief.

"You're sick?"

Boris dabbed at his mouth. "The doctors at Sloan-Whatever say I have a few months left, but what do they know?"

"Christ. And you're still smoking?"

"Why not? You want me to—how you say—close barn gates after horses have escaped?"

"Close enough."

"Well, that is not for me. I want to enjoy my last days. Vodka and cigarettes. And settling my affairs."

"But they have drugs these days, for all types of cancer," Hefflin protested.

"No, it is everywhere. It was there in Bucharest. That is yet another reason I asked you to come, because I thought I did not have much time left. But after all things were finished, which I will tell you about, I knew I would be able to come to New York where they could buy me some time. So, I postponed our little tête-à-tête."

"You've been in New York all this time?"

"No, not all of it. I did other things, too, which I will tell you about if you stop asking questions." Boris sat back and sipped his vodka. "Now, let us talk about you. Your future. You are made for bigger things than an analyst's desk. And that is why I am here. I have a story to tell you. It goes back many years, to the War."

"Which war?"

"The fucking Second World War. Is there any other?" His head eased back; his eyes focused on the far distance. "It was 1942. I was a stupid nineteen-year-old soldier in the Russian army. We were being invaded by the Germans; they were closing in on Stalingrad. Together with the German army was the Romanian army. As you know, the Romanians were on the side of Germany for most of the War, then they switched sides—whores who went with whoever they thought was on top. But never mind." He waved his hand. "It was in the middle of the miserable Russian winter. While we were engaged in a counteroffensive, I was wounded by shrapnel. As I lay dying in the snow, praying to God that he take me without further suffering, a young Romanian soldier appeared. He looked lost. He was holding a pistol, though I could see by the way he was handling it that he was an amateur. Then I saw the red cross on his armband."

"A medic." Hefflin felt a shiver pass down his spine.

"I was hoping he would just shoot me and put me out of my misery," Boris said. "I had lost a lot of blood and my wounds were still bleeding badly. But he put away his gun and started to tend to my wounds. He placed a tourniquet on my leg and told me how I was supposed to loosen it every hour or so. Then he listened to my chest and said that my right lung was collapsed. He clicked his tongue, probably like his mother used to do, then inserted this big needle into my chest. At that point I did not really care what he did, I could barely breathe. As soon as the needle was in, I heard air coming out of it, like out of a tire. A tension pneumothorax, he called it. The Russian doctors later told me I would have died in a short time if he had not acted quickly. Pretty soon I started to breathe better. By that time, I trusted him enough to let him inject me with penicillin.

"When he was finished, he said he was going to fire a flare so my comrades could find me. He was lost behind enemy lines. If he fired that flare, Russian soldiers would take him prisoner. But he did not care. He was a doctor and I was his patient, he said, and he could not just leave me. Can you believe it? What a man. I told him not to fire the flare yet, that he would never survive as a prisoner. I told him that he had to go back to his unit. So I took his flare gun and pointed him in the right direction, toward the Romanian lines. After he was gone for a half hour or so, I fired the flare and my comrades found me."

"That was kind of you to show him the way back," Hefflin said.

"He was the kind one, a prince of a man. He saved my life, an enemy soldier, though at the time I did not think I would survive. But just in case, before he left, I asked him his name."

"So, who was he?" Hefflin held his breath.

"That is the funny thing: he was not Romanian at all, but Greek. I think he hated the Germans as much as I did. I thought, 'What a crazy world.'"

"What was his name, damn you?"

Boris smiled. "Spiridon Argyris."

"My father?"

"None other."

The Russian bear story.

CHAPTER FIFTY-TWO

New York
November 1990

Tears blurred his vision. His father. Papa.

"My father used to tell me a bedtime story of a reluctant hunter and a wounded Russian bear," Hefflin said. "After the hunter saves the bear's life, they become lifelong friends."

"Ah." Boris sighed with satisfaction. "He tried to teach you a good lesson. We are all the same mortals with the same problems, except that the rotten politicians screw it all up for everyone. Anyway, do you remember at the Athénée Palace Bar you asked how I knew your father? I told you to read the Greek tragedies, especially the *Oresteia*. Did you?"

"I did, but couldn't quite figure out the riddle."

"I told you to turn one of the themes on its head. One of the great themes in Greek plays is that the sins of the father transfer onto the sons and daughters, who pay the price. If you turn it on its head, in your case it is the good deed of your father that has transferred onto his son, who reaps the benefit. Do you like that? That's pretty good, no?" Boris was beaming. "I told myself that if by some miracle I survived, I would never forget the good doctor. I vowed that I would repay him, whatever it took. But how do you repay someone, an enemy soldier no less, for saving your life? So, for the rest of my time on this earth, I have tried to do everything in my power to help him and his family."

Hefflin sat back, letting this unbelievable story filter through his mind. A Greek tragedy turned on its head to become a tragicomedy, with both happy and sad endings. He dreaded to broach the subject.

"How did you know Pincus in Romania in 1947?" Hefflin asked.

"He was a good friend of your father from their university days, may their souls rest in peace," Boris said. "I helped Pincus escape in 1948 with his wife. He was a Jew who pretended to be a Christian. That is how he avoided the Romanian pogroms during Antonescu's time. After the War, he was afraid he would be found out by the communists and did not know how they were going to treat Jews. Anyway, he hated the communists as much as your father. In the end, I helped him escape because he was your father's friend, another one of the many ways I tried to pay your father back."

"I found out who killed Pincus and why," Hefflin blurted out.

He quickly recounted the events regarding Pincus's assassin, his recognizing the assassin in the picture on Stanton's desk to be the same man that was in the picture with Stanculescu in East Berlin; that the assassin had acted on Avery's orders to kill Pincus to convince the U.S. president to start a bloody revolution in Romania; that the same assassin killed Stanton because Stanton had discovered the plot.

Boris took it all in with a stoic face. "So Avery did this on his own?" he asked. "And Bush doesn't know?"

"Nobody knows. At least that's what he told me when he came to see me after I got back." Hefflin recounted the evening with Avery and Avery's ultimatum—for Hefflin to either join him or face elimination.

"He wanted to keep you under his thumb for the rest of your life." Boris spat. "So? You are still alive. What did you do?"

Hefflin's guts churned, but he managed a tight smile because he knew that was what Boris would want. "Your little present came in handy."

"You coated his glass with my poison?" Boris slapped his thigh, his face aflame with pride. "Bravo, Vasili! You are turning out to be a great field agent." He poured some more vodka and raised it up in a salute. "That miserable man got what he deserved. So, back to my story. After the War, I joined the KGB. I was good at it, partly because I was no longer afraid to die. The life your father gave me was a bonus. I was not supposed to be alive."

"Maybe fate had decreed that my father would save you," Hefflin said.

"You believe in fate?" Boris asked. "Remember the movie *Lawrence of Arabia*? 'Nothing is written,' Lawrence says to the Arabs after he saves the boy's life. I love that line."

"But the boy eventually does die, by Lawrence's own hand," Hefflin said. "So fate still won in the end."

"Yes, I know. Still, I never believed in fate. But after you hear the whole story, you will see why even I changed my mind." He lit another cigarette even though he still had one burning. "So, as KGB I had a lot of freedom to move around, especially in the Soviet countries. I asked to be posted in Bucharest because I wanted to keep an eye on the good doctor and his family. We quickly became great friends, even though I told him I was KGB. We had many discussions late into the night sitting at the dining table in your house. He helped me realize how evil Stalin was and how communism could never work."

"You sat at our dining table? I don't remember you."

"It was before you were born. After a few years, I stopped coming to your house because I thought people should not see us together. But, yes, we sat around your dining table, the same table you saw in my apartment."

"That was *our* dining table?" Hefflin gasped. "That's why you commented on my inability to notice. I thought it looked familiar, but it never occurred to me that it could be the same one."

"It had so many memories that I bought it from your parents when they left the country. Which brings me to another example of how I tried to repay my debt."

He took off his suit jacket and started pacing back and forth in his vest.

"At one point your father told me your family had applied for visas to immigrate to Greece, their homeland," Boris continued. "They were still Greek citizens, after all. But, of course, the government did not let anyone leave. Their visa applications had gathered dust on some bureaucrat's desk for years. After some—how you say—bending of wrists—"

"Close enough."

"—I arranged for the visas to be approved on the grounds that you were undesirables. Bad for the communist ideal. A corrupting force. It was not that difficult, for I was a colonel in the KGB by then, the station chief in Bucharest, and I knew where all the skeletons of those bureaucrats were buried." Boris laughed, then started coughing.

"I remember it well," Hefflin said. "We were all surprised. I was sad to leave."

"Yes, your sweet Pusha, the love of your life, but we are getting ahead of the story. So, where was I? Yes, you and your family immigrated to Greece where you lived in a refugee camp for over a year. Your father, seeing the lack of opportunity in Greece for his son, decided to come to America—a brave sacrifice for a man in his fifties."

"My mother didn't want to leave Greece," Hefflin said. "She cried."

"It was all for the best," Boris said.

"You think?"

"I am sure. Your parents suffered, yes. But you grew up in a rich country, attended great universities, and are living in New York, the greatest city in the world. None of that would have happened if you had remained in Greece, and certainly not in Romania."

Hefflin had to admit all that was true, but it didn't take into account his suffering all these years—his lost childhood, his beloved Pusha. But he decided not to mention any of this.

"So, if Pincus and my father knew each other from the old days, they must have been in contact in America."

"Of course. They were hoping you would get admitted to Harvard."

His stomach sank. "I thought I got in on my grades."

"You did, my boy. No one fixed your admission. But once you were in, Pincus already had his eye on you for recruitment. He and your father had great arguments about that. Your father wanted you to be a doctor, like him, not a spy. After you joined the CIA, he did not speak to Pincus for months."

"You knew they were recruiting me?"

"Of course," Boris said. "Pincus had already arranged for you to join the Fly Club, one of the traditional places for CIA recruitment. Your three friends, who had already committed to join the CIA, were there to give you a taste of the select life of the chosen few."

Reginald Tyler, Tom Drier, and Allen Gainsworth the Third, or was it the Fourth? He wondered whatever happened to those guys. He hadn't seen or heard from them since graduation.

"Personally, I thought those spy games were a little amateurish, though not insignificant," Boris went on. "Some of the intel you provided on your targets was quite useful to the CIA."

Hefflin's chest tightened. "They told me the information would be destroyed."

"Ha! You think the CIA would throw away good intel? Because you discovered that one of your married professors had a lover, the CIA was able to blackmail him into admitting he was one of ours, then turned him to spy against us." Boris laughed. "And the Arab kid, the son of the Saudi defense minister, what was his name?"

"Abdullah bin Sultan."

"That's it. You found out he was gay—a big no-no in Saudi Arabia—and that he had orgies with his buddies in his dorm room. Well, he later became an important man in his country, a big banker . . . and one of the CIA's best assets. There were others, but let us not dwell on it. For you it was just a game, so let us leave it at that."

Hefflin wondered if Catherine had known that the games were for real.

"Let us go on. Now, as to Harvard and Columbia. All expenses paid both times. How did that happen?"

"I've always assumed it was the CIA," he said.

"And they let you assume it. Why not? If you thought they were responsible for your education, you would feel even more obligated to join them. They were only too glad to let you keep believing it."

"But if not them, then who?"

"His name is not important." Boris winked. "Let us just say he was a very wealthy Asian businessman who made his money in casinos. And let us say that during my travels I discovered that he was also heavily involved in the illegal arms trade, mostly to Africa. It did not take a lot of convincing for him to donate some of his ill-gotten gains toward your education. I considered it a form of penance, to get him past the pearly gates when his time came. Besides, for him, it was just pocket change."

"So, it was you?"

"Just further payment toward my debt."

"My God, I owe my entire life to you."

"You don't owe me anything. I owed your father. The CIA has a great deal of influence with the universities. As I told you, Pincus and I had been friends for many years, often working together. Whenever there was a crisis between our two countries, we tried to smooth things over, to avoid misunderstandings. Our leaders can be hotheaded at times. So, I told him I was interested in your future and that I would be paying for your studies. In turn he could try to recruit you to the CIA. If you joined, I told him I intended to become your mole, and make you a leading analyst at the CIA with a very valuable asset. He got what he wanted, someone high up in the KGB passing vital information to the Agency, and I got what I wanted, your success, all in the same bargain. A good arrangement, no?"

Hefflin sat back, trying to take this all in. "But why did you decide to spy for us? Surely it wasn't just to make me successful at the Agency."

Boris beamed, the way he did when he was going to talk about Hefflin's father.

"Ever since my marathon discussions with your father across your dining table, I had already seen the writing on the wall.

Communism was doomed. It was a corrupt system. The only question was when it would fall. But I knew that the State could hold on to power for many years using fear tactics. I wanted a way out. I realized you could provide me with that, when the time came. You were my insurance policy."

"In case you wanted to defect?"

"Why not? Kill two birds with one stone. I would provide great intel to help bring down my corrupt system, and you could vouch for me when the time came. But it was your welfare that was my main motivation, believe me."

He saw the sincerity in Boris's face. "I remember you told me at the Athénée Bar that the real smart guys would come after the Soviet system fell."

"It will happen as I said. Just wait. Which brings me to my main point." Boris picked up his suit jacket from which he removed several folded pieces of paper, then dropped them on the coffee table. "Let us go back to the day when the Ceausescus were executed. It was a grizzly affair, no point masking that fact, but they deserved what they got."

"A kangaroo court."

"Of course, it had to be. Nobody—not the politicians, not the generals—wanted Ceausescu to testify in public. They were all guilty and would be ruined. In fact, the only reason they did not execute the two of them immediately was because they were waiting for the green light from Moscow."

"Gorbachev?"

"Who else? He personally gave the order, through me. That is why they were waiting for us. He considered Ceausescu to be a criminal, a murderous tyrant who destroyed his country and the image of socialism. Anyway, the point I want to get to is something completely different: Elena Ceausescu's handbag."

"Her handbag?" Hefflin remembered it clearly. "Yes, she kept it close to her chest. At one point you took it from her and examined its contents. And . . ."

"And?"

"I saw you take out a piece of paper and slip it in your pocket."

"Ha! Bravo! And what do you think was written on it?"

"I have no idea."

"You can take a look for yourself." From his wallet Boris removed a small square of paper, which he unfolded and placed on the table. It was yellowed and fragile.

CHAPTER FIFTY-THREE

New York
November 1990

THERE WAS A column of numbers, each followed by two or three letters, written in pen.

"What are these?" Hefflin asked.

"Just to show you what kind of woman she was, even as they were fleeing for their lives, barely ahead of the mob, she had the clarity of mind to bring the numbers of their offshore accounts."

"Offshore accounts?"

"The letters after each number refer to a bank. You recognize UBS, for example. The banks are located in Switzerland, Luxembourg, and Lichtenstein. It took me months to track them all down." Boris broke into laughter again. "Funny, no? All the time we were trying to get the offshore accounts from Ceausescu's money man, and in the end it all fell into our hands. Fate, again."

"You found them?"

"Yes, all of them. A total of two and a half billion dollars." Boris sat back down, his eyes beaming.

Two and a half billion. Hefflin's heart was rushing like a bird's. "What did you do with it?"

"I transferred most of it to other offshore accounts, many times over, so that the transactions would be impossible to trace. I left a few hundred million for the Swiss. I knew the Swiss and Romanian investigators would need some encouragement to come to the same conclusion: that there were no foreign accounts belonging to the Ceausescus."

"And that was exactly their report," Hefflin marveled. "You mean the Swiss paid off the Romanian investigators and kept the rest for themselves?"

"Corruption does not belong exclusively to the Romanians," Boris said. "The Swiss have a long history of keeping forgotten money."

Boris now unfolded the sheets of paper he had dropped on the table. "Here we have a list of my numbered accounts all over the world. To get access you need the number of the account and the password. The accounts also have a name attached to them in case the numbers or passwords are lost. There are two names, in fact, on each account: mine and yours. Either one of us can access them without the other."

Boris fished for two passports from his jacket pocket, one Canadian and the other American. He opened the Canadian first. It had his picture on it, without the beard, and a name: Vladimir Kopsin.

"It is an alias, of course, one of many," Boris said. He opened the American passport in which Hefflin saw his picture attached to another name: James Blake.

"This is a real passport, not a fake," Boris said. "Another contact in your government. So, Mr. Blake, you are now the proud inheritor of a fortune of over two billion dollars, the culmination of my lifelong vow to repay my debt to a kind Greek doctor in the Romanian army who saved the life of a young Russian soldier." Boris's face was lit by an ethereal glow.

Hefflin was unable to speak.

"I suggest that after I am gone you move these funds around so that any traces of Vladimir Kopsin disappear," Boris said.

"I can't accept this," Hefflin stammered. "This is dirty money, stolen by Ceausescu from the Romanian people."

"Actually, most of it was stolen from American and European companies who paid big bribes to Ceausescu to do business in Romania." Boris smirked. "They bought grain and minerals from Romania at below market prices, which they then resold at market value for big profits."

"Still—"

"Still nothing. Who are you going to pay it back to, the thieves who head the large corporations that bribed Ceausescu? Or perhaps you want to give it to the thieves that are now running Romania. Either way it is all going to end up in those same offshore banks."

Hefflin didn't say anything. His brain was moving in molasses.

"Anyway, after I am dead you can do whatever you want with it," Boris said. "But I suggest you use the knowledge you gained in that high-priced school of economics to manage the money properly. If your heart bleeds for the poor, set up a nonprofit organization to help stamp out hunger or disease in Romania, or whatever. But do not throw it away on those kleptocrats in Bucharest." Boris cursed in Russian, then swallowed another shot of vodka.

"I knew you would respond this way, so I took measures," Boris continued. "One of the accounts is in the Caymans, and has special provisions. It has one hundred million dollars, getting a guaranteed five percent interest. You are not allowed to touch the capital. Only when you die can the money be withdrawn by your heirs. Even if you squander the rest, you will still have five million dollars of interest per year to live on."

Boris was breathing heavily, excited about his revelations.

"But if I were you, I would think of doing something more interesting with the money," Boris went on. "Why not invest in a company? Personal computers, for example. It will be the next revolution. A thousand times bigger than now. Go to Silicon Valley. I have friends there. This guy named Jobs started Apple, then the idiots threw him out. The company is not doing well. But Jobs is a genius. I met him. He has started another company called NeXT, which is very innovative. Look into it. In fact, I told him James Blake might be interested in investing."

Boris lit a cigarette and leaned back into the couch. "There is one remaining matter, the most difficult for me to approach."

CHAPTER FIFTY-FOUR

New York
November 1990

HEFFLIN DRANK DOWN another vodka shot. He didn't know how many more surprises he could take.

"This is a matter of the heart. Two hearts, in fact." Boris's eyes grew misty.

"Oh, anything but love," Hefflin moaned. "I've already given up on it."

"What about your Pusha?"

"Beyond reach or hope. After my fiasco with Soryn, I realized it was a foolish dream." He waved his hand in dismissal. "Even if she had been the real Pusha, our encounter would have been a failure. We are now adults. We've had different paths in life, different experiences, and we've developed into different people. We would be two strangers."

Boris drew on his cigarette. "Sad but true. You two only knew each other as children. It would have never worked. Well, then, what about your second love, Catherine?"

"Catherine?" He sat up; his mind suddenly alert despite the vodka. "I've never told you about her. How?"

"Because I am a spy, like I keep reminding you. I know everything about you. Your *amore* from Harvard. So?"

"I lost track of her after she graduated," Hefflin said. "She just disappeared. A few days later, I read she was engaged to the son of a French banker. I didn't hear from her for years, then she showed up in Timisoara, of all places, out of the blue. She was supposedly working as a reporter for *Le Monde*."

"*Le Monde?* Is that what she told you?" Boris laughed, shaking his head. "So, what happened?"

"What usually happens in my life: she vanished again. I received some postcards from her from various parts of the world she was supposedly covering. Then I found out she never worked for *Le Monde*. I think she's working for the Agency, or some other clandestine service. One lie after another."

"Poor boy. The two loves of your life, and both disappear on you. You must be dejected."

"More like catatonic."

"The lowest point in your love life, yes?"

"If it were any lower, I'd be dead."

"Perfect. It could not be any better if I wrote the plot myself." Boris lit another cigarette, preparing himself for another story.

"What are you talking about?"

"You are the writer, you tell me." Boris winked.

"Haven't written in years. Decades."

"Well, correct me if I am wrong, but the structure of the classic plot is that the hero wants something, in this case love, but he has to go through many obstacles before he finds it. Right? Up and down he goes, hope then dejection, hope again then dejection again, over and over, until finally . . . deep hopelessness, the deepest one, almost catatonic, right before—"

"—the climax, when he gets the girl. I always thought the sexual connotation was obscene."

"What are you, an American Puritan? So, right now you are in the deepest dejection possible. Catatonic. Right? Perfect! So, I have to tell you my story first, so you can understand." Boris's eyes were sparkling. "About a year and a half after you and your family left Romania, I passed by your old house on Strada Sirenelor. I wanted to make sure that the people the government had put there were taking good care of it. You can call it nostalgia, protecting your parents' house in case, some day, when the politics got more sane, your family might return."

"You're kidding."

"A foolish idea, I admit. Anyway, when I got there, I found the gypsy woman I had already met before, during the time I was visiting your father. She was sitting under an apple tree smoking a pipe."

"Tanti Bobo."

"The same. She said she was expecting me. Strange thing, no? 'How could you be expecting me?' I asked her. 'You are needed,' she said. She started telling me about a little girl named Pusha, how you loved each other so much and how she was now an orphan. At first, I did not understand why she was telling me this, but then she said, and I remember her exact words: 'Fili and Pusha have loved each other over many lifetimes. Pay your debt by saving her and bringing them together.' I almost had a heart attack. How did she know about my debt? And what was this about many lifetimes? I almost became religious then, I have to tell you. Maybe I have always been religious, I do not know."

"What did you do?" Hefflin's heart was now racing, his mouth so dry he could hardly swallow.

"She told me the girl was at St. Bartholomew's orphanage, so I immediately went there to find her. When I saw her, I realized why she was called Pusha, which I knew came from the

Romanian word for 'doll.' She truly had the face of a doll. The prettiest girl I had ever seen. I asked if she remembered you, and she started to cry. Well, my heart melted. When I left that horrible orphanage, I swore I would get her out somehow."

"And?"

"I spent the next few months planning the operation. It just happened that at that particular time the KGB decided to send me to France to recruit new assets. A coincidence? I do not believe in them anymore. While in Paris, one of the people I tried to recruit was a young State Department official working in the American Embassy. As it happened, he and his wife were also looking to adopt a child. They could not have one of their own, apparently. Although they originally wanted a younger child, when they took a look at a picture of Pusha they immediately fell in love with her and wanted to get her out of Romania."

"They adopted her? Your communist recruits?"

"They were communists like your actors in Hollywood were communists. They were stupid, young idealists, a little like you, who imagined a communist utopia. I quickly set them straight about real communism and told them to forget about it. We became good friends. When Pusha arrived, I became the 'uncle,' like in the old novels."

"But how did you get her out of the orphanage?"

"When I returned to Bucharest, I just entered the orphanage at night and took Pusha with me. It was quite easy. The place was totally unguarded. They would have been only too grateful for someone to take an orphan off their hands."

"She just agreed to come with you, a stranger?"

"She had no one, alone. I told her we were going to France, that I knew you and your family, and that we would look for you in Greece. She was very excited. She cried with happiness at the thought of finding her little Fili. I took her dossier with me to make it more difficult for them to report her missing, and we left."

"But how did you succeed in getting her out of Romania?" Hefflin's head was spinning.

"We drove. As simple as that," Boris said proudly. "At the Hungarian border nobody asked any questions when they saw my KGB papers. Hungary was a staunch Soviet ally at the time. At the Austrian border I used a fake French diplomatic passport. I have many of those, for practically every country in Europe, as do your CIA operatives. Pusha was hiding in the trunk. I was waved on. Pusha and I arrived in Paris a few days later."

"I can't believe you did this. You're a guardian angel."

"Of course. I am Boris." He rubbed his hands together as if he were starting a fire. "When do I ever fail? Okay, I failed in the coup, but that was the exception that proves the rule."

"So, what was the name of this State Department official?"

A smile burgeoned over Boris's face.

"Stop dithering and spill it!"

"John Nash."

CHAPTER FIFTY-FIVE

New York
November 1990

HEFFLIN WAS BARELY able to breathe. "Catherine Nash is Pusha?"

He tried to put the two images together, the little girl he'd left over twenty years before and the sophisticated woman he'd met at Harvard. "No, it can't be," he cried. "All this time she was right there, and she didn't say anything."

Boris shifted in his seat, then lit another cigarette.

"Stop stringing me along like a puppeteer and tell me what's going on."

"She does not know who you are," Boris said. "The last letter she got from you was from Greece when you were in the refugee camp. Then her parents died and she was traumatized, alone among strange people in that horrible orphanage. She could hardly speak for the first few months. When she got better, she couldn't even remember your address in the Greek camp. Later, when she was older and living in Paris, she tried to find your family in Greece, but by then you had already left for America. It was hopeless."

"But *you* knew. Why didn't *you* tell her?" Hefflin could barely keep himself from strangling the old man.

"At first I wanted to, believe me," Boris said, "but by then she had loving parents who doted on her, the best French schools, a society of diplomats and intellectuals who passed through her house, summers on the Riviera, winters at St. Moritz, a privileged life. Her mother was French and her side of the family had money, you see. I came to the same conclusion you just did: that you cannot base an adult relationship only on childhood memories. You two were now growing up in very different circumstances. Your life as a poor immigrant in America was the opposite of hers, a privileged life in Paris. The only way you two could ever come together was by meeting each other as adults, and falling in love all over again. On your own. That is when I had my grand epiphany." Boris was beaming, his face red with excitement—and vodka. He paced back and forth, obviously trying to extend the tension.

"It was a crazy idea, totally improbable. Still, I thought that if the old gypsy was right, that you two were meant to be together, that you had lived many lifetimes together, as she put it, it might work. So, I decided on the solution: put the two of you in the same place and see what happens."

"You got her into Harvard?" Hefflin gasped.

"She was an excellent student and was accepted to many fine universities," Boris said. "At first, she wanted to go to Vassar where Jacqueline Kennedy went. But I convinced her that Harvard was it, the best school in the world. Her parents agreed. In the end she took her uncle's advice and that is where she went."

"But how did you know I'd get into Harvard?"

"She went to Harvard first, since she was a year ahead of you. But I knew you were an excellent student, too, and that you would apply everywhere, including Harvard. So, I made it easier for Harvard to accept you. I told them I was creating a fund for gifted students. Harvard tuition at the time was five thousand seven hundred dollars—I remember it very well—so I gave them half a million dollars that I'd extorted from my Asian gunrunner. I told them the first student to receive the gift was to be William Hefflin, aka William Argyris. They told me they were going to accept you anyway, but that my donation sealed the deal."

Hefflin's mind was in a daze. "Okay, then what? Harvard is large. Catherine and I could have been there for years without meeting."

"Since she was a year ahead of you, it would have been difficult. In fact, you probably would not have met at all if it was not for the Fly Club."

"It was you, my sponsor?"

"It was Pincus, actually, using his CIA contacts. Like I told you, we were working together. You were a perfect candidate for him to recruit. You were an immigrant from Romania who spoke the language fluently, and you were a loner, a drifter. He had his fellows in the Fly Club already recruited. Catherine, one of their friends, was already being primed for possible recruitment, on my suggestion. Like you, she was a person with no sense of belonging, a drifter, though on a wealthier scale. So, when you met Catherine, I knew fate was working, that the old gypsy was right. You two fell in love for the second time. Without even knowing who the other person was. If that is not a love made in heaven, I do not know what is."

"It did feel like magic, as if it was meant to be," Hefflin murmured. "But then she left me to marry a banker."

"The Ambassador's idea. He knows nothing about you. But no, no, I am the wrong person to tell you that part of the story." Boris picked up the phone and dialed.

"Who are you calling?"

"Can I speak to the young lady with the black beret sitting at the bar, please." A pause, then, "Katia, darling, it is time." He hung up.

Hefflin's heart was still. "Was that Catherine? Where is she?"

"At the bar across the street. She has been waiting for the call."

CHAPTER FIFTY-SIX

New York
November 1990

SHE WAS WEARING a black beret and black overcoat, an apparition standing in the doorway, unsure of whether she was welcome. No words, his soul a sea of wild emotions. Her embrace was timid, careful. He took her coat and beret.

"Katia!" Boris spread his arms and ambled over to hug her. "A vodka to warm you up?"

"Of course, a vodka, Uncle. It's freezing outside."

Boris poured a glass for her. "A toast," he declared, and they all raised their glasses. "To long-lost friends."

They drained their shot glasses, and Hefflin poured refills.

Boris put on his suit jacket and gathered his coat and hat. "No more vodka for me. I will leave you two alone. You have a lot to talk about, and you do not need an old man around. Call me in the morning. I am staying at the Pierre."

Boris closed the door behind him, leaving the two of them to face each other and the many years that lay between them.

"So—" she tried to smile— "here we are again. We seem to keep losing track of each other."

"No, *you* keep disappearing." He looked at her for a long moment, trying to sift through the adult image for clues of his Pusha. But his memory of Pusha was like an impressionistic painting: indistinct, smudged, only the broadest strokes of a bird in flight. Had he finally captured her, or was she going to fly away again?

"You don't work for *Le Monde*—" The words flew out of his mouth. But why? What difference did that make?

"No, never did. Sorry. DGSE."

"The French external security service? Why them?"

"Why not? It's better than the CIA in some respects. Smaller. More personal."

"I always thought you'd join the Agency. You were part of the Fly Club group, after all."

"That was Uncle's idea, to have someone in the CIA to vouch for him in case he wanted to defect. But I've never felt American. I've lived in Paris for much of my childhood. French was my first language, English only my second. Even though my father is American, my mother is French. I feel more French than anything else."

Boris was right, another displaced spirit, like him.

"You mean French was your second language," he said, "English your third."

Her eyes focused on his, her face dark, fearful. "What has Uncle told you?"

"Your story, from when you were a child in Bucharest."

She frowned. "Oh, he shouldn't have. That part of my life is too painful. I've tried to forget it."

"You lost your parents—" He trod lightly.

"Yes, I lost my parents, my childhood, my friends, my innocence. Everything."

"Your time in the orphanage must have been traumatizing," he said.

"Yes, a horrible place."

"But then you went back to Romania, even after all that," he said. "And we ran into each other again, in Timisoara."

"The DGSE sent me because of the revolution, because I can still speak the language," she said. "The French don't like to depend on the Americans. I was taking pictures of the atrocities when you saw me. I was also there because Uncle needed me."

"Oh?"

"I had to help him with a little job."

"What kind of job?"

"A certain minister . . . of agriculture," she said. "He was the money man for Ceausescu. Uncle was trying to get him out in return for Ceausescu's offshore accounts. I arranged for a van and driver to get him out of the capital, then put him on a train to Constanta where he was supposed to get on a boat. But when he arrived, the Securitate was waiting for him. It turns out his wife turned him in. Can you believe it?"

Hefflin began laughing uncontrollably, causing Catherine to laugh with him. But then she stopped laughing and began to worry because he continued on.

"Are you all right? What is the matter?" she asked.

"Your uncle is a great spy, that's all," he said, finally controlling his hysterics. "He used me and my cousin, the minister's lover, to convince him to go for the deal."

Catherine now broke into new laughter, which started him laughing again. The two of them continued on until they were exhausted.

"But how do you know Uncle? He hasn't told me anything," she said.

"Your uncle's code name is Boris, the CIA's most valuable Kremlin asset. I have been the lucky recipient of his intel for the past several years. And I bet you were Hermes, as the Agency named you, the cutout for his messages."

"To Pincus? Those were for you?"

They stared at each other, both incredulous at Boris's machinations.

"All this time and I didn't know." She crossed herself. "Uncle sure has a complicated life." She sat thinking for a moment. "But how did he originally contact you?"

"That's a long story, which I will tell you later, slowly, so that you can savor it," he said. "So, did you visit your old neighborhood while in Bucharest?"

"Yes." Her eyes lit up. "I avoided going back there at first because of the painful memories of my parents. But for some reason, after I saw you in Timisoara, I got this strange need to find an old woman I used to know. But by the time I was free to go see her, it was too late. She had died a few days before. I feel so guilty."

"A gypsy woman."

She looked up at him. "Yes, how did you know?"

"No need for guilt," he said. "We would all be prisoners of guilt if we let it in. So, what else do you remember of your childhood?"

She hesitated. "There was a boy I loved very much. We grew up together. We'd meet under the apple tree where Tanti Bobo— that was her name—would sit and smoke her pipe and we'd make up stories and share dreams."

"Whatever happened to him?"

"I don't know. I lost track of him. When I joined the DGSE, I tried to look for him all over the world, even in America, but there was no one by that name."

Hefflin realized his parents had passed away by then, and he had changed his name. And she never knew he had a cousin,

Irina, in Bucharest, who might have known he was in America. Still, Irina didn't know he had changed his name.

"So many years ago. I lost hope. But in my heart, he is still there." Her eyes glistened.

"You were the princess in white silk and lace and he the knight in shining armor riding in on a white stallion," he said.

She looked up, amazed. "Yes, that's it exactly."

"And you used to sit under the apple tree and drop berries into his mouth, one for each kiss."

"But how—?"

He went to the bookcase and pulled out an old paperback. "You can read about it in here." He handed her the book.

She looked at the cover and gasped. The title, in bold letters: *Pusha*. Underneath it was the single name of the author: Fili. She glanced up at him, her eyes shining with tears. "He wrote a book about me?" A single tear rolled down her cheek. "How did you get this? How do you know about him?" She opened to the first page. He recited the lines to himself as she silently read.

> *My name is Vasili, but when I first tried to pronounce it, it came out as Fili, so that's what everyone calls me. I was born on Strada Sirenelor number 36 in Bucharest, Romania, where I lived until the age of eight. It is sad to say, but those were the happiest years of my life. I was in love, you see, my one and only love, with a girl named Pusha. She was the princess in white silk and lace, and I was the knight in shining armor on a white stallion.*

"He never forgot me, my Fili." She burst into tears and hid her face in her hands, her body shaking, her cries coming in a torrent. "All these years," she cried, "and I'm still that girl waiting for the boy in shining armor to come riding on a white horse and rescue me."

She cried for a long time, finally wiping the tears away with her hand. "Stupid, isn't it? But that's my illness, and I could never inflict it on you. That's why I left you, why I could never give myself to you." She started crying again. "I'm sorry, but I have to find him, that boy. A man now. What does he say? You've read it, tell me."

"He's been suffering the way you have," he said, "a drifter, an observer of life, keeping the image of his little Pusha safely in his heart. But the book was written when he was a senior in high school. He doesn't yet know about the second girl he'll meet and fall in love with."

She grew silent, her face lifting up full of sorrow and fear. "Another girl?"

"He meets her at Harvard"—he switched to flawless Romanian—"and he falls in love with her a second time."

She stared at him, her eyes searching into the corners of his soul. "And she with him," she said in Romanian. "But it can't be. The world doesn't work that way."

"Tanti Bobo's world does."

Her mouth rounded in shock as the meaning of his words sank in. "Fili?"

"Pusha!"

They both burst into tears, then embraced with the fury of two people who had finally found their other halves. As he clutched her tightly, he felt the pall of sorrow that had weighed him down ever since he had left his childhood now rise and float away, and a new lightness now lifting him into a joy he had imagined only existed in the afterlife.

They dropped to their knees still embracing, as Hefflin murmured thanks to the gods, to Tanti Bobo, to Boris, and to any other deity or sorcerer that had toiled to bring them together. As their lips touched, the feeling for Hefflin was both new and familiar, as if he were kissing her for the first time and yet had been kissing her for many past lifetimes. They touched each other tenderly, their passion measured by a sense of enchantment, of a whimsical fate that had toyed with their lives, finally culminating in a magical union. But then she sat back, her breasts heaving with passion, her lips swollen.

"Lord, make me chaste—but not just yet," she quoted Augustine. "Take off your clothes or I'll tear them off with my teeth!"

He smiled, then shook his head.

"Oh, so that's how you're going to be." She giggled, then let her passion drive her to bite and tear off each morsel of his clothing until he lay naked for her to devour. He remembered the first time they had made love after he had lost the chess match—her dominating him and yet with a sense of play.

"The hidden bishop," he gasped. "You learned that from my father."

"I was there when he sprang it on you. You don't remember?"

She tore off her garments and declared, "We're not wearing any clothes for a week."

Their bodies entwined, their mouths searching for each other's lips, her wetness dripping and glazing his skin like aloe. As he breathed in her scent and tasted her body, he felt himself melting into her, his mind no longer resisting, becoming one, as the poets always claimed. He knew he was living a blessed existence, for out of all the possible universes, he was alive in the one that had given him both Pusha and Catherine.

CHAPTER FIFTY-SEVEN

New York
November 1991

THEIR NEW APARTMENT was a penthouse in a majestic building on Fifth Avenue overlooking Central Park: three massive bedrooms, a paneled library, a chef's kitchen, a formal dining room, a living room large enough to roller-skate in, and a terrace with a veritable forest of dwarf fruit trees and potted plants.

It had been decades before when Hefflin had first set eyes on this enchanted city whose spires were shrouded in a magical mist. He remembered stepping off the gangway of the *Saturnia,* an Italian ocean liner, and being picked up in an Oldsmobile by one of the Romanian immigrants from Worcester, a car as large as a boat, and dreaming of one day living in New York, among the wealthy. And here he was now, one of the privileged, with the love of his life next to him, raising glasses of champagne, watching the sun go down. They were toasting Boris. The first month anniversary of his death.

"May he rest in peace in that big spy ring in the sky," Catherine said with a grin.

"May he cash in on all the favors owed to him," Hefflin added.

Boris had chosen this apartment for them—his wedding present—and had stayed there during his final months. It had been a relatively kind passing, vodka and pills taking care of the pain, then a morning when he just didn't wake up. They never knew his real name. He had many. To Catherine he was Uncle and to Hefflin he was just Boris. To the Agency he was an asset who had simply disappeared—assumed to have had his cover blown and been shot.

Hefflin was no longer with the Agency, and Catherine, now that she was pregnant, had also resigned her position with the French DGSE. Yes, they decided to start a family, despite his vow to his parents to never have any children. And they were drinking alcohol-free champagne due to her pregnancy. Hey, things change.

He did receive a request from Boris, his last, when the Russian found out Catherine was pregnant. "Do me a favor," he said. "Do not name the kid Boris. I never liked that name. Or Natasha, if it is a girl. Okay?"

They hadn't decided on names yet, though she was leaning toward French ones, Phillipe or Gabrielle.

Tanti Bobo's black-and-white pictures, which she'd kept in her tin box, now blown up and framed artistically in black, covered an entire wall of their master bedroom. Every night he and Catherine gazed at Fili and Pusha sitting under the apple tree, he with his mouth open and she about to drop a berry into it. Around it were several of his favorites: Tanti Bobo bouncing little Fili on her knee; Fili, as a baby, suckling on Tanti Bobo's breast; his family standing together, Tanti Bobo's hands settled proudly on Fili's shoulders, laying claim, giving a tantalizing sliver of credence to the traditional Romanian tease that he used to hear from the boys in the neighborhood: "You were bought from the gypsies for a sack of flour!"

She had told him that her child had been stolen by her father when he found out it was a boy. But would a gypsy *voivode* who had ostracized his daughter for having an illegitimate child with a *gadjo* really want that child? Would that child ever be accepted into the gypsy clan?

Another story had formed in his mind, a branching of the algorithm of fate that existed either in this universe or in one of the infinite universes in a quantum reality. What if Tanti Bobo's child never was stolen? What if, instead, wanting her child to have a better life, she gave it to a kind Greek doctor to raise as his own?

Could such a secret be kept? How could his mother explain her never showing her pregnancy or the child just appearing out of nowhere?

His mind had created a possibility. What if the decision was made while Tanti Bobo was in early pregnancy and living with the kind Greek doctor and his wife, the doctor who had saved her life? And what if this Greek woman started stuffing her dress with pillows to feign her own pregnancy? At a time when most deliveries occurred at home, the doctor could easily have said that he had delivered the baby in their bed, next to that ceramic fireplace that warmed their room on winter days. When Tanti Bobo delivered the baby, it was declared stolen and the Greek woman, her pillows now removed, claimed him as her own. In this way, the circle of secrecy could have been closed.

Was that story so fantastic? He'd certainly read more complicated plots in novels. But why was he even contemplating such a possibility? His parents had certainly shown him the same love they would have shown their own child. Was his loss of identity so powerful that it had pushed him to this preposterous explanation? His sense of alienation could easily be explained by his immigrant experiences. And yet, the story rang true, felt true.

He had looked up the history of the gypsies. The word *gypsy* came from the Greek *Egyptos*, meaning Egyptian, due to the common belief in the Middle Ages that the gypsies were itinerant Egyptians. But the Roma, their preferred name, were originally from Northern India, having migrated into Europe around a thousand years ago. Their true numbers were unknown. In some parts of the world their resistance to integration, their lack of official identity papers, as well as their reluctance to declare their true identity for fear of discrimination, made a true calculation impossible. It was estimated that one million Roma lived in the United States and between two and fourteen million in Europe.

But did he really care if he was Greek or Roma? His identity didn't depend on biology. His personality had been formed by his growing up in a Greek family, first living among Romanians, then among Greeks in Athens, then among Greek and Romanian immigrants in Worcester, and finally among Americans. Pusha's story had been similar, though her travels had taken her to other countries, following her adopted father's postings, but mainly growing up in Paris. In some ways it was a universal story. In America everyone was a gypsy.

He raised his champagne glass. "To us gypsies, then."

They drained their glasses then hurled them into the fireplace. In this world they were free to write their own history, to truly become self-made.

"What are we going to do now?" he asked. "I mean, with our lives."

"We're both trained operatives," she said, "and we have all this money, Uncle's gift. We should give it the honor it deserves."

"The world is full of places where we can create history," he said.

"Or not. Maybe history should be left to itself." She shrugged, and then gave him a mischievous, secretive smile that was pure Pusha. "It's all up to us. We are citizens of the world, traveling light."

AUTHOR'S NOTE

I was born in Bucharest, Romania, of Greek parents and came to the U.S. as a young boy after spending two years in a Greek refugee camp. I have returned many times since then, still have relatives and friends living there, and speak the language fluently. I know firsthand how the people suffered from and tried to cope with the forty-odd years of communism, which I hope adds a deeper dimension to the Cold War spy story that forms the spine of this novel. Even during one of the bleakest periods in Romania's history, the flame of hope still burned brightly in the hearts of those that endured it.

Even thirty years after the Romanian revolution of 1989, the questions of how it started and why it became so violent have never been adequately answered. This novel provides a plausible scenario based on the facts as I know them.

Although this is a work of fiction, it is loosely based on events that occurred during that tumultuous time. Many of these, such as the trial of Nicolae and Elena Ceausescu, including their execution, were filmed and can be viewed online. While most characters are fictional, a few are based on actual historical figures, amplified by a bit of poetic license.

I did not write this novel to catalogue the misery the Romanian people endured during those communist years or the revolution's atrocities. Nor did I write it to illustrate the corrupting effects of a police state upon those who suffered it. These have been well documented in many nonfiction books and articles, as well as in a few fictional works. I wrote it to show how love can prevail despite these dire circumstances. Thus, we have a love story within a spy thriller within a historical novel, fictional yet, at times, personal.